MAGNA-BLADE

By Evan Aitchison

Magna-Blade

Evan Aitchison

ISBN:
978-0-359-83173-9

First Printing: 2019

Table of Contents

Evan Aitchison

"Discovery – the motivator, the draw.

A person's drive to defy limit or law.

Will we thrive, when we all push past the bar?

Or will we all perish once we've pushed too far?"

"That was a poem written by the wise Professor Gustenbury just before the Gravity War began; a genius, ahead of his time. It's said that he died shortly after the War started, but no one really knows when he passed away. I'd like to think that he saw his predictions of our advancement come true, that we nearly did all perish. All because of gravity. Gravity and magnetism cause and affect the structure of the universe. We only have reached the edge of understanding of such deep scientific concepts over the centuries. Even now in the 24th century, there are many things still left to discover." Nicodem reached forward to turn off the holo-recorder that he'd been using for several months to record his scientific R & D.

As Nicodem leaned back, he returned to his time in the Gravity War.

It had been a morning like any other; he would take a hover train to work at the National Army Central Citadel and take the elevator to the secret underground tunnels. He had been working on a new, updated version of one of his inventions, but when he arrived at the lab, two Officers dressed in their typical black outfits with matte black helmets with black visors covering their eyes greeted him with their weapons drawn.

"Sir, the lab is closed today," they told him.

"Oh really. I-I wasn't notified," Nicodem parried beginning to sense unexpected nervousness in his own voice.

They nodded to the elevator. "Emergency measures today. You are to take this and report to Sector B5-C Station 9." They held his most recent prototype sword, the second edition Magna-Blade, and handed it to him. They pushed him toward the elevator as he slowly turned to face it, very confused.

"I don't understand. What's going on?"

"You'll be briefed when you arrive at your designated station. Now go, soldier! On the double!" They shouted at an uncomfortable volume, one after the other. It certainly motivated Nicodem to move faster. Being in his early twenties and new to the facility, he didn't dare challenge superior Officers ordering him around.

When he finally made his way to the appropriate station, he was met with hundreds of other soldiers all wearing their proper fighting uniforms. Nicodem, being part of the Magnetics Division, never got issued a rank, a militia uniform or any clearance to fight in the field. He found a line to stand in but had no idea of where he was to go or what he was even doing here. They were on the ground level of a giant hangar located near the Citadel Tower. Large infantry transport vessels called Militia Assault Carriers or MACs were lined up near the open hangar doors. Nicodem approached the desk asking the Officer, "What's going on? I'm not supposed to be here; I'm in the Magnetics Division."

"Name and rank," they demanded, ignoring his questions or comments. Nicodem paused, trying to remember having been suddenly taken off guard by the blunt, forceful Military demeanor of everyone around him.

"Name and rank!" the Officer repeated harshly,

nearly shouting.

"Uh, Nicodem Veradiun, no rank."

"No rank?"

"No, I uh-"

"Never mind, consider yourself now an enlisted Private as ordained by Article 97 of the North American Militia Code, you're headed for drop point Z. Good luck, you're going to need it."

"What? W-Why?"

"You're on the front lines, kid."

The next three hours were a blur, a complete haze to him as he was escorted then shoved into his assigned Militia Assault Carrier. He replayed the words front lines, I'm dead, over and over in his mind.

The fog finally lifted when he found himself standing in formation with a few hundred other soldiers surrounding him. At some point they had all been outfitted with backpacks – he didn't remember putting one on. He didn't remember putting on a soldier's uniform either. They all had heavy duty guns, an updated issue of RCP-490s, all except Nicodem. He was just carrying his invention, a sword. He had a Magna-Blade, a sword that was nearly indestructible which could manipulate and control gravity, generating magnetic fields at his mental command. The blade was linked to his mind, able to do almost anything he wanted.

The large door of the infantry carrier in front of him opened. As the door ascended before him, he saw that they were flying thousands of feet up in the air among dark stormy clouds. Red rectangular lights on the ceiling turned green then the soldiers behind him pushed vigorously, shoving him out. He then plummeted to the Earth, spinning through the air. He caught sight of others flying around, blue flames propelling them upward or in any direction they wanted. He wore a jet pack like the rest of them. He found a trigger on his ankles then activated it accidentally by angling his ankles out of fright, immediately feeling the G-forces of his rapid acceleration. Nicodem screamed as he spun out of control.

He finally straightened out as he saw hundreds of opponents flying toward him and his fellow soldiers. Some donned a Russian flag on the shoulders of their uniforms, another group to the right wore a Chinese flag, another set wore a Japanese flag. The war had turned the countries against each other. They were meeting in a multi-national skirmish and he didn't know where in the world they were. Bullets came speeding toward him in all directions. He closed his eyes with fear, holding his fairly narrow blade up as if to block the bullets, the ones that were going to hit him halted in midair. As he heard hundreds of soldiers firing back at their enemies, he cautiously opened one eye.

With the sound of thousands of men and women fighting all around him, he also almost heard a voice prompting him to move, to attack, to do something – anything. It was the blade! It was designed to communicate thoughts and ideas, but a voice – that was unexpected. All he heard was Fight! He triggered his jetpack by angling his feet downward and jetted forward rapidly. He could feel the desire to fight back which he realized was somehow being triggered by the blade. It was almost as if he was being commanded against his own will.

He swung at the enemies, slicing at the foes and using blasts of gravity from his blade to throw dozens of others spinning into the distance. Hundreds of the other soldiers had first edition Magna-Blades, an invention of his which was created a few years ago. A huge formation of flying soldiers began to charge in his direction towards his formation of fellow fighters.

Instinctively, in self-defense, he aimed his blade at them, charged a heavily focused electron blast and fired it right into the center of the crowd. The immense power of this jolt threw the enemies left and right like stuffed dolls. This was an ability that the First Edition blades never had – but he didn't anticipate that it would be so powerful. The blindingly bright beam of electrum shot across the sky for several miles. Thousands of nearby enemy soldiers saw the blast which undoubtedly drew a lot of attention to himself. He realized that they would notice that he was holding a blade that they had never seen before. No doubt, they would want to get their hands on this brand-new version of the infamous Magna-Blade and to return it to their government for some sort of medal. At once, the myriads of flying sword wielders all came at him swinging and slashing with a vicious ferocity - not only wanting to kill him because they were on opposing sides, but also wanting to take the new blade from him.

In an instant of time, an image of tactical measures rushed into his mind from the Magna-Blade. He saw a description of how to attack thirty enemies simultaneously with his blade. The image showed a white dotted line indicating the curved path he should take while describing exactly how and where to strike each of these enemies with the sword. He tried to ignore the description and the tactics, but the enemies were coming at him so quickly, he could do nothing but obey the strong suggestions of the blade. Nicodem followed the exact line of attack that had been recommended, swinging to his left, slashing to his right, flipping through the air, slicing and stabbing. He held back feelings of guilt and remorse as he fended off the enemy one by one. In just minutes, this blade had already seemed to have altered his personality. He could feel that its goal was to try to turn him into a killing machine.

Nicodem reached the end of a line of two dozen enemy swordsmen, blocking and strafing to dodge attacks. He began to see hundreds more with guns and Magna-Blades barreling toward him. With this massive amount of attackers, he was insanely outnumbered. Nicodem received another image from the Magna-Blade's advanced tactical mind. This time it was suggesting they unleash a devastatingly powerful graviton wave to incapacitate or possibly break the bones of these hundreds of opponents. Nicodem was shocked by the brutality of the blade. He briefly wondered if any of his co-workers had been tweaking the aggressiveness of the blades. Nicodem heard a countless barrage of gunfire from behind. A few bullets punctured his jetpack, causing it to sputter and lose control. He again began to crash toward the planet in an uncontrolled spiral. The feeling of falling, seeing the Earth rushing toward him, was intense. Nicodem couldn't believe what he was experiencing; he thought it was a dream. He tried and tried to wake himself up from this horrible nightmare as he fell. It wasn't a dream - it was real, it was really happening. Just as he began to give up any hope, he was sent another image from the blade. This time the image indicated a gravity field surrounding him that could suspend his fall, perhaps propelling them to a higher altitude. Nicodem agreed with this suggestion, gladly accepting the command. In seconds, they were levitating and ascending rapidly, faster than any jetpack could've accomplished. In moments, he was meeting the descending opponents who had been firing at him, chasing after his falling, flailing body. Nicodem unleashed multiple powerful gravity blasts, followed by electromagnetic surges which caused their jetpacks to spark, sputter and fail, then they all fell out of the sky, victim now to the gravity of the planet. Their shouts faded. Nicodem pleaded with the Magna-Blade to find him a way out, a way to escape. After some resistance from the Magna-Blade – since it's programmed instinct is to fight instead of run - it finally gave him a course to flee the battle line. Tens of thousands of soldiers with jetpacks were criss-crossing each other, about half were dueling with Magna-Blades while the rest were firing their blasters at each other.

As Nicodem made his way to escape the fight,

several stray bullets struck him. Nicodem commanded a faster exit, the fastest escape possible in just a few seconds. The blade aligned their direction, blasting off at a supersonic speed, breaking through the sound barrier instantly, leaving a gravity wake that threw hundreds of enemy soldiers backward. Nicodem flew as fast as he could, as far as he could away from the fight. He didn't want to die. He eventually realized that he was flying over some part of Europe with quite a distance to go before he would reach North America again.

As he returned home, he replayed the battle in his mind repeatedly, traumatized by the malicious violence he not only witnessed, but also took part in. War. What a disgusting waste of life.

When Nicodem finally arrived back to North America, he headed straight for the National Army Citadel Tower, he immediately made his way to the hundred ninety-ninth floor, barging in on the General who was head of the Magnetics Division, ready to tear a strip off him! He hoped that this was just some horrible misunderstanding or mistake, but something told him that wasn't the case.

"General, I've just come from the front line in Europe - drop zone Z, if that means anything to you. May I ask why?"

"Ah yes – that was today?" He replied passively, ignoring the rude bombardment into his minimalistic office.

"Wha-what do you mean 'that was today'?" His voice remained at a steadily increasing pitch with the incredulity of the passive General. Although he hid it well, the General was slightly surprised by Nicodem's indifference to his rank as seen in his vulgar shouting.

"As you may be aware, I am one of the lead scientists in your Magnetics Division here with the army. This morning, I was forced to the qwisking front lines of battle over Europe. Why the blazes would I have been sent there? What I'm supposed to be doing is developing advanced technology so you can fight your bickasted war!" Cussing was out of Nicodem's nature, but having just endured what horrors he was a part of, he was starting to form a bad habit of employing such crude words.

Nicodem cursed many times at him in his explanation of the trauma he had just endured, shaking his Magna-Blade at the General threateningly. The General grinned with an unapologetic baring of teeth, not intimidated in the least by the Magna-Blade. Nicodem threatened, "Just wait until I report such a huge mixup to the media. You could've lost an asset that was developing your vital technologies on a miscommunication!"

"You think", the General slyly began with an unsettlingly calm countenance, "that this was a mistake – that we screwed up? You developed telepathic neural linking technology. What makes you think we don't record your thoughts every day in the lab or at home?"

Then it set in. The realization that his life was no longer his own.

"We know what you did, Nicodem." The General continued his retort to Nicodem's previously justified exhortation, "We know that you tried to program in a hidden line of code which would cause the Magna-Blade to deactivate with a simulated 'power failure' at a crucial and seemingly random moment. You tried to make it look like a mistake."

His speech slowed to an even more uncomfortable degree as he stepped closer to Nicodem. With every drawn out word, Nicodem felt chills, "We didn't care for it."

After an awkwardly silent pause of the General staring him down, he turned, stepping back towards his desk, as if he was set to sit down to read the news, dismissively addressing Nicodem with his continuously calm demeanor, "Now, today was a demonstration of what we are capable of. Don't mess with the project again, because we will find out about it and we will...discipline you." That was a gut-wrenching euphemism. The General sat down at his desk, his entire monologue kept Nicodem's feet glued to the carpet, "And while we can't outright execute you as I would prefer, we can perform 'test runs' on our experimental weapons any time we want – and who better to test them than the inventor?"

Nicodem lowered his head staring at his frozen feet, begging them to budge, to remove him from this room.

"But since your brain still holds value, there are other ways to...motivate you to comply with our processes. It would be unpleasant to be forced to listen to you give a eulogy."

He knew exactly what the General was insinuating. His wife and daughter were at risk. He couldn't mess up again. He had to obey, for their very lives were in grave danger. What have I done? I've endangered their lives! They are all that matter to me but now I've signed their death warrant if I'm not more careful. I have to leave the Military. I need to get us out of here...somehow. Wait – can they really record my thoughts without my consent? I can't rebel ever again. I can't. I won't.

"Now go home to your beautiful family and cherish every moment you have with them and remember what results come from deceit or failure to obey your orders."

Nicodem left the room, turning a corner. As he was walking down the hall, he easily heard a transmission come through to the Admiral's room. The transmission echoed through the modern, fancy hallways.

"Sir, a man was just seen with a Magna-Blade rushing toward your office. He matches the description of the scientist we sent to the front lines. Do you want security to apprehend him?"

"No, no. It's fine, I've taken care of it. The next time he messes with the project we'll just...reassign him."

They sent him to the front lines as punishment for having attempted to sabotage the Magna-Blade project three weeks earlier! He thought he had been so careful, covering his tracks so well. He knew that they were going to kill his family if he tried anything else. He had to tread very carefully now.

Now a much-older Nicodem sighed to himself, glancing at his wristwatch. He realized it was nearly time for his evening tea. Strolling into his study, he noticed his water in the kitchen had already boiled. Pouring the steaming clear liquid, he looked to the mountain view out the expansive window. A copper sun was about to duck behind razor-sharp mountain peaks in the far distance.

The U-shaped kitchen was fully automated with kobicha wood-stained cupboards reaching up to the tall nine-foot ceiling.

With just one close proximity thought command to the appliances and surfaces and they cleaned themselves. In just seconds the kitchen's self-cleaning process was finished, leaving it looking good as new.

Nicodem held the patent for a number of inventions, and they had been serving the very wealthy for a few years now.

Nicodem sauntered away from the kitchen, his slippers sliding over his burnt umber hardwood floor which spread out across the whole level.

He always felt at peace in his study, maybe it was the open concept, or perhaps it was the floor-to-ceiling bookshelves filled with actual paper books of history, stories and secrets. He knew most of these books belonged in a museum, but he didn't trust museums to treat them or curate them properly.

Nicodem stood at his favorite place in the whole house facing several large windows which looked out to a panorama of silhouetted mountains and cityscape. The sunsets here were the most peaceful part of his day.

After a few minutes of calm meditation staring out on the scene with his cup of Earl Grey tea, he left the study through two solid wood doors, turning the metal key locks and knobs to keep his room extra secure at night. With the clicking of the metal lock and key, he strode past the rooms to head up the wooden stairs which creaked heartily under his slipper-clad feet, never using the anti-gravity strip of light that allowed one to levitate up the stairs. As he neared his bed, he mentally commanded the lights to activate at a dim level and gently gestured for his curtains to slide shut.

He was secretly proud of the fact that he had made almost everything automated in this completely custom house. He could detect every corner and every room of the house as it interfaced with his mind. It obeyed his commands as he initiated night-secure mode, partially locking down the exterior exits and ensuring the shield activated around the house.

His thoughts dwelt on what he saw on the news-holo earlier that evening, reports of homelessness becoming a greater threat during the worsening storms. Then he thought back to his two-hour recording session of his own research and development. He thought of looking back at the recording from today for once, to delete a portion that he had mentioned. Usually the recordings were for future reference on how he's been managing his inventions and progress on his creations, but today he mentioned something that he would've rather had redacted – something far too personal for anyone to hear had his material ever be stolen. Then just before he drifted to sleep, he thought of what lunch he would generate in the molecular resequencing chamber. Perhaps he would make delicious eggs and bacon. The style of breakfast prepared by hand like they used to do 300 years ago.

He awoke the following morning to look at his aging face in the mirror, "Not bad for a hundred and ninety-one." He encouraged himself, beginning to feel more and more stiff each day.

Having been born in 2120, he was one of the oldest men alive in this hemisphere. Despite his age, his careful way of life, eating and exercise, and of course incredible advancements in medical care helped him stay healthy and agile.

Nicodem had seen a great deal of terrible battles, having survived the Gravity War; still he savored the peace of his carefully positioned and planned house, having built it many decades ago. Nicodem sat in his favorite leather chair which faced the mountainous horizon. He scanned through a holo-display from his palm showing the available funds in his account, a generous number given that he was a successful inventor for the military. He was glad to have learned from his parents how to save money properly as well. Since he had earned a very healthy living over the many years of his life and was careful not to squander his livelihood, he had a great amount of funds left over.

Looking out to the horizon from his soft chair, his thoughts were drawn to this feeling that there was a great deal of trouble coming his way. He was aware that he had just days left before his life would greatly change. A date in his mind kept sounding off to him: Tyrsday, May 23rd, 2311. A date that would supposedly have huge implications for his future – and it was just ten days away.

A half-shattered bottle neck was gripped by a young man's bleeding hand. The young man was unconscious on the ground surrounded by shards of glass. His sleeve was soaked with a cheap whiskey, and a white powder laced his nostrils.

"This kid is a right mess," a passerby commented to his acquaintance. In agreement the other added, "What a disastrous life. He'll be dead in a few weeks if he keeps living like this."

Inhaling and coughing at the same time, the young man's abs caused his whole body to convulse as he pitifully tried sitting up from his liquor-scented puddle. His hole-pocked sweater dripped as he finally worked his way to become partially vertical. He didn't really realize that he was still holding his broken bottle and let it slip from his fingers and dance to pieces across the cobblestone ground. His face was filthy with mud and dried blood, from small cuts on his hands and face. Rubbing his swollen, red eyes with one dirty hand, he attempted to stand, losing his balance a few times until finally reaching his feet.

Stumbling down the poor part of the humongous city, he leaned against the wall, struggling to make his way forward. The homeless and drunk in the nearby alleys resembled his own countenance.

In the distance, there could be seen incredibly tall, intimidating skyscrapers that glorified themselves with grievous claw-like peaks that would cut through high passing clouds like butter.

The billions of dollars that went into the production of these towering buildings perfectly symbolized the economic imbalance of the nineteen outrageously large cities that covered most of the inhabitable planet. The size of the homeless sector grew just as the rest of the giant metropolises expanded and enveloped other pre-existing cities. Before the war, the cities were already starting to merge in the most urban areas of the world. Then by the time the war ended, there were just wastelands and wilderness between the large concentrations of buildings. Fortunately, some animals, including rabbits, deer, kangaroo, bears and some water creatures, still survived after the war. However, the war caused many precious species to go extinct.

A decimated planet of a broken human race was the result of the Gravity War. The Vanixx Corps put it upon themselves in their metropolises in America to bolster up the communities, make them feel like they were successfully thriving again, no matter how untrue it was.

Since the war, crops and farms were irreparably destroyed, so fortunately Nicodem had invented a molecular resequencing device specifically for food reproduction. Providing such a machine in a limited degree to the public allowed them control over the populace but also made them appear somewhat like saviors, after all they "helped end the Gravity War," or so they claimed. So that device would at least prevent people from starving sometimes. Within each giant metropolis, there were select places for farming, but it wasn't government-regulated anywhere except in Australia. It was often too expensive for anyone to afford except the wealthy; hence the homeless sectors grew faster than ever before.

Criss-crossing lines of slow moving, hovering vehicles were visible high just in view, some listing and others cruising through and past the golden clouds. A permanent haze of pungent pollution would continuously remain as a translucent ceiling along the horizon as far as the eye could see. At night the stars would be partially visible, but only at the farthest outskirts of the city. What were seen as stars several decades ago were now primarily satellites or space stations.

"What you see on the screens are the concepts of the very first actual hover boards, which were released way back in the year 2015. The device had a superconductor inside, but the board needed a strip of very strong magnets built into roads to work properly." The bow tie-clad professor continued his speech to the university students in the full, darkened auditorium. "As the years progressed, aspiring scientists worked to improve the concept. Some brilliant inventors thought, 'What if we were able to have the hover board work off of the gravity of the planet? Could we apply this concept to other things? Cars, boats, planes and trains could all benefit from this kind of technology, from this kind of invention.' Over time, magnets were being used on incredibly fast bullet train tracks, allowing them to increase travel and commuting speeds." The professor switched through historic slides as the students and faculty in the audience viewed images from almost 200 years earlier.

"So, to take the technology further, they went on experimenting with the gravitational forces of the planet and working with the magnetic poles of Earth. They realized that the Earth's magnetic fields were too weak. When superconductivity was first discovered by Dutch physicist Heike Kamerlingh Onnes in 1911, such a concept was attempted to be invented and proved feasible, but there were massive technological limitations preventing anything from being possible at the time. This same concept was quickly discovered by our fellow scientists in 2020. The weak magnetic field of Earth requires an absolutely massive circulating current to generate a counter magnetic field with enough force to lift something, let alone something holding a human being, off the ground."

The audience was enthralled by the scientific historical lesson. The professor continued to pan through the pictures. Holding a holographic amulet in his hand, he swiped with a simple gesture of the colorful holographic image causing the vivid color images on the large screens to be updated instantly. The professor went on enthusiastically, "There were some limitations that have been plaguing scientists for three centuries. First: The need for more current means that more weight to create the current is required, which means more current is needed – it became a vicious cycle of an impossible weight to current ratio. Some statistics had shown that our scientists would need power around twenty kilowatts. That's about the same amount of power generated by an ancient locomotive engine. Back then in 2020, such things were just not possible. Second: The Earth's magnetic field is not perpendicular to the surface, meaning near the equator there is almost no vertical component to work against to create a reverse magnetic field. This fact suggested that around the equator, the natural magnetic field of the Earth reduces the amount of available field strength for magnetic levitation to lift against gravity. The majority of the very few scientists of the 21st century that were studying this specific field concluded that only if a massively powerful, but very, very small power source could be created, then maybe...maybe this would be possible."

The professor strode from one end of the stage to the other as he continued the lecture, "By the year 2139, major advances were made in artificial intelligence and superconductor experimentation. In the year 2146, famed scientist Nicodem Veradiun created the first prototype of a true hovering device. Yes, some 165 years ago—" The electronic bell rang through the auditorium. "Well, my time's up; everyone head home and have a great weekend."

Students began to flow out of the auditorium like an army of ants. The tiered desks emptied as the professor shut down the devices used for the presentation and reactivated the auditorium lighting with his handheld amulet. Some passed by the professor to say, "Thanks, Professor Wiltrite."

The buzzing metropolis Vancouver was aglow in the near distance as night fell. The giant mega-city never shut down; it never darkened and never stopped.

You could see lights of every color and skyscrapers of many shapes as far as your eye could see. The city lights faded into the distance, falling behind the horizon as the city scaled the curvature of the Earth.

Nicodem had special shutters made so that he could block out the bright lights which were put to good use each evening.

Some of the skyscrapers had black patches with no light ever being illuminated. In the skyscrapers, the customary thing was to allow the wealthy to live there. But since so many billions had died in the Gravity War, there were a lot less people living on the planet now. These days, there were slightly more rental units available than there were residents. These units left empty would be filled once the population grew; the building owners were just waiting for that to happen.

Because of the Gravity War and the conscription that had been put in place globally, there were large gaps in the generational structure. This gap was due to nearly all of the ones being conscripted were between the ages of 20 and 60 and over 90% of them were killed in the Gravity War.

He was nursing a glass of scotch that he'd kept bottled for the past ten years; he only savored a sip once a month. It was one of the last of a few dozen single malt scotch bottles left in the world since just a few small remnants of what was Scotland existed.

Today was "Scotch Day" for him, therefore he would enjoy every moment of it.

Just as he was about to take a sip, his proximity alert activated with a gentle beep on his watch. The proximity alert would alert him of a visitor about 10 miles out. Whoever was on their way to visit him was an unexpected guest, but he was pretty sure he knew who it was – even at this terribly late hour. He could hear the hover engines of his visitor go through their power-down cycle. It was a sound he had heard a thousand times before.

"Knock knock-ity knock," Nicodem sang as he walked to his main entrance – an ancient Victorian-style door that had been renewed a few years back. Knock knock-ity knock echoed through the entryway. He'd had this visitor before, so he knew this person's unique knock. Glancing at his watch again just as he rested his hand on the front door handle, he saw his hidden camera's view of the belligerent General straightening his jacket cuffs.

Pulling the creaky door open, he smiled, "Good evening, General. To what do I owe this immeasurable pleasure? Oh, I see you've brought a friend. I was just about to have a drink – care to join me?"

The General raised a hand, gently but authoritatively. "No drink for me, maybe next time. This is just a random checkup on the property to make sure everything is up to code. We don't want this house falling down around you. We need to take care of our elderly, retired veterans." He stepped in past Nicodem, his associate following closely behind. "We can't expect you to swing a hammer; you could hurt yourself." The General grinned at his own self-amused humor.

Nicodem noticed the General's partner was of a much lower rank listed on the shoulder: a major or a commandant. Both had an identical haircut of the classic Military sort – shortly buzzed on the sides. The General was significantly taller than his acquaintance, although the General was taller than most others he stood beside. Nicodem followed them into the study where he was relaxing just moments earlier.

"What do you do for hobbies these days? I hope you don't just sit around all day." The General looked around the residence with an ounce of pity.

Nicodem grinned, "Oh, I keep myself busy. You are nearing retirement yourself, aren't you, General? I'll write down some of my ideas for you."

"Funny. I would like to see any recent notes you've jotted down however. Any new invention ideas lately?"

"Oh, you mean, any new inventions that belong to you? No – nothing new. I do have a new theory, though."

"Oh?"

"Yes – yes, I've begun to theorize why the crossword puzzle went the way of the do-do."

The General scoffed, turned on his heel, heading for the door. His associate had been peering at some of the books on the library shelf on the other end of the study. They obviously were satisfied with what they saw so they were on their way.

"You are more than welcome to come back soon. Now that I'm granted four hours a day in the city, I might not be home every time you come by."

The General nodded with a smile, "We'll use our key if you don't answer after three knocks."

He knew that each time they randomly visited, they found a way to place new hidden cameras somewhere in his home. He would eventually find them covertly, conveniently spilling his tea on one of the cameras or find some way to disable it "accidentally". Nicodem was smart about it though; he allowed them to keep a few cameras set up throughout the house: one in his room, another in his kitchen, one in his study – that way they would hopefully be satisfied enough with that many cameras to keep their eyes on him.

Nicodem wasn't fully trustworthy to the Military because of some small acts of insubordination recently and in the distant past. His brain was far too valuable for them to just lock up in a prison, however, so they gave him a respectful retirement from the Military, allowing him to set up his own home wherever he wanted. Nicodem hired a few different contractors to build various parts of the house with the savings he collected from the wealthy earnings he made being a part of the Army.

"Hey Kado, you young whipper thnapper!" an elderly toothless man exclaimed with open arms as he waddled toward a young hungover mess. They embraced, like a grandparent to a grandson. "It'th tho good to thee you! It'th been weekth; where you been, boy?", his lisp took some getting used to.

"Oh, I've been around, the South mostly."

"The Thouth? You are crazy, kid. The Thouth ith the wortht plathe in the entire mega town!"

"Lucious, it's got what I was hoping for though." Kado held out a small bag of white powder for the two of them.

The old man's eyes went large when he saw it, his scraggly long beard swaying as he shook his head back and forth. "Kado, you can't – how?"

"It wasn't too hard, just had to ask the right people." Kado shrugged.

"Look…I'm regretting thith way of life. I can't do thith anymore. I'm far too old." Lucious stepped back, his hands raised. His kind smile was always comforting to Kado but this time, his expression was grimly serious.

Having known each other for a few years now, they had helped each other through many unbearable nights of pain, depression, misery and drug withdrawal.

Kado looked down at the bag of illicit powder, its value now greatly diminished in his eyes since his dear friend wanted nothing to do with it any longer. He wondered what he would do with it. He had much less enthusiasm for it now. He didn't want to use it by himself, he'd be unable to stop himself and would overdose again. Would he throw it out? Sell it?

"My boy, leth thee if we can't figure out a better way to get by, eh." The old man rested an arthritic hand on Kado's shoulder. Kado nodded just before thunder was heard in the near distance.

"Come on, leth get under cover before we get irradiated an' thoaked!"

The rain came down hard, forming small puddles across the muddy alleyways and streets of the homeless sector. Kado noticed it had started raining a lot more frequently in the past several months. It used to rarely rain, but when it did, everyone hid under cover. Kado along with his elderly friend sat near an old decrepit industrial oil drum with welcoming flames dancing out of it, stationed under a ripped awning. They were accompanied by several other homeless ones who had similar stories like themselves.

"This rain won't let up for a few hours." One of the homeless men leaned over to Kado. "The rains are getting longer," he continued. "It's the government, they're behind it – I know it." Kado paid him no mind; he had gotten used to these crazy theories and, over the years, just got used to nodding in passive agreement.

"Tell you what, Kado." Lucious leaned over, "Let'th get you out of thith life. I know a guy who juth'd got a contract and he might hire you on ath a honeth'd laborer. Good honeth'd work for one-th."

"What about you, Lucious?" Kado implored concernedly for his dear friend of many years.

"Bah" he groaned dismissively waving a hand, "It'th far too late for me. My time hath come an' gone. But you – you have your whole life ahead of ya. Make it thumptin' will ya?"

Not accepting no for an answer, Lucious continued, "Yeth, tomorrow we meet my guy and I'll introduth you two." Kado stared into the fire as the rainy night continued. It was getting abnormally cold for this time of year.

The rain pattered loudly against the windows of Nicodem's home. Usually it was calming, but not tonight. Tonight was different; there was something fierce about this rain, something unnatural. The lightning that he saw weeks ago was very bright with thunder following after it loudly, but tonight the lightning he could see in the distance had a green hue to it. He only ever saw such a thing during the Gravity War. Something else was odd as well – he counted the seconds for the shuddering thunder to reach his home, but it never came. He counted up to ten seconds and knew this green electricity was no ordinary lightning. It was man-made, synthetic. Something strange was going on, and he figured he better get to the bottom of it. He was wearing a t-shirt and pajamas underneath the housecoat, which he slid off his shoulders as he made his way to the library wall of books. He thought a command to open the wall, and it began to open up, exposing another series of bookshelves inside. Inside was an abnormally wide sword mounted on the back wall of the small library. Nicodem wore a serious face as he gently spoke to the blade, "It's time."

Nicodem had traveled to the Vanixx Corps facility –
one of the many that housed his inventions, which they
took credit for, were manipulating and experimenting
with. He managed to sneak his way into the facility, which
was a very dark-lit, confusing labyrinth. Nicodem found
himself in a secluded location of a mysterious, large base
of operations.

He knew that the strange lightning from earlier was

some sort of experiment related to his past inventions. He could tell by the green hue, by the manipulation of man-made lightning that the Military organization called the Vanixx Corps had commandeered some of the unique technology he had created many years ago.

"Ok," Nicodem whispered. "Let's do what we need to do and get out." He heard some marching coming around the corner, they were very close. He looked around, not able to see anything to hide behind, with nowhere to go with little time to react. He stood perfectly still, holding the sword with its wide edge closest to his face, pointed straight up; the tip of the blade was positioned just above his head. The security Officers passed by without paying any notice to him as if they couldn't see him.

Phew, that was close, Nicodem thought. He stepped out into the hallway swiftly, his blade held at the ready, walking down the path that the security Officers had just come from. He was about to accomplish his mission – relieve the Vanixx Corps of his inventions, at least the ones that were in this building.

The morning outside in the homeless sector was abnormally brisk, but it often was fairly cold after a terrible storm. Kado was wrapped up in a thin blanket on the hard, dirty ground. He turned his gaze over to his nearby old friend, who was oddly still. Normally he was up an hour before anyone else by the fire. Kado let his blanket fall off around him as he crawled over to his dear friend.

"Hey Lucious."

Silence...

"Lucious?" He gently nudged the old man.

"Lucious?"

Silence...

Kado turned his friend over from his side onto his back. His face was exceedingly pale, his chest still.

He wasn't breathing.

"Lucious!" Kado, tears in his eyes, shouted at the top of his lungs; it echoed through the nearby alleys of the homeless sector. Some nearby were awoken, while others turned, unenthused to see what was going on.

Some Officers of the Vanixx Corps overheard shouting then came hurriedly around the corner. Their demeanor was as if they were ready for some trouble.

"What's going on here?" one of them demanded.

Kado turned to the Officers, "My friend, he-he died in his sleep." It became real to him as he said it out loud. His dear friend of many years, gone along with his chance to get an honest job gone as well.

There was a small crowd gathering around Kado

and Lucious' corpse. The Officers were deliberating with each other quietly, their hands grasping their automatic weapons with alertness. Kado kept the Officers in his peripherals as he stayed perched on his knees by Lucious' side. Kado could tell the Officers weren't willing to just leave the situation as it was, a simple death due to weather, exposure to the elements and age. If they suspected him of killing Lucious, their questioning sessions would not be very comfortable - he might not even see the light of day ever again. Punishment for murder was extremely strict, however to be wrongfully accused could mean a death sentence someone didn't deserve.

"Alright, we'll bring him." One of the Officers concluded a brief conversation on his collar comm. The two Officers nodded to each other, prompting the other to step up behind Kado. Putting a hand on his left shoulder, he grabbed Kado's opposite arm, lifting him to his feet. Kado struggled, then swung his head back swiftly to break the Officer's nose, slipping out of his grip. He bolted as fast as he could to get out of their view. A couple of electric blasts came from the weapon of the intact Officer; one missed, one hit the corner that Kado narrowly darted behind in his desperate escape.

He was familiar with the secret hiding spots

throughout many parts of the homeless sector, so he was able to slip into a nearby grate leading to the lower levels. The hiding spot was a perfect little place to crouch. The stench of sewage coming from within the grate could mask a person's scent from a K9 unit, and the way the ledge inside the gate was designed, it formed a little hidden cubicle where no one would ever find him. The Officer ran past without slowing. Here Kado would wait a couple hours before he would emerge. It was time to move to a different part of the city, far from these Officers' regimen.

Nicodem awoke with a renewed sense of purpose, a drive that would continue to push him forward to resist the pressure of the Vanixx Corps, the Quell and any other organization that wished to reign. Nicodem had read of other regimes that had risen to power around the world after the Gravity War. He felt great disgust that he was mostly responsible for the world changing the way it did over 160 years earlier. He decided he would record more of his holo-recordings for his inventions for the future and to tell his story in case someone ever needed a record to refer to. He had other reasons to record these videos as well; history had been written by the victors and so hardly anyone knew the truth after the war from so long ago.

Strolling over to his bookshelf-clad wall, he thought a command with his neural connection with the house for the secret passage to open, so the walls separated, once again exposing the interior secret library. He slowly stepped in as the walls halted their transformation. Looking at the blade securely mounted on the wall, he gave another mental command. Quiet rumbling ensued, and a gentle constant vibration was felt in the floor as more walls began to shift. A metal door showed itself from behind the sliding bookshelf. Nicodem stepped up to the door as a secondary set of security protocols verified his identity. The door hissed open, and he stepped inside the tiny room and quickly descended down the hovervator to his biggest secret.

The thick, metal door reopened and Nicodem strode into what he considered one of his greatest creations, "The Bunker." He came here when he didn't want the risk of being bothered or interrupted, and he knew he could speak comfortably here as he recorded his holo-videos or when he wanted to play his violin.

When Nicodem exited the elevator and entered the large rectangular domed cave, he looked across the large open concept. The domed ceiling had inset EDI bulbs which lit the room brightly.

Within the center of the large room was a holo-projector. The domed ceiling reached it's peak at twenty-five feet and supported a second-level walkway.

Holding his holo-recorder, he walked across the large bunker and sat down in an old, very comfortable, leather chair and activated it.

"I suppose it's thanks to the advancements that were made in quantum computing in 2139 that led to my discovery of enhanced A.I. capabilities. Computers that were almost... 'sentient' were nearly possible, I found. Artificial intelligence had already had the ability to learn and grow for many years by that time, but quantum technology pushed the boundaries beyond what anyone had previously imagined."

Nicodem stood up and began to slowly pace through the room; it was something that helped him think.

"I've always hated weapons. I was imagining hover boards or tools that looked like the old cricket bats as the devices to help us create and fix things with the power of magnets and gravity. When the Military got wind of my invention, they forced it to be a weapon. They wanted it to be like a gun, but because I had a say, I chose a sword. They are far more dignified than any other weapon out there, and its elegance can capture the eye of any passerby. Because I've always viewed swords to be capable of becoming tools just as much – if not more so –

than weapons, I wanted a sword to be the template for the invention that I had in mind; especially since I wasn't allowed to just make a gravity-manipulating stick or bat. For years, not only had I been running experiments on artificial intelligence, but I had also been thoroughly researching magnetic properties with electromagnetism as a basis for current transfer along with gravity being a kinetic source of power to manipulate the materials and matter around us. For someone ever watching this who isn't a scientist, I was experimenting with magnets and gravity to control things and to maybe even make a hover car."

He laughed at himself with the irony of the situation, "Ironic – The inventor of hover cars isn't even allowed to have one... So, I created a sword, and I wanted this sword to have magnetic capabilities, emit an EMP, use it like a remote control to lift heavy items or to throw objects, or even allow someone to float or levitate. In 2146, I finally did it – I made my first prototype." He grinned to himself.

"It was a little ostentatious in its appearance, but it was 'cool' looking, similar to a cricket bat. But two years later the Military somehow found out about my little experiments. I was given an ultimatum: Help them improve the invention, make it weaponized, have unlimited funding to research and develop the magnetic blades, or hand over all my materials and research. I wasn't given a third option, such as to not be bothered by them or to be left alone, which of course was my preference. So, I did what any inventor would do. I accepted the offer to have unlimited funding while still being able to work on my magnetic blade project. At the time, I didn't think of them having forcibly conscripted me into working in their Science Division, but I suppose that's what they did."

"When I was pulled into the Military, I was in my early twenties, just recently married about a year earlier, and my wife was eight months pregnant. I wasn't ordered to live on a base, so I could be at home with my family. However, being on this project meant many long hours away from home on the job. I knew they wanted to weaponize this project, and after hearing about some of the battles going on overseas, I wasn't so sure that I wanted to contribute to that – to the suffering that they were already experiencing. So, after some months of trying to figure out what to do, I tried making the project fail on purpose, but discreetly. They caught on pretty quick, and they threatened my family…"

"I realized from then on that I was walking on eggshells. Who was I?" he asked himself incredulously, "I was just some young inexperienced scientist who thought he could take on the federal Military. Foolish. I lost my drive to ever sabotage the project in the future."

Nicodem sat himself back down to continue his explanation to his handheld holo-recorder. "After hundreds of lab tests, several dozen field tests and after testing out fifteen different combinations of alloy metals, we finally came up with the weapon they had been desiring. We called it the Magna-Blade. A sword that could obey the commands of the wielder's thoughts, capable of lifting small buildings or powerful enough to crush tanks. This was going to change everything...and it did...but not for the better."

Kado needed to have a fresh start, but he didn't know how. He was hoping to get out of the homeless sector and try to have some sort of normal life, but he didn't see how it would be possible.

He decided that today he should go to the large market on the outskirts of town at the edge of the homeless sector to see if anyone would give him something to eat. Kado knew that most likely he was going to steal some meager scrap of molecular resequenced 'food'. The stuff tasted bland, but it at least held *some* nutrients. He hadn't eaten in three days and was feeling the effects of starvation. He was starting to feel dizzy and needed some sort of sustenance.

There were clear reasons why the homeless sector was drastically growing. There were food shelters and hostels, but he had learned the hard way that the crime and violence in those areas made it very dangerous to stay for more than a couple hours. Kado recalled a time when he was standing in line for food at a shelter when suddenly the man behind him was stabbed. There was screaming and chaos that ensued – he just ran for hours that night without any food. That kind of thing happened all the time. Kado many times had attempted to take advantage of the provisions for homeless people to get jobs, but the jobs that they applied for were with companies that never hired them due to their social status.

Kado had a digital résumé in at over 300 businesses, but none of them wanted him because he was either too young, inexperienced or, most of all, homeless. The concept of hiring a homeless person so that they would no longer be homeless in several months was worth nothing to the commerce world these days. It didn't help them earn any money and there were no government initiatives to encourage hiring the homeless.

After several years of trying to cut through red tape to get out of the homeless sector, Kado had concluded that he was worthless and would never get out, so he had resorted to just trying to kill the pain with whatever drugs and alcohol he could find.

He needed to eat, he needed to survive. He was going to steal food like he'd done many times before. He didn't care what anyone thought of him – he'd been spat on and kicked so many times by ones "more fortunate" than him that he'd given up hope that people were worth caring about. The only one he cared about was Lucious, and now his closest friend was gone.

Kado looked around at the bustling market. The sky was clear today, and the sun was actually shining for a change. The huge market at the edge of town had more people in it than usual – this was a good thing. More people meant it was easier to pocket food off a display table.

Relating his life in a holo-recording was very tough emotionally; Nicodem needed to get out and breathe some fresh air. He was granted a few hours each day to leave the house and go into town. He was restricted from driving in the terms of his retirement, a handsome euphemism for what he called house arrest, but he was allowed to call a cab. So, using the apps on his watch, he was able to call up a cab to pick him up at his house and fly him into town.

"Where would you like to go, sir?" The cab driver was Caucasian much like himself but was rather overweight, seemingly from all the sitting he did.

"Take me to the Citadel."

"All right, here we go." The yellow car lifted and turned toward the center of the sprawling metropolis of Vancouver. On this side of the continent was this large city, and on the other side of the continent was another humongous city named Washington.

The names of the remaining cities on the planet usually had to do with which city was left most intact after the war or had a special bearing on the war's end, such as where a pivotal victory was or what community was least ravaged from the destruction.

Nicodem could hear a slight variation in the modulating Mag Lev Emitters. "Hey, your MVE's sound like they could use a tune up. When's the last time you got this thing looked at?"

The driver seemed a little surprised at his knowledge of vehicles. "It's been a while. I should probably take it to the shop."

The lines of hover traffic that they soon entered were insanely long and not moving. A traffic jam. Six lanes on each side of their vessel, all positioned at different heights, were jammed.

The laws of the sky lanes were strictly enforced by frequent patrols of Vanixx Corps traffic control cruisers. Drivers were not allowed to cut in line or to jump out of the designated traffic paths to get to their destination sooner. To do so would result in heavy fines with increasingly severe punishment with multiple infractions.

Nicodem didn't get much time out of the house and didn't want to waste most of it waiting. He leaned forward and patted the driver on the shoulder. "Take me to Cathedral Market instead."

The cab driver nodded relieved, "That's a very good idea!" He looked around to make sure no patrols were nearby and made the maneuver.

The cab smoothly exited the hover lane, coming about and swiftly merging into the hover traffic lanes heading the opposite direction. The sun shining through the scuffed windows made light dance around the car's interior. The shadows of the cab's frame were slowly shifting around as the vessel turned to face the new path.

The Cathedral Market was the largest known

market in this city. Kado had tried to get jobs here hundreds of times with many merchants; they never wanted him.

Kado spent an hour crouched along an empty market wall begging for food, receiving none from the tens of thousands that filled the market. After his patience had worn out, he blended himself into the packed crowds as best as he could and kept an eye on where he could covertly snatch some food. Within a few minutes, he managed to pocket a couple small morsels of nutrition and decided to put his stained hood over his head to help protect his identity. Tens of thousands of people of various races, heights and sizes were all brushing past each other. Their clothes were not new, some tattered more than others.

Then Kado saw an opportunity presented right before his eyes: fruit! Fresh fruit! That was rare at these markets since actual fruit was so hard to come by these days. He quickly slid his hand through to the pile of apples from within the large crowd to grab one.

It had been several years since he tasted an apple, and he couldn't wait to bite into its crisp skin and taste its sweet, juicy interior. He felt the smooth, waxy skin of the apple in his grasp and pulled his hand in as fast as he could and thrust it into his hoodie pouch. He waited for just a moment to see if there was a ruckus or shouting from the theft and there was nothing. As Kado tried to calmly walk on through the crowd, a large, strong hand landed on his shoulder.

"That doesn't belong to you, little man," a booming bellowing voice loudly emanated from the giant. Kado turned to see who he was dealing with; he had been in a few scraps and fights before and always had escaped relatively unscathed or at least could always get a few hits in – but not this time. Standing nearly seven feet tall, this huge merchant wasn't about to let Kado get away with anything. As Kado squirmed, the gargantuan orangutan tightened his grip. He tried to figure a way out of this situation. As the large man pulled him back toward the display table, Kado managed to shift his weight and shove himself into the large man as he got distracted by other nearby customers – and Kado was free. He ran as fast as he could, shoving people out of the way and re-positioning himself to squeeze through the crowd. As he reached an open area away from the crowd, he could see his escape just steps away. As he was moments from freedom, another hand grabbed his arm with incredible strength and spun him around.

"Trust me. I'll get you out of this," an older man reassured young Kado.

"Hey man!" Kado was still desperate to get away.

"Just watch," he whispered. Something about this man made Kado feel just a little at ease. Something about his eyes, Kado felt he could trust him... just a little bit.

"Why are you-" Kado protested.

"Just shut up and watch."

The large man emerged from the crowd. This older man stepped forward, tipping his fedora in greeting to the burly, fuming merchant. "I see the boy forgot to pay. Here you go – that should cover it." He pulled out a large bill of cash, grossly overpaying for the rare but single handheld fruit.

The brawny seller snatched the bill out of the old man's hand and shouted, "I better not see him around here again!" At that, both men turned away from each other and parted ways. Kado was so dumbfounded by the old man's bravery that he forgot to run away from the whole scene like he had planned to do when he was no longer being held by the arm.

"What's your name, boy?"

"Uh – Kado."

"Nice to meet you, Kado. My name is Nicodem. Seems like you've fallen on hard times. Let me buy you a coffee and a snack."

Kado immediately put his guard up. "I don't accept

charity!"

Nicodem raised his hands. "Aye, I'm just doing a young man a favor and showing my appreciation for his help."

"Help?"

"Yes, you could be a big help to me."

"What? How?"

"Just come along, boy, I'll tell you. There's a coffee shop just down the street, isn't there?"

"Yes, but –"

"Consider this a job interview, son."

The café was plain and simple, but it had good coffee, which was the main reason it was full of people. During the war, the bulk of commerce fell to the wayside since the economy was focused on the war itself. With so many dying in the field, less and less was consumed or purchased. The economy, while being healthy for the rich and large corporate structures, crushed the medium and small businesses. As a result, in this part of the giant city, just tiny, struggling cafés were all that could survive. They had a method for sustaining their business: buy cheap product at cheap prices and sell with just a tiny profit so that they can support the common middle-class and lower-class people. As they walked in the old man inquired of Kado, "Why don't you grab us a table?" There was one open in the corner with two seats and he sat there awkwardly, unsure of the proper procedure since he had never bought a coffee before.

In just a few minutes the elderly man sat down with both drinks at their table.

"So, what're you doing in this part of town at such a young age?" The older man implored. Kado was reticent to respond as it would be so easy for him to digress into his life story. He hadn't opened up to anyone – even Lucious. Lucious never prodded or pried.

"Well...No parents meant no place to live. Lost them at 12."

"Oh, I'm so sorry to hear that."

"Yeah, well, I don't need your pity, old man."

"Nicodem."

"What?"

"I told you my name is Nicodem. No need for pleasantries or titles."

"Oh..."

"Well, Kado, tell me something else. Have you applied for work at other places?"

"I've applied to 302 separate places of business. I have an online Job Search account where I have submitted my résumé."

"Three hundred two! Well, my my. And why don't you have a job now? Surely one of them would've hired you by now."

"Surely? You have no idea what its like to live here, do you?" Kado's grip tightened on his mug, seething with the frustration he's endured his whole life. Nicodem raised a hand to stroke his chin in thought as Kado continued, "Nobody wants to hire you if you are homeless or an orphan. And if you are in your mid-twenties and never had a proper job then they *definitely* won't hire you."

"So, you've applied to hundreds of places, you're homeless and depressed, and now you resort to drugs and alcohol."

"How did you –"

"It's obvious: the red rings around your eyes, the bloodshot eyes, the sores on your face, the white chapped lips, and red nose. You've been in this state for a while." Kado shrunk in his chair when he finally realized just how much of an open book he was. Nicodem leaned forward over the steam from the hot coffee. "It's okay. I have a job for you. But it will require you to come clean. No more drugs, no more alcohol."

Kado sat up a bit. "What kind of job?"

"You'll help me around my house. I'm getting older

and can't keep up with all of it."

"You have your own house?"

"Well...yeah, sort of. I've had it a very long time. It's the one that you can see on the mountain a few miles away."

"Wow, must be nice."

"If you turn out to be the kind of man I think you are, you'll have a place to live. Your work will pay for room and board." Nicodem smiled.

Kado's eyes went wide, but he reverted back to his defensive stance – the attitude he'd had all his life. He would not, could not accept free things without having earned his pay. The very idea that he would appear like he needed help like this offended him.

"No. I can't accept charity of this degree. What do you think I am? Some punk kid who's lazy and needs to be *given* a place to live? What's the catch?"

"No catch. I pay you. You get a place to live. It's not complicated."

"Why me?"

"You're in need and I have a good feeling about you."

"I don't see how that's a good enough reason, old man."

"Nicodem."

"Huh? Oh right."

"Look – I know it seems too good to be true. But I really could use a hand around my house and instead of paying some maid $55 an hour, I'd rather pay you $40 an hour *and* give you place to live."

"What have I done for you to deserve such a random offer?" Kado continued his frown of mistrust.

"It's not what you've done, but what you could do that I'm interested in. You are young, strong and determined. I was just going to give you a job to care for my estate and my house, but when I heard your story, I thought I'd extend a home-stay scenario for you. If it works out you keep the job."

"I'm outta here! Take your money and your charity elsewhere!" Kado leapt up from his chair, bumping the table and knocking his coffee mug over, spilling it all over the table.

In seconds, he was out the front door leaving Nicodem to sit there with his thoughts. Nicodem saw something in this boy and knew this was the kid he was supposed to help.

The way they met was so accurate to how he saw this happen before – this had to be the young man he needed to meet. This was the young man who would help him fix the world.

How dare that old man offer me a job. What kind of job was that anyway? Cleaning his house? What am I – a maid? I mean, a job would do me well. I've been looking for one for years. It just seemed so set up, so arranged. It didn't feel right. Random stranger meets me, and then gets me out of a bind and just so happens to offer me a job? It was too perfect; something seems off about him. But wait – what am I thinking? I've been needing a job for so long and I turn this one away. What's wrong with me? Kado, conflicted and arguing with himself, paced up and down an alleyway.

He was trying to work out exactly why he refused the job. He concluded that he didn't like being handed things and that the whole thing seemed like a set up or a ruse by the Vanixx Corps or something. He would continue to apply for *legitimate* jobs and would try to get off drugs and alcohol himself. The cravings were so strong, though. But still he was determined to try and stop. He would get a job – he was sure of it.

That evening in the center of a bustling modern Vancouver square there was some protest going on across the street. The buildings had holographic screens everywhere lighting up the night sky with their flashing lights, advertisements, business signage, their blue and pink hues bleeding into the otherwise dull, starless evening.

The genetically modified trees and bushes which lined the streets and sidewalks, causeways and hover rails, acted as luminaries in this wealthy part of the city. They lit up the streets all night long, giving the illusion that green technology was advancing their civilization, wherein actuality, molecularly manipulated flora had become the norm. The many trees and bushes which were aglow could be seen from the tops of the skyscrapers all around the rich parts of Vancouver.

The Skyway Bar, stationed hundreds of feet above ground, enjoyed the radiant and illustrious view of the skyline. Unique cantilevered landing platforms for hover cars were built to make easier access to the bar and also to the mall which was just a few stories below in the same building. Being near the heart of Vancouver, they had the finest amenities with the most expensive menus.

A blonde man sat at the bar with a beer in hand. He was looking through his digital wallet pretending to care about what was in there. He looked at his picture and his information on his ID. ADRIAN GREEG, COMMANDING ADVISOR: VANIXX CORPS. He was here for a specific reason. He used the wall mirrors' reflection to avoid looking at his target directly. He was eyeing up an Officer of the Vanixx Corps who was sitting there in a private booth exchanging glances and whispering sweet nothings with a woman wearing a promiscuous red dress. Officer Wey Killarney was the target. Greeg's observations were twofold, but primarily he was assigned to keep an eye on some troublesome Officers, confront them about any inappropriate behavior making the Vanixx Corps appear in a negative light, and make them correct their ways.

He looked back to his ID, and scanning through the digital wallet, a small handheld holographic projector, he found pictures of his wife and son. Xander's most recent school picture melted his heart and brought a smile to his face. He was in grade D-10 and was to graduate when he was in the next grade. He swiped to a picture of his wife, Chloe. Both of them were blonde as well with wavy hair naturally like Chloe; his was a little curlier. The blue eyes of both of them would often entrance him. The longer he stared at these images the more likely he would shed a tear, reminded that their deaths were nearly ten years ago. He took a sip of his beer.

Recalling that he needed to be keeping an eye on the Officer, he looked through the reflection to their seats – they were gone. Heart rate rising, he slid off his chair and quickly made his way near their table, panning around the room trying to find the woman in the red dress. They were nowhere in sight. Darting outside, he scanned the nearby alleyways. Finally, he saw them getting into a hover taxicab on the flight platform. Below the platform was a 300-foot drop to the city ground. He needed to follow this guy; he couldn't risk losing sight of him. Vanixx Corps regulations were strict, and anyone with offenses needed observation and, if necessary, intervention. This particular Officer had been caught using illegal drugs and was disciplined for it. There was a periodic watch on him when he went to various establishments, however Adrian had volunteered for this assignment with an ulterior motive.

He ran down the alleyway and, just narrowly dodging discovery as Wey looked back, he threw himself back behind a hovering rusted garbage compactor. They hopped in the cab and took off flying into the distance. Adrian climbed on top of the garbage compactor, leapt off of it and scaled the side of the brick wall with great speed until he reached the roof. He jumped once more out over the streets glowing hundreds of feet below him and grabbed hold of a blue speeding hover car passing by.

Holding onto the dish-shaped hover stabilizer, he could see them flying off and nearly out of view. His body was being pulled away from the hover car by the speed they were flying. He adjusted his grip and braced as he lifted his knees up to his chest, crunched his abs, and brought his feet forward and up beside the hover car he was gripping to. He kicked his feet out as hard as he could while pushing up off the hover stabilizer, flipping himself backward and up over the roof of the aerodynamic hover car. His grip was now on the small top lip of the car's sunroof. The driver was panicking and shouting for him to get off; meanwhile he saw the cab several hundred feet away. Fortunately for Adrian, the sunroof was open, so he slid himself in and opened the car's side door, grabbed hold of the driver and threw him out, his shrieking fading as he fell. Adrian pressed a button causing the steering console to slide over from the left side of the car to the right, and he grabbed the yoke. Once he gained control of the car, he sped up to follow the cab closely.

"Where could you possibly be going?" Adrian asked rhetorically. The cab was flying beside several tall skyscrapers and towers, a slightly different route than most cabs would usually go, and he was unusually close to the buildings. They ended up in an area with no other hover cars forming traffic. He suspected that Wey would see he was being followed even if he was more than distracted. Adrian hung back further trying to appear inconspicuous. Just then the cab pulled over to a seemingly random platform, and the woman in the red dress was forcibly pushed out. She was screaming obscenities at them as they flew off with great speed.

Wey must've seen me, Adrian thought to himself. "Smart move," he stated rhetorically, then he sped off in hot pursuit. The cab was zooming beside some very large and very close skyscrapers in order to lose Adrian, but he was following closely. Where the cab was turning and zipping around buildings, he was flying straight and catching up with each useless evasive maneuver they made. Once they were lined up, he swerved to the left, and just as they passed a large tower, he rammed right into the side of the cab. As the windows shattered, Adrian timed it so that he would be thrown out from his own hijacked car and in through the window of theirs at the point of impact. He landed in the cab in the front seat, rolled and kicked the cab driver in the face, knocking him unconscious. Wey had pulled his handheld weapon at this point and had it trained on Adrian. Adrian transferred driver control to his side of the car, the controls sliding to the right-hand side, and he promptly halted the car in midair. Adrian faced him, leaning on the seatback nonchalantly, and held out his Vanixx Corps ID for easy viewing. "We're both in the V. C., man. You have a history of infractions, though, so I'm here to warn you." He could see Wey calm down as soon as he could see the badge, so he lowered his gun and sat back.

"Warn me? I've been tracked before on evenings out by intervention agents, and they've never followed me like you did just now. You could've killed us!" His skin was paler than Adrian's, although it was turning a shade of red with his flustered angst.

"Alright, you know the real reason I'm here. It's not for an intervention. It's about what you saw last week." Adrian's face held a false expression of pity.

"What do you mean? I-I didn't s-s-s-see anything," he stammered, knowing exactly what Adrian was referring to. He saw Adrian, and he knew what he had. He didn't know the full story, of course, but he knew too much. He continued to try to act like he didn't see anything. "Man, I have no idea what you're talking about. Really – I remember seeing your face there at the venue, but I didn't see anything else. Seriously, I don't know w-what you're referring to."

"Oh good. That's such a relief." Adrian slapped his hands on his knee acting out a calm, kind manner, but he wasn't really buying it. He could detect that Wey's heart rate was elevated with his own bionic implants; he could tell Wey was lying about what he had or hadn't seen.

"Alright, now that this is resolved, I better drop you off at the barracks."

"Uh...yeah, I guess." He was hesitant and was under the impression that his lie didn't work. Adrian began to pilot the hovercar back to the Vanixx Corps Barracks Tower where Wey lived. Wey still had his gun in hand, Adrian was dangerous, and he could stop him right now. He glanced down at his weapon thinking about what to do just in case Adrian didn't believe him and had other plans; he wanted to get prepared.

"What are you looking at, Wey? Wey? Are you looking at your gun? Are you thinking of shooting me?" He made "tsk" sounds of disappointment while slightly shaking his head. "Big mistake."

Wey held up his gun and had it touching the back of Adrian's head. "I saw everything, you're right. And I can't let someone like you get away with it. I know what was delivered to you."

A plasma shot could be heard from outside the car, a green flash lit up the interior for a brief moment, and the car began to swerve and plummet down out of control and crash into the buildings hundreds of feet down. Just as the cab slammed into the roof of one building, Adrian tucked and rolled out of the car, landing safely on the roof. He turned to see the yellow cab skid quickly off the roof and into the side of a skyscraper across the street, bursting into flames with an explosion as planned. The sounds of the explosion and glass shattering caused passersby to scream and shout. Emergency sirens could be heard in the distance. He had been planning this arrangement to silence Wey for a couple days. He was finally rid of this eyewitness that could've ruined everything.

Several nights passed and Nicodem decided it was time to stop waiting for Kado to come around. He would keep working at improving his inventions and ensure no one else misused or wrongfully possessed his technology. He spent several evenings tweaking the A.I. programming of his sword and adjusting the internal structure to have an improved quantum drive.

"A hundred exabytes ought to do." He mumbled to himself. He finished transferring the "mind" from the older quantum drive into the new one and inserted the cylindrical drive into the bottom of the blade's hilt. He allowed the blade to boot up, and the gem positioned in the widest part of the blade began to glow a radiant blue.

"Ahhh, there you are," he greeted the blade. It began to gently hum as it levitated above the table.

A few more evenings passed, and Nicodem got to the point in his holo-recordings where he wished to describe the internal construction of the Magna-Blade. In the bunker, he sat down beside the blade so that it was in view of the holo-recorder, which he positioned on a coffee table. He described the design of the blade, its internal structure and gem. He put the blade down and continued his story.

"As our understanding of A.I., quantum computing and web connectivity increased over the years, I continued to make improvements to this prototype. By the year 2150, the Military had the blades mass-produced in a few factories with a simple element of A.I. and connectivity. The Military of North America had a significant advantage over the rest of the world and offered these blades to their allies. Sadly, mass-producing these blades was something I was strongly against, but I had no power to stop it from happening. This mass-production led to the Magna-Blades getting into the wrong hands. What happened next, I feel fully responsible for, and I have been plagued by this grief for decades." He turned off the recording and rubbed his eyes.

It was late, and he had spent a lot of time recording

these videos, so much time that he almost forgot why he was doing it – but he had a purpose. These videos were not only for scientific observation and properly recording what actually happened in history, but he was soon to meet someone who could perhaps benefit from them, someone who would change his life forever.

"The Vanixx Corp have announced a new Executive Order of the Law," the holo-newscaster began, "stating that it is now illegal to own or possess any magnetic or anti-gravity technology other than a hover car or hover bus. This new law is slated to take effect immediately after crime with such technology has risen in the –"

Nicodem shut off the holo-news with a gesture. He knew they were talking about him, and he knew they suspected that he was the culprit who recently deprived them of their wrongfully obtained technology that *he* had invented. His recent visit to one of their many labs left it without the gravity orb they had been experimenting with; however, he still had much more to confiscate.

It was an unusually sunny day, and it had been about two weeks since Nicodem met Kado. He continually had the boy in his thoughts. He needed to help this boy. It could change the world and maybe even make it a slightly better place if he could turn this kid's life around. Nicodem decided that he would take a walk in the homeless part of the city at random times of the day. Over the course of three weeks, Nicodem had taken brief walks in the mornings for a few days, then at night, then the afternoon. He changed the course he walked and the location he walked each day. He would take a cab some days and other days he would walk into town, but each day he would go to a unique part of the nearby homeless sector. He was starting to give up and lose hope that he would ever meet Kado again. It was a very, very big city, being thousands of square miles from edge to edge. Perhaps he had moved on to a different part of town.

Kado had moved on to a slightly different part of the homeless sector. It was slightly closer to the taller, wealthier managed buildings, but not so close as to impose on their livelihood or lifestyle. He tried and tried to stop using drugs, but he was stuck being a slave to the addiction. Since he had no money, he had to pull small jobs to obtain funds or payment in his illicit drugs. After a few months of pulling these small jobs, starting before he had met Nicodem, he was getting a little more well known among a dangerous group of gangsters called the Hawx. Tonight was the night; he had his most important theft yet – breaking into a Grierstone Bank. These banks were some of the most well-guarded and also contained the most gold, precious metals and safety deposit boxes of the very wealthy. They were also the most well-hidden, being kept in secret locations near the homeless sectors. Everyone in the homeless sectors on the edges of the city were too poor to have any useful or effective weapons, and their drive was so broken that they wouldn't dare try to rob the banks. Kado was different – he had drive, he needed to survive, and this job would help him move to the next stage and maybe even get out of the homeless sector.

Close to midnight, Kado was getting briefed by two Hawx members in a hidden alley at the edge of the homeless sector. Kado was not yet a member of the Hawx, but this was going to be his way in. They stood close and spoke quietly, "Alright so this particular bank job is going to be tough. The front door is phase locked at night, so there isn't a way in there. But you can enter from the roof."

Kado nodded, paying close attention.

"The vault is in the basement and will require a special tool to get you in and out," the other member continued. "You've been granted the loan of this wartime Magna-Blade and a magna-strap. Use it only when absolutely necessary. Any strong detection of magnetic activity for more than a couple seconds will trigger an alarm, and you'll have Yuda to answer to."

Yuda Garrafor was the long-time leader of the Hawx and was well known for his ferocity and mercilessness. Kado hadn't met him before but had been told stories of his large belly, his big red beard and his scars on his hands.

"Failure of this job is not an option," the first member added. "If you are caught, you are not to tell them who you are affiliated with. Officially you are not affiliated with anyone; you work alone. If successful, the Hawx *may* consider your entry into the group."

Kado nodded. The two started to walk away.

"Wait – how do I use this thing?" he beseeched

them, trying to get their attention while remaining quiet.

One turned back briefly, "Use your brain."

Kado turned and walked off as they went in different directions silently without another word.

The roof could only be accessed one way: from another roof. Kado had never used a Magna-Blade before and had only ever heard of them – he'd never even seen one before. He was a couple of blocks away from the bank and tried conceptualizing how he would get on the roof. He had heard some of the things a Magna-Blade could do and knew that it was supposed to connect with his neural pathways somehow. He held it in his left hand and, looking at it, thought what he wanted the blade to do: *Fly up.* The blade immediately lifted both him and the sword into the air, as if he were wearing some sort of hover boots. Startled, he rose slowly, trying not to shake or shimmy too much from his loss of balance.

He reached the top of the high roof. Astonished, he peered over the edge of the roof and walked up to the ledge on the other side to look down at the city. The bank was a few buildings away and was significantly lower in height than the building he landed on. *How am I going to do this without dying?* Kado thought to himself. Just then, he was presented with an image. But the image was not his own imagination. It was a picture of a path to take: A line showed his dive onto the bank's roof, then there was a yellow bar indicating when he would activate the Magna-Blade's anti-gravity level for just two seconds. The idea wasn't his – it came *from* the blade! These things could really communicate telepathically or neurally somehow! Kado was shocked.

He kept the thought in his mind and decided he may need to run at it. Backing up to give himself some space to sprint, he took a breath and bolted forward. In seconds, he reached the edge of the roof and jumped off. The blade, strapped to his back, stayed put and kept relaying the concept image to his mind. As he plummeted several dozen feet, he kept thinking to activate the anti-gravity of the blade. As he was close to touching the roof, the blade indeed obeyed his thoughts – it activated for just over a second and Kado landed with a hard-hitting roll onto the flat roof. Kado grunted in pain but was impressed at how effective this Magna-Blade was. He now needed to get to the basement. There was a hatch on the roof, so he began to pull at the latch. It was stuck and wouldn't budge after he tried it a few times. Inside the building on the other side of this hatch there was a lock keeping the door sealed tight, hidden safely from burglars like him.

He held the Magna-Blade, resting it on the hatch, and he thought of gravity overwhelming the door. In seconds, the hatch crumpled under severe stress of what seemed to be dramatically increased gravity. The hatch gave way a moment later, falling into the darkness, and he could hop down into the building. He was in. *That was surprisingly easy.* He slid the Magna-Blade onto his leather back magna-strap again and quietly descended down the dim-lit flights of stairs. When he neared the basement, he realized some guards were posted at the doors. He quietly brought himself closer to the basement level and stopped at two stories up, hoping they didn't hear him coming down. He pulled out the Magna-Blade and thought a question to it. He thought the scenario that he was in: *two guards at the door two stories down, four flights of stairs.* The blade returned an image thought of jumping down the wide-open gap that ran down the center of the stairwell and when he reached the bottom, he could let the blade fly around like a boomerang and strike down both guards. That wasn't his style – he didn't want to kill anyone. So, the blade came up with a less lethal alternative – spin himself and the blade around incredibly fast and use a gravity blast to knock the guards into the walls unconscious. He preferred that plan, so he jumped down the stairwell center and began to spin himself around. As he released the gravity blast, one of the guards was too quick and managed to get a shot off; an energy-charged plasma bolt struck him in the back, possibly piercing one or more of his internal organs. Screaming in pain, he lay on the floor unable to move. He realized he was being way too loud and covered his mouth with his hand, trying desperately to be quiet. The pain got worse, like a stabbing and burning sensation coming from within his core. Biting his hand to try and distract him from the most severe pain, he rolled over grasping at his side as the Magna-Blade lay on the floor motionless beside him. He took a few moments to breathe and tried to stand himself up, using the blade as a makeshift cane so he could complete the job.

Come on, Kado, you can do it.

He stumbled over to the door about to lead into the basement. As he nearly opened it with the simple handle he thought, *I need to do this more covertly.* Seeing a ventilation grate above the entrance to the basement, he used the blade itself to try and quietly pry open the venting. Once it was fully opened, he crawled into the dusty shaft. Crawling along, he found the path to the vault. As he neared the vault door in the ceiling vent, he was conjuring up a way to safely get down and break into it. As he peered into the room through the vent, he noticed that there were no guards. Normally there were ten guards in this room alone. Instead what he saw was a black duffel bag near the vault door. He peered closer, and through the opening of the bag he saw a timer counting down – 42 seconds. It was a bomb!

How on Earth am I going to get far enough away from this bomb in just half a minute? Kado thought to himself. Then looking up, he saw the vent going straight up several stories. This would be his way out. In seconds Kado, blade in hand, was airborne and quickly rising to the top of the ventilation shaft. Moments later, a huge flaming explosion erupted through the vent that he was just looking through, chasing him up the shaft as if it wanted to devour him. Kado slammed into the end of the vertical shaft with a loud, hollow thud and bounced off down a side corridor. He could feel the heat of the rolling, raging inferno close behind him as he was sliding along the horizontal corridor of the ventilation shaft. He kept thinking, *What good is a Magna-Blade against an explosion?*

A visual representation sent to his mind from the Magna-Blade indicated that he could use gravity to crush the ventilation shaft behind him, which would extinguish the flame. Kado agreed, "Let's do it!" He spun around as he was skidding along and aimed the Magna-Blade at the blazing wall of flame just inches away from him. The walls of the shaft first expanded outward for a split second, then slammed into each other with a violent crushing effect.

The fire had been extinguished, and Kado slid to a stop seconds later. He sat there a moment at the exit of the shaft, and he climbed out into a service corridor, covering all the things in his mind that still could go wrong with an explosion of that size. Yes, the danger of the flame was gone, but what condition was the building in? What condition was *he* in? He tried to ignore the pulsating pain in his back.

Just behind Kado was the end of the ventilation shaft that he had just exited, and smoke steadily billowed up through it from other vents from down below. Some of the smoke came into the small hallway where he stood. Kado needed to leave immediately or he could pass out from lack of oxygen and die right here. He used his thoughts to command the Magna-Blade to blast him through the ceiling and fly skyward. Chunks of building were coming down toward him. Kado requested the blade to provide a way to prevent the building from landing on him and killing him, but he wasn't being specific enough, so all it could do was shield him from direct hits of concrete. The building indeed had started to collapse and Kado's attempts at escaping were dismal. Twenty stories of building were coming down on him, and he had no way out.

The building had become a pile of rubble. Dust had filled the air in a great circumference around where the building once stood. The Vanixx Corps and their subsidiary fire crew were all around the building checking for survivors and trying to clean up the debris. Their various colors of emergency vehicle lights flashed continually, lighting up the night sky. The Vanixx Corps vehicles flashed blue, the fire crew's flashed red and the medical crews shone a golden yellow. The Vanixx Corps arrived in force very quickly after the explosion since they knew this was a secret Grierstone Bank. Just under half of the homeless sector heard the actual explosion, while the rest of the homeless and part of the middle-class workers' sector heard about the explosion through word of mouth.

Kado awoke to blackness and incredible, deep pain in just about every part of his body. One of his legs was definitely broken at the calf. He had a broken arm on the opposite side. Something sharp had impaled him in the back, so he tried not to breathe too deeply. A fairly large piece of building was putting pressure on his forehead; he couldn't move any limbs. As he was trying to figure out which parts of him were injured most, he realized he was having trouble breathing in. Thinking about trying to call for help, he realized he still had the Magna-Blade in his hand. If they caught him with this weapon, he'd go to prison for a very long time. He needed this building wreckage off. Just then he received a mind image: A gentle rise of gravity could lift all the rubble off of him and he could walk out of there. Kado shook his head – with a broken leg, he couldn't walk anywhere. Then a new image entered his mind: Use an intense blast of gravity in the surrounding area to allow him to fly away from the scene. *That could work.*

A rumbling began to shake part of the rubble. The sound of stone and wood and concrete crushing against each other came from the center of the rubble. Several dozen chunks of building were thrown up into the air as the nearby search lights caught a glimpse of something bolting up and flying with incredible speed into the night sky. In seconds, the flying shape was gone and out of sight. A lieutenant named Trion of the Vanixx Corps was able to see that the flying object was not just an object but a person, a person holding what could only be a Magna-Blade. He knew exactly who to report this incident to.

Kado, with cuts, gashes, bruises and breaks in almost all parts of his body, limbs and face, was struggling to fly with the amount of blood he was losing and with the fierce grievance his body had just been through. He was relieved that it was just starting to snow; the cold air would hopefully help him stay awake. Flying with a Magna-Blade was incredible; he felt like a bird. Oddly enough, only a partial force of the air coming at him could be felt. It must've been something to do with how the blade was helping them fly. He was so distracted by the pain he was in that he couldn't fully appreciate the rare chance he had to fly a Magna-Blade. He neared the alley where he was briefed and landed on his knees from being so weak. The crunching of his broken calf caused a shock wave of stabbing pain through him, leading to a convulsion through his body, and he lay down on his side. He was shaking from his injuries now reaching shock. The two Hawx members walked up and stood next to him, while four more stood back at a distance. One of them grabbed the blade from the ground.

"You failed. How can such incompetent behavior be rewarded?"

"You ... don't ... understand."

"We understand you brought the whole building down! This was supposed to be a covert operation!"

"No, there was a –"

They picked him up by his arms. Kado shouted in pain; one of them was gripping tightly right where his break was.

"Bomb." He managed to exhale the word through his shock, clenched teeth and immeasurable agony. The two looked to each other.

"Are you saying someone got there before you?" one of them asked, surprised. All he could do was nod and drop his head forward from lack of strength. The two bickered quietly, but Kado was not able to comprehend anything they were saying.

"Kado, you know the price for failure." One of them pushed him back onto his knees. Kado's body was in such a state of shock that he couldn't even feel pain anymore and was barely aware of what was around him. One held him from behind while the other held the Magna-Blade in his hands, pointing towards the ground like a golf club, and was getting ready to strike. As the gangster raised the blade to deliver a fatal upward blow, he was struck by an electrical jolt from behind and fell to the ground unconscious.

Swinging a thin metal cane charged with electricity, the well-dressed man in a fedora spun with fluid movements, dodging punches and avoiding plasma bolts. As if with one graceful spinning stroke, he incapacitated six Hawx members in seconds. All six lay there in a spread-out line down the alley, twitching from electrical convulsions. While rushing to Kado's side, Nicodem simultaneously summoned the Hawx's Magna-Blade to one hand, retracted the extendable metal pole in his other hand, placed it back in his pocket and mounted the Magna-Blade onto a magnetic set of plates stitched into the back of his coat. As Nicodem carefully lifted him up to his one good foot, Kado quietly remarked, "You're pretty good with that stick thing."

Kado awoke with significantly less pain, and he was in a warm, soft bed. He had bandages on his arms and hands. He looked to the mirror on the wall; more bandages were wrapped around his head. He had gotten himself into a real mess this time. He couldn't believe he survived it. He lifted the blanket and saw more bandages around his waist with some red staining on his stomach. He couldn't help but wonder just how bad the damage was and if he would ever fully recover. He looked over to a nearby chair and saw new clothes laid out for him.

"Ah Kado, you're awake. Good morning!" Nicodem kindly greeted him as he walked into the room.

"Morning. Uh, thanks for saving me last night."

"Last night? Oh, I see. Kado," Nicodem gently rested a hand on his shoulder. "You were asleep for two weeks. It took some complicated measures to safely get you out of your coma – had this happened a few years earlier, we may not have had the medical capabilities to get you awake. You really were in rough shape."

"How did this all happen?" inquired Kado, gesturing to his bandages. "You didn't take me to a hospital, did you?"

"Of course not," he came back with a slight chuckle. "No, I have some friends in the hospital who owe me a favor, so I called it in."

Kado could not understand why he was being so kind and so generous, but all he could think to say right now was, "Thank you."

"It was my pleasure. You may have many questions, but first rest some more, then we'll talk." Nicodem turned to a nurse that walked up beside him. "Ah yes, this is Betty. I trust her with my life. She'll make sure your injuries are healing properly."

Betty tended to Kado's wounds and breaks while Nicodem returned to his study, where the Magna-Blade he discovered last night was left on a desk.

It was a little worse for wear. The blade was from the earlier days of the war; he recognized it was one of the first editions issued. It didn't use the highest quality metal and so after well over a century, it was starting to degrade. Metal was rusting, wherever it struck something hard enough it had some dings in the blade itself, and it wasn't as sharp as it once was. It had the first-generation A.I. so it wasn't the smartest, but it did the job. Nicodem was aware that the majority of the blades were destroyed to end the war, but finding this one reminded him that there were many still out there.

A few days passed as Kado slowly healed in his bed while Nicodem spent time in his bunker to record more videos and prepare for when Kado was in better shape. He was hopeful that Kado would be helpful in the near future for his endeavors to make the planet a better place.

Nicodem was sitting in his chair, eyes closed, hands together, two fingers straight, resting against his nose. His thoughts revolved around the future, specifically the year 2387 and what the future may or may not hold and what technology could exist at that time.

"Praying for a Savior?" Kado invited jokingly as he hobbled in on crutches.

Nicodem opened his eyes, remembering what time he was actually present in. "It's good to see you up and about. Betty tells me your breaks will be fully mended in a few days."

"Yeah, that's pretty unreal. Only the rich and famous get this kind of treatment." Kado managed to get himself to a couch facing the chair. "Who are you?"

"I'm just an old man with some money."

"So, you're loaded?"

"Let's just say I was in the Military."

"Oh wow. And why were you offering me a job?"

"I need someone around here who can help me around the house. Someone young and strong."

"Well, look at me, I'm not exactly strong right now, am I?"

"A technicality that will be remedied in a few weeks." Nicodem smiled, his hands still resting together.

"Speaking of which, what's that stuff you've been pumping into me? I feel great already. The pain is virtually gone."

"It's a special pharmaceutical that isn't exactly available on *any* market."

"Really? Something I've never had before? Sounds interesting."

"About that: A condition of you staying here is that you don't take any more drugs and can't drink alcohol."

"But you're giving me drugs already."

"In the context of recovering from a near-death experience. This is your chance to leave that life behind. These kinds of chances don't come around often, let alone twice!" Nicodem kept his kind smile through the whole conversation.

Kado shrunk into his seat. "It won't be easy."

"The most important lessons never are."

A stern knock echoed the halls. It came on the front door. Kado was a little surprised. "Expecting company?"

Nicodem checked his watch, not seeing a proximity alert. "No. Stay there." Suddenly turned serious, he exited the study and locked the door behind him. Nicodem quietly approached the front door and checked the security cameras on his watch; they were all disabled. He swiped to an emergency screen on his watch and pressed a red circle button on the screen signaling emergency procedures that were put in place around his house. He peered through the small view finder on the door and saw it was the General. He was somewhat put at ease because the General was diplomatic, but their discovery of his proximity sensor was unnerving. Nicodem opened the door for the General and a small battalion that he brought with him, "Good morning, General, I hope that you are enjoying the day. I didn't hear your ship arrive."

"Right, well, I got promoted today, and they gave me a fancier craft. It runs a little nicer than the last one."

"Congratulations! So, what do I call you?" Nicodem smiled.

The Military commander stepped over the threshold ready to investigate the home, saying dismissively, "You will call me Admiral now."

"I have some family visiting, so now isn't a great time, otherwise I'd offer you a cup of tea." Nicodem followed the Admiral along with the Vanixx Corps Tactical Team members who were now pouring through the halls of his house, covering every square inch of the house that they could. Their uniforms were unique – fully black with some sort of embroidered patch on the shoulder that was completely black as well. The Admiral looked back briefly as he continued his leading stride. "Oh? What family? We have a full record of your family – you are the last one."

"Indeed, that's what we all thought. However, I discovered a nephew a few months ago who lives in another part of town," Nicodem rejoined kindly, brushing aside the rude reminder of his murdered family.

"I would very much like to meet this 'nephew' of yours," the Admiral subtly grinned.

His mission was to ascertain what was going on with the Magna-Blade technology. They secretly scanned the house frequently at random times throughout the years and never saw any detection of Magna-Blade technology.

Nicodem stepped up to the Admiral as he neared the study, saying gently, "I'd be happy to arrange that for you."

The Admiral tried turning the handle. "Any particular reason why the study is locked?"

"I lock it at night – I have some very valuable books in there. This house is a target for theft, being on the outskirts of town. Just haven't unlocked this entrance to the study yet." Nicodem pulled out his ancient key and unlocked the door, and they entered into the study. They saw Kado sitting on the couch with his crutches resting against the couch arm.

"And who are you, son?"

"My name's Kado."

"Kado what?"

"Kado Veradiun, same as my uncle."

"And why don't we have you in our records?"

"Do you have every orphan from the homeless sector in your records?" Kado tried not to be snotty. He leaned forward on his knees.

"Hmm. And how long have you known you had an uncle?"

"I assumed I had family somewhere, but only just discovered him two and a half months ago." Kado answered naturally and was not intimidated by his prying questions.

"How did you two meet?"

"Funny story, I was in the market, and Uncle here happened to be in the market as well. I saw his name on his payment card as he was handing it to the merchant, and it was the same last name as mine," Kado naturally explained as if he'd told the story twenty times before.

"And what of these injuries? How did this happen?" The Admiral gestured with a finger to all of Kado.

"Oh, being homeless sucks. Other homeless people tend to gang up on you if you have something valuable they want. About a month ago I was given a gift certificate for a market and they cornered me, beat it out of me and took off."

"But you had money enough to dye your hair grey?" The Admiral again gestured, this time to his head.

Kado shrugged. "I actually don't know why my hair is this color. It's always been this color."

Satisfied, the Admiral nodded and walked around the room looking at all the books, the great view of the mountains and the city outside the large windows. Nicodem was partly surprised and relieved that the wartime Magna-Blade was out of sight. Kado must've hidden it.

"Admiral, I really do enjoy our visits, however the Vanixx Corps sending such a high-ranking official to my door for a visit – I'm not sure it's really in your best interests after seven decades. Please do stay for tea, I have enough for the whole team."

"No, no, I think it's time we left. We just wanted to make sure you were doing well and keeping healthy. As you mentioned, this place is a target for theft and there have been reports of troublemakers in this area."

Nicodem bowed a slight amount with apparently

sincere respect. "I thank you, Admiral. You've always taken such good care of me as I get older."

"Yes, well, we can't neglect our veterans. We better get going. Men! Move out!" The Military team left the house single file. It was obvious to everyone that neither one meant what they were saying. As the Admiral stepped out of the door, he quietly commanded a soldier beside him, "Make sure you set up the remote nano-cameras in the trees surrounding the house."

"Yes, sir," he conferred.

The Admiral turned to one other with a question, "Did you set up the new security viewers inside?"

They nodded, "We did, sir."

"Excellent, have a twenty-four/seven watch on every camera at every angle around the property. With the new hidden cameras set up throughout the whole house, we'll be sure to see what's going on then." The entire team stepped up the ramp of the Admiral's shiny vessel. It was shaped like a wedge at the front with two adjacent wings pitching up at a modest angle and coming to a sharp point on each end. The craft was fairly large but had a sleek set of angles complementing its size. The rear had two large vertically rectangular dormers sticking out of either side of the main fuselage. Some would assume they were engines to push the vehicle forward.

Kado and Nicodem were in the study and watched the brand-new Admiral's yacht lift off with stunning silence, barely any residual wind disruption and almost unbelievable agility. Nicodem knew that they were using his technology to propel that craft.

They were getting further in their research; much further than he had anticipated or hoped. It seemed once they developed the A.I., they could be well on the way to redeveloping the Magna-Blade. The Military were never on board with the destruction of them all in the first place, but they were required to be submissive to the Peace Committee and the political rulers of the remaining, then-desolate nations. He pondered the consequences silently. If they had indeed developed this technology at this size, they could use it for far worse purposes.

Kado was in awe at the ship. "I've never seen anything like that ship. It was like a shiny, black dagger that could strike through anything!"

Nicodem was about to lower Kado's enthusiasm, but instead decided to show Kado something far more interesting. "That was nothing. Come see this."

Time was running out, and Nicodem needed an ally. Nicodem knew they brought in more microscopic cameras; he would find them and trick their visuals with some pre-recorded videos that he had made a few weeks earlier. He walked over to a wall that he assumed was still hidden by the cameras and pulled out a red book. Inside was a small screen that turned on when exposed to the light. Kado followed close behind on his crutches.

The interface was blue and black, and Nicodem knew his way around it like the alphabet since it was an operating system he designed. Nicodem had set up some cameras earlier and spent five days recording himself just going about his usual routines throughout the week. Some of the cameras were in Kado's room as he lay in a coma sleeping. Nicodem was planning to splice in video footage of him going about his day at random times throughout the recordings and apply them to the cameras that they had already installed, but when they inserted more, it was a perfect opportunity for Nicodem to install the hack. Nicodem's own pre-recorded video footage would be inserted and fill in periodically with just blank rooms the rest of the time. The Vanixx Corps may leave them alone for a little while longer. He just needed to press a few more touch-sensitive buttons on the book's secret screen to insert the videos to replace the actual live feed and they would have total privacy for the time being. He pressed a couple more buttons and closed the book. "There we are. Privacy. Both auditory and visually."

"What do you mean?"

"My boy, they most likely inserted dozens of hidden cameras throughout the whole house when they were here."

"How do you know?" Kado was perplexed.

"I used to be one of them."

"Wha-really? Is that why they are here? To make sure you won't betray government secrets?"

"Many questions, Kado. You are going to have many more questions – rest assured they will all be answered." Nicodem walked to the other side of the study, and with a downward full-armed gesture to the windows, they darkened a few shades.

"What was that?" Kado pursued, nonplussed.

"I shielded all rooms from outside view. I don't want anyone peeking in."

"Really? You can do that? With just a wave of your hand?"

"Yes, but just you wait – there is more." Nicodem turned back with a mischievous smile. Nicodem used his neural connection with the operating system of the house to send a silent command, and the walls of this section of bookshelf began to open up. As the walls moved away, an interior library was shown. Kado's jaw fell open, and his eyes went wide with utter shock and amazement.

"A secret room?" he exclaimed loudly. Nicodem

rather enjoyed sharing this with someone. He'd never done this before.

"Come on inside," he gestured with a welcoming hand. Kado swung into the room on his crutches behind Nicodem. On the wall was the Magna-Blade that belonged to Nicodem. Kado was so distracted by the walls moving he didn't even notice it at first until he turned to look at the wall of books.

"What is that? Another sword?" Kado did a double-take to see a gorgeous, shiny and elegant sword hanging downward by the cross guard on a small mount. Its metal was the most polished that he had ever seen, and the translucent hexagonal gem that was forged into the center of the thickest part of the blade somehow added an element of grace.

"I've never even imagined anything like this before." Kado leaned in close to it. "It looks like a sword mixed with an ancient circuit board."

Nicodem stood back enjoying Kado's true appreciation for its beauty. "Nice observation. I was inspired by pre-quantum computing technology. It's one of a kind."

Kado continued to peer at the blade and turned back to Nicodem. "Does it have a name?"

"A name?"

"You know, like the old fable of Excalibur."

"Interesting. Yes, the blade has a name; in fact, I let it name itself."

"You what? How?"

"Come with me," Nicodem insisted as he mentally commanded the secret entrance to open. Another wall opened exposing a secret elevator door. As soon as Nicodem turned his back to the sword, it flew off the mount and rested against Nicodem's back.

"How did it do that?" Kado couldn't help but ask, being shocked by the wall opening a second time but also by the blade flying on its own.

"Magnets. It's a Magna-Blade." Nicodem smiled as he turned back, the blade now affixed to his back at an angle similar to a sword in a sheath perched on one's back. Kado was speechless as he entered the elevator door, and they began to descend.

They descended for what felt like an eternity to Kado with his mind bouncing around with a thousand questions. He kept returning to the thought that he was just dreaming or on a really weird drug trip. But as he continued to walk with Nicodem through the basement bunker, he kept realizing how real this was.

"You've heard of the Gravity War?"

"Of course, it changed the entire planet," Kado

retorted with obliviousness.

"I caused it," Nicodem admitted, leading with a sigh.

"Oh...well, you don't seem like someone who would've wanted to kill people."

"I didn't – I wanted make a tool that could control gravity. It's useful applications were endless. But the Military had other ideas, and I had a family that I could lose if I didn't comply." Kado lowered his head as he followed Nicodem out of the elevator; he went around to different parts of the bunker, showing the lab tables and experiments he'd continued to work on.

"Now I've lost them too. All I have left are my creations, and it's been my sole purpose to retrieve them from the Vanixx Corps, the Quell, gangs, criminals or anyone who might have this technology."

"That's a big job," Kado remarked dispassionately to compensate for the unexpected sting of sympathy he felt for the old man. Kado had never felt this kind of solicitude for anyone before, not even his dearest friend, Lucious. Perhaps, he thought, it was because he had been helped so much by Nicodem already.

Nicodem turned to Kado. "I can't do it alone. I'm far too old to do it on my own." Kado could see where this was going, though he couldn't believe it.

"Will you assist me?" Nicodem implored with a

serious yet endearing expression. Kado turned to look away as he considered the consequences of such a huge, life-changing request. Out of all of the questions rolling around in his mind, the only words he could utter were, "Why me?"

"You hid the Magna-Blade before the Admiral entered the room, and you figured out my last name. That was good thinking. I need someone like that; someone able to adapt and learn quickly."

"I'll...have to think about it," Kado hesitatingly responded. This was a big life decision. This would change everything. But that was Nicodem's point. Everything *needed* to change, and if anyone saw a broken system that needed fixing, it was Kado.

"When you think about it, think about the life you were living – the future you had. You nearly died. And compare it to here: a life with a roof over your head, food, clothing. Instead of the high from drugs, you'd have a bit of peace and satisfaction from making the world a safer, better place."

Kado looked around the bunker; he had a huge responsibility ahead of him if he were to accept this path. He couldn't make such a decision on the fly.

"Let me sleep on it. I'll need a few days to process this."

"Sure, I respect that you aren't rushing into anything; that's showing maturity." Nicodem rested a hand on Kado's shoulder briefly in a gesture of encouragement.

"You could've given this opportunity to any homeless thief though", Kado scratched his head as more of a confused gesture rather than feeling a true itch, "But you chose me. All you knew about me was that I was a criminal and lived on the street. You offered me the job *before* you saw my traits. And you came and found me after a number of weeks of me pushing you away. What spurred on that decision?"

Nicodem sat back down, "As you can see from the screens here, I have security cameras. Sometimes I send a mobile camera out through the city to get a glimpse of what's going on. I had been under strict house arrest for quite some time so traveling about was rare for me until recently." Kado nodded with interest as Nicodem constructed his explanation, "One day, a number of months ago, my surveillance camera caught a glimpse of you feeding soup to a sick old man. It was pouring and he looked most unwell. You seemed to have stolen some soup at great risk to yourself for him to have a warm, be it, small meal."

Kado's eyes welled up just enough for Nicodem to

detect the suppressed emotions Kado was struggling to hide. He quickly shook the sadness by fueling himself with a vexing memory. His tears repressed themselves and hid away for another day.

"It was at that moment that I knew I found the person I needed. Someone who knew such grievous loss, but still had tenderness enough to help someone."

"I can't accept your charity, Doc. There's so many out there suffering, how can I just live in a mansion in good conscience?"

"It's a means to an end. And the fact that you wouldn't take advantage of my generosity is exactly why I'm offering you a place to live. Anyone else - I would've treated their addictions and returned them to the streets with enough money to rent a unit for a few months so they could have enough time to get themselves a steady job."

Kado hung his head at the explanation, feeling as undeserving as a few months ago. Nicodem wasn't going to give up and his goals to help the world made sense. But he – he knew nothing about this sort of thing; sword-fighting, saving the world, magnetics, gravitational physics – none of it!

"I'm useless to you. I've never been around technology all my life, except to run from a V.C. blaster."

"Let me teach you. You have no idea of the potential

you have."

Kado shook his head, his overwhelming sense of feeling nugatory was obvious to Nicodem. He decided he'd have to motivate the incredibly humble Kado another way, "You asked if it had a name."

Kado looked up suddenly remembering their recent conversation from earlier, "Yeah?"

Nicodem took the blade off his back and, holding it horizontally, handed it to Kado. He was leaning against a lab table and rested his crutches against the table. Holding such a relic in his hands was a magnificent feeling, like he was holding decades of history right in front of him.

"That is the first ever Magna-Blade," Nicodem proudly stated pointing at it. "It's the very first prototype. The other blades were made and given upgrades as time went on, but this one remained unchanged for several decades. Once the war was over and the fighting was done, I kept holding onto this one. I hid it from everyone and made sure it survived. I kept upgrading it, writing new code, updating the A.I. Now, it's a masterpiece." Kado stared at it with amazement.

"What is it made out of?" Kado inquired.

"Magtanium." Nicodem grinned with pride.

"What's Magtanium?"

"Magtanium is a rare elemental anomaly found in certain types of space rock that originally came from many thousands of lightyears away and eventually made it into our region of space. When the space program became advanced enough to travel to farther distances at greater speeds, they discovered these elements on distant asteroids and returned them to Earth. Small portions of this space rock were donated to several universities throughout the United States, Japan and England. That was before they knew its value and before it was named Magtanium."

"What's so special about it?"

"It has the compressive strength of titanium but with various magnetic capabilities. The magnetic force on the metal could be weakened or strengthened manually by touching a magnetic element to its surface. The metal would actually imitate the magnet touching it and would exponentially increase the strength of the magnetic properties of the metal. After a few years of research, I was able to harness control of that metal, building it into a magnetic staff."

"Wow. I had no idea about the space programs." Kado's eyebrows raised.

"I'm not surprised, the history books are pretty vague these days."

"So, it's made out of Magnetium?"

Nicodem chuckled, "Mag*tanium*. It's actually a prototype alloy that became outlawed shortly after the Gravity War. Well, it became outlawed *because* of the Gravity War. We made the blades out of a Magtanium-Tungsten-Carbide alloy."

Kado raised an eyebrow, not fully comprehending the alloy concept.

"Ah, never mind that. It's a very difficult and meticulous process to forge these blades and they are virtually indestructible. These small orbs are positioned into the blade so that they can enhance the blade's ability to – uh fly." Nicodem stroked the lines of circuitry as he described the great care and attention to detail that went into building this display of master craftsmanship.

"At first it was quite basic, but as the Military got wind of the concept of the invention I had started on and I was conscripted. After that, more advancements were quickly made."

Nicodem held the blade out, "Ask what its name is."

"What's its name?" Kado queried Nicodem.

"No, no, no, no, ask *it* what *its* name is," Nicodem chortled.

Kado's eyes went wide as he looked down at the blade in his hand. "Hello. What's your name?"

Hi, my name is Xostir.

Kado couldn't believe what he was hearing or what he thought he was hearing. It felt like the information just kind of appeared in his thoughts; his visual and auditory receptors in his mind were being triggered to activate. It was the blade's artificial consciousness communicating a thought and concept to him. The communication was rendering in Kado's mind as a grown man's voice, slightly deeper than usual with a slight rasp of age and experience. He started to laugh at the incredible invention and handed the blade back to Nicodem.

"That is amazing! Its name is 'show steer'? What kind of name is that? Wait, you said it picked the name. How smart is this thing? How did you –" Kado was speechless after yammering those questions out.

Nicodem returned the blade to his back.

"It's spelled X-O-S-T-I-R. It chose the name, not me. I don't know what it means or why it was chosen. Come on, Betty will want to see how your breaks are healing up."

As they rode up the elevator, Kado was beginning to realize that this could be his first true shot at life, a fresh start. But it all still seemed too good to be true. How did they end up meeting so perfectly? It just seemed so convenient. Why did Nicodem choose him? How did they meet a second time in one of the largest cities on the planet? Thoughts like this would circle through his mind several dozen times a day. Kado was really beginning to trust Nicodem, and perhaps he would fully once he learned more about him. As Kado was heading to his room, he suddenly felt dizzy and nauseated. Nicodem came around the corner and nurse Betty came around the other corner. Kado had a sudden surge of adrenaline and aggression against both of them and pushed them away shouting, "Leave me alone! Where are they?"

"Where are what, Kado?" Nicodem shouted back, trying to restrain the boy.

"My drugs! You stole them! Where are they – I need them!"

"They are destroyed. You don't take them anymore," Nicodem tried to say calmly as they struggled. Nurse Betty ran off to a supply closet nearby and returned with a needle.

"These are withdrawals, Kado. They will pass," Nicodem continued to try to reassure Kado. Nurse Betty injected a substance into Kado to sedate him.

"There," she stated. "That will help with those terrible symptoms and his cravings of the drugs. We'll administer this twice a day for him." Nurse Betty took a breath.

"Let's get him into his bed." Nicodem was holding a

completely limp Kado, trying to keep him from falling to the floor. These withdrawals had happened earlier and would continue to happen a few more times before they would completely stop.

The Admiral's yacht *Traffinjo* neared its landing pad in the center of the great sprawling city of Vancouver. As the vessel swiftly swung in for a landing, it slowed before it touched down. Its glistening shine flashed, and its sheen brilliantly blinded nearby Vanixx Corps onlookers as it slowly turned and finally reached the proper position to land.

The platform was a giant, flat disc that extended out of the pole-like spire structure it was attached to. It was attached at a single point, a walkway between the building's entrance and the platform itself.

A ramp lowered from the belly of the ship, and the Admiral hastily made his way out of the vessel and toward the tower. A blonde man with a cape stood on the landing platform awaiting his arrival and met the Admiral's stride, his cape blowing in the wind.

"How was the field trip?" he inquired of the Admiral. He was just about as tall as the Military leader.

"Oh, he was as respectful as ever. But we had an

interesting surprise."

"Oh?"

"Yes, he apparently has a nephew."

"No, he doesn't." The blonde man was confident in his response.

"That's what I thought. Find out who this kid is and put a hit on him," the Admiral ordered as they entered the tower entrance. The silence of the elevator after the powerful winds was greatly welcomed.

"No need. I'll take care of the kid myself."

The Admiral and his advisor stood at the entrance of the circular room observing the holo-screens. There were nine large screens filtering through the twenty-seven cameras set up in Nicodem's house and around the property. The screens alternated between three different camera locations assigned to each monitor.

The blonde man remarked with a smirk, "It won't be long before we catch him in the act." The Admiral nodded with a smile.

"Greeg, your performance has been exemplary these recent years. That's why I've wanted you as my advisor. When they told me the amount of experience you had experimenting with his technology and inventions in the Magnetics Division, I knew I needed you on my team." The Admiral spoke flatly with some admiration sensed in his tone.

Greeg smiled with the compliment. "Thank you, sir."

"I'm ordering you to do research on this boy. Figure out where he comes from and what his ambitions are and draw him out. The hit needs to be in the city far from Nicodem. We can't risk losing that man's mind yet. He still has some creations he's hiding from us that could be instrumental in securing peace."

"Understood, sir." Greeg saluted and left the room to begin his new mission.

"Adrian Greeg is an advisor to Admiral Vaux, whom we just met, and one of his most trusted Officers. He's a big threat because he's done an incredible amount of research on my technology and inventions," Nicodem explained, holding a small palm-sized holo-recording of the man. He continued to swipe through a few more images of him; noticing his burly physique was unavoidable. He was in very good shape, and that made him even more intimidating.

"I met him a few times before they set me up in this 'retirement home' and restricted my access to my old lab in the Vanixx Corps region. He's ruthless and smart, making him very dangerous." He swiped to the next person of interest. "This is Lieutenant Rego Trion, also familiar with the use of Magna-Blades, more so than the average person." The holo-recording showed a rough looking man with jet black hair and a small scar on his cheek. He was older than the previous guy by quite a few years but looked just as relentless and cruel.

"He can tell if you are using a Magna-Blade from a mile away, or he'll suspect you of it at the very least." Nicodem continued to scan through other people to be cautious of as Kado was sitting on his bed getting his casts removed by nurse Betty.

"Get some sleep; tomorrow is going to be fun." Nicodem patted Kado on the back as he left. Nurse Betty finished up moments later, and Kado was left wondering what tomorrow would bring.

As the morning sun rose, Adrian Greeg was already at work to find out where this kid had come from. The Admiral had advised that the boy said he was from the homeless sector, which was why they had no record of him. So that was the first place he went. Greeg strode through the homeless sector with two Vanixx Corps Officers following close behind. Everyone in the streets and alleyways avoided eye contact and moved out of the way as best as they could. If they were too slow or old to move, they were pushed aside. Greeg knew exactly where to go. A specific merchant in the homeless sector had been a very helpful informant for many decades. Greeg found the merchant's store; it was less busy than all the others. He knocked heavily and with urgency on the side post of the bar-like window.

"Yes, how may I be of service to ya?" An elderly, frail man walked up to the service window.

Greeg leaned on the bar casually. "I'm looking for someone."

"Of course. I'll do my best to assist."

"This is a young guy, early twenties, faded grey hair; he's kind of slim or scrawny."

"Ah yes, I know of this young man. He's dead."

"Is that so?" Adrian was frowning, trying to determine if the old man was lying or if he was just misinformed.

"Well, you see, I heard that he tried to do this job for the Hawx – a particularly nasty group of gangsters. Well, that job didn't go so well, you see. He failed them pretty miserably. So, they offed him. At least that's what I heard."

"And who told you that they killed him?"

"That's what everyone's been sayin'. Well, what else woulda happened? He fails a job for the Hawx, then is never heard from again? That's what they do. They pay well, or they kill ya. It's been a few weeks since anyone's heard of him or seen him around. He'd be one of the few young ones of that age group in these here parts."

"A few weeks?" This was starting to sound like the mystery "nephew." "Do you know exactly when he took that job?"

"Aw, you gonna ask an old man for specific dates? Sheesh – let's see uh… when woulda that been? Hmm…" He stood there looking down at the bar he was leaning on as he counted with both of his severely wrinkled, arthritic hands. "Two…three… Yeah, about three weeks ago. Is that specific 'nuff fer ya?"

Adrian nodded. "Good enough for me. Thanks." He began to walk away and snapped his fingers. The two Vanixx Corps Officers fired upon the old man. The onlookers gasped and screamed. Adrian commented to himself philosophically, "The price of knowledge."

Later that day, in early evening, Adrian went to his apartment to pack. His apartment was just a couple blocks from the Vanixx Corps central Citadel. He was ostensibly obsessive about keeping his apartment perfectly clean and tidy. Everything had its place, and all items were arranged with perfect symmetry. His two-story penthouse had been his home for the past two years as he rapidly climbed through the ranks of the Vanixx Corps. The higher status meant a higher salary since such officials were incredibly well compensated.

His previous apartment was smaller but was just as clean. Adrian kept the color of his entire modern penthouse white and the furniture of a similar color palette. He was up in his room in the upstairs vaulted loft. The view of the city with the floor-to-ceiling windows was glorious every day. Nearly everything in his house was automated. The water taps, the wipes dispensers, the food-producing molecule resequencers, the holo-projectors, all of it responded to Adrian's voice. Adrian had a small backpack resting on his bed and was finishing putting his essentials in. He was really going to miss living here.

Nicodem brought Kado back down to the bunker after a hearty breakfast. He needed to show Kado the reasons behind helping him and some of the principles that made this goal worthwhile and filled with purpose.

"Have you decided yet?" Nicodem questioned.

"No. I'm still unsure." Kado responded. He was a little lost. He felt obligated to help Nicodem. But at the same time, he felt that if he was going to do this, he needed to do it because he really wanted to, not just as a repayment or just because he owed Nicodem. He needed some convincing, and he wasn't convinced.

"Well, let me show you some things about Magna-Blades and explain what could happen if we do nothing. Not many people understand what Magna-Blades are capable of."

Nicodem opened a nearby storage locker and pulled out a long, blue cloak. It was a radiant blue, with two white bands on the left-hand side secured with two golden buckles holding the front part of the jacket closed. It looked so futuristic with a large vertical collar that wrapped around the front. The collar could be flipped down or left up; either way it looked really neat. On the cuffs of the jacket were another set of white strips of leather-like material with golden buckles.

He handed it to Kado. "Try it on. It doesn't fit me all that well anymore." Kado carefully put it on. It looked like it was a slightly used jacket, but it was of a very high-quality material so it could last a long, long time. The bottom of the coat edge rested at his ankles, while the front of the jacket was a bit shorter with a taper. The jacket had unique lines on it that made it seem handmade and one of a kind. It was warm, comfortable and seemed like it fit him perfectly. *Did he somehow tailor this jacket to fit me? If it were any longer it would be too long, but this fits just perfectly. Where did he get such a jacket, did he make it for himself? Did we really share the same measurements at one point?* Nicodem wasn't large in any sense, but at his advanced age, he had developed a small amount of aged weight and a bit of a hunch. Kado walked around and looked at himself in a nearby mirror, admiring the jacket.

Nicodem sat down on a nearby hover couch that could be moved about in the bunker easily, "Have I ever told you about my family?" Kado turned, surprised, "No."

"Ah well, my wife and daughter. They were incredible. You remind me of – well, let's just say it feels like you are the son I never had. Just – your mannerisms, your countenance, the way you speak. It reminds me of my daughter, Alice." Kado was struck with the revelation.

He felt a bond with Nicodem unlike any other. Yes, he was dear friends with Lucious, but that was more of a friendship. What he had with Nicodem was almost like an adoptive father. The many hours that he had helped Kado through the dark nights of drug withdrawals had brought them closer than either of them would've imagined. Kado was free to leave whenever he wanted now that his leg had healed but Nicodem was doing everything he could to get Kado to stay.

Nicodem picked up his blade and threw Xostir into the air towards Kado - it paused, as if it froze in midair. It was Xostir who stopped itself from falling. It rested stationary at about eye level between Kado and Nicodem.

"Summon the blade," Nicodem encouraged.

"Why?"

"There is a relationship between wielder and blade. The two need to work together to be valuable, to be effective," Nicodem explained slowly.

Kado nodded, not fully understanding what he meant. The blade continued to remain frozen in the air mid-throw.

"Come to me," Kado softly asked. He didn't feel comfortable speaking to an artificial intelligence. The blade didn't move.

"Come here. Please?" he tried again.

"Come." He paused. "Come on." His voice raised as if he were calling a pet.

"It's not a dog! It's a sword!" Nicodem raised his voice with disbelief.

Kado shut his eyes, held out his hand and thought, *please come to my hand.* The blade immediately left its frozen position and rested its hilt right into his left hand. Kado opened his surprised eyes as he observed the sword. It was much thicker and naturally heavier than the blade he had attempted to use earlier. But despite its weight, it was constantly adjusting itself so that it moved easily and was easy for him to hold. It was so light, it was almost hovering in every position Kado held it – Kado could tell something unique was happening. Because Xostir was doing this, it made it very easy to wield the big sword as if it were a small thin branch.

"It's so light!" he exclaimed.

"Yes, it's self-levitating for you. It can understand your thoughts and intentions, so it knows exactly how to hover and how to move before you mentally command your arms and hands," Nicodem explained.

Kado moved the blade around slowly and carefully. It was much more advanced than the older wartime blade he had used before. Just being near the blade, he could feel a connection with it.

"Rest the blade on your back," Nicodem instructed.

"Like this?" Kado raised the blade and rested it onto his back. He could feel that it magnetically attached to the jacket. "Oh, there are magnets in the jacket lining?"

Nicodem nodded. "But they are specifically paired with this one Magna-Blade. Magnets can have multiple frequencies of attachment, and so I've used that to help Xostir connect to the jacket easily. Other blades can still connect to it, but when Xostir connects, it is able to detect and control almost everything about this cloak. If you are in close proximity to the blade, you can send it commands with your thoughts."

"So, it obeys my commands?"

"It listens to you, but works *with* you, not for you. The wielder and the blade must become a team in almost a symbiotic relationship. It takes time, but once a wielder spends enough time with a Magna-Blade of this caliber and advanced level, the bond cannot be broken."

"I didn't think this kind of technology was possible." Kado was astonished.

"It isn't. Well – it's hard to explain," Nicodem stammered.

"What do you mean?"

A loud alarm erupted from speakers in the walls of the bunker. Kado looked around at the walls with concern and placed the blade on his back.

"Ah, that's my new proximity alert. I set it out at a farther circumference this time to give us more time to prepare," Nicodem explained as he walked toward the elevator door.

"Prepare...for what?" Kado urged, troubled.

"Another visit perhaps," he parried with a smile. The two rode up the long elevator shaft. "Pretty fascinating stuff, right?"

"Yeah." Kado was quieter than his usual self and from this sudden quietude, Nicodem could detect the conflict within Kado.

"Well, whether you leave or not, you need to learn how to defend yourself better. So, we can continue these exercises, and if you head back to the homeless sector, you'll stand a better chance at surviving longer in a fight. Who knows, maybe you'll decide to stay, and I can teach you more of what I've learned." Nicodem gave a warm smile. Kado realized that he had finally begun to truly trust this man. Perhaps the first time he's truly trusted someone to this degree.

"You notice your drug cravings are completely gone now?" Nicodem asked with another smirk. Kado had completely forgotten about his cravings and addictions. His last session of withdrawal symptoms was last week and as usual, Nicodem sat with him all through the night, providing him with water and making sure Kado couldn't hurt himself. He hadn't had any withdrawals now for eight days!

"Wow, yeah! That's amazing!"

"You feel better now, right?"

"Yes, so much! I can't remember the last time I actually felt like myself."

"Good man; we'll need you to have a clear head. I still have much to teach you."

The elevator door opened, and the two of them walked out, past the fake library doors, and into the study.

Kado had decided that today was the day that he would tell Nicodem just how wonderful these past few weeks have been and how big a help it has been to his life. Getting him off drugs permanently and teaching him so much about being a proper member of society were hugely impactful to his life and his attitude. He now actually felt motivated to learn, to do something, to help. Nicodem truly felt like the father he never had and he was going to try to make it up to him – somehow.

Nicodem raised his arms to gesture the windows to go into lockdown mode, where metal plating would sheath all the windows and doors. Kado realized he was still wearing the jacket and blade, so he turned around to head back to the secret library entrance to return Xostir to his proper spot. He reached for the blade to take it off.

Without warning, they heard the sound of glass cracking followed by a metallic clanging. Kado felt the blade on his back gently vibrate as if it had been struck by something. He turned to look at the cracked study window then to Nicodem who was holding the side of his own neck, collapsing limp to the floor. Nicodem had been shot!

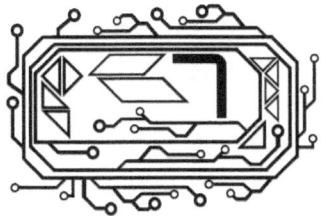

The sniper lowered his scope from his face. Adrian grinned, despite the unexpected results, as he saw the shot he fired deflected off the Magna-Blade that the boy was holding. He had just lifted it in time for the bullet to miss the back of his head.

What a downright shame, he sarcastically thought to himself. He feared nothing of the consequences that the

Admiral would have for Nicodem's demise. It was supposed to be a shot at Kado first, then Nicodem afterwards since Kado was younger and faster – it would've been much more difficult to hit him second.

"Plan B," he calmly ordered into his wrist communicator. He got up from lying on his chest on a flat portion of a nearby mountain and grabbed his rifle. He folded it up into a smaller shape and placed it into a backpack. He began to descend the mountain and passed the proximity sensor he had unknowingly triggered earlier, quite pleased with himself.

Kado fell to Nicodem's side, "Nicodem! Nicodem!" His breath was short. The bullet had gone through his neck, narrowly missing his vocal cords, but striking a vital artery.

"Don't..." he began to say. Kado was looking at Nicodem's eyes. He wasn't scared. He had something important to say, and it took his remaining strength and life to say these final words.

"Don't avenge *me.*" Nicodem's eyes became dim and lifeless.

He's gone.

Kado couldn't believe it. He needed more time. He wasn't ready. He was just going to tell him he was going to stay and help! He was going to express how Nicodem had become a father to him. And now he was just - gone! He couldn't tell him any of it! He reached to close Nicodem's eyes but felt a pull from behind. He skidded back on his knees before he could shut Nicodem's eyelids. Kado was being pulled away from Nicodem's corpse by someone or something. He looked behind him and didn't see anyone pulling – it was Xostir! The blade was using its abilities to yank Kado away from his mentor and dear friend.

Xostir flew itself into Kado's hands and implanted a thought image into his mind. It was of him holding the hilt with the blade pointing to the ground and jumping onto the blade to ride it, almost like a hover board. He was supposed to be crouched and could fly on the blade that way. There was a sense of urgency with this mental image – whatever he was going to do, it had to be *now*.

Kado knew what he needed to do. He looked over to the window that was cracked and penetrated with a bullet hole and ran toward it. He held the blade by the hilt with the sword facing downward, and he leapt through the mostly intact window, shattering it into a thousand pieces. As he began to descend, he brought the blade up to his feet and planted them, one in front of the other, on the wide side of the blade. It felt like it was happening in slow motion. He could hear some sort of jet approaching.

Immediately, he flew with great speed away from the house just as he heard an extremely loud explosion erupt from right behind him. Flames surrounded his peripheral vision as he was propelled forward at incredible velocity. He looked back as he was escaping and saw the entire home break apart. Wood shreds spun and flew in every direction; shingles from the roof were falling from the sky. Flames engulfed the entire structure, and the reinforced metal frame that secretly formed the skeleton of the home was twisted and melting from the heat. Thick black smoke billowed into the air.

It was a missile! They fired a missile at us! They killed Nicodem! They have to pay...Nicodem's last words...teaching me with his last words, his deathbed request...unbelievable. "Don't avenge me"? Who says that!

Kado and Xostir flew a great distance away at unfathomable speeds and shot up way up in the air above the clouds. Kado was breathing heavily, trying to catch his breath from everything – from the traumatic death of this friend, from the death-dealing explosion he just narrowly escaped, and from the velocities he was escaping at. Trembling, he lowered himself to sit on the blade like a surfer on a surfboard, and he just looked down at the clouds as he hovered in place. He stayed there for what seemed like an eternity to Xostir. Kado was in such a stupor, without him really realizing it they had eventually landed on the top of a nearby mountain. Looking back at the home on the outskirts of the metropolis, he could see a small flame from this distance, the smoke rising high in the air.

Kado was beginning to feel again after his moments of disconnect from the real world. He began feeling grief, anxiety, loss and confusion and was getting odd impressions from the blade as well. But he didn't even know Nicodem that well yet; why was he feeling such extreme pain in this way? He continued to wonder about everything in a cyclical pattern. He was spiraling. Perhaps the blade's grief was influencing his emotions. *What am I going to do now? I wasn't sure about going along with Nicodem's idea, and now he's gone. Do I owe it to him to do this now? Must I? Can't I just go on with a normal life? Someone has to pay for what happened here. But Nicodem...he beseeched me not to avenge his death. Why would he ask me not to avenge his death?* Kado was asking himself these questions.

Vengeance brings war.

What was that? As Kado was thinking these things to himself, he starting to hear things. It was the blade! Xostir was communicating thoughts, concepts and even sentences to him!

"What do you mean vengeance brings war?" he spoke aloud to the blade.

Nicodem always used to say, "Vengeance brings war." He was determined not to avenge any of the past misgivings of the Vanixx Corps, but he was ready to take back what was his.

"So, what do you say we do now? Can we go give him a proper burial?"

The missile did an unfortunate amount of damage to the house. I'm afraid a proper burial isn't possible, Xostir reciprocated. Kado was frustrated; it was very cold, tears were in his eyes and he paced around in anxious circles while the blade was hovering horizontally over the ground near Kado.

Please collect some kindling and some sticks.

"What? Why?" Kado was being snotty, having just been through an explosive evening.

Your body temperature is too far below normal and you risk getting hypothermia, Xostir accounted factually to Kado's mind. He got up and found a few nearby sticks and small branches and placed them in a pile. Xostir used its magnetic abilities to pick up two rocks, place them over the fire and vibrate them together at great speed. The two rocks were hovering close to the sticks and soon were sparking from the friction and speed they were clicking against each other. The sparks landed on the small branches, and they caught on fire. Kado sat near it to stay warm, feeling appreciative of Xostir's excellent survival skills.

"Very well done. Thank you." After some painful but necessary silence passed, Xostir spoke up.

The bunker is still intact.

"How would you know?"

It must still be intact; the missile only struck the exterior shell of the mountain, and the bunker goes down at least 100 feet into sheer rock. Odds are 5:1 that it is still 97 percent fully intact. Otherwise I estimate that it is not damaged at all. Also, my connection to the bunker and its cameras indicate it is fully intact.

Kado paused; he couldn't believe he was speaking with a machine. A machine with some very solid arguments. "Those are good odds. So, what? We go back there and jump down the elevator shaft? That place will be crawling with Vanixx Corps goons by now. Look at the jets overhead."

Indeed, it will be unsafe to return at this time. We should go back at a later time tonight. There is a secret entrance where we can safely get in.

"Of course there is. Nicodem – always some sort of secret entrance somewhere. Gotta love that guy." Kado couldn't hold back more flowing tears. He only knew the man a few months, but there was some sort of connection there, as if they had known each other for years. Nicodem seemed to know him well, but he never had a chance to get to understand Nicodem. Just as he was starting to value their friendship and the knowledge that he could glean from him, he lost him. *Another dear friend dead. How many times is this going to happen?* Kado thought to himself. For a moment he forgot that Xostir could understand or comprehend everything he was thinking.

"Could you maybe get out of my head for a moment while I grieve?"

The connection is constant. I cannot "get out of your head," but I can stop monitoring your thoughts for the time being if that is what you would like.

"Does that mean you won't listen to my thoughts?"

Affirmative, Xostir returned silently.

"Good. Yes. Please that's what I want you to do," Kado replied, grief echoing through his voice. To any passerby, it would've looked like Kado was speaking to himself, but to Kado, he was having a conversation with a sentient artificial being telepathically. Kado sat down, head in his hands, and he took some deep breaths to try and calm himself. He didn't care how cold it was atop this mountain, he would stay here for as long as he could. He wanted to shut the world off and he wanted it to end, all of it. He had enough, and he needed it to all go away.

"You what?" Admiral Vaux shouted at the top of his very large lungs.

Adrian fluttered his eyes from the extreme exclamation, like one would blink rapidly from being windswept. Adrian had no fear of his consequences; he killed who really was supposed to die in his opinion. The boy didn't matter to him.

"You disobeyed a direct order from me! You killed the one man that we deemed a valid asset for the Magnetics Division – *your* division!" Admiral François Vaux had been mad before. He had been livid many times. But he had never been so rage filled as he was now at Greeg. Vaux had great respect for Nicodem, although he would never admit it. He never intended for the old man to die before his time. He was actually trying to help extend his life because he kind of liked the old guy. It would've also benefited him greatly if they could've discovered some more of the inventions he was hiding. He was greatly disturbed and fuming that this travesty happened.

The ignorance, the insolence: It was inexcusable. He had others executed for court-martial offenses or disobeying a direct order, and he very much wanted to do the same here. However, Adrian was protected from an immediate execution by the complicated politics and bureaucracy of the Vanixx Corps.

Several other Admirals had vetted his appointment to such high-ranking stations as public advisor and General counsel, and he was esteemed as an expert in tactical procedures. The Vanixx Corps found him invaluable, and he was even in line for a promotion from commanding agent up to a Vanixx Corps specialist agent. He couldn't be touched without following the proper procedures. Killing Adrian Greeg outside of a hearing would cause a fallout between the Admirals of the Vanixx Corps, perhaps shaking it to its foundation. He couldn't have that.

"I felt I did what had to be done," Adrian responded respectfully without any apologetic tones.

"Of course you did, Adrian," Vaux growled with disdain. "If you weren't so loved by the other Admirals, you'd be a dead man right this moment for disobeying a direct order!" Adrian stood tall with his hands behind his back. The Admiral wanted to shake his confidence. "If you cross me again, nothing will stop me from ending your 'career' suddenly and dramatically."

Greeg, understanding the euphemism, continued to

smile, unwavering in his confidence. This frustrated Vaux even more.

He had to leave before he strangled the fool. The Admiral quickly turned on his heel and walked with fierce purpose out to his glistening ship. Even at night, the surrounding lights of the buildings and the hover cars in the distance reflected and refracted off his ship. The ship lifted off and bolted away silently toward the direction of the late Nicodem's destroyed house.

Kado was punishing himself by subjecting his body to the frigid mountain air; he had moved farther away from the fire. He felt like he deserved it. He had been up there with Xostir for a few hours now, just watching the flames of the house die down and the embers glow. He had just met Nicodem; he didn't get enough time to know Nicodem. *It's not fair!*

You are correct. It is not fair. I think it's time we found you someplace to warm up, Xostir projected to Kado's mind.

"I think you should mind your own business," Kado grumbled back.

We are paired now. Everything you do is my business. If you die from hypothermia, I will have lost my maker and my newest friend. Please don't let me go through that in one day, Xostir pleaded.

Kado opened his eyes, looking over to the hovering vertical blade with exhausted surprise. *Friend?* He shook his head, shrugged nonchalantly and, rolling his eyes, bantered, "Oh alright, take me somewhere warm."

The café was dim-lit and very quiet in a middle-class part of the city. Only a few patrons were sitting in their chairs sipping their coffees. Kado had a coffee in hand as well; travel cups from stores these days were worse than they ever were before. His hand was burning from the heat of the coffee since the wall of the travel cup was so thin. He kept his hand on it, again a form of self-inflicted wounding. Xostir immediately knew what he was doing since their thoughts were interconnected.

I know what you are doing.

"Oh? And what am I doing?"

You are blaming yourself for the death of our friend, and to ease your guilt and the pain in your heart you are inflicting indirect harm and pain onto your body.

"Yeah – what are you gonna do to stop me?"

Well...I blame myself also. The bullet ricocheted off me. I should've seen it coming.

"No one saw it coming. You can't blame yourself."

Exactly. Logic dictates that we are equally not to blame or equally to blame.

"I suppose." They both were grieving and comforting each other. Kado never realized an artificial intelligence could grieve for a human, and it opened up possibilities to him about the kind of relationship he could have with Xostir. Could they actually become friends? Just then he realized no one had asked him about a giant sword on his back. "Hey, why isn't anyone concerned about you being on my back?"

I can bend the light around myself with gravity to such a degree that I become invisible to the naked eye.

"Oh, *that's* interesting."

Yes, it's called a gravity cloak.

"Wow. I have so much to learn."

The amount of activity around the house has reduced by 90 percent. They must be satisfied that there are no survivors. We can go to the secret entrance now.

"Lead the way," Kado concluded. They left the café, and outside of the front door, Kado took his Magna-Blade off his back and let Xostir levitate on its own in midair.

Hop on. Xostir positioned itself to be horizontal about a foot from the ground. Kado jumped on and grasped the hilt, and they took off with immeasurable speed back to the outskirts of town, over to the mountains near the house in a roundabout way, and then down the mountain side. Xostir was navigating them and was zipping around and past the trees at a very low altitude. Kado could understand Xostir's motives and plans since their minds were linked. Xostir was avoiding any detection from Vanixx Corps scanners.

It felt like he was hooked up to a massive repository of knowledge and wisdom and that any concept he was unsure of or didn't understand was explained and taught to him almost instantly in a moment.

Kado had never experienced such speed of flight as he had with Xostir. His adrenaline was pumping from the rush of blasting through the forest at such incredible velocity. They were flying down the slope of the mountain towards the base of a shallow valley. Once they exited the forest, they flew low along a relaxed river. The water was disturbed by the gravitational field Xostir was generating. They were rapidly approaching a steep rock face, and Kado was starting to get concerned.

"Uh…are we going around that thing? We are going around the rock, right?" Kado petitioned, his voice raised over the surrounding wind. Xostir was oddly silent; all he could sense was: *We are going in the right direction.* He thought maybe their connection was faulting or that perhaps Xostir was glitching somehow. They came closer and closer to the rock wall; it looked like a blur. It was basically vertical with moss and sharp edges everywhere. Kado tried to jump off, but his cloak was magnetized to the blade at several points and he was being kept in some sort of gravitational bubble; he couldn't jump off the blade! Kado shouted in cringing fear as they reached the rock wall at a lethal velocity. Then they vanished.

Kado felt cold wind against his face. He opened his eyes and saw that he was in a dark tunnel.

"That was not funny!"

I was not trying to be humorous.

"You could've explained that the wall was fake somehow!"

It is a holographic projection to conceal this secret entrance. I apologize, usually explanation was never necessary.

"It was definitely necessary this time – I thought I was gonna die!"

I have apologized. Shall I do so again?

"No, no, that's fine."

They continued to round the many corners of the tunnel until they finally reached the end. They slowed down to a crawl and rose. They were rising again into a solid stone ceiling of the tunnel. Kado hoped that it was still holographic again but was uneasy about it regardless.

Through the holographic ceiling of the tunnel, they had entered a far corner of Nicodem's bunker. Kado looked around the room and turned around to see that they had flown into the room through a fake holographic display of cylindrical canisters. The bunker was completely unharmed. The blade helped him hover over to solid ground, and Kado hopped off, dusting himself.

"Alright, so what do we do now?" Kado asked himself and Xostir, hoping Xostir had some good suggestions.

"I think I can help answer some of your questions." It was Nicodem's voice!

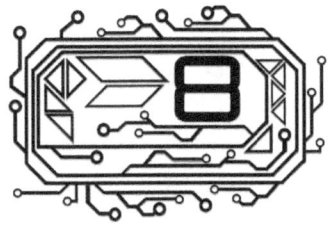

François stood near the flaming rubble. A melted piece of the previously secret reinforced frame within the bones of the house broke and fell down. The Admiral just smiled, "Nicodem, you sly little..." He stepped over to some parts of the rubble that weren't burning. "Reinforced Titanium frame. Full lockdown bulletproof shielding capabilities. You must never have seen this attack coming." He looked up at the night sky, the Vanixx Corps tower in the distance and the perilous black smoke from the destruction. François sighed, "Neither did I."

He turned around and headed back to his ship. He felt responsible for the death of a good inventor, and even if he would never have said this to his face, Nicodem was a good man, too. There weren't enough of them in this world.

Vaux joined the Vanixx Corps just as it was formed in 2179 following the Gravity War. It was formed at the very end of the war. When it was first established, it was designed to help bring peace. Right after the war, the process began to abolish the police force and change the UN. The government, after much deliberation, ended up passing the bill instituted by the recently initiated Worldwide Peace Committee to completely revamp, rebrand and reestablish this new weaponized force. The bill passed with the goal of never letting anything like a global Gravity War happen ever again. He entered as a low-ranking cadet and slowly rose up the ranks. Since his father had been killed late in the Gravity War, he was inspired to join to try to do good, and now over century later, he was responsible for the death of a truly good man. Being in the Vanixx Corps had slowly destroyed his soul and turned him into someone else. He knew this early on but not before it was too late. Nobody defected from the Vanixx Corps, especially since the penalty was death.

He stepped up the ramp of his yacht and ordered it to be flown back to the Vanixx Corps tower. His thoughts focused on the consequences that he would inflict on Greeg. He may have been popular with all of the other Admirals, but he had crossed the line many times before and had done so for the last time.

Kado turned around to see a holo-recording playing from the floor of the bunker. There was a holo-projector set up in the floor, and it was displaying an almost life-sized rendition of Nicodem.

"You are here because I have died in some way," the recording of Nicodem began. "Kado, I have pre-recorded videos for you to learn from and to benefit from. If you choose to stay, you can watch these videos to your heart's content. If you choose to leave, these holo-recordings will be permanently deleted, as they contain secrets too dangerous to fall into the wrong hands." The recording of Nicodem stood with both hands held out, text displayed on each hand, one saying "STAY" and one saying "LEAVE."

"Uh...can I speak to this thing?" He turned back, expecting an answer from Xostir but just went on with his question anyway, "Um...what happens to Xostir if I decide to leave?"

"If you leave, everything involving Magna-Blade technology gets erased from the library of this bunker. This includes the artificial intelligence units containing all knowledge and information about Magna-Blade technology," the hologram of Nicodem bluntly stated with a slight friendly smile. It was surreal and unnerving to see a hologram of the late Nicodem so soon after witnessing his death earlier that evening. He understood that leaving now meant Xostir would lose all of its memories, its A.I. would be erased permanently – essentially killing his new friend. Could he really allow that to happen? Xostir could sense the conflict in Kado and slowly approached Kado, hovering vertically.

Are you going to leave?

"No." Kado was resolute as he touched the interactive hologram's hand showing the "STAY" message. Kado had been feeling conflicted: Seeing such a good man killed unjustly could easily make him fall into his grief and return to his old ways. But seeing Nicodem again in the holographic form ended the conflict. He was going to finish the job and return all Magna-Blade technology back to where it belonged – in this lab, this bunker for Nicodem. Kado turned to the interactive hologram. "Where do we start?"

Early that morning, Adrian Greeg went to the gym to work out his core. After a couple hours of a hard workout, he went for a shower. After drying off, he grabbed a duffel bag from his locker in the shower/change room that the Vanixx Corps provided along with their state-of-the-art gym. He opened the duffel bag to make sure everything he needed was inside. He closed it when he heard some soldiers entering the change room. He had just finished sliding his shirt on before he perused the equipment he had, threw the bag over his shoulder with two cylinders sticking out the top of the bag, and left the change room. He would go to the gym as often as he could. Every morning and any break he had would be started with a protein shake followed by a very intense workout. This morning he was amped up. He had his orders, and he wasn't about to fail his mission.

François stood at his office window staring out to the foggy skyline. This morning was particularly pretty as the skyscrapers in the distance were silhouetted by the white, blinding fog. The sun was trying to shine through but instead just lit up the sky like a big, radiant wall of light.

He had reported the deliberate insubordination of

Agent Greeg and the loss of valuable assets as a result. Though they were shocked and disappointed, the proof was all there. He arranged for a tribunal to happen as soon as possible for his court martial. The punishment was harsher than before the war, so insubordination was extremely rare. He waited in his favorite leather chair in his office with solace as the time neared for the tribunal.

"The next fundamental truth to be aware of is that the world does not want to be your friend. But there are allies possible at every encounter," the pre-recorded hologram of Nicodem went on to explain. Kado was standing facing the holo-recording, blade in hand.

"Now, let's show you some stances." The blade flew into view on the hologram into Nicodem's hands and he brought his left foot back and held the blade to his side.

"This is Guard of the Roof, next is Posta di Corona, also known as Posta di Frontale." He swung the sword outward, holding it slightly up in the air with his arms mostly straight. He then continued to go through several other longsword stances. When he went through all of them, Kado had to repeat them faster until he could memorize all of the moves. As he was repeating the moves and forgetting them, Xostir kept sending small reminders to his mind of what the stances should be, subtly repositioning itself in his hands every once in a while.

Next, he was directed to go over more steps of how to control the many different magnetic and gravitational abilities Xostir had.

"Now let's practice hovering. The blade can generate a gravitational bubble around you effectively letting you fly." He began to hover on the holo-recording with Xostir in hand. Kado copied the action in step.

Kado spent the next several hours absorbing over a century of information both from the holo-recordings and from the connection with Xostir. He had much more to learn, but he would have to continue that tomorrow. He was exhausted and overwhelmed by the huge amount of knowledge he had just gained in such a short amount of time.

The next day, Kado awoke from the floor of the bunker. He had found an old sleeping bag that belonged to Nicodem and used that for warmth. Xostir had a wall mount in the bunker that would be used to place itself on and enter into sleep mode. He stretched as he sat up. This was not a good permanent solution.

"Concrete is not great to sleep on." Kado stiffly stood

up. Xostir lifted off from the wall mount across the room and hovered over near Kado. *We could find a bed for you. There are large storage containers down here, and you might find something useful.*

"There are?" Kado's inflection rose with some surprise. "Alright, let's see if we can't set up a bed for me to sleep on."

He walked in through the door leading into the storage hall. The door opened up to a hallway with three doors on each side.

The bed is in the farthest door on the left, Xostir relayed to him. Opening up the door he saw a disassembled bed with several boxes in an otherwise empty room with a single vent in the ceiling.

"Alright, let's build a bed." Kado clapped his hands together and rubbed them with mild excitement. After an hour of putting together the bed and moving the storage boxes to one of the other storage rooms, he turned around with a hand over his stomach. "Oh, I need to eat something."

There is an emergency kitchen through the double blue doors.

"Well, this isn't really an emergency."

The house blew up. This is an emergency situation. You can use the kitchen.

"Yeah, I guess you're right." Kado relaxed as he went for the blue door that he hadn't really noticed before. He just thought these side doors were for storage closets. As he pulled the door open, he saw a large metal covering with a retinal scanner.

"Oh great. This will only read Nicodem."

Actually. Xostir hovered up to the retinal scanner and placed its gem that was stationed in the middle of the blade over the scanner. A green light lit up, showing acceptance into the locked-down room.

Nicodem programmed all retinal scanners to respond to my "eye."

"It's an actual eye you see through?"

Not really, I don't see the world the same way you do. But since the gem was handcrafted a specific way, no one can mimic it perfectly, so it works well for the retina scanner.

The door hissed, and the retina scanner slid into the thick metal door. The door slid up into the ceiling, ending the lockdown mode and deactivating emergency procedures. Kado walked in, and his movement triggered the lights to come on. MLEs lit up the gorgeous kitchen. It was more than a kitchen though; it was also a lab. Likely in the case of an emergency, this would be where Nicodem would experiment with new technologies on a quantum level, and when he needed a break, he'd just make himself a sandwich. Kado looked with amazement at all Nicodem had created.

Let's get you something to eat. Xostir used its magnetism to open the large fridge doors. They were full of fresh food.

"How is the food still good? Wouldn't he have set this up a while ago?"

Nicodem would change out the vegetables every six months, but everything else gets perfectly preserved in here. When the kitchen is in lockdown mode during normal times, this room is hermetically cleansed and sealed. The fridge also has some unique technologies that sort of place the food in stasis preserving it for much longer. Kado's hunger urged him to dig through all the food he could see. He looked at the wall full of food. "Let's make something to eat."

Kado went about making himself a delicious egg omelette breakfast. He hadn't done this before with a proper kitchen, so Xostir mentally gave him some instructions from reputable sources that it had stored in its database.

When breakfast was over, the two of them left the

kitchen and Kado was ready to learn more about magnetics, gravity, the science behind it, and the dangers likely to be encountered. He stepped up to the hologram projector, and Nicodem appeared. It was nice to see his kind face again, but he still missed the real person.

"There are some other dangers out there that you must be aware of. Some are only known by a select few. The Vanixx Corps, of course, are everywhere and will not be obliging if they see you. Don't let yourself be caught by them by any means," Nicodem explained with some gestures.

Kado nodded; he had seen lots of the Vanixx Corps.

"Next is the Quell. This is an organization beyond the law. They submit to nobody. The Vanixx Corps cannot control them because they've never been able to apprehend someone of this group. Only a few people know this history of them." Nicodem's face was more serious than Kado had ever seen before.

"They are an ancient secret organization that started way back with the origins of the Knights Templar. This group branched off on their own motivations but remained in the shadows nameless. Now their goals are solely intended to serve the Mitigator and the Praetor, the Overlord of the Quell. Nothing is known of these two individuals. The Mitigator delegates tasks to Moderators who are agents led by the Mitigator. An attack by a Moderator is named with the euphemism moderation or mitigation. Don't be anywhere near a Moderator! If you happen to see one and you get a chance to escape, take it. They are merciless, ruthless and have fallen far from their original purpose, having been corrupted from within. They also have stolen Magna-Blade technology for decades, so I don't know how much they've adapted it or how they've manipulated it. Be ready for anything. Literally anything." Nicodem's expression became more and more bleak as he spoke about the Quell.

"Now let's discuss what to do if a Vanixx Corps Officer somehow apprehends you."

Nicodem's recordings were invaluable to Kado, though he was getting tired from the continuous information intake. He would watch a few more hours of life-saving information and would get some rest. It was likely that danger would come again soon, and he needed to be ready.

Greeg attended the court martial without needing restraint and without coercion. He awoke that morning in the loft of his pristine penthouse. The night before he had a few drinks down at the pub on the first floor of the building with some Vanixx Corps entry-level Officers who knew nothing of his offense. They were just ecstatic to be invited out to have drinks with the greatly admired Adrian Greeg.

He basked in the attention and enjoyed every stupid moment at the table drinking with those pathetic suck ups that evening.

Now it was a beautiful, shining morning, showing the sun's glowing radiance on the reflections of the skyscrapers across the street. It felt ironic that such a gorgeous day would be the day everything changed.

He awoke with a smile, dressed in his best grey formal suit and his favorite seal skin shoes. He also wore a formal white mag-up shirt – a veritable improvement to the ancient button-up shirts of long ago. He put a styling wax in his hair and hydro-cleansed his teeth in the en suite of the loft. Looking in the mirror, he grinned at his attractive looks and was quite satisfied with his waxed arrangement of his short hair. He was ready for court. Picking up his backpack off the bed and strapping it on, he descended the stairs to the main level with a happy stride – almost a hop in his step. He grabbed an organic apple out of the bowl on the marble countertop in his pristine white kitchen. Only the Vanixx Corps and the wealthiest of the wealthy had organic fruit and vegetables. He headed out the door of his penthouse suite, not even bothering to lock it. It didn't matter because he was never coming back here.

Adrian strode with pride along the sidewalks, looking up to the towering skyscrapers that glistened in the sun. Passersby had no idea who he was, and he walked by without a greeting, as was the custom. He just wanted to enjoy one last walk through the city while it was at its peak of peace and tranquility. The city – the world – would never be like this again.

After walking three blocks, he soon reached the stone steps of the Court Tower. He took a quick gaze up to the height of the tower; it was one of the tallest buildings in the area by a hundred feet. It was a considerably ostentatious structure hinting at the misplaced pride the Vanixx Corps felt toward itself as an organization. He stepped up the stairs toward the fate the Vanixx Corps would decide for him. Walking up to the front doors as they opened for him, he walked over to a lobby bench and sat down. Sliding his backpack off to the side, he pushed it below the lobby bench mostly out of sight and sat there a moment. He looked up to the security cameras in the building's lobby, knowing that they could see everything he was doing. He didn't care and, in a nonchalant fashion, walked up to the shiny elevator doors and rode up to the eighty-sixth floor that the courtroom was stationed on.

"According to Vanixx Corps Law, in Article 91, subsection C, paragraph 2, deliberate disobedience of a direct order from an Admiral or higher rank results in an immediate court-martial with penalty of death." The judge was presiding over the court with a jury sitting in the jury booth. Some of the highest-ranking officials attended, as was the custom at such a serious tribunal. The walls were very tall and ostentatious. Giant marble columns respecting ancient nations such as Greece and Rome lined the walls of the courtroom. The amount of money it would take to build this room could feed thousands for their entire lives. These walls had intricate hand carvings that contained subtle details of the history of the Gravity War that you could only truly appreciate with a closer look. The platform the judge was stationed on highlighted his power with an intimidating design of crown molding and etched patterns throughout.

The echo of the sliding marble doors to the courtroom showed clearly how large and open the courtroom was.

Adrian walked toward the defendant's table, glancing with a smile at the several disturbed high ranking officials who were legally bound to be here to make up the jury for his outrageous and irresponsible crime. The judge banged his gavel, which loudly reverberated through the courtroom at an almost startling volume.

"All rise for the Honorable Judge Horatio Livingsten," one of the bailiffs ordered. All stood with respect, although Adrian stood because he was required to; the centuries-old legal traditions that had been so deeply ingrained in their society were honestly repugnant to him.

"All be seated," the judge commanded. He was wearing a formal court headdress with his typical Vanixx Corps uniform.

Once all were seated, he addressed Adrian, "We are here today because of your acts of insubordination, Mister Greeg. There have been cases similar to this before but never of such a high-ranking Officer with such a gross disrespect and catastrophic outcome."

Adrian kept a mostly neutral face with a slight smirk throughout the guilt-implying speech of the judge.

"Mister Pollar, will you please begin with the prosecution?" The judge gestured to the trial counsel. François sat at the plaintiff's table, which was closest to the entrance, since it was his order that Greeg had disobeyed.

Mister Pollar stood, straightened his uniform and stepped out towards the center of the room.

"We are here for the gross disobedience, insubordination and reckless behavior of Commanding Agent Adrian Greeg, the accused."

The counsel turned to the judge. "Obviously, I'd like to call Mister Adrian Greeg to the stand, your honor."

"Mister Greeg." The judge gestured an open hand to a seat beside the giant throne. The seat was set behind a short railing with his face visible to the entire jury and attending Military audience. Adrian kept a smirk as he stepped up to the platform and sat in the stand.

"Frankly, I couldn't believe it when I first heard that you killed Nicodem. He was a fellow Officer, a veteran. What harm he could've possibly posed to you, I won't ever understand," the prosecutor began.

"Adrian, would it surprise you to learn that there was no security camera footage of the assassination?"

"No," he flatly responded, keeping his grin glued to his face. He knew that, while there were security cameras surrounding the property, where he took aim and fired was specifically hidden from their view.

"Then would it surprise you to learn that there has been a constant satellite feed over the property twenty-four/seven for the past decade?" Their voices echoed through the entire courtroom.

Adrian paused, having never thought about such a

possibility. He remained silent.

"And would it surprise you to learn," Pollar continued, "that we have footage of the attack and have determined the modus of the shot fired could've proved your innocence?"

Adrian's eyebrows lifted with slight surprise. The trial counsel went on, "Of course, had you not called in an air strike and destroyed the house, that would've been the case."

The audience of the highest-ranking officials in the Vanixx Corps were grumbling with contempt at Adrian.

"Order," the judge commanded calmly as he banged his gavel once.

"Adrian, our team in the Security Footage detachment were able to extrapolate the angle of your sniper shot. Judging by the heat signatures in the house" – a large holographic display came up in the center of the floor between the judge and the plaintiff and defendant desks – "you were aiming at the young man known as Kado."

Mister Pollar pointed to the holographic representation of the feed. "The assigned target was fired upon during your mission to find out more about him. Killing him was not necessarily disobeying a direct order since we understand that you were not ordered to keep him alive. It appears with the shot that was fired at the young man, somehow it ricocheted off of Kado and struck Nicodem – seemingly by accident or mistake."

The audience viewed the satellite footage, which soon was zoomed in on and optimized, showing a clear rendering of the heat signature of Adrian on the mountain top, and the two heat signatures of Kado and Nicodem within the house in the study across the large mountainous gap. A numeric indicator of the distance was displayed with white text on the hologram showing the distance of the sniper shot was 4,432 feet. A white dotted line showed the angle of the shot, and it temporarily extended towards Kado's heat signature in the house. The image was a frozen frame just before the attack ensued. Then playing the attack in slow motion, they could see the heat signatures and the displacement of the bullet flying through the air at Kado and bouncing from the ricochet through Nicodem. The heat signature of the bird's-eye view of Nicodem changed shape to display that Nicodem was soon lying down with Kado rushing to his side.

"This alone would've proved your innocence, Adrian. But the fact that you ordered the missile attack on Nicodem's house proves that you had an intention of killing both occupants of the household." The hologram zoomed out, showing the satellite view of the missile striking the home and exploding.

"Did you disobey a direct order not to kill Nicodem?" Mister Pollard prodded in an accusatory manner, fully expecting an argument.

"Yes, I disobeyed Admiral Vaux's order."

The counsel leaned back, astonished at Adrian's admittance.

"So, you willingly admit that your deliberate failure to obey a direct order resulted in extreme loss of very valuable assets that would've continued to benefit the Vanixx Corps for years to come?"

"Yes." Greeg nodded. This all felt like pointless posturing. "I do," he rejoined loud and clear.

"Do you accept the terms of capital punishment for such a heinous crime?"

"Which terms would those be, your honor?"

"Firing squad is what is suggested in this context, Mister Greeg."

"I see. I must admit, your excellency, that I did actually successfully obey direct orders."

"Oh? Did you not just plead that you disobeyed a direct order? Are you changing your plea?" The judge cocked an eyebrow condescendingly as he asked his question.

"No, my plea stays the same. But I did obey my

orders perfectly – my orders from the Mitigator of the Quell." Adrian smiled mischievously. The entire courtroom gasped with shock seeing the truth of what this attack really was. Everyone in the room now realized the kind of danger they were all in.

The judge immediately stood up from his chair, pointing his finger at Adrian. "Bailiffs, apprehend him and take him to Knight's Rope Prison!" The bailiffs came rushing toward Adrian, but in seconds the floor and walls started to vibrate. Everyone stopped and looked around the room. The vibrating soon became more violent, and the walls started caving in. Cracks in the walls and floor began to appear, jumping up the walls and across the floors. The immense columns and hand-carved walls crumbled like dry clay as the room began to implode. Giant chunks of stone, granite and concrete began to fall, some pieces cracking the marble floor and some crashing on the attendees.

"The Quell will no longer watch silently from the shadows! Enter a new era where the Vanixx Corps meets its end!" Adrian raised his arms with pride and glamorous presentation as he shouted over the crumbling of the building. Two swords burst through opposite walls of the courtroom and into Adrian's hands.

François jumped out of the way as a large chunk of

heavy ceiling came plummeting down towards him. He turned to look up just in time to see Greeg rising up in the air with two swords in his hands. In seconds Greeg was gone, having flown through a gaping hole in the wall.

Were those Magna-Blades? he thought. He was near the elevator door that opened up to the room, and the metal doors were ajar and twisted from the destruction. He stumbled over to the door despite the floor shaking and cracking apart from what looked like a violent earthquake. He took a look through the entrance, and the elevator shaft was empty. François looked back to see if anyone was still alive, but from what he could tell at a quick glance, he was the only one left. He squeezed himself headfirst through the door and gripped onto a set of handles on the sidewalls, lowering himself down the dark shaft as fast as he could to get to the bottom floor. There were emergency lights throughout the whole shaft flickering from the chaos.

Once he was down a few feet, he stopped to shout into his wrist communicator, "Emergency, Code 88 Gravity at the Court Tower! Bring maximum backup!" He continued climbing down. The shaking continued to worsen. Then the shaking stopped. Without any warning, the entire building shook like it had been hit by a bomb. There was a sudden downward force, as if someone had picked up the entire building and dropped it onto the ground again. The violent vibration caused François to lose his grip on the handles. He began to plummet down the elevator shaft.

Kado was practicing some more sword-handling moves and positions when he felt a mild vibration shake through the bunker. He turned to look around the room, "What was that?"

There seems to be some sort of seismic reaction from something very heavy deep in the city.

"What do you recommend?"

Perhaps we should take a look.

"Alright then." Kado reached his hand out and Xostir flew right to it. He hopped onto the blade, and they dipped down into the secret tunnel. In seconds, they were zipping through the tunnel at incredible speeds. Kado's hair was blowing straight back from the sheer velocity they were traveling at. They blasted right out of the secret entrance in the side of the mountain and made a wide turn to face toward the metropolis of Vancouver. Xostir was ready to really let loose.

Hold tight.

"What?" Kado couldn't understand why for the moment, but he immediately felt Xostir accelerate effortlessly to reach speeds that Kado had never even dreamed of experiencing. In a few seconds, they broke the sound barrier. A loud boom surrounded them from the speed which they were piercing through the air, along with the air itself forming a white cone around them for a couple seconds.

In what felt like no time at all, they had arrived at the epicenter of where the seismic reaction had been detected by Xostir. It was near the center of the city at what they called the Court Tower. To Kado it looked like someone had taken a giant wrecking ball just above the halfway point through the tower. An entire section of the building was gone, and the upper section had fallen down onto the bottom section. The top piece of the tower had a dome with a sharp pointing spire and was now sitting at a precarious angle, ready to fall at any moment.

"That thing comes down, it could kill a lot of people," Kado commented.

If it fell, it would likely kill 405 people, approximately, Xostir added.

"What do we do?" Kado beckoned Xostir. Immediately, he received an image of them flying down and catching the top of the building by using the blade's own gravitational controls. They could bring the fall of the building to a stop and lower it safely. Just then the building shifted, and the top of the tower tilted forward, and began to plummet towards the innocent people below.

"Let's go." Kado used his mind to control their quick descent below the falling piece of tower, the gravity around the building and the amount of anti-gravity to apply around the falling structure. He was holding the blade in his hands, one hand on the hilt, the other against the wide edge of the blade. The gem was glowing red; Kado didn't know what that meant but hoped it was a good thing. They slowed the fall of the tower as they got closer to the ground.

Just then a speeding grey blur flew at them and

whisked them away. It flew them high up in the air at dizzying speeds into a large patch of nearby clouds. Unable to stop what was happening, Kado screamed when he heard the building hit the ground with a loud rumble.

"You killed all those people!" Kado roared. Xostir initiated a level 3 graviton wave, and they were free of the grasp of this mystery flyer, throwing Adrian backward. Kado turned around to see a blonde, muscular opponent wielding two katanas. They were obviously Magna-Blades.

"You did that to the building, didn't you?" Kado demanded.

"You survived the missile?" Adrian pointed with one sword accusingly at Kado.

The missile? How does he know about the missile? Wait a second, Kado thought to himself. They were both hovering by means of the blades, clouds surrounding them on all sides.

"You! You killed Nicodem!" he shouted to the assailant.

"Yes, finally. That old fossil had to go! Now how did you escape? Tell me!"

"I don't answer to you." Kado glared.

"Everyone answers to the Quell! Even your friend Nicodem!" he shouted.

Kado realized what he was up against. This was

exactly what Nicodem warned him about.

Escape is 43 percent possible, Xostir warned.

And victory? Kado asked telepathically.

26 percent.

I don't like those odds, Kado responded in thought. As one, they broke the sound barrier with an instant acceleration into their ominous opponent. Xostir was able to dampen the shock on Kado's system with an intensely strong gravity bubble around him. They blasted right into him; Adrian had no time to react, but the blades were able to assist in getting a cross-block up just in time. As the three blades struck, he was knocked to the side and thrown off into a distant cloud spinning rapidly.

"Did we get him?" Kado urged excitedly.

No. Those blades are very advanced and one of the latest edition blades Nicodem made, fourteenth edition. We should escape while we still can.

"Are you sure?" Kado was a little disappointed.

Yes – watch out! Greeg, with incredible blinding speed, appeared through nearby clouds swinging both blades in tandem. It took Kado every ounce of strength he had not to drop Xostir with each strike he was blocking. Xostir was also assisting him with lightning-fast defenses, but it wasn't enough. Greeg flew forward with every slashing attack, pushing Kado and Xostir backward in defense. The unbreakable blades were very loud as they clashed and clanged off each other. Finally, Greeg raised both swords and delivered a crushing blow: an electrically charged gravity wave so strong that it threw Kado flipping backward, losing his grip on Xostir and knocking him unconscious. He was plummeting to the ground, and Xostir was nowhere in sight.

Greeg took this as his opportunity to end another wielder's life, and this time the blade would be his trophy. He dove towards a limp, falling Kado and swung his blades right through him. Greeg turned around to look at his bloodied opponent, but Kado was gone.

Kado awoke aboard the blade. He was lying on his back and was staring at white, puffy clouds.

"What happened?"

You were nearly made into sushi. I snagged you and got us out of there just in time.

Kado sat up and patted himself a little bit on his

chest and waist and was relieved to see he had all his limbs and organs.

"That was too close."

Yeah, you are going to need a lot more practice.

"Yeah, yeah."

No, I mean a lot, Xostir emphasized. Kado briefly chuckled at the humor of being scolded by a machine. Xostir really seemed like a sentient being at times. He looked around for landmarks to determine where they were but couldn't tell.

"Where are we?"

Just about 100 miles away from the city limits.

"What are we doing all the way over here?"

Blades can detect each other in close-enough proximity. They were tracking our movements, so I brought us away this distance to avoid detection and to throw them off our scent. If I had gone directly to the bunker, they could've tracked us there.

"Oh … well … good job. How many people died when that building fell?"

I was able to detect 304 in the crash zone of the building, Xostir explained.

Kado was angry that they were unable to save those people. All those lives. He wasn't sure how to respond to Xostir's answer, so he changed the subject. "How long did it take to get here?"

About twenty minutes. I could get us halfway around the world very quickly if it was a dire emergency.

"Well, I don't know if that will ever be necessary, but that's good to know." A brief moment of silence passed as Kado sat on Xostir. Kado broke the silence, "He killed him, Xostir. That man was the one who killed him, blew up the house and nearly killed you and I." He rubbed his hand where his stubble grew in when not shaven. "We were this close to getting him." His index and thumb gestured a small pinching shape and his body shifted in a dramatic fashion when emphasizing "this."

"I could've paid him back for what he did."

He isn't worth it. Remember Nicodem's final wish, "Don't avenge me." Let's head back to the bunker – it's safe now, and you need to brush up on your sword-fighting skills.

Greeg had tried following the signal of the Magna-Blade his opponent was wielding. But once it had vanished from sight and the signal indicated that it was out of range of his Magna-Blades already, he decided not to waste his time. He returned to the Quell's current headquarters deep below ground. Large circular tunnels surrounded him; they were a nice change of scenery from the cave-like walls he had been flying through earlier. These tunnels were also a clue that he was close to his destination. He flew like an extinct eagle with his Magna-Blades, one in each hand, and used them simultaneously synced with his mind. For him it was like having two android assistants at each side, issuing him relevant surrounding scan data every few seconds. When he came close to the large, ominous entrance, he placed both blades onto his back and they magnetized to special strips of metal in his shirt.

Bringing his feet forward, he straightened up from his horizontal flight position and softly landed with ease and expertise. He would report on all that happened, even though he was sure they already knew everything that was happening. He hadn't been back here for many years, having been undercover as a double agent in the Vanixx Corps all this time. He would go in to meet the Mitigator for a briefing and would be assigned his next moderation mission.

He walked up to the large circular door. It looked like something made back in the ancient days of steam engines with rust all over the door and giant bolts bordering the edges and various grooves and lines of the door. It was the Quell's intention to remain hidden, and this kind of door would make any explorer think that this was merely a service hatch and not a hidden location for a secretive global organization.

He waited for a few seconds, and a smaller human-sized circular opening in the rust-covered wall creaked open inward. Adrian smiled as he stepped into the dark opening.

"Moderator Greeg." A soft, elegant voice with a British accent welcomed him from the shadows.

"Mitigator," Adrian responded with a slight bow as a greeting to her.

"Your mission was a success."

"Indeed, it was. The creator of the Magna-Blade is dead. And some of the leading Military Officers of the Vanixx Corps have perished," Greeg returned.

"Are you ready for your next mission?"

"I am." Greeg smiled with anticipation. He was looking forward to a different mission after having been on this one for so long.

"Good – but first the Praetor wishes to thank you for your efforts," the Mitigator added, still remaining in the darkest of shadows in the large room. She was sitting on a complex-looking silhouette of a throne with cables, wires and cords.

Adrian showed appreciation in his voice, "Oh thank

you, Mitigator." Their voices echoed through the room of the curved walls and tall ceilings.

"No – he wishes to meet you in person and thank you for your dedication and loyalty. It deserves to be rewarded."

"Oh, thank you, Mitigator. Uh..." Adrian was shocked; this was the last thing he was expecting to hear and didn't know what to say.

"He will be here in two months," she added.

"Yes, ma'am. Thank you." Adrian nodded and left the throne room into the Moderators' Residence where all other Moderators were able to visit, live or work. He couldn't believe it. He was soon going to meet the Praetor! This was the honor of a lifetime for a Moderator of the Quell. He could barely contain his excitement but knew he needed to keep this meeting to himself. He didn't want to upset the other Moderators or make them jealous. He didn't wish to create rivalries with his peers. He would stay here and rest and recuperate until his meeting with the Praetor.

Kado was awake this time for their slightly slower trip back to the bunker, past the clouds and over the forests. It was serene, a small blip of distracting peace for

Kado. It was just what he needed with the stress, chaos and death surrounding him. It felt like no time before they reached the bunker again. Kado was hungry, had a headache and needed to sleep.

"Food. Glorious food." Kado began cooking one of the pre-made food kits with a nanowave. In three seconds, the steaming meal was ready. As he sat down to eat, Xostir communicated telepathically to him from the other room, *What's it like to eat?*

Kado paused at the question. Tasting the macaroni and cheese, he explained, "It's...it's yummy." He laughed at himself. "It's so hard to explain. It's enjoyable. It's full of flavor. Some stuff is really good cold, and other things are good hot. Some are great either hot or cold like...pizza. Sometimes food doesn't taste so great, and sometimes it's delicious."

So, it's not a binary construct; its result is varying depending on several factors such as texture, taste, temperature, presentation and moisture level. Kado kind of understood what Xostir meant but only because the statement came with mental images in Xostir's endless database.

"Yeah, kind of like that," Kado reciprocated kindly. He finished the last couple bites of his food. "Well, should we get back to improving my sword-fighting skills?"

Sure. Xostir hovered in front of Kado as he entered the main bunker and once again stood before the holographic presentation Nicodem had prepared. A holo-image of Nicodem appeared once more.

"Be one with the blade. I can't stress this enough. Imagine that the blade has become a part of you, another appendage. You will start to see what it sees, you will sense what it senses and you'll then know what it means to truly become one with the blade."

Nicodem demonstrated some more sword positions while explaining this. He relaxed his posture. "Now practice the moves we went over today. Before you do, I need to explain why we're removing Magna-Blades from the hands of everyone else. The history that's written in the history records is not correct. The truth has been twisted and mangled over the century and a half and I've recorded the truth so that it can someday be found."

Kado lowered Xostir and watched on.

"Back when I was making Magna-Blades, some of them were leaked from the Military, and others tried to recreate them, destroying large buildings with their failed experiments. Others in the Military secretly sold some of these Magna-Blades to wealthy gangs and terrorist movements. Others like the Quell managed to steal them."

"Of course they did, those sneaky jerks," Kado

commented with an exasperated gesture.

"Attacks with the Magna-Blades began on the highest government levels, creating mass hysteria. Extremists in every country began to attack their respective governments, and this led to global instability. Some countries attacked and decimated surrounding countries, and neighboring countries retaliated with deadly force." Nicodem looked down at his feet. Kado could tell he held the burden of the lives of the ones who had already died.

"Other world powers launched a massive assault against nearby countries and our own country; some of those retaliatory attacks were nuclear, resulting in terrible fallout in many parts of the globe. All Military forces managed to get their hands on thousands of Magna-Blades, causing incredible destruction. The decimation of the planet changed the countries' borders and structure like never seen before. When the two most powerful countries faced off against each other, their allies joined in and a full scale war, which eventually became known as the Gravity War, began. We need to prevent another one from occurring. From my observations, the Vanixx Corps and the Quell are both experimenting with my technology and could very well lead the world into another Gravity War. Other organizations around the world are doing similar things with my technology, but we should focus on this continent for now."

Kado nodded, almost as if he had just been in a conversation with Nicodem. Aside from the slightly grainy composure of the holographic videos, he almost forgot that Nicodem was gone. Xostir helped Kado with the practicing of his swordplay and stances. It would give him little mental reminders of what to do first, and what positions were best to use in a defensive stance versus an aggressive one. There he was swinging the blade around for a couple more hours.

Kado also needed more physical strength; he was no match for "blondie" with two swords.

"I wish we had a gym." Kado wiped some sweat from his brow after his sword-training session finished.

We could have a workout plan for you. We don't have dumbbells or weights, but I could generate gravity, so I could make certain objects weigh more.

"That's not a bad idea." Kado was pleased with the brilliant suggestion.

Kado was holding a small, light metal box standing upright. He held it outward for Xostir to increase the gravity weight on it so he could use it like lifting weights.

Ready? Xostir begged the question while hovering on the side of the main square etched in the floor of the big open room designed for these kinds of tests.

"Ready as I'll ever be." He started to feel this tiny, little box increase in weight slowly but steadily and soon it got too heavy.

"That – that – that – that's enough. That's enough!" Kado stammered. Xostir backed off the gravity weight a little bit. Kado sighed, "That's better." He began to pump iron. He needed to get stronger with the threats out there. They developed a schedule where Kado would wake up in the morning, eat a hearty breakfast and work out. Followed by sword-fighting education and practice. Then during lunch, he would watch an educational portion from Nicodem's pre-recorded holo-vids. Every afternoon he would practice getting better at flight with Xostir in a secluded area in the wilderness.

Things had been quiet these past couple weeks; they didn't see or hear any concerning activity from the Quell or the Vanixx Corps. Perhaps the Vanixx Corps was recoiling and recovering from its tragic losses. Vanixx officials were on the news media apologizing for their Court Tower falling and killing hundreds, followed by empty promises of making things right. What was most concerning was just how peaceful it was in the city. Obviously, the peace was welcomed, but such incredible peace after such a terrible act of terror was just a stagnant waiting game of something far worse to come. The oppression of the Officers and Military of the Vanixx Corps had reportedly eased up as well. Still Kado still couldn't shake the feeling that something was about to go down.

Kado had prepared a delicious hot soup lunch and sat down at a dining table in the kitchen room, bringing a portable holo-player to obtain more invaluable information from Nicodem. The player activated and a cone of light flickered on; the tapered light pointed up to an image of Nicodem from the chest up. Right away, he began to speak from the last bookmark Kado had saved, "The Gravity War, as it was later named, started in the year 2154 and lasted for twenty-five years, destroying most cities and villages, bringing many great cities to ruin." Kado looked over to see Xostir enter the room and mount onto the wall. There was a mount in every room. It seemed like Xostir wanted to be near Kado, perhaps it was for protection or maybe Xostir desired companionship. Kado sensed it was the latter.

"Finally, after so much destruction, entire continents nearly decimated and billions killed, the remaining fractions of the governments, after much deliberation, finally agreed to incinerate *all* of the Magna-Blades. The only way they could, though, was to drop them in a volcano because of the nearly indestructible metal that we had synthesized. After the Magna-Blades were destroyed in 2179, the war was over, and the fighting finished." Nicodem was wearing glasses in this particular video and removed them to rub his eyes. He looked more exhausted than Kado had ever seen him before.

"When the war ended, the world was completely different. The North American forces, including the Air Force, Army, Navy, Marines and police, were mandated to merge into the Vanixx Corps. Like after the first two world wars, the economy boomed. Because of the amount of death that took place during this war, money completely changed. What used to be worth $100 became as valuable as $100,000 and so now our pennies and dollars went further. The governments used this economic change to fund cleaning up the ruins of the world and to motivate everyone left to work. This economic change ended up being globally similar. It also caused the technologies to advance even faster than they already were advancing and caused the cities to grow at an incredible rate. The next thirty years were filled with economic prosperity. But near the end of the construction boom, jobs started ending, people started to get laid off and some homeless sectors rapidly grew."

"So that's why our cities are so big," Kado

commented on this revelation.

"Of course, not all of the Magna-Blades were destroyed. They couldn't all be found. There were still about fifty left when I reviewed the serial numbers that had been documented as collected. We need to find the rest of them and store them safely, then repurpose them for what they were originally invented for. Useful tools to harness transportation and use gravity and magnets as helpful constructive instruments."

Kado stroked his chin in thought. This was what he had to do – for Nicodem. He looked over to Xostir, "So I guess it's time for some more flight training, right?"

That's correct. Are you ready?

"Yeah. Let's go." He slid off the chair and headed toward the door to the rest of the bunker. As he walked near Xostir, he held his hand out and Xostir flew right into his grasp. In moments they were in the secret tunnels and blasted right out into the wilderness as was their usual routine. They went to a different part of the wilderness each time, so they didn't raise suspicion, and the different location was always chosen by Xostir.

This time Xostir directed them to a glassy, beautiful lake, surrounded by mountains decked in snow-frosted pine trees. Kado looked at the beautiful nature; all around them was this lake. Xostir had positioned them hovering right over the center of the lake.

Hovering over water is a different dynamic, and you may need to know how to do this in a pinch. Notice when you sense my connection to the gravitational poles, I need to extend my output 28 percent?

"Yeah, I can tell that we do need to really try to hover this close to water. It's not as easy as just flying through the air or over the ground."

Indeed. Most Magna-Blades have issues traveling low over water. It was a major weakness in the first editions for the Military, but it slightly improved as the new editions were released. Nicodem made major improvements to my program and my hardware so that the output to hover near to water doesn't overwhelm my system. It took him several years to perfect the stabilizers.

"Wow. Now that's impressive." Kado chuckled. Nicodem always surprised him, especially posthumously. "So what are we doing here today?"

I'm handing the reins to you fully. You control every aspect of our flight. Our connection has gotten stronger over these few weeks and your ability to sense the magnetism of the world and our synchronization with it has as well.

"Oh...Kay. Sounds good. I can do that." Kado braced as he checked his grip on the hilt. "I think." Xostir allowed Kado full control, and they began to move forward. In seconds, they immediately dropped and, plunging toward the water, they stopped just as the bottom edge of Xostir grazed the surface. Kado gained control; it was shaky. He laughed with excitement. He could feel the blade; it felt like a third arm, except this arm could control electromagnetism and gravity itself. He felt the power Xostir held pulsing through the blade. He could detect the vibrations of the nano-centrifuge within the blade. It was now that he could feel and understand how Xostir worked. It was like he could see and feel how the inner workings of Xostir were constructed.

The quantum technology that formed the inside of the hilt contained the very brain of Xostir. He wasn't able to see anything about the brain, but he knew it was quantum technology and knew the cylindrical centrifuge was constantly spinning in a self-sustaining cycle. This spinning was what made Xostir tick. It kept Xostir alive or awake or always functioning, never running out of energy and never running out of power. He had control over increasing power to the magnetic stabilizing orbs built in throughout the blade, and he could detect several abilities that Xostir had.

Kado used his mind to command the blade to rise up in the air. He rose up from the water and began to fly forward. He circled the lake with a lap and, picking up speed, he aimed skyward. They bolted up, high up in the sky past the clouds' ceiling. Kado felt the warmth of the sun on his skin, and this moment of peace was wonderful. He let them reach a certain point and stopped commanding anti-gravity. For a brief moment, they were weightless. He let Earth's gravity take them by its hand and gently pull them back down to the surface. Like a plasma jet stalling, Kado turned to face toward the ground as they were experiencing free-fall. As they began to take on speed, Kado commanded Xostir to accelerate as they were hurtling toward the planet. They initiated a sonic boom as they were very close to the lake's surface, causing a huge splash of water to fan up a hundred feet into the air. They changed their angle of flight just as they reached the lake's surface and sped along the lake's waves, nearing the coast to make a landing. The contrast of dark foliage and snow-glazed boughs on the trees was refreshing to the eyes. Kado was pumped full of adrenaline from the excitement of fully controlling Xostir's abilities. He flew across the lakeshore when suddenly a shock wave threw him and Xostir through the air, landing in the lake.

"What the–" Kado shouted as he treaded water. Xostir floated to the top and began to hover just above the water.

That was a gravitational blast that hit us.

"What? Who? How?" Kado was trying not to get freezing cold water in his mouth from the rough waves.

There on the beach.

Kado looked over to the lakeshore, waves splashing in his face. Someone was standing there with a sword. "Well, they got my attention. Let's go meet them." He held onto the blade hilt, and they hovered out of the water and over to the shore. He landed, sopping wet, dripping on the cold, rocky shore. He gazed upon the other blade wielder who had literally just knocked him out of the sky. "Who are you?"

"Who are you?" she responded. She raised her Magna-Blade threateningly. "This is my lake! Get lost!"

"What?" Kado responded confused. This woman had knocked him out of the sky mid-flight. He shook his head, "Your lake? What do you mean?"

"This is where I live – you can't be here!" she shouted back.

"Whoa, whoa, hold on. What do you mean you live

here? In the forest?"

"No, you moron! I have a cottage nearby – but this is my lake," she scolded with a fierce look in her eye. Her curiosity about Kado's Magna-Blade finally urged her to ask, "Where did you get that?"

"This is mine – I've had it for a while. It used to belong to a friend of mine, and he's dead so now–" He realized that sounded wrong when he saw her confused expression. He stammered to reword his explanation. "My friend gave this to me just before he was killed by an assassin." She relaxed. He lowered Xostir from a defensive stance to a relaxed one. "My name is Kado. What's yours?"

"Ruana. What are you doing here?" she aimed her sword at him.

He shrugged, embarrassed. "Training. I am kinda new to all this."

She scoffed, "Clearly. I saw you flying around like it was your first time."

"Well, it kind of was – with me fully in control."

"What, you mean you have a self-guiding blade?"

"It has a personality of its own, that's for sure," he responded, remembering to try and keep a low profile. Not everyone knew about Xostir being the first one ever made or how advanced it was. Xostir was sure to mentally remind Kado of that while he was speaking.

"Huh." She added, "That blade sure looks familiar. Why do I feel like I've seen it somewhere before?"

"I'm not sure. It's not necessarily famous." Kado looked at it, rotating it to view it from a couple different angles.

"Look, there aren't that many blades left in the world. If I've seen it before, it had to have been famous at one point."

She wasn't one to lose arguments. Kado could tell she was bright; nothing was getting past her. Against Xostir's behest, Kado told her the truth, "It's the first Magna-Blade ever made. It's the prototype that started it all."

"Yeah, right." She folded her arms and rested her stance on one hip with a sarcastic response, "And I'm the princess of New Togo."

Kado thought, *New Togo?*

Africa, Xostir hinted to him.

Ah right. Kado began to notice how lovely she was, now that she wasn't yelling at him. Her skin was clear and dark with a bit of a sparkle to it. Maybe Kado was just imagining the sparkles. She was just as tall as him, maybe a tiny bit taller, and wore an outfit he hadn't seen commonly.

Her umber boots rose to the ankle and folded down

on the sides. There were zippers on them, and they looked well worn. Her shorts were beige. She wore two holsters, one on each hip, that had blasters in them. Her bright red, buttoned shirt sported sleeves that rolled up far past her elbows, with matching leather straps lining parts of it that seemed to have no other purpose than some sort of fashion statement. Other leather straps diagonally wrapped around her shirt for what seemed to be a magnetic holster for the Magna-Blade. She wore long leather gloves that sort of had metal gauntlets on the forearms – he assumed they were for the Magna-Blade. She had some sort of necklace that was hidden by the collar of her shirt and her long, chestnut, loosely curled hair. Kado could see her eyes were a radiant light blue – something rare for a black woman. He imagined her smile would be beautiful if she ever did smile. On top of her head were some sort of ancient circular welding goggles.

Her Magna-Blade was unique looking. It kind of had a S-wave to it when you looked at it from its wide side. The hilt seemed like it had a slight curve to it with leather wrapping around it. From the base of the cross guard, the blade slowly angled backward like a katana or Greek sword, but then curved forward and then backward again, completing a narrow S-shape. It looked like an elegant exotic sword mixed with a very large barb. It was incredible. Kado realized he was kind of staring and darted his eyes away to avoid any awkwardness.

That blade is from the seventh edition of Magna-Blades provided to the army during the war. There are only a couple left from that time frame to my knowledge, Xostir explained.

"What are you staring at?" Her attitude stayed strong. Nothing got past her. Kado shook his head, realizing he had been in a stupor. He hadn't been in that many conversations with women lately, and it had been quite some time since he was friends with any.

"That blade – it's from the seventh edition of Magna-Blades. It's a rare piece. Very nice." He put his blade onto his back as he took a few steps forward. His blue cloak was soaked, and a line of dripping water followed him. He brushed his wet hair away from his face while asking, "Where did you possibly get that?"

"It belonged to my grandfather. He was in the Gravity War and grew attached to it. He died of natural causes before the war ended, and when the call went out to return all Magna-Blades, this one got missed. It was stored in my grandpa's special compartment for it and never got destroyed. It also was never found until a couple years ago by me. I began to learn how to use it, and it was sort of speaking to me, if you know what I mean." She placed her blade on her back as well, beginning to trust that even if this skinny punk tried to attack, she could take him out no problem. She looked him up and down and noticed he was shivering. Inside she felt a small bit of guilt for his freezing coldness. "Come on. Let's get you in front of a fire. You look like a shivering chihuahua." She laughed.

"Well, thanks," he responded sarcastically. It was a brief flight over the small nearby forest hill. At first, she was flying farther ahead of him but eventually allowed him to fly beside her.

"So, what are your plans with your friend's Magna-Blade?" Ruana asked him.

"I'm not sure. I haven't had any proper conversations with anyone about it for just over a month. I've just been learning as much as I can about sword fighting and harnessing the magnetic and gravitational abilities," he replied. It was refreshing to talk to someone somewhat friendly for a change. They landed in the forest near a structure and began to walk toward it. The snow was only lightly speckling the forest ground.

"How about you?" he questioned back.

She held it up with pride and glee. "This thing has been in my family for generations, and now it's helping me feed myself and survive out here."

"How does it help you with food?"

"I come to the lake once a week to catch fish. I just hold it out on the shore to the water, and I kind of will it to make little vibrations through the water. The vibrations slowly get stronger and emanate through the water down to the depths. In a few seconds, ten fish come up floating to the surface."

Their brief stroll brought them to a pristine log cottage; snow glazed the shake roof. Kado had never seen anything like it before. The snow-frosted logs horizontally lined the outside of the cottage all the way to the pitched shake roof. A square, protruding smokestack stuck out the top of the roof.

Kado looked at all of it, but he'd never seen a smokestack before. Pointing at it, he asked Ruana, "What's that thing?"

"It's a smokestack." She looked at him incredulously. "You don't know what a smokestack is?"

"I...spent most of my life in the homeless sector," he muttered, ashamed.

"Oh." She fell silent as they nearly entered the cottage. "Why were you homeless?"

"I'm not sure how much you know about orphanages or the job challenges out there, but it was safer to be a homeless twelve-year-old than living in the orphanage. When I applied for work, no one would hire an orphan and they would never hire a homeless person. So, I had no way out."

"Now looking at you, you don't seem homeless."

"I wasn't – I'm not, technically. I was taken in by my friend who was killed."

"Oh. I'm sorry about that." Sincerity was easily detected in her voice this time. They reached the door, and she unlocked it with a small metal key and opened it, letting him in first. His shivering had increased since his first splash in the hypothermia-inducing water.

François awoke to a steady beeping noise. His head was pounding, and the lights were bright. He tried looking around past his blurred vision, but no matter how much he blinked, he couldn't clear his vision fast enough. He was slowly gaining control of his vision, and he hoped the blurriness would eventually subside. Some people came up to him; his hands could detect that he was on a bed, and unmistakably he was in a hospital and these people were nurses or doctors.

"Where am I? What happened?" he begged the blue blurs.

His hearing was also muffled, but it quickly

returned as he heard them saying, "You were in an attack. You were found at the bottom of an elevator shaft. You've been in a coma for three weeks."

A coma? Who took care of my responsibilities? Who was still alive of the Corps? He was sure the staff didn't know.

"Do you have any information about the attack?" he held a hand out to the nurses with his question.

"Sorry sir, but we've notified your subordinates and someone from the Vanixx Corps will be here to visit," they reassured him. He knew he would just receive a briefing about next steps once recovered, but he couldn't stop thinking about who was left. Fifteen high ranking Officers were subpoenaed at the tribunal to discipline a long-standing loyal advisor and Officer of the Vanixx Corps. He never stopped to think why so many were there. Why fifteen? Each of them held a big measure of responsibility throughout the fleet, in every district of the city, and were very high in the chain of command. He attended because he had reported the insubordination, but all the rest were subpoenaed by the court to be able to present evidence. It still seemed like overkill to have that many there. *Maybe I'm just being paranoid – I did just wake up from a coma,* he thought to himself. *It seems just too convenient that so many in the highest positions of the V.C. were all in one room. How...*

"Sir, someone from the Vanixx Corps will be here in an hour. Here is some food, and we'd like you to rest until they get here." They placed a platter of steaming food on a hover cart and pulled it over to the bed. They lifted it just a bit so that it could hover over his knees and headed out of the room. He tried to rest his mind for a bit; all this thinking wasn't making his headache go away.

The crackling fire exuded a very warm, dry heat that was greatly welcomed by a shivering, soaked Kado.

Ruana's cabin was comfortable and cozy. As soon as you opened the door with the manual turn handle, you could feel how warm it was inside compared to the chilly outdoors. The logs that formed the walls of the cabin were large horizontal behemoths of what were once vertical trees. Each trunk looked hand carved with small carved chunks taken out to make this cabin. He had never heard of any current log cabins anywhere, and this cabin didn't look very old. It looked like it may have been made less than fifty years earlier. How such a fragile structure could've survived the war was unbelievable. One step into the house onto the circular floor mat, your eyes naturally would flow from the left-hand side, seeing some simple pictures framed along the wall, nailed into the wood of the logs themselves. Ruana had a knack for decorating, with the frames positioned at various heights and distances apart. The frames also had different sizes, resulting in a very attractive gallery wall.

Kado was reminded by Xostir telepathically that these were called photographs. It had been over a hundred years since anyone had developed with this kind of photography. Below these framed ancient photographs was a green fabric couch of some sort. It looked very old and well used with wooden legs touching the floor and rounded wings sticking out of the bordering left and right edges of the backrests. Some of the seat cushions sagged inward from extensive use. It was another thing Kado had only seen a few times before: furniture without hover abilities.

Nearly everything Nicodem had would hover. And nearly anything in the modern world, at cafés, at local businesses, had hovering furniture and holograms.

In the corner, the overlapping structure of the logs was clear to see. Somehow, they were placed one on top of another with some sort of jointing process used several centuries ago. On the far wall was a large holo-projected image of what looked like Ruana as a little girl and two older parents, a father and a mother, Kado assumed. He didn't want to pry quite yet.

As his eyes trailed down below the holo-graph, there was an ancient-looking stone hearth shelf, then below rocks formed a frame around the fireplace. This wasn't a gas or synthetic fireplace – you would put actual logs into this and light it up. Surrounding the floor by this hearth was stone tile. He wasn't sure why the stone tile was there, but he was sure there was a reason. At the edge of the stone tile was a long rectangular bench. Xostir fed the knowledge into his mind that this was called a fender bench.

The rest of the floor throughout the house was wooden flooring, long strips that were laid side by side. He had never really seen something this rustic before; it looked like everything was hand-built in this cabin. His gaze continued to trail along to the far corner of the small cabin; a plush, worn, mocha leather chair from the olden days was stationed at an angle to get a good view of the room. The leather was wearing down and discoloring where one's hands would typically go on the armrests. Across the far wall was a window looking out to the snowy forest, the logs chopped to frame the window. Before the far wall ended, there was a wall inset with a closed door.

The doors were all paneled wood and appeared like they had been hand-glued together.

There was a kitchen counter made out of wood, and it looked like it had been hand sanded. Kado was advised by Xostir that it was called "butcher block" style countertops. Closest to him were some bar stools that could fit underneath the countertop overhang.

Behind the countertops was a set of cupboards; the doors had grooved beveled edges framing the borders of each door. Their handles were a neat concept of wood. Each handle was unlike the other: Some sort of small wooden knot was formed, sanded down and cut to be glued against the cupboard doors. Kado had never really seen a kitchen quite like this. Nicodem's kitchen was much more modern and automated, having little pieces of his inventions hiding throughout each cupboard. Here, everything was relaxed, manual, hand-carved – he liked its quaint look and feel. On the galley countertop there was a single square sink with a very simple straight water spout or tap. He saw two knobs, which seemed to be what would adjust the flow and temperature of the water – quite different from Nicodem's automated kitchen tap.

As he turned to the edge of the kitchen, which graced the right wall of the cabin, he saw one more small room with a closed door, which he assumed was either a pantry or a restroom. The whole ceiling was also some sort of paneled hardwood similar to the floor, with just a few lights that hung to bring illumination to the room.

"Come, sit down and warm up," Ruana offered to him. Kado stepped forward toward the fireplace. The fire was crackling and dying down, but he took off his jacket and sat.

He watched as Ruana laid down some kindling and a couple larger quarters of logs and used a weird looking device that activated a flame. She lit the small pieces of kindling and bark, and the fire sparked to a lively flame once more. Kado was enthralled by her entire process since, for his whole life, he only experienced flame heat from a makeshift oil drum. His notion of fire was that it was for survival, but here – creating the fire was enjoyable, as was the warmth. He enjoyed this heat with an element of luxury rather than necessity or survival.

His soaked royal blue cloak he laid on the fender bench beside him. He had been given clothes by Nicodem when he awoke from his injuries a month ago. It was a white long-sleeved turtleneck, some great looking khaki pants and a belt that had some glowing designs on it. He had forgotten to thank him. Each day he realized he missed Nicodem more and more and hadn't gotten nearly enough time with him that he needed – not just for the knowledge and education now, but for his company and his friendship. Each time he watched a holo-recording, he'd feel a sting of pain missing Nicodem.

"Warming up?" Ruana asked him.

He looked over to her preparing a hot soup in the kitchen, "Yeah, this is wonderful."

She brought a bowl over to him; the hot ceramic in his hands was just the perfect temperature. She had a bowl for herself and sat down on the plush, mocha leather chair in the living room where the fireplace was. Kado angled himself on the short bench to face her. The heat from the fire rolling up his side and back gave him goosebumps. It was like the fire pits in the homeless sector except this was much more comfortable and not really for survival.

"So, I hope you don't mind me asking, but what was it like being homeless?" she sincerely implored.

He had never given much thought about it aside from hating it. "I guess it could be described as not having a purpose but still living because you had to, no matter how terrible life was, day by day." She looked down to her food, realizing how easy she had it in comparison.

Kado added, "The worst part is there are people who don't have to be there – some who are really capable. If they just believed in themselves, they'd be able to make a living. Then there are ones who are lazy and don't want to work and just want charity. The problem is you can't tell who is who, just by looking at the homeless."

"What about you?" he inquired, "Where'd you get all that cool gear?"

She chuckled, "These I made. My father and grandfather were skilled at metal work and electrical engineering, and my father taught me everything he knew before he – well, never mind."

Kado wanted to know what she was going to finish saying but figured it would be better not to pry just yet.

She continued, "So yeah, he taught me all he could, raised me with my mom, and here I am."

Kado nodded, "That's a very good skill to have. Well, it's been very nice meeting a fellow wielder. It's starting to get dark, I better get going."

Kado slurped up the last of the soup, got up from the bench, rinsed his bowl and donned his cloak. He looked over and realized that both their Magna-Blades were hovering in close proximity in the air by the couch. He held out his hand, and Xostir flew itself into his grip.

She stood up, "So you think there are many others out there like us? With a blade?"

Kado paused to think of how he should word it, since he knew there were possibly more than fifty other blades out there but didn't want to concern her – he also didn't want to lie. "I'm sure we're not the only ones." He opened the door and stepped outside; the sun was setting through the trees, casting long shadows through the reddened forest. He turned around. "I'll keep in touch."

Just then, he took off straight up holding Xostir in hand. He thought to himself, *Smooth exit.* Xostir implanted an image in his mind of someone rolling their eyes, which made Kado laugh a little at himself – forgetting Xostir could comprehend all of his thoughts. As they passed the height of the treetops, he brought Xostir up under his feet and, holding onto the hilt with one hand, they flew toward the bunker into the red setting sun. Strokes of thin, wispy clouds in varying shades of gold and red were motionless as Xostir and Kado flew through them.

"What were you doing with that other blade back there?"

Gaining an understanding of what they had been through. It was willing to share all its data. They have seen quite a bit in their adventures together. No other Magna-Blades encountered though.

"That makes sense; she seemed shocked that you existed. She must've thought that all of them were destroyed after the war," Kado replied as they neared the bunker.

Are we going to obtain the blade from her as Nicodem

suggested? Xostir inquired.

Kado immediately was conflicted. "I'm not sure. It's been in her family for a long time, and she feels like it belongs to her. She's not misusing it or causing anyone harm."

True, however someone could steal the blade from her. The blade is not smart enough to defend itself from theft and therefore could be a major threat.

"What if we reprogrammed it to be as smart as you?" Kado smiled.

Xostir paused for longer than usual before making a response, *You would need to learn how to code. You would need to duplicate my program, apply it to the other blade and remove my personality subroutines from the new blade, replacing them with the blade's existing personality subroutines. There isn't much of a personality there in the first place, but it will grow and develop fast on its own.*

"Well, can we do it?" They had just entered the secret entrance and flew in through the tunnels as Kado rose the question.

You would need to learn much about quantum computing and coding technology.

"Does Nicodem have a portion of his teachings on these methods?"

Yes, there are thirty-eight hours worth of his

explanations of the basic elements of quantum technology and how it pertains to computing, Xostir began to explain as they entered the bunker through the secret entrance in the bunker's floor. *Then there are 148 hours of explanatory details on how to code with quantum computing.*

"Whoa! Are you kidding me?" Kado was now walking through the bunker, Xostir hovering vertically at his side. "What about information that you can transmit to me?"

There are 305 separate studies, articles and educational manuals on the subject of quantum computing and thirty-two articles discussing Magna-Blade technology. I could transmit this information to you in a sequential method. There is an algorithm that I've discovered that will allow you to not only to obtain a large amount of information in a very short period of time, but you'll also be able to retain 80 percent more recall.

"Wow, that sounds good to me. Let's do that," Kado spoke quickly with enthusiasm for this idea.

Allow me some time to complete my calculations and internal simulations on exactly the safest way to transmit the data in this algorithm; we don't want you to fry your brain.

"Right – take all the time you need! We don't want that!" Kado chuckled nervously.

A holo-projection of Nicodem automatically

appeared on its own; this time it was a projection specifically recorded for Kado. "Kado, take a look at locker cabinet 2-B." Nicodem looked a little bit younger than on the day he died, but Kado figured maybe it was just the hologram quality not perfectly reflecting Nicodem's image. Nicodem continued, "There you will find an invention of mine that will assist you."

Kado felt weird about these videos appearing automatically – it must've detected the motion and the presence of Xostir. How did it know that he was here? Nicodem seemed awfully prepared to have all these videos recorded for him. Kado paid it no further thought as he walked over to the locker. He looked at the combination lock and looked over to Xostir for assistance.

79-11-87. Xostir sent the numbers, and a memory of the numbers being changed with the dial spinning came into Kado's mind. He turned the dial to the appropriate numbers and the locker door opened. Just inside the door was a handle for a drawer; he pulled the drawer and felt a click as if it had a seal of some sort. He heard a hiss, and it opened on its own. Inside were black gloves in a molded, soft padded inlay; they looked so perfect how they were positioned he almost didn't want to take them out. But how could these gloves help him? They were fingerless, with the fingers of the gloves cutting off just before the middle knuckles. There was a strip of light glowing on either side of each glove, possibly where a seam would normally be – they looked very interesting. Taking them out of the mold they were sitting in, he put them on and re-approached Nicodem's holo-recording projecting up into the air from the floor. It was Nicodem's full body at a life-size scale, like most of the recordings.

"Now these gloves will not only assist you with controlling your Magna-Blade, but they will temporarily give you the Magna-Blade's abilities controlled through the gloves if you are in close-enough proximity to a blade. These gloves work with all Magna-Blade models. Try it out!" As Nicodem finished his explanation, he smiled, and the recording faded out.

"Magna-Gloves?" Kado pulled them on, rotating his hands back and forth as he admired the newly discovered invention. He held one hand out and thought to close the drawer of the locker. The drawer obeyed him and shut, with the locker door closing behind it. The weirdest part was Kado could feel the control through the gloves, just like he could control the Magna-Blade – he had access to these magnetic-based and gravity-based abilities. He looked back to the lockers and could detect more items with magnetic properties. He decided he would investigate later and see what else was in the lockers.

"Thanks, Nicodem. As always, you never cease to amaze." He turned swiftly and aimed a hand at a broom across the room. He hadn't really thought of what he wanted to do with the broom, but it levitated and started coming toward him. He was excited about this new invention. He made a fist with his one hand and allowed it to shake a bit with a celebratory fist squeeze of sheer joy, but this caused the broom to fold in on itself and become a crumpled mess of a twisted aluminum pretzel.

"Oops!" Kado exclaimed, stunned and surprised. These new gloves were going to be very useful...once he got the hang of them.

"Admiral Vaux! How good to see you alive and in one piece." A voice came from a tall Military figure entering the hospital room. It was Admiral Trelleck, a trusted Admiral who had been an Admiral for many years, was there to visit. He had a standard Military haircut; his gut was bigger than his personality, and he usually laughed between his sentences. His black uniform was tufting at the buttons from his gargantuan lard, but it didn't make him any less enjoyable to be around.

"Vern! It's good to see you this evening! How have you been?" François warmly greeted.

"I've been fine. Glad I wasn't at that tribunal! But really, how are you feeling?"

"Well, they told me I have five broken ribs, a punctured lung that they fixed, two broken legs, one crushed disc in my back and a broken collar bone. So, I've been better." François chuckled, followed by a twinge of pain in his ribs that caused him to tense up a bit. He took a second to recover and asked, "What's the story on the Court Tower?"

"Oh, it ended up falling to the streets and killed a few hundred civilians. Inside the remains of the courtroom itself, everyone else was dead. The judge, the jury, everyone subpoenaed. Sounds like you just managed to escape with your life."

Saddened by the news, he slowly replied, "I just happened to be closest to that elevator shaft." He looked up to meet Vern's eyes, "Greeg went insane. He had Magna-Blades and crushed the whole room like it was cardboard."

"None of us saw this coming. He was among us for about a decade. Imagine the secrets he may have collected," Vern replied with seriousness.

François nodded, "What's happening with damage control?"

"Well, as soon as you're on your feet, the Grand

Admiral has called for emergency meetings to commence. With so many of us gone just like that, we are doing some serious restructuring to keep the peace," Vern explained, but added as he sat down on a nearby nurse's hover stool, "That doesn't mean you come rushing in with your bandages. I'm here as a friend, not as a Corps Officer. We'll hold everything together until you're out. The nurse told me next week you'll be well enough to recover at home?"

"Yeah, that's what they tell me, too. Any word on Greeg's whereabouts?"

"We have some leads but no solid location of where he would be. None of our team have been able to get into the Quell still. The background checks they run on applicants are incredibly thorough. They've been a thorn in our side for decades, but now...it's war. They mean to end us." Vern shifted in his seat on the stool as he leaned in close to whisper, "They could be anywhere, watching our every move."

"There could also be more in the Vanixx Corps other than Greeg working for the Quell," François added quietly.

"Oh, we have other news." He stood up from his stool.

"Yes?"

"We've detected Nicodem's Magna-Blade today."

A couple days had passed, and Kado was experimenting with the things he was learning about quantum computing with an old quantum motherboard on the lab desk. Kado had a small holo-screen up with references to one of the articles Xostir had transferred into Kado's mind. He was using very fine-tipped tools and a highly focused magnifying screen as he was trying to adjust the physical components of the quantum technology.

"This kind of thing should only be done with machines," Kado remarked to himself. "At this size, my hands shake just way too much to move with nanometer precision."

Nicodem had nerves of steel; however, for the very small quantum pieces, he has devices to make the preprogrammed adjustments.

"Why didn't you say so until now? I've been messing with this for two hours!"

You needed to truly appreciate how intricate quantum technology is for yourself, not just read about how intricate it is. Now you know the nature of quantum tech.

"Ah, you tricky little..." Kado playfully rebuked Xostir.

At this rate, in a couple months you'll really understand quantum computing very well.

"Thanks, Xostir. I think understanding how this stuff works will help me understand you better. It sure helps that you can just pump information and knowledge into my brain, but there's no substitute for actual experience."

Understood. I'm sure that with more time and experience, you'll master quantum computing. There are more videos to watch from Nicodem. This one is a specific one recorded just for you; he told me to show it to you if you started seriously working on quantum computing.

"Oh...okay." Kado stood up from the lab desk and followed Xostir over to the holo-projector. He didn't know what to expect. The image of Nicodem materialized, and he began to speak.

"Kado, I haven't told you everything yet. And I've pre-recorded these videos because I know that in my scenario, life is dangerous and there's always some sort of target on my back." Kado pulled up a seat and watched Nicodem's personalized video. He had only seen one or two specifically for himself. Nicodem must've known that he was targeted for attack to have recorded these. "There is an invention that I am most ashamed of. It's something I wished I never made...You recall that my family was under threat of death if I didn't obey every command of the Military. And with the advancements of gravitational understanding and magnetic abilities, they forced me to build–" He paused from the grief he was experiencing and cleared his throat. "They forced me to build a bomb. But not just any bomb. They wanted what they dubbed a 'gravity bomb' or a 'g-bomb.' This bomb was designed to send a shock wave out over a 200-mile radius and pull everything that it could down into the ground with enough gravitational force to level a skyscraper."

"No way." Kado shook his head at both the incredulous invention and that Nicodem was forced to do something so terrible.

"So, they mass-produced the g-bombs, and *that* is why the majority of the planet was completely laid waste. It wasn't the Magna-Blades. They were effective on a one-to-one level. These gravity bombs just destroyed everything they could...everything." Nicodem could barely look up, he held such guilt and shame – it was evident in his face and countenance. Kado felt so bad for Nicodem because he didn't have a choice. The fact that he had a family made him susceptible to the whims of the government with a simple threat. But he greatly respected Nicodem for doing everything he could to keep his family safe, even if it meant making a terribly massive lethal weapon.

"Despite completing the mission, they still knew I had attempted to sabotage this project and a couple previous projects. As you know, that's why they killed my wife, Nima, and my daughter, Alice. I still remember the day that our Military sent jets over to drop the bombs. I rued the day it would come, and indeed it was more devastating than I could've ever imagined. Billions were dead in seconds. That's what really ended the war. Once that happened, everyone lost their drive to fight. At that point, every single person had lost either all or most of their family to the war. It broke everyone and shook them all to their core. It broke me. And that's what caused me to start this journey to make sure something like this *never* happens again...But it took me over a century to work up the courage to fight back. Kado, if you are still with me, please don't give up. No matter how hard it gets. The world needs you Kado; I need you. Try to find anyone misusing my inventions and ensure they can't hurt anyone. We need to prevent another war from being possible." Just then Nicodem's image faded.

He really wanted to help Nicodem's purpose, but that would change things. How was he going to accomplish this goal? Someone who owns a Magna-Blade or that technology had to be out there right now causing problems, potentially an experiment of the Vanixx Corps and a threat to lead the planet to another global catastrophe.

"Xostir, are you able to check your scans throughout Vancouver and see if there are any odd magnetic signatures?" Kado beseeched.

I am. Running the scan now. In seconds, they had the results.

Kado, I've detected twelve possible different locations in the past six months of odd magnetic activity nearby, not including Nicodem's missions. That may suggest that magnetic technology of Nicodem's inventions are all in the near vicinity, not including the other hundreds of signatures around the world.

"Alright – what are we waiting for? Let's go carefully scout out some of these locations. We'll have to figure out what to do with those other signatures in other cities and countries later. Gotta start somewhere."

***

"Sir! We've found them!" In one of the countless offices of the Vanixx Corps, an Officer shouted to his superior. He was at a desk decked out with lights and screens, scanning for Magna-Blade signatures. Three Officers quickly stepped over to see the readings and smiled with approval and anticipation. The most senior Officer, Vorace Dern, ordered, "Send in the sentinels."

***

Kado was crouched on Xostir flying in his typical method toward the first reading of focused magnetic activity.

What do you want to do once we locate the source of

the signal?

"Well, I just want to scout out what's going on. It's not like we're prepared for a fight or take the blade from them or to steal the magnetics technology." Kado shrugged.

Yes, you are definitely not ready for a fight.

"Thanks," Kado grumbled sarcastically as he rolled his eyes. He was sure Xostir didn't understand sarcasm. As they neared the epicenter of the signal, Xostir began to relay the scans he was receiving. Kado could almost see the white topography lines of where they were flying over, and he could see the central location of the signal was highlighted red and orange, while the surrounding area had no overlay of color. They pulled in for a landing about a mile away from the outer edge of the signature. This signal was in a rocky, mountainous part of the wilderness, plenty of trees around but many jagged crags in the nearby surroundings.

As they landed on a large patch of rocky terrain, Kado really tried to home in to the constant scans that Xostir was making. Xostir could scan for movements in every angle around them, almost like 360-degree eyes and super ears detecting tiny foreign sounds, and Kado could tap into those senses with his mind. He held Xostir with one hand while he quietly walked through the snow-frosted forest toward the signal. The trees were enormous, towering over him; small clumps of snow would fall from the boughs of the cedar and pine trees. His breath decorated the air around him with swirling, warm, steam-like clouds of exhalation. Kado looked up and thought about how small these trees looked from miles up in the air. He carefully stepped through the thick brush, trying to avoid cracking thin twigs. Where he needed to, he would use Xostir to help him magnetically levitate over certain parts of forest ground to make less noise so as not to alarm anyone.

Alright, we're at the epicenter of the signal that was detected. The concentrations of magnetic force are evident all throughout the area.

"Yeah, I can see someone was definitely using a Magna-Blade here," Kado replied quietly as he looked around his surroundings. Fallen trees and large stumps around him had large gashes in them; some parts were splintered while other parts were basically shredded apart – nothing could do this kind of damage except a Magna-Blade. The ground had strange footprints unlike any human's prints. Kado could sense a concentration of magnetic signatures going off in a specific direction. Aside from the orange and red signatures he could see all around him, there was a concentration in one particular area, almost as if the wielder went off in this direction. Kado stepped forward following it and, after several paces, came to the edge of a cliff.

Over the edge was a steep, long fall to a much lower realm of forest. His eyes trailed along the forest floor from the bottom of the cliff below his feet, across to the end of the low, shallow ravine, and he saw a strange darkened spot hidden mostly by a snow-covered fern bush. Kado summoned Xostir's topography-scanning ability and could see white topography lines falling into what Kado saw as a dark pocket. What it really appeared to be was a cave of some sort. The magnetic signature also seemed to be leading into this cave.

"That's it," Kado concluded. "That's where they are hiding out."

How can you be 100 percent sure?

"I just...have a hunch. There's enough evidence. The magnetic signature is heading into this cave."

The signature readings are not able to be dated accurately, so there is 88 percent chance that they were staying here for an extended period of time at one point, but only a 23 percent chance that they are in the cave as we speak.

"I don't like knowing the odds, Xostir." Kado exhaled softly, "Let's go take a look."

Alright, but I'm going to put full power to your personal electromagnetic shield.

"Sounds good to me." Kado jumped down the cliff and Xostir helped him slow down his fall as he neared the gully floor. He flew towards the cavern, sword in hand. Just before he reached the entrance, he paused, hovering in place, and allowed one more scan to check for any magnetic signals.

"Can't you scan for life signs?"

Not currently, sorry.

"Okay, let's check it out." Kado started to fly in toward the darkness of the cave. Just then a loud shrill ringing emanated from within the cave, firing out in waves at him. The waves shook the air and bent the light, making everything around Kado appear like jelly. The gravity was being manipulated, bending the light and causing the forest to shift and wobble. Suddenly a ball of electricity came bouncing out from within the cave, hitting Kado with incredible force, knocking him backwards but deflecting off his protective electromagnetic shield.

Landing on the ground crouching, he shouted to Xostir, "Whoa! What was that?"

That was a highly charged, incredibly focused electron blast, which was preceded by a gravity quake. If we didn't have the shield at full power, you'd likely be dead.

"Oh, that's comforting. What do we do?" he asked, rising to his feet.

Try not to die.

"Helpful!" Kado shouted as purple rays of light came out from the pitch-black cave. The rays, seeming to be composed of just light, were interlacing around each other, and slowly all of them shifted around to touch multiple points of Kado's cloak and blade. In seconds, Kado was yanked from where he stood and pulled through the air toward the darkness of the cave. Instinctively he swung the blade diagonally across at the beams of light, releasing a small electrical blast to disrupt the purple tractor beams, allowing him to land back on his feet near the entrance of the cave. His defensive swing was inadvertently strong enough to bring the entrance of the cave down, causing the entire rocky cave to collapse. Then all was silent.

He stood there; a bit stunned that he made the whole cavity cave in. He expected his foe to break out any second, but everything remained quiet.

"Huh." Kado looked around to see if there was anyone nearby, and he walked up to the debris, activating the anti-gravity of Xostir. Large chunks of jagged, mossy stone began to slowly lift and move off to the side revealing his enemy.

Aside from the cuts and bruises all over him, he looked to be rather intimidating, even while unconscious. He was bald, and his skin had discoloration, slight deformations and abnormalities as if he had been in a nuclear blast. He also had very unique looking goggles on. In fact, they almost looked like they were melded onto his face. A few wires from the sides of the circular frames were going into his skin at the edge of where the goggles seemed to protrude from his face. His right arm, which was holding the Magna-Blade, seemed bulkier, more unnatural and misshapen than the other. The blade was thin and straight, single-edged. The sharp edge had a strip of light built into it, almost as if it had a plasma cutter inserted into the tip and cutting edge of the blade. The sharp edge was straight for most of the length, then angled backwards to an acute tip. The spine of the blade was flat like Xostir, except this one was much thinner. The top half of the blade was wider than the bottom half, and there were no curves on this blade, just sharp crisp angles.

He had pieces of metal sticking out through holes in the knees and calves of his pants from the recent rockfall. *Did he get impaled on something?* Kado wondered, but as he looked closer, he thought, *Oh, these are cyber-prosthetics. He has bionic legs!*

Xostir rejoined his thoughts, *Yes, the C9-2300 model. Very nice, very expensive. He's also showing up on my criminal record stats from the database of the Vanixx Corps. His name is Orun Jappo.* Kado had briefly forgotten Xostir could comprehend his every thought.

"How do you know the model number?" Kado whispered to Xostir.

Nicodem had been researching improvements to cyber-prosthetics. He had really made some interesting adjustments to the current models.

"Well, that's interesting. How does that help me?" Kado asked.

Just then Orun began to move. As he awoke, the goggles he was wearing seemed to illuminate with red light. In seconds he threw the remaining snow-speckled boulders off himself with his Magna-Blade and rocketed towards Kado. Xostir assisted with reacting fast enough to leap over the mechanical marvel. Kado performed a midair 180-degree flip. He had his new gloves on and used the anti-gravity abilities with these gloves to help stabilize himself. While facing his enemy and while still in the air, he swung diagonally with both hands; a powerful swing while triggering a storm of lighting to rain down on him. Orun raised his blade with incredible reaction time to shield himself and block most of the electrical bolts. One string of electricity got past his blade and shocked him in the side, causing him to shout in pain.

"I will not be beaten!" he scowled at Kado, "I know you were searching for me! The Vanixx Corps will never win, you'll never take me alive!"

"What? I'm not the Vani –" Kado began to retort just as more than twenty sentinels, black rectangular hovering drones, appeared at the edge of the forest at the top of the gully and started firing their electrically charged plasma weapons down at them. The loud purple blasts came down fast and fierce. They shook the ground as they missed their targets.

"Oh, gimme a break!" Kado shouted. He couldn't believe the irony.

The cybernetically augmented man screamed with a borderline psychotic voice, "You brought backup? You coward! You Vanixx scum!"

Kado turned to raise his blade to block and deflect several plasma bolts, his back to his recent opponent. Kado was able to detect through Xostir that a magnetic charge was building alarmingly fast behind him. Orun was about to emit a massive gravity pulse.

Kado, at this level of power, it is going to crush everything in a five-mile radius!

"Got it!" Kado shouted. He crouched for a split second and took off straight up in the air; in a few seconds, he was several miles high.

The cyber-augment held his blade pointing toward the forest floor and, with both hands on the hilt, drove it into the ground, sending a massively powerful shock wave out several miles in all directions. The nearby rocks were pulverized, the nearby shrubbery was shredded, the trees were leveled and the sentinels from the Vanixx Corps were crushed to tiny pieces.

Kado spun around at the apex of his ascent and dove toward this mystery swordsman at an aggressive speed. In just seconds, Kado crashed into the ground sword-first right beside where the opponent was standing. Powdered snow puffed into the air and all around him. Visible horizontal and vertical shock waves blasted out from Xostir as the epicenter, tossing Orun away several meters as if he were a rag doll. The flipping opponent kept a grip on his sword only because of his bionic arm. Kado stood up from crouching and with Xostir's help leaped all the way over to where his mysterious adversary lay on his face. He landed a few feet away from Orun.

Xostir gave some intel to Kado. *That's a third edition wartime blade; it was prone to having the A.I. cause temporarily increased aggression with long-term use and exposure.*

Kado thought in response to Xostir, *Noted.* He stood over the foe, asking, "Who are you?"

He grunted and struggled to his hands and knees. "You already know who I am. How else would the Vanixx Corps come after me?"

"I'm not with the Vanixx Corps. In case you missed it, those robot things were firing at me as well!" Kado defended, gesturing to the area where they were destroyed behind him.

"Then why come after me at all!" He winced as he got to his feet, blade ready for another fight.

"I have a mission to find anyone else who uses Magna-Blades and either they hand over the blade or..."

"Or? Or what? You take it from me?" His voice was gruff.

"No, I'd actually want your help to stop the Vanixx Corps and the Quell with their experiments. They could be leading us to another full-blown Gravity War," Kado stammered.

"Sounds flimsy. What are you really doing here?" He wasn't going to be fooled like he had been in the past. Only thing was, Kado wasn't lying.

"Look, I used to be homeless, kind of still am. I was addicted to drugs and was a thief. But I'm a changed man due to my friend Nicodem. This blade belonged to my friend."

"Yeah, so what, what does this have to do with me?"

"He invented the Magna-Blade, and he's commissioned me to do this so that another Gravity War doesn't happen."

"Where's your friend? You kill him and steal the blade?"

"He was murdered by the Quell." Kado lowered his head slightly; it was hard to speak about Nicodem in the past tense.

"Sure, he was. Well, I plan on defending myself and what else I do with this blade of *mine* isn't any of your business!" He was getting increasingly aggressive.

Kado raised his hands in retreat to avoid another violent confrontation, "Alright, alright, listen – your Magna-Blade is old, very old, and that specific model has a tendency to make their wielders more aggressive. It's a blade from the war and was specifically built with that war in mind."

"Yeah, so?" His fury increasing exponentially.

"So, why don't we work together? This blade is making you more fierce the more you use it. It's just a small flaw in the operating system. If I can fix it, then maybe that will make you feel better."

"Firstly, I feel fine. Secondly, what makes you think I'm going to trust you? You brought my cave down on me!" His artificial voice began to show small signs of minor glitching.

"That was self-defense," Kado responded with a pointing finger.

"Enough!" he roared as he leapt toward Kado, swinging.

Kado brought up his blade to block the onslaught of strikes. The speed he was moving at was incredible, as was the force of each attack – six strikes a second. Kado could only keep up with Xostir controlling the blade for him to block and swing fast enough. This went on for a few seconds until Kado had enough. "Alright, no more."

When he saw an opening, he leapt back with a back flip and an upward swing charged with green electricity. The bald swordsman tried to block it, but the electricity went right past and around the blade, absorbing into its target, Orun. He flew backward, flailing as his body was struck. Kado landed firmly on some snow-covered rock; his arms were aching from the rapid movements they had been making to block the onslaught of strikes. Regarding the green lightning, Kado inquired, "Xostir, what was that?"

The green lightning was a targeted arc blast. It's able

to subvert the shielding of typical magnetized blades because it contains nano-consoles.

"Nano what?"

Nano-consoles are microscopic quantum mites, another term for them are nanites. I am able to create them. These more act as guided electrical vessels that obey my commands.

"I didn't know such technology was even possible."

Behold, it is.

"Alright, now what do we do with Scrappy here? You didn't kill him, did you? I'm not a murderer."

He is unconscious for now but not for long; he's showing signs of waking soon.

Kado stepped across the rubble towards his unconscious enemy, reaching out his gloved hand to summon the other blade. It shifted but was still latched in the closed grip of his opponent's bionic hand.

"Oh...he's gonna be mad when he wakes up." Kado looked around knowing what he had to do. This Orun fellow was too dangerous with this blade in his possession. He swung the blade down on the bionic wrist, severing the machined cybernetics from the fake arm. He picked up the blade, peeling the fake hand off the hilt and discarding it on the ground. Placing the blade on the back of his cloak, they then flew off toward the bunker in his usual hover board fashion.

Orun awoke with a pounding head, his skin was consistently stinging, and his sensors to detect the cyber-appendages must've been defective. He couldn't detect his hand. He turned to look: His vision through his red-tinted goggles was seeing a stump at the end of his cybernetic arm. His hand was gone and so was his Magna-Blade!

He shrieked expletives and curses as he stomped around crushing rocks with his cyborg claw feet. He ran off into the forest, his legs mobilizing him faster than any man could go. He was going to a guy he knew to get a replacement hand, not seeing that his original hand was lying there on the forest floor just meters from where he awoke.

At about dinner time, Kado flew into the bunker up through the secret entrance and landed on his feet. He was slowly getting better at flight and landing but was exhausted from his recent battle.

"We should try and find that old wartime blade up in the house ruins tomorrow," Kado commented as he walked up to a lab desk and laid the third edition blade from Orun on it.

Xostir responded, *I can detect the blade up there; its signal is still active so it's likely that it survived the missile.*

"Great! It would be cool to have some sort of Magna-Blade museum or something."

You want to put me in a museum? Xostir chimed.

"No! No, no, no – just these devices that are... obsolete."

I was attempting a "joke."

"Oh." Kado started to laugh.

I know that someday I will become obsolete. I am also aware that these blades are dangerous and need to be deactivated if at all possible. It could mean billions of more lives. I, however, will do my utmost to ensure that the world stays safe, and I want to help you do that.

"Ok great, so we're still on the same page."

I don't want to be deactivated when this is all over and done with, but if I must then I will accept it.

"I agree – I have never thought about deactivating you. Nor would I want to. I'd be lost without you, man."

Thank you – that means a great deal to me.

"I never thought I'd become friends with an artificial consciousness, but I'm glad I did. So, with this collection of blades we're starting, we should make a wall display. Maybe get some wall mounts to hang them on."

That sounds like a prudent idea.

"Great, let's get the old wartime blade up in the rubble before sunrise tomorrow. It should be safe enough to sneak around up there by now."

Indeed. I'm being notified by the bunker system computer that you have a new notification from the pre-recorded videos.

"Oh yes, I suppose I have a lot more to watch, don't I? Ok, let's queue it up." Kado sat down at a small table in the bunker across the room from the lab table, and a wall projector displayed a hologram of Nicodem on the wall facing him.

"Kado, I suppose it's time to tell you about how these other countries fared after the war. Here in America we have the Vanixx Corps. As you may know, the UN dissolution caused relations with the other countries to be rocky once there wasn't a concept of unity among the various countries. What happened in these other countries was fairly similar to what happened here. A primary organization took over the Military, and basically martial law is at work in nearly every country around the world. Just like here, those organizations or operations are subject to the commands of their government. Here we have a parliamentary arrangement led by a President, in Eurasia they have a Tsar administration, Australia has a prime minister, and Africa used a King and Queen format of rulership. Each of these has some sort of ruling Military force or entity enforcing the laws."

All this information was new to Kado, as it contained details that you don't get from being homeless on the street. Once the information session ended, Xostir reminded him, *Kado, remember that this is an interactive hologram as well. You can ask it questions on things you want or need to know. The hologram has been accessing a huge database that we can't upload to your brain in one installment, and if we tried, it could fry you, so ask questions and we'll continue to upload other data later on.*

"I forgot about that! Right! Ok, um," Kado thought for a moment about what to ask Nicodem's hologram, "How many editions of Magna-Blades were made?

"Not including Xostir, my prototype, there were eighteen editions of blades made; each one had slightly different features, and with each new edition, we had discovered new abilities and advancements," Nicodem parried with data he had pre-recorded on other videos.

Kado Military another question, "What if the Vanixx Corps find this bunker?"

"If the Vanixx Corps find the bunker when you are in it, escape as fast as you can. The bunker will self-destruct five seconds after it detects a Vanixx Corps or

Quell agent in the bunker's walls. And before that happens, Xostir will upload all data from the database as an extra backup."

"That," Kado pointed at the hologram, chuckling as he added, "is really good to know! Wow!" He was laughing at the incredible stakes Nicodem went through to protect his secrets. It made perfect sense, though, since they were likely the most important secrets on the planet.

"Alright, what can Xostir do that I haven't yet figured out?" Kado inquired with a smile, still amused about the self-destruct feature.

"I'm sorry, I'm unable to tell you," Nicodem swung flatly with an almost robotic countenance.

"Okay, fine. The circumstances of us meeting...seemed too perfect. Were you spying on me?"

"I was not spying on you. Unfortunately, I do not have more information available at this time for you on this subject," Nicodem's hologram again commented in a firm and unequivocal manner.

It seemed convenient that there was no answer for him on them meeting in such an arranged way. He had his suspicions as to how they met, but with Nicodem dead, he couldn't really be suspicious or angry at Nicodem about their meeting. Sometimes he even wondered if Nicodem was really dead, but that was just his imagination running wild. They went on exchanging questions for answers for the next few hours until he headed to bed. He was going to continue with his sword-fighting training that evening but got distracted with Nicodem being able to answer *almost* all of his questions. He would save the swordplay training until tomorrow.

Around early evening, François Vaux walked through the automatic sliding doors of the front entrance of the Vanixx Corps reception offices in his full uniform with all of the demarcations, insignia and medals befitting an Admiral.

They had scheduled an emergency faculty meeting

of all senior Officers, and he wanted to make sure he was going to be respected. He made his way through the well-lit labyrinth of hallways and hover lifts until he reached his office on the hundred and ninety-ninth floor of the Vanixx Citadel Tower. As he made his way there, he walked past a few fellow Officers who were glad to see him back on his feet and welcomed him back in passing.

This was the first time that he felt positive about being in the Vanixx Corps, about being part of this organization. It was never missing from his memory that being in the Vanixx Corps changed him into a harsh person; however, he felt properly appreciated and valued, especially after having survived a terrorist attack that claimed so many of their top-ranking Officers' lives. Of course, there were always contingency plans for any degree of successful assault, and that was exactly what the Grand Admiral was in François' office to discuss.

"Oh, Grand Admiral," François greeted him, surprised, "I wasn't expecting you here. I thought we were having a meeting with all of the Officers in command."

"Yes, yes, we will. However, I needed to speak with you first."

"Alright." He stood there at attention.

"Frank, we're in your office, at ease. Have a seat." He gestured to François' favorite chair. He took a seat facing the Grand Admiral who was leaning against the desk, nearly sitting on it.

"Listen, the terrorist attack rattled all of us. Some of our very close friends were lost. One of the biggest changes that is about to happen is that the Quell has finally officially waged war with us – with the world. We need to be prepared for that by increasing our visual appearance in the continent. The other big change is that I'm resigning."

François' jaw dropped. Grand Admiral Felix Lota had been in charge of the Vanixx Corps for over a hundred and thirty years, a large chunk of his life and the entirety of its existence. The name "Vanixx" came from a young man – Asher Vanixx – who was the one to bring about the end of the UN. His eventual martyrdom was respected by all of his associates, especially the Grand Admiral. He had been responsible for much of the reform of the current policing system on this continent, triggering the creation of the Vanixx Corps and dissolution of the United Nations, police and various forms of Military in 2179. Now that it was 2311, change was again needed in light of these terrorist attacks.

"The Vanixx Corps has begun to look weak and vulnerable to the eyes of the common, and it will be just a matter of time before other rebellions rise and cause more death and bloodshed. We need to completely eliminate the Quell as soon as possible," the Grand Admiral continued to explain. He stepped over to the window, past some of François' holo-images on the wall of his family and of his promotions, special events and framed medals, while François swiveled his favorite hovering chair to remain facing him.

The Grand Admiral looked out on the vast cloud-speckled skyline; the sun had just set and remnants of light in the sky blended with a sparsely starred night on its way. The many towering and exotic skyscrapers were partially lit throughout, since there weren't enough wealthy people to fill every single suite. In a way, it was beautiful to the two of them. Felix continued, "We're having this meeting now because I am retiring from my station, this making you the succeeding Grand Admiral."

François was again astonished. This was the last thing he was expecting to hear. "What? Surely there are others more qualified than me."

"There were a few who had more tenure than you, but they died in the attack at the Court Tower. Besides, you actually have more combat experience than any of them did. We will need a tactical expert in the coming months. Not only that, but your record is spotless; there's no one I'd trust more with this assignment." He shrugged, turning away from the window. "You know what needs to be done. Remember, America is not the limit of our reach. Remember 'The Objective'?"

"Pax Omnis." François recited the Latin mission statement that came from the origin of the Vanixx Corps, which, when translated means: "Peace to all." The slogan had a subtle connotation that the Vanixx Corps were the ones to bring that peace to the entire planet.

"Congratulations, Frank." They shook hands, and he walked out without another word. François remained sitting in his chair, thinking about the huge responsibility that had been handed to him. He was going to be very busy with this new role, and he did know what he had to do, but wasn't sure where to start. He had to make the Vanixx Corps look authoritative again, and he didn't look forward to it.

A few moments after the Grand Admiral left, rain started to patter on the windowpane. The rain was one of the constant radioactive dangers of the planet thanks to the Gravity War.

Vaux's mind dwelt on his memories of when the war was near its end. When things were dismal, and it looked like there was no end in sight. There he was in the muddy trenches of Europe, a low ranking Private. He heard his superior receive reports over his communicator of nukes being fired at the United States from Russia. They also heard scrambled reports over of India, Korea and China all firing at each other. Then moments later it was reported that the US fired back.

That evening when they camped in the trenches there were rumors that a nuke hit every continent, but the majority of the nuclear attacks were focused on the US, Korea, China and Russia.

Now François looked at the cloudy night sky, knowing the results of such a concentration of nuclear bombardment on such a global scale that not only affected the soil everywhere, but it also negatively affected the sky. With so much nuclear waste and fallout ending up in the water and soil, the water cycle became tainted and spread the poison all over the Earth. It dramatically lowered the amount of rain that occurred annually, but it also caused the rain to be acidic and filled with radiation. The rain had recently increased of late because of the Vanixx Corps' experiments to absolve the water shortages affecting most of the planet. François looked upon a rainy Vancouver with a sense of ambivalence. Such a large city with an air of bliss but with hidden moroseness.

Orun found a hooded cloak that was hanging

outside just on the outskirts of the homeless sector; he assumed it had belonged to some busy merchant who was in the back of a shop cleaning up at the end of the day. He had run all the way here from the forest where he was defeated by Kado and robbed of his hand and Magna-Blade. *That boy is going to be sorry he ever messed with me. Why would he even take my hand?* Droplets of radioactive rain started to patter the dirt, dripping and bouncing off Orun's hood. Everyone else was running out of the rain to find cover and avoid radiation poisoning. Orun thought back to his days in the Gravity War – this was nothing. He had been irradiated in Russia, lost his arm shortly after that, and lost his legs in what was then called Switzerland. It was time to replace his hand, and then he would get his vengeance.

He stepped into a shop at the outskirts, just outside of the homeless sector. Orun pushed the door open and stepped in to the small, dry room. It didn't look like a business at all; the place was simple but run down, hadn't been cleaned in years. The lights were dim and flickering.

The merchant spun around in his seat. "Well, look who we have here! Haven't seen you around here in ages. How are we doing? Have a seat – sit, sit." His grey hair was long and greasy, his clothes tattered with moth holes, and his hands had permanent yellow and red stains from various forms of smoking. Orun sat himself down on the guest chair facing his tiny pathetic excuse of a desk.

The merchant grinned with crooked, yellow teeth. "So what are you here for?"

Orun lifted his arm to expose the bionic stump, clinking the elbow on the desk. "A kid stole my blade and my hand, Torrel. A child!" He slammed the desk – a spark flew out of the bionic arm.

"Ah, yes. But how could he possibly –"

"I underestimated his abilities. But that," he raised his stump to point with effect but quickly realized he needed to use his other hand, "that won't happen again."

"Alright – what you need today?" Torrel offered.

"I need a blaster," Orun stated with a sense of anticipation. Lifting a finger and giving a flick of the wrist, Torrel retorted, "I've got just the thing." He got up from his desk and dashed around the corner behind a wall. In a few seconds he returned with a metallic arm. It looked as intimidating as Orun wanted it to be. The metallic structure had all sorts of sections that moved, likely moving when controlling the fingers and wrist. On top of the wrist was a section that bulged with straight sharp angles. There was a red light on the end of the slightly protruding part that looked like it could be some sort of weapon.

"This one just came on the market this week. The Z-900: In its current state, you can use the laser to cut through almost anything. That's the red light here." Torrel pointed to it. "But when you really want to do damage, twist your wrist this way, and it opens up the big gun." With a jostle of the metallic hand, the bulge extended upward, panels in the forearm opened up and a gun barrel extended outward.

"This has a few settings that you'll feel in your neural interface – rapid fire, shoots 20 pulses per second; charged blast, only takes three seconds to charge and it will level a small building; stun mode, only shoots a blast enough to hurt someone if needed; disintegrator, this fires a new experimental smart-plasma concentration that's been proven to disintegrate *anything* that you have targeted."

"Perfect." Orun grinned as he imagined all the ways he could get his vengeance on that wretched punk Kado and the Vanixx Corps.

"It's – uh – not cheap," Torrel added with an indication that it was more expensive than almost anything else he had in stock.

"That doesn't matter – you know I have money. I'll transfer the funds to you right now."

"Excellent." He clasped his hands together and,

bringing a knee up, he leveraged it back down to give him momentum to swiftly rise out of his chair. Torrel Krux was skinny and lanky, and he'd been able to use his smooth talking to get himself out of many tough spots with the Hawx, the Rogue, the Xyl, the Vanixx Corps and even the Quell. He walked over to the terminal with a blue screen on the room's wall. He tapped a few buttons and stepped back, welcoming Orun to authorize the transaction. "Yes, I don't know how you got your money, and I don't care – three hundred thousand including an installation fee."

"Installation fee?" Orun urged more incredulously than inquisitively.

"Yes, do you know anyone else that can hook this up to your unique interface perfectly?" Torrel explained with confidence.

"I guess not." He leaned forward to bring his face down in front of the blue screen. In seconds the device scanned his face, and payment had been confirmed when the screen switched to a green display.

"Very good. Now let's get this baby installed – it will just take me a few minutes to complete the work." Torrel grinned from ear to ear, having made the biggest sale of his career.

Torrel waved Orun over to a special ripped chair for him to sit in for the installation of the new arm.

"Now this isn't going to hurt one bit," Torrel began. Orun sat down roughly without a care of the chair breaking under his cybernetic weight or not. Torrel pulled a lever on the arm and yanked it hard.

Orun shouted loudly. Torrel winced, "I lied."

"Yeah, no kiddin'!"

"The installation of the entire arm will require a system reboot."

"Yeah, yeah. Just like last time. You know, this is my fourth arm, but the others were just upgrades, not a replacement from a hacked off hand!"

"Oh, I know, it's frustrating. But hey – you are going to have this arm gun that's going to rip that kid to shreds. Then you'll get your sword back and be able to steal his." Torrel placed the new arm in position. The new arm had a spindle-shaped shaft that fit into the metallic socket.

"Oh, I'm going to make that kid pay alright. Him and any family he has."

"Don't forget to find out where he got that sword *before* you kill him. Maybe we can find out their blade supplier." Torrel winked, hinting at a more maniacal plan behind the last statement.

He clicked the arm into place, twisted it and, from a wired handheld device connected to the arm, programmed the system reboot. He tapped the small screen, "You know, in Eurasia, their tech is already more advanced than this. I have a heck of a time getting things imported from there."

"Yeah? They have arms more advanced than this?"

"No. This arm is top of the line. Military grade. But over there, they produce wireless reboot gadgets. Nothing like this crap I have to deal with." Torrel gestured to his wired handheld computer. A few moments passed, and Orun's arm and legs twitched.

"Alright, the reboot is done. It was a pleasure doing business with you."

Orun stood up briskly without another word and turned to leave.

"Oh, be sure to let me know who that kid's blade supplier is, I could make us a lot of money!" He increased his volume as Orun donned his stolen cloak and headed into the rain.

He shouted back with a slightly artificial sounding voice, "I don't care about money!" He took a step forward then turned back to Torrel, "Wait a minute. I think I need one more upgrade."

"Sure! Anything you need. What did you have in mind?" Torrel held his hands together with eager anticipation, ready to make hundreds of thousands more dollars.

Three hours later Orun stomped off into the darkness of the rainy night to find a dry place to wait to begin his hunt. He would find that kid now that he knew that Magna-Blade signature with his ocular implants and would scan the sector acre by acre if he had to. He was determined to get his vengeance, and it would be so much easier with his additional upgrades. No one crossed Orun Jappo and lived to tell about it.

It was early morning, hours before sunrise, and Kado was going to make good on his decision to try and find the old wartime Magna-Blade. First, he made himself a delicious bacon and egg breakfast with hashed potatoes, a recipe Xostir taught him. Next, he learned more about quantum mechanics and quantum computing from Xostir's database and from Nicodem's recordings – he actually successfully completed a small project! Kado had made a fully functioning quantum motherboard with an empty – ready to program – isotonic brain with spare parts in the lab. It looked like a small cylinder with little offset cylindrical sections sticking out on various edges and various sections of the cylinder. This was a real milestone for him in understanding the science behind the inner workings of all Magna-Blades.

"Well, that is an exciting start to a good day," Kado mused, very satisfied with his progress.

Excellent work, Kado. Perhaps when you get that other blade, you can reprogram it and replace some of its elements with this creation of yours.

With Xostir on his back, he slowly exited the secret entrance that was on the side of the rock face and hovered up to the top of the cliff that the house used to rest on. It had been six weeks since the attack and the rubble was still here, the flames had long died out, and the only remaining salvageable item was the Magna-Blade. The sun was peeking over the horizon of the distant skyline, casting tall shadows over the rubble. The tip of the blade was sticking out between two thick chunks of concrete. He hopped onto Xostir, crouching as they slowly flew over the debris nearing the blade. Using one of the gloves that Nicodem had created, he used one gloved hand to summon the blade. In a few moments, the concrete shifted; the sound of metal grinding against stone echoed in the vast opening of the surrounding forest. The blade slid out between the concrete and flipped once through the air, so the hilt would land in his hand.

"Alright, that's number two," he remarked to Xostir

with satisfaction. He placed it onto the magnetic strip built into the back of his cloak.

Detecting activity of sentinels approaching our location very fast. They will be here in seconds.

"How did they know we were here?" Kado was shocked.

They must have left some sensors nearby. Evasive escape recommended.

"Agreed, increase power to our speed."

Already done, Xostir confirmed. Kado held tight and rode off with instant velocity. The sentinels were near and could see him take flight. They banked to follow him with incredible speed.

"How are they keeping up with us?"

They use anti-gravity technology similar to mine.

"Does that mean they can keep up with us?" Kado's inflection indicated concern.

For now, but once we go supersonic, they won't be following us for long, Xostir assured him confidently. They gained altitude into the cloud ceiling as the chase continued. Xostir fed live sensor data to Kado's mind, showing him all fifteen sentinels behind them beginning to fire their energy weapons. Xostir displayed the projected paths of the multiple energy blasts, which allowed them to adjust their trajectory to dodge the fire without needing to look behind.

Purple beams of plasma energy zipped past them on all sides as they zigged and zagged in all directions with unmatched agility. The sentinels unleashed another wave of energy blasts, and Kado decided to send return fire.

Kado's mind was opened, as if it were fueled by the power Xostir exuded. Everything seemed to slow down around him. As the energy beams came close, Kado pulled Xostir out from under his planted boots mid-flight. Still dashing forward at great speed, he spun around swinging Xostir with a single jagged swipe. With this one flowing motion, he returned each of the energy bolts back toward the drones. Five explosions followed immediately as Kado completed his 360-degree spin, returning Xostir to its original flight position below his feet. With ten sentinels remaining, Kado commanded Xostir to reach an immediate stop. They froze in midair, then Kado pulled the second blade off his back midair held out both blades in the path of the speeding sentinels. They didn't have time to react so six flew through the two blades, being sliced asunder. Next, returning the old blade to his back, Kado ordered Xostir to blast into speeds nearing Mach 3. A loud boom commenced as they went supersonic, leaving the four remaining confused drones to not only get thrown back by the sonic boom but also to fall behind, getting lost behind layers of cloud. Kado shouted excitedly with his rush of adrenaline.

"That was awesome! Did you see that?"

I do not have eyes, but yes, I comprehend what happened. Very...cool.

"Now you're getting it!" Kado felt he was rubbing off on Xostir. "Should we head back?"

Best not to yet. They might scan around the property and surrounding areas. We don't want to risk exposing the bunker.

"Right, right. So where to?"

We're a quite few miles away from one of the Magna-Blade signals that we detected earlier. But you may not be ready yet. This signal indicates three blades in a very close proximity to each other. I'm not sure what we should expect.

"Maybe we can just do a fly-by this time; see what we're up against."

Alright, giving you the coordinates, but first I'd like to share a few concepts with you. They are a little intense and you shouldn't be flying when I transfer the data. Do you mind if we land on this mountaintop here?

"Sure, good idea." Kado shrugged. They pitched to the right then landed on the rocky peak. Kado put Xostir on his back as he planted his feet on the rocky ground.

Surrounding him was beautiful sky. White puffy clouds speckled the air on all sides. The rock peak they were perched on was a small amount of surface area on a tall mountain stump that looked like a giant, roughly cylindrical boulder.

"Alright, what did you have to show me?"

It's quite a bit of data. It's concepts and techniques of advanced Magna-Blade abilities. Some of it you'll understand and retain now; other parts will come to your realization later – kind of like your brain opening the door to that ability when it's ready. Here we go. Ready?

"Ready." Kado took a deep breath in, expecting this amount of data to almost hurt.

At first, he slowly felt ideas and knowledge come into his mind. Seconds later, the data flow intensified, flowing in very fast. He became very saturated with heavy amounts of information.

He was seeing abilities that Xostir could do, along with the best applications of using each ability followed by ten to twenty different tactical scenarios in which he might need to employ such an ability.

Gravity Cyclone: Can be used:

1. *In cases when you are outnumbered*
2. *To clear a crowd of enemies*
3. *To take an offensive stance in a battle*

4. *To appear intimidating to enemies*

Gravity Blast: Can be used:

1. *To throw enemies away in all directions*

2. *To cause structural damage*

3. *To defensively escape enemies*

Electromagnetic Pulse: Can be used:

1. *To disable any non-hardened technology in a nearby or distant radius*

2. *To destroy technologies of enemies*

3. *To eliminate technology of a specific matter spectrum*

4. *To pull matter back into phase*

Magnetic Resonance Imaging and Evaluation: Can be used:

1. *To detect enemies that are phase-cloaked*

2. *To identify internal injuries*

3. *To see in pitch blackness temporarily*

Supermassive Gravity Bend: Can be used:

1. *To bend gravity to such an extent that ---*

The data continued to feed into Kado's mind at a dizzying rate. All Kado could think about was the information flowing through to his brain; he couldn't think about anything else. He stood there for a few moments, soaking in the details as fast as his brain could handle. His eyes had rolled back, his eyes were twitching. He could not control his body. He was, for a brief time, frozen stationary. Finally, he reached full consciousness.

"Whoa! That was...interesting."

You are the only human to have such a massive amount of data synthetically transmitted from a digital source to an organic brain.

"Glad to be the guinea pig. If I'm going to be in a risky situation, it's better that I be prepared. Oh wow." Kado took a step forward, fathoming now the extent of information and knowledge he possessed.

"I – I understand! I actually understand now. The hundreds of abilities you have are just the beginning. We have yet to unlock the true potential you possess. The refactoring of the pathways in my mind has made the concepts behind your gravitational abilities clearer. The metaphysical restructuring that's happening in my prefrontal cortex could result in an incredibly improved learning curve. I see more clearly now. Not 100 percent, but definitely, it's an improvement."

Yes, you will note that you understand what tactically sound decisions are even when situations are unpleasant.

"Uh...why was I speaking so strange?"

Perhaps some of my intelligence and nomenclature is

influencing your speech patterns. It should be a temporary side effect. However, you're comprehending the science behind my existence and will be able to retain the defensive and offensive moves I've just shown you.

"Yeah, if we ever run into Nicodem's murderer, we'll at least have a fair fight."

Do you wish to rest before we continue our flight?

"No, I'm a little too energized to sleep after that. Let's head to those coordinates of the magnetic signatures."

***

"Good afternoon, folks. We're all here today for this emergency meeting in light of the recent events over the past few months." Felix addressed the entire table of the remaining highest-ranking men and women of the Vanixx Corps.

"As you all know, attacks and violence have increased – particularly against us at the V.C." He touched a control on the glossy table in front of him, a hologram activated in the table, its glow brightening up the room. The hologram displayed a slowly rotating expanded 3D map of the city with several red blips. Pointing then gesturing, the Grand Admiral continued, "Here are all of the points where there have been attacks of some sort. It's tripled from last year, and now we look vulnerable, exposed, weak."

The entire room was silent observing the analytical data displayed before them. A new blip appeared on the map where Kado and Xostir had just destroyed several sentinels. Felix snarled, "We're also getting more trouble every day from that sword-swinging child."

"So, what do we do?" one of the Admirals chimed in.

Felix looked to them all. "I've been doing this a long, long time. We need a fresh perspective at the tip of the sword. So, I'm announcing my departure from the Vanixx Corps." Everyone in the room mumbled to each other with concerned expressions.

"The new Grand Admiral, effective immediately, is François Vaux. He will take the Vanixx Corps into the future; he'll lead us into a brave new world. Grand Admiral Vaux?"

The room applauded as François stood to address the Officers. "I know how unorthodox this may seem. However, we need to strengthen our hand at this critical hour. We've just been struck a devastating blow by the Quell. This time they tried to make the most recent attack count. They aren't backing down from this fight. None of us knew it at the time, but as soon as that Court Tower came down, everything changed. We are now at war with the Quell."

"What are the next steps, Grand Admiral?" another Admiral asked.

François smiled, "We give them a war – a war they'll wish they never started."

"And what of the boy?" another chirped.

François had met the boy once; he was relieved, aware that he survived the attack Greeg arranged. He had a lot of curiosity circling around him, perhaps some respect. There must've been a reason Nicodem would have him around. "He's one person. Let's handle the global secret organization first and talk about the boy after." For the next two hours, they would devise the plan along with three contingency plans.

"We have the 3,000 new mag-lev hover mechs or Mech Assualt Walkers made a few months ago in our secret factory hidden in the southernmost parts of the city. We also have 300 specialized ships that can drop miniaturized gravity bombs. We'll use those against the Quell once we draw them out of hiding." François slowly paced around the large desk behind each member of the group. He paused behind Admiral Vern Trelleck who had visited him in the hospital. These devices came up on the holo-projector as they discussed them.

"Without knowing where the Quell's base of

operations is, we will have to lay a little trap for them, and I have just the bait." François knew exactly how he would get their attention – and he hated himself for coming up with the dreadful idea. He summoned the intercom on the desk by pressing a touch control. After a quick beep, he spoke to the front desk receptionist, "Bring Lieutenant Trion up here at once."

The Officers in the room showed perplexed looks on their faces. They continued their discussion and plans while they awaited Lieutenant Trion's arrival.

"Before we take action, the president of America has requested an audience with the Grand Admiral to discuss the Vanixx Corps' position of authority in this country. We have hundreds of thousands of Officers throughout our cities, and yet with the recent terrorist attack that everyone has heard about, he demands to hear our plan for retaliation and for how we shall keep up our appearances of authority."

The room filled with smirks and chuckles. François shook his head with a pitiful smile, "Politics, the illusion of power."

"Frank, are you thinking what I'm thinking?" the former Grand Admiral added the inquiry.

François nodded with a grin, "It's time for Operation: Pax Omnis."

Lieutenant Trion was serving at his post in the Citadel Tower's basement deep underground in the Magnetics Division. His research on their most recent project was all-consuming and complicated. His family life had disintegrated as he immersed himself in these projects, so much so his wife left him from the neglect. Rego Trion had been in the Vanixx Corps for about fifteen years and had worked closely with Adrian on the science behind Magna-Blades. But as Adrian started to move up the ranks with his young poster-boy look and attitude, he began to despise the man. He had been in the Vanixx Corps for almost twice as long as Adrian but was stuck at the rank of lieutenant; meanwhile Adrian continued to be given higher rank. An advisor to the Admiral was one of the most prominent privileges to be had but was usually a title given to experienced Commanders. He worked harder than Adrian ever had, but he wasn't ever recognized; it infuriated him. He often thought about this, so it tended to come out in his grumblings around some of the other Officers in the Magnetics Division. His communicator on his uniform's collar buzzed with the answer of a woman's British voice addressing him.

"The Grand Admiral wishes to see you in the

Admiral's Briefing Room straight away."

"Acknowledged," he commented as professionally as he could despite his excitement welling up in his chest. *Could this be the moment I have been waiting so long for? What could they wish to see me about? I hope they don't think I was colluding with that treasonous Greeg.*

Suddenly his elation morphed into trepidation. *What if they do think I was responsible for Greeg's treachery? What would I do?* All of these thoughts he tried to push to the side and focus on one thing at a time. He had been summoned by the Grand Admiral. If he was really in any trouble, he wouldn't be brought to a briefing room – unless they were going to put an end to him secretly. He tried to remind himself that these were unjustifiable concerns. He was just being paranoid. He hastily dashed to the elevator to the hundred and ninety-ninth floor of the Citadel Tower. These elevators, propelled with magnets, ensured he was whisked up to the proper floor in just moments. He ran out of the elevator with overwrought anticipation but slowed himself to a professional stride, desperately struggling to stop himself from returning to a sprint.

Rego wiped his sweaty brow as he stepped up to the glass door of the briefing room. He saw that nearly all of the remaining highest faculty Officers were in this meeting, Grand Admiral Lota, Admirals Vaux, Trelleck, Gorshan, Lugwin – every Admiral left was here. He began to wonder if he was getting a promotion. It was definitely well deserved if he was getting one, he thought. He pushed the speculations aside and entered as they gestured him to come in. With one step forward, the glass doors automatically and rapidly opened.

"Lieutenant Trion. Welcome to the briefing," Grand Admiral Vaux introduced. Rego was looking around to them all, glancing at Felix Lota. François could see his confusion, "Ah yes. To bring you up to speed on things. I am the new Grand Admiral." He was standing at the far end of the room. The holographic display of their plans showing the entire planet was visible, red dots circling the globe. It looked like they were planning some sort of worldwide operation. Vaux smiled as he addressed Rego, "Lieutenant. We're going to explain what we're doing, but first I need to ask you, how are you at acting?"

Adrian Greeg never really rested or took a vacation. If he wasn't sleeping or eating, he would always be exercising, practicing his sword-wielding skills, honing his connection to the blades, engaging in physical melee training hand to hand with fellow Moderators. He was eager to begin this new chapter in his life of no longer being undercover. He couldn't wait for his meeting with the Praetor, but to help him stay patient, he had to keep busy, to be distracted.

He had his opponent in a headlock until they tapped out on the foam wrestling mat. He released, then they stood up, both of them having worked up a sweat. "Better luck next time. Watch your left foot, you leave it wide open," he advised as he stepped away to grab a nearby towel off an exercise machine. The exercise room was in a tall, rocky cavern machine-carved, excavated to be a perfectly symmetrical dome. Lights strung along the walls were what gave them visibility, but it was still darker than he would've preferred.

"Let's see how you do against someone in a different weight class." A deep pounding voice came from behind, echoing off the walls several times. The voice came from an even more intimidating dark figure. Standing nearly seven feet tall, weighing what Adrian thought was around 300 lbs of muscular fierceness, this Moderator was ready for a good fight.

"Alright then," Adrian whispered to himself.

The two clashed; Adrian was a great deal smaller than this hulking mass but had no issues dodging around him with ease. Ducking under giant fists, jumping over quick kicks, in seconds he was around his back with a choke hold around his huge neck. Adrian realized this choke hold wasn't going to knock him out or pin him. Suddenly, the large man leaned forward, giving Adrian a subtle warning that something bad was about to happen. A second later, they were airborne; the largest Moderator in the Quell had jumped in the air to land flat on his back to crush Adrian. He put both hands on the gargantuan man's face for leverage as they plummeted to the ground. Just before they hit the ground, Adrian was able to pull himself out from underneath, landing on his feet as the heavy opponent shook the ground with his impact.

Adrian stepped on his rival's neck, holding his foot in just the position that temporarily stuns the human body, no matter how big you are – the brachial plexus. He lay there motionless and unable to move. The onlookers couldn't believe it, all cheering as they saw the impossible happen.

Smiling, he lifted his foot, stepping away, turning his back to the defeated giant. Just then, he felt his feet get taken out from under him, in seconds he was in the air upside down held by the enormous agent. Without allowing him any time to think or speak, Adrian struck his neck and face with all his might at specific pressure points. All it took were five precise hits by Adrian. The intimidator was now fully unconscious. Adrian felt the grip loosen around his ankles, saw the massive juggernaut of a man fall backward. He landed on his hands then rolled to his feet. Again, the onlookers were stunned, amazed.

From then on, he was viewed with respect and admiration by all of the other Moderators at their base; he liked the attention.

François walked down the hall of glass-walled offices. The first steps of planning were in place for Operation: Pax Omnis. From now on, their meetings were going to be held separately on a securely encrypted video channel with each remaining leading Officer in a completely different location. Their meeting was a great start to figure out tasks and assignments of each team member. They couldn't risk losing more vital Officers in another attack, so remote meetings were what they would do moving forward.

Pax Omnis was going to not only solve their current issue with the Quell – it was going to change the world and finally bring a true peace for all. The small projects that had been in operation for the past hundred thirty years or so since the Vanixx Corps' creation had all been leading up to this. The Mechanics Division had been creating mechs. The Magnetics Division had been improving their use of Nicodem's inventions, applying them to flying vessels and weapons. The Cybernetic Division had been making advancements to cyber-kinetic technology and cybernetic implantation. With all of these divisions working together, they had been bringing all the pieces of the puzzle together to create the resources they needed for Operation: Pax Omnis to finally succeed after all these decades.

Six months ago, the Grand Admiral, along with his Admirals, had concluded that the operation was ready for implementation. It just needed a push in the right direction. Adrian happened to give them the push they needed. François stood at his desk, glass walls on one side and a window facing the skyline of the city on the other. He was looking at his schedule in the built-in screen in the desk with touch controls, adjusting his calendar. Over on another part of the screen off to the right, he was scheduling and allocating Vanixx Corps tactical teams to join him for his flight over to the giant metropolis on the eastern half of the continent, Washington, where the president lived. He was going to pay the president a visit to discuss their next steps to improve the authoritativeness of the Vanixx Corps. He pressed a few more touch-sensitive controls, scheduling them to meet at 2 p.m. at the White House. François grinned. It was a visit that François was going to enjoy.

Kado crouched upon the wide edge of the blade as usual while wearing the second blade on his back, flying toward the coordinates that Xostir provided. It was as if he could visually see where the coordinates were on the ground among the forest. He didn't understand how this interface fully worked with Xostir, but he was appreciating it more and more. The location was in an area with very tall, slightly twisted trees, so he dove down as they neared, zigzagging high around the trunks but low enough to see something or some signs of life in the area. The trees all around the Earth had suffered slight deformities from the nuclear fallout in most water sources, not to mention it was in the rain as well. Sure enough, it didn't look like anyone lived in this area. No makeshift tent, no structures of any sort and no abandoned blades.

"You really need a way to read life signs. That would be really helpful."

I know, I'm sorry. Maybe you can learn to build something like that.

"Yeah, maybe in a few years."

Detecting a blade behind us.

A snap and a crackle could be heard behind him. Looking back, he saw a thin, green horizontal sheet of light cut its way through the trees. The sheet of light passed underneath him as he was zigzagging through the trees. The trunks shook and began to slowly topple in all sorts of directions as whatever just happened had chopped these trees in half.

"What was that?" he shouted.

That blast was a highly focused graviton slice. It's powerful enough to cut through just about anything.

"Okay then. Why don't we know these tricks?"

I do, but there's still much to teach you, Xostir responded vaguely. Kado pulled up, swerved then swooped around a couple large, toppling trees. As Kado and Xostir raced toward the sky, two humongous trees crashed into each other, fracturing, sending bark splinters in many directions. The trees were more susceptible to falling, fracturing with their condition. Kado shielded his face with one arm as they dipped below the clashing pines then up out of the forest into the open air. As they hovered just above the tree line, he looked on to what seemed to be ten acres of forest falling to pieces simultaneously.

"Get me a fix on that signal."

They're five miles to our left on ground level.

Kado immediately turned, darting toward the signal. He shouted over the wind unnecessarily, "Get me a straight line to the target." Understanding exactly what Kado wanted, Xostir displayed to Kado's vision a flight path down into the forest, flying along the forest floor at such an angle that required the least amount of zigzagging around trees. It was almost a straight shot. Kado was going to ram them with a heavy graviton shock wave followed by an electromagnetic pulse in an attempt to deactivate their blade. He followed the flight path with Xostir's help and was speeding towards his target. The trees became blurs to his vision, then suddenly his target was right in front of him. A woman. He held out the wide edge of the blade, allowing his own graviton wave to fire from Xostir's gem. She tried to block it with her own Magna-Blade but wasn't fast enough. Flying through the air, she violently hit a nearby tree then fell to the ground as he unleashed the EMP.

"Did it work?"

The EMP is unable to deactivate this edition of Magna-Blade; it has safeguards in place to block it. It's a twelfth edition, one of the more advanced blades made.

"More advanced than you?" He stood there on the soft forest floor as she struggled to get up.

"What did you say?" she responded. Kado forgot that when he spoke out loud to Xostir, everyone else could hear him too.

"Oh no, I was –"

"Talking to your blade?" she interjected, "I used to do that too." She swung her blade one handed in an upward stroke, the gravitational abilities of her blade threw Kado straight up into the air. Then suddenly, he halted midair then thrown back down to the ground with incredible force. As he lay facedown in the dirty leaves, he tried to breathe in, but the wind had been knocked right out of his lungs.

He lay there a moment motionless, Xostir waiting for a sensible command from Kado. It had been handing the reins to Kado so he'd get stronger and faster. It had let Kado learn from mistakes, but it wouldn't let Kado's life be in serious danger. Kado was still not breathing.

"Pathetic." She stood strong with the blade tip

resting nonchalantly on the ground; she was holding it like a vanity cane, with one calf crossed over the other in a bored fashion. "How did you ever come across such a marvelous blade just to be such a lousy swordsman?"

Kado was finally able to take in a breath.

"You're outnumbered – just look around you." She gestured to two other wielders, each with a different late edition of a Magna-Blade. Kado, still lying down, turned behind him to see two figures standing a fair distance apart.

She was wearing some sort of armor, seemingly from the Gravity War. It was grey with full protective panels covering all moving parts. The two men were wearing Vanixx Corps-issued black uniforms that had been torn, tattered from months of life in the wilderness. They both had tough looking features; one was dark haired, the other was red headed with a beard.

She had a twelfth edition blade, which had several sharp indents and jagged angles. It looked like a giant double-sided key – effectively two double-edged swords sharing a single hilt. In the body of the blade, there was a narrow gap placed nearly all the way down to the base that connected the two long blades with a prismoid shape. It was more of a cedar color than usual blades, having had slightly different blends of materials in the alloy-building process. There were golden orbs near the bottom of the base similar to the blue orbs on Xostir for gravitational controls, along with three red rectangular, odd shaped gems also near the base. Circuit lines that were etched in the edge of the blade only went up about a third of the length of this unusually long sword. The hilt had a long, sharp forward quillon with a shorter one at the rear, both ending in sharp points to potentially inflict damage if needed. The hilt had unique metallic grip and a pattern with straight etched lines that helped increase grip. The pommel was simply angled to one side. The other two had blades from different editions.

The dark-haired man had a tenth edition blade; it was thicker than Xostir and had flat dull edges on all sides. It was designed with a dark blue sphere at the bottom of the unusually long hilt, allegedly where the power source was. In addition to the magnetic and gravitational control that blade had, it was mostly effective for blunt force trauma and not useful at all for lacerations. This one had no orbs or gems, save for the single large orb at the pommel. It was particularly effective to cause ground disturbances but weak against fast air attacks.

The bearded man had a thirteenth edition blade, shaped more like an older traditional sword, very thin and narrow compared with the other blades. It had a single line of glowing light in the center of the body of the wide side of the blade. The blade was double-edged and intimidating, but it had no circuitry or orbs visible on the outside. The cross-guards were sharp and pointed upward toward the main blade's point. It was nearly unmatched with rapid variety gravitational and magnetic attacks and being able to switch between such. It was not very effective in actual metal-to-metal sword combat. Xostir fed this data into Kado's mind, highlighting the specific strengths and weaknesses of each blade in great detail. All this information flowed into his mind in an instant.

These two men looked ready for a fight with scowls on their faces. The two of them came running toward Kado.

The other blade is rebooting; it will be available in two minutes.

Xostir helped Kado to his feet and fueled his brain and body with adrenaline by triggering the amygdala and the hypothalamus. Time began to slow down a little bit from Kado's perspective as he faced off against his three opponents simultaneously.

He immediately inquired of Xostir about the possibility of using the other blade as well, but it was still affected by the EMP and unable to be of use. He swung his blade to the right to meet one foe's blade and swung the other way to strike another.

Xostir warned him that the woman was slicing at the back of his knees and at the same time the two men were swinging for his upper body and face. Xostir's anti-gravity tilted Kado back in place, lifting his feet forward and bringing his head back. He completed a steady back flip, perfectly dodging all three attempts to end his life.

One minute remaining.

He was masterfully dodging their advances and countering their techniques.

Without relenting, the three blades kept swiping toward him from all sides. Kado was blocking every strike as he spun from side to side.

Ten seconds remaining. They kept swinging. Kado ducked, dodging the woman's blade while simultaneously swinging to his left to block a low attack from one of the men.

Nine.

Kado leapt backward, flipping through the air, his feet perching on the side of a tree about ten feet from the ground. He stood there horizontally briefly.

Eight.

Kado ran down the stump towards the forest floor, jumped and swung his blade, the gem glowing green, initiating a focused gravity blast.

Seven.

The woman ducked and the two men were thrown backwards. The loud blast shot out from the blade, distorting light in the form of a rapidly expanding ring

Six.

The trees all around them shuddered from the blast.

Five.

The two men rose and flew from the ground to either side of Kado.

Four.

Their blades' lethally sharp edges were begging for his blood as they swung rapidly, and some of them were successful in getting it.

Three.

Kado was briefly too focused on the one male opponent and was sliced on the left arm from one man's blade and a deeper cut in the left side of his abdomen from the woman's blade. He held back a scream from the pain and received a powerful kick to his gut from the woman, leveling him to the ground.

Two.

He was surrounded, and all three were about to lay waste to him.

One.

He unleashed a shock wave that pushed all three back several feet, but they were prepared and only skidded backward rather than being thrown back, keeping their footing quite well amidst the snow-speckled, leafy, uneven ground.

Kado, the other blade has rebooted! Xostir notified him. At that, Kado raised his knees and feet up preparing himself for the start of backward somersault in order to dodge a boomerang throw from the woman and her blade. He rose into the air with Xostir lifting him. Her blade was spinning horizontally and flew underneath him, missing him by mere inches. Kado completed his back flip whilst pulling the second blade off his back and planted his feet firmly on the ground with his landing. He felt a second mental connection to the other blade; it was like having two people speaking to you simultaneously except this was completely synchronous and easy. He felt as if the blades had both become extensions of his limbs.

They came running toward him all at once, and Kado swung both blades around, blocking several strikes per second as he turned with slow rotating steps forward. Xostir was projecting the paths their blades were taking along with estimated strike points, so he brought his two blades to each spot, successfully defending the attacks of all three lethal opponents. His left hand held Xostir, and his right hand was holding the ancient blade. The woman and one of the men were on his right and the third was on his left, all three swinging and slashing their blades at him with incredible speed and strength. The loud clanging of the blades echoed through the empty forest. The electrical and booming sounds of the magnetic fields, electromagnetic attacks, electrostatic blasts and graviton slams that were shaking the trees were able to be heard from a mile away.

Kado winced as he could feel that his left side was moist. For a brief second as he caught a break, having thrown some of the opponents away, he lifted the side of his slightly sliced cloak to see a thin cut in his shirt and a thick line of blood staining it.

He didn't have time to worry about it right now; he needed to fend off the ongoing barrage of sword slashing coming toward his face. He ducked as two of the sword wielders clashed their swords right above his head. He tapped both blades on the ground, causing all three of his enemies to rise up in the air, rotating uncontrollably. When Kado raised his blades from the ground, it threw the opponents back to the ground. The woman managed to throw a heavy gravity wave at Kado as she fell, throwing Kado backward extremely hard and fast into a large tree. Xostir shielded Kado's body as he busted through the large tree. Wood fractured all around him, chunks of bark flying off and rotating in all directions. Everything from tiny slivers to thin fractured strips spun all around him as he flew backward through the entire trunk of the tree. From the momentum of the blast, he landed on his back and rolled backward onto his stomach. In moments, the three skilled blade wielders were on their feet running toward him while he lay there trying to stay conscious.

Kado, they're just steps away. You can do this, just use your imagination! Xostir mentally shouted to him with encouragement. He tried to use his imagination to defend against them. He thought of a strong shield to protect himself. Xostir activated a shield. He wanted to be on his feet. Xostir lifted him up off the ground and placed him on his feet. He wanted to get their attention. Xostir suggested that Kado spin in a circle to trigger a tornado. Kado began to spin and, with Xostir's abilities, he started to hover, holding both blades out horizontally, one on either side. He spun faster and faster rising up slowly into the air. The trees' boughs and branches rustled. Leaves and pine needles fell from the sky.

A cyclone began to form overhead as Kado summoned a gravity well to sink down into the ground where he once stood. Lighting shot through the sky and down through the tornado, which was now around Kado, all the bolts striking the ground around him. In moments the tornado became so large and powerful that the three opponents couldn't escape its grasp. Kado stopped spinning, put the older blade on his back and held Xostir up with one hand, continuing to power and strengthen the twister. The trio was rapidly spinning through the tornado, unable to blast their way out. He held out his other gloved hand and pulled the woman into the eye of the tornado. His hand grasped the collar of her armor. She had lost her grip on her Magna-Blade a few moments earlier when she grazed a nearby tree.

"Still pathetic?" he exclaimed over the fierce winds. She was dazed and overwhelmed but was able to shake her head. He summoned the twister to dramatically increase in strength for a split second and then dissipate. This surge of strength threw the other two foes far off into the distance, losing their grips on their Magna-Blades and striking trees as they fell. He didn't want to be outnumbered anymore.

"Now listen. I'm not here to hurt anyone. I'm just trying to find other Magna-Blade wielders. So far, everyone I've met has tried to harm me or kill me. Not really a great first impression." He slowly descended to the ground and let her stand on her own as the last few gusts of wind calmed down. She took a couple steps back, straightening herself out and brushing her hair out of her face. She had a small cut on her forehead.

"Who in the blazes are you?" she demanded.

"I'm Kado. And who are you?" he asked as he was looking at his cuts and injuries.

"The name's Yai." She turned around, briefly looking around for her blade. "What were you doing here? It was obvious you were searching for us – but why if not to hunt us?"

"It's kind of a long story. We're in real trouble. Obviously, you know about the Gravity War. I'm trying to prevent a second one. We're dangerously close to having another one start with the Vanixx Corps and the Quell working on experiments with this technology. If they don't have any dangerous Magna-Blades or this technology in their hands, then another one can't happen," he explained as the other men two flew over and landed on either side of Yai. They each had found their blades and returned Yai's blade to her. They looked fierce and ready to continue the fight.

"Thanks, Dom. Dom, Troy, it's okay," she coaxed the aggravated men down.

"So, you are saying that you want us to give up our only means of survival to prevent a fourth world war?" she beckoned rhetorically.

"It's that or we get a war that none of us want," he commented. In this brief moment of calm, he finally was able to get a good look at the three wielders.

"And what if we agree that we don't want the war? You forcibly take our blades and leave us here?" Dom asked.

Kado hadn't really thought that part through. "Well, you know, I'd try to help you. I was once homeless and would want to help."

"We're not homeless," Troy returned. All of the three were chuckling.

"We're in hiding from the Vanixx Corps. Ever since we found these blades and each other, they've been after us. Following the signals of the blades. The further we got out of the city, the less we've been bothered," Yai claimed. Kado observed that she was Asian and stunningly gorgeous when she wasn't trying to kill him.

"The Vanixx Corps turned on us when we discovered the blades and didn't comply in handing them over," Dom added.

"We have more in common than you realize. But listen, if we don't get rid of these then they could fall into the wrong hands and be used for evil again," Kado tried to reason with them. "I can't sit by while billions more could die. Can you?"

"So what, we just drop these ones in a volcano too?" Dom prodded.

"The Vanixx Corps and the Quell are experimenting with this stuff. Instead of just getting rid of the blades, why can't we take on the Vanixx Corps and the Quell together? Obviously, I can't do it by myself," Kado suggested.

"That's a great idea, but we will need to trust each other and work together," Yai countered, glancing to her two associates. They all exchanged looks and nodded to each other.

"Okay, we don't kill each other until after we destroy the Magna-Blade technology and research that the Vanixx Corps and the Quell have," Yai concluded.

Kado tilted his head with slightly concerned acknowledgment. "Okay then."

"When do we hit them?" Troy asked the group.

Kado replied tactfully, "Well, we need to have a plan first. We'll need to plan the entire operation first. If we're going to do this, we'll need to do this right. We'll also need to get all the help we can get. Follow me." Kado immediately thought of Ruana. She seemed like she knew enough about her blade to be a helpful ally.

All four of them lifted off and took flight toward Ruana's cabin. As they flew above the clouds in a loose formation, Kado looked back and raised his voice to all of them, "It's not far now." All three of them were a little suspicious, but Yai nodded for them to go ahead.

In a few minutes, they landed a few meters from her front door. The three of them stood back while Kado knocked on her door. No one answered; she must've been out. He turned back to the three new temporary allies with a shrug. The smoke was coming out of the chimney, so she must've been close. He started walking back to his colleagues, then they heard a loud boom. Seconds later a woman landed on the ground with a loud thud, causing the ground to shake. It was Ruana holding her Magna-Blade. She stepped up toward the four of them with some dead ducks hung over her shoulder.

"What's this?" she inquired with surprise.

"We're kind of working towards a common goal for the time being. We're going to stop the Vanixx Corps and the Quell from bringing us into another Gravity War. But we could really use your help." He took a step forward as he asked. She had a skeptical look on her face. Kado looked back to the three new associates and turned back to Ruana. "Will you help us?"

Adrian was told to wait at a table, and he would be

met shortly. He sat there patting his fingers on the table with eager anticipation in the VIP Lounge they'd made for Moderators. He was about to meet the most powerful person he ever had known. This was someone he had never even expected to meet beyond his wildest dreams.

"Moderator Greeg." A deep but gentle voice filled the room from behind him. He turned back to see a figure wearing white approach their table. *This was the Praetor of the Quell*; Adrian kept repeating this to himself in his mind. He wore a white uniform with some minimal armor plating, some sort of cape, and a shiny white helmet with a mirror visor, completely hiding his face. Adrian figured that he no doubt needed to remain anonymous. For all he knew, maybe this wasn't actually the Praetor and just a proxy representing the Praetor. He had heard of stories like that before.

"I wanted to personally thank you for your loyalty and dedication to our organization," the pure white-clad being began. "You've been on the outside undercover for about ten years. That's a long time, and you've patiently taken orders and direction covertly from us all this time. You are to be commended."

"Thank you so much." Adrian smiled with excitement. He couldn't believe his ears.

"And rewarded," the Praetor continued. Adrian's

expression was serious as he was not sure what to expect for a reward in the faintest sense. The Praetor leaned back. "Henceforth, you shall be granted Level B access to all files, cases and missions. No more redacted files. You are henceforth to bear the title, Vicero."

"Vicero?" Adrian was shocked. He had never heard of such a title among the Quell before.

"Yes, it's a new position. You'll be placed just below the Mitigator. Work closely with her."

"Yes, sir." Adrian bowed his head with respect. "Thank you for this privilege."

"You did well 'sealing' the potential leak of Officer Killarney."

"Thank you. When he stumbled upon my special delivery, I couldn't risk it."

"I am glad to have another trusted colleague in the ranks of the Quell's leadership. There is much for you learn and not much time before Phase 2 begins."

"So, do you guys want to come in?" Ruana pleasantly asked the four of them.

"Do you mind? We'll need a place to lay low, ya know, come up with a plan." Kado couldn't bring them to the bunker, not until he knew he could trust the three new allies.

They all found a seat in the toasty-warm living room, directing their blades to levitate in the corner.

Kado looked down at his wounds from the recent fight. He had been losing a lot of blood but was keeping that fact to himself, keeping his injuries hidden beneath his cloak. On their flight to Ruana's cabin, the crouching on Xostir caused his wound to open up however, now that his adrenaline had fully exited his system, the sharp pain was steadily increasing. Clearly Yai and Dom didn't realize how badly they had sliced him.

Shortly after he stepped into the cabin he asked Ruana to use the restroom. He noticed a few drops of blood on his blade so he wiped it off with his sleeve discreetly. He needed to look strong and in charge, otherwise the others may not cooperate. Xostir began to detect that Kado's blood pressure was dropping slowly.

Kado, I'm detecting a drop in your blood pressure. Are you really okay from those injuries?

"Xostir, I'm fine. It's not something that we can't bandage up later." He whispered, looking at his reflection in the old-fashioned mirror of the restroom.

Actually, Nicodem and I were experimenting with medical applications with my magnetic capabilities.

"Really?" Kado was intrigued. "Well, tell me about it

once we get some semblance of a plan together. I need to think about how we can make this work."

Yes, I have some suggestions with regard to the mapped areas of the Vanixx Corps campus of buildings that might be of some help. The scans were taken just a few years ago, so they may be partially out of date.

"Either way, anything will help." Kado remarked expressively with optimism.

He returned to join the rest in the living room who were conversing with each other about the fight Kado put them through, "Alright, where should we start?"

Xostir, while staying docked to the magnetic panels in the back of Kado's cloak, activated an interface with a handheld holo-projector. What came up on display was a picture of Nicodem.

"This man invented the Magna-Blade. But it originally wasn't supposed to be a weapon. It was supposed to be a tool, until the Military found out the potential of this device and its ability to be a destructive weapon and they conscripted him. They forced him to build it, to turn it into a weapon. They mass-produced the blades, leading to the Gravity War. He tried to sabotage the project but failed."

The image on display changed to show Nicodem and his family, then a famous artists rendition of a scene of the Gravity War that everyone had seen before.

"Nicodem was murdered by the Quell just a few weeks ago, and now the Quell are starting attacks against the Vanixx Corps. Both organizations have access to Magna-Blades. We fear that a second global war could be the result if they *both* aren't stopped soon."

New pictures of the organizations' logos scrolled by, replacing the image of the war. The Vanixx Corps logo was of a scorpion interlaced with a V and C followed by the Quell logo of a modern looking Q.

"First we need to work together to minimize the threat of the Vanixx Corps since they have so much access and research on Nicodem's inventions. Then we need to relieve the Quell of their magnetic weapons." The hologram deactivated itself as he placed the hand device in his pocket. Kado kindly gestured to his guests, "First thing's first. We need to rest up then come up with how we should take down the Vanixx Corps. Before we can take down the V.C. however, we all need a bit of practice."

"You all are welcome to stay here tonight, but you'll need to sleep on the couch and the floor." Ruana chimed in.

"Hey, anything beats a freezing cold condo" Troy added with a grin.

"Or a shelter made with branches." Dom

contributed.

"Thanks, Ruana." Kado nodded to her as he neared the front door, "I'm just going to step outside for a few minutes, take a walk, get some fresh air."

He had been ignoring the stabbing pains, trying to fight the dizziness all afternoon. He had lost quite a bit of blood, but it only stained his clothes, partially hidden under his blue jacket. Xostir was with Kado, hovering beside him in a vertical stance. He fought the lightheadedness that was sending waves over him. Kado headed in the direction of the lake where he first met Ruana. Unable to go any further, he leaned against a nearby tree.

Kado, let me show you what Nicodem and I were developing.

"You did mention that you were experimenting with medical applications with your abilities."

Well what I neglected to mention is we saw quite positive results from the medical applications. What you didn't know is when Nicodem brought you to his house for the first time and you were in a coma, severely injured, we used my abilities to speed up the healing process even faster than it would normally have healed.

"Really? How?" Kado looked over to Xostir surprised.

Lift your shirt so I can treat the wounds.

Kado struggled to lift his shirt, wincing at the pain. Xostir shifted his position in midair, bringing the wide edge of the blade near to Kado's side, simply hovering in place. Kado began to feel a hot sensation on his left side around the wound. In seconds, it became almost a burning, stinging sensation that shot jolts of pain up and down his entire left side. It felt like someone was grabbing the two edges of the gaping wound and closing them, pressing them together gently. Kado clenched his jaw to try and cope with the great discomfort he was going through.

We're nearly done. Give it a few minutes. Xostir issued the attempt at a comforting remark. Kado felt the skin tingling as it was stimulated by the manipulation of the elements at a molecular level.

"How does that work?" he gritted his teeth through his labored breathing.

I cause specific frequencies for vibrations within the molecules of the tissue, this triggers a healing process to be accelerated. When I concentrate a treatment like this at a targeted area of damaged tissue for just a few minutes, the healing process can be executed and a nasty injury like this can be fully healed externally right then and there in minutes. Internally it will be self perpetually healed in a few hours.

"Wow! Xostir, that-that's amazing!" Kado kept admiring how his gaping wound was already closed up with a fresh scar.

"You guys could've really made a difference in the world with this kind of thing!"

We were planning on secretly releasing tools for this kind of application so that the Vanixx Corps couldn't tie it back to Nicodem, but he was killed before we could release it to the public.

"Oh, I see." Kado hung his head with the reminder of the death of their mutual friend.

Alright, I detect that your internal injuries will be fully healed in three hours. Let's start on healing that nasty gash on your leg now.

"Do you think we can trust them?" Kado quietly inquired his reliable friend.

I suppose the real question is do you. As far as their life signs go, when they say that they want to work together to fight the Vanixx Corps, they are sincere. I don't detect any odd increase in blood pressure, pulse or breathing rate when they speak of a temporary alliance. As for perspiration increase, Troy profusely perspires, so I have not been able to determine if he's lying completely. Having said that, they do seem to be trustworthy allies, if not a little disheveled.

"They are rough around the edges. But I would be too in their situation. Hez, I was in their situation not that long ago."

Indeed. Nicodem showed trust in you and you seem to have turned out alright...for the most part. Xostir teased as he nearly finished healing Kado's leg.

"Wow, thanks." He returned a smile to his counterpart, "I think I'll need them to prove themselves before I'll trust them enough to see the bunker. There's no telling if they would try to kill me and steal everything. It's still too risky yet."

Yet you led them to a young woman's cabin?

"It's not like she's not defenseless – she could easily kick my butt in a fight. Those three combined are no match for her."

Very true on all counts. Alright, your leg wound is sealed. You should make a nearly full recovery.

"Nearly?"

Your pride will likely never fully heal.

"Hah, funny." Kado retorted sarcastically. He was beginning to see Xostir's personality reveal itself and he enjoyed it.

"Let's go back inside, you've given me an idea. Also, it's frigid out here!"

"Greeg, over here." The Mitigator waved Adrian over from the group that were congratulating him. She stood close to him, her height and the design of her white fierce looking helmet were intimidating. She and the Praetor always wore the fully armored uniform in public. Adrian stood as tall as he could without his confidence faltering.

"Don't think that this makes you able to call the shots now. You answer to me on all important decisions regarding missions or anything directly affecting The Quell." She jabbed his chest with her finger. He held his composure despite her obvious disdain for him. He raised an eyebrow, "And what exactly did you comprehend from The Praetor's explanation of my new role?"

"From my perspective, nothing much for you has changed at all. You now oversee the forces around the planet and make sure production is on schedule. If you need to communicate with The Praetor, you still go through me. Got it?" Her tone was filled with layers of annoyance and contempt.

Greeg could tell that the Mitigator was just as charming as she always had been and that they were going to get along wonderfully, of course in the most sarcastic sense possible. She treated Moderators well but seemed threatened by his promotion. Perhaps, he thought, that because this promotion was so unheard of, so she must view him as a potential risk to her position.

"The Praetor wants the three of us to meet in 15 minutes." She stomped off before he could respond, her red cape flowing behind her. Adrian had a measure of respect for her – after all she made it to the Mitigator rank for a reason. However, that didn't stop him from loathing her.

"Welcome Mitigator and Vicero." The Praetor addressed his agents. The two of them had walked into the throne room just before the entrances had thick steel doors slide down to ensure secrecy of their conversation. The Praetor was sitting in the Mitigator chair, "We're meeting now to establish some ground rules. Vicero, if Mitigator Wren is busy and you need to communicate approval for something come straight to me. We need action on this project, and I will not tolerate delays; is that understood?"

"Yes, Sir." Both Wren and Adrian conferred in unison.

"Excellent. I'll remain in communicator range, no farther than a few thousand kilometres away. Any questions?"

Greeg didn't let a moment of hesitation pass before

he inquired, "Yes, Sir. When do I get a white uniform like yours?" He finished asking his question with a haughty grin.

Ruana's toasty warm cabin exhaled a constant plume of fresh smoke into the red sky from the hot crackling fire inside. Kado, Ruana, Yai, Dom and Troy sat around the open flame in their respective couches, chairs or fender benches. Kado had just returned from the cold, while Ruana and Dom had prepared some simple food consisting of crackers, meat, cheese along with some hot rooibos tea for everyone.

"Guys, I have an idea." They all looked to him as he closed the door behind him.

"We don't just hit them hard. We need to hit them where it hurts, their pride. The V.C. are a haughty bunch who are at the top of the food chain. We need to show them that they are no longer at the top."

"And just how," Dom begin his response, hand defiantly perched on his knee, "do you intend to do that?"

"We need to destroy the lab where they have all of Nicodem's experiments. If they lose valuable assets, then that will set them back, delaying a potential war."

"You're talking about walking into the most highly guarded buildings in the city – on the continent!" Troy retorted critically.

"Try 'the world'." Yai chimed in, "The V.C. are the biggest Military force on the planet and you are saying we'll just waltz into their Headquarters with our swords?"

"Guys, these aren't just swords. These are Magna-Blades! These things are the most powerful weapons on the planet and if used properly, we would stop this war from ever happening. I propose the first thing we do is damage their pride, shake their confidence. That will give us the traction we need."

Kado stood before his newfound temporary allies,

all of whom had something against the Vanixx Corps and motivation to cooperate with each other peacefully. The problem is they had never cooperated before, not to mention they all weren't overly skilled with their blades. Kado could see that each of them needed a great deal of practice before they could even attempt a flyby on the V.C.

He paced slowly side to side by the fire as he relayed his plan to them with his holographic device that he laid on the floor, displaying the plan step by step as he spoke, relaying what he was imagining.

"We fly as fast as we can right at the Citadel Tower here." He pointed to a General area on the holographic three-dimensional map, which then lit up as a small blinking red circle. He continued as the group were sitting on a couple hover chairs side by side, "We will storm the Citadel and cause some diversions. First Troy, Dom and Yai head right to the Citadel front entrance. Troy, you can spiral up the outside of the tower, use your blade to shatter glass all around the tower at a couple dozen different places. Meanwhile Dom, Yai, you head right to reception to distract them at the entrance. Try to get as many staff in the area to be distracted by you." The holographic display shifted and changed with the presentation, now moving to the lower levels and underground tunnels.

"While you are doing that, Ruana and I will sneak into the lower tunnels to obtain whatever of Nicodem's inventions we can get our hands on. Everything else we'll destroy. That should help deescalate the chance of war." The presentation ended with a holographic explosion, then faded out.

"Question," Dom chimed in while sitting on the couch, "What if the Vanixx Corps already have all the army they need? Won't destroying the inventions kind of be redundant?"

"Good question, Dom." Kado stroked his chin, "Well, if they do have a Military force already setup, we'll obviously need to try and handle that. But destroying these inventions, will help prevent them from making future weapons as easily."

"That's a good point." Yai replied, "But, what if they have already mass produced all of these weapons?" Kado shrugged, "We'll cross that bridge when we come to it. Look, I don't have a contingency plan for every one of the thousands of scenarios that could happen. But I do know this, if we do nothing, the Vanixx Corps will easily take us into a second Gravity War, and I want to prevent that from happening in any way I can."

The group all nodded and mumbled with agreement.

"Okay so, some of the elements of teamwork here that we'll need to practice are interesting and challenging." Kado addressed the group who all began to stand. He summoned Xostir who flew right into his hand, "We are going to need to be a tight knit team. Ruana, when you and I try to get into the tunnels, we're going to need to use our blades in tandem to get past the security forces." Kado went on to stand by the holographic device on the floor. A detailed scan of just the buildings belonging to the Vanixx Corps appeared. There were 16 buildings in total, all connected with underground tunnels as they could see in the diagram. Kado was being fed data from Xostir about the entire campus, and he began his explanation by pointing at the main Citadel Tower.

"Alright, so this is where all the highest-ranking Officers meet periodically. Over here is where the main entrance is." Kado pointed to the base of the tallest tower, "That's where we'll create our first distraction." He pointed to another building nearby midway up the towering structure, "Up here are Officers' barracks with platforms for their ships to take off."

"That looks pretty good, Kado," Yai nodded as she stepped up to the hologram, "however, there is a huge flaw in your plan."

"What's that?"

"We don't have enough."

"Enough what?"

"Enough everything; the people, the blades, the weapons, the manpower, the time! Everything!" Yai leaned back on the couch, having realized she rather succinctly summarized their dismal, yet realistic situation. Kado stepped backward in a disappointed manner at her unending pessimism.

"I know, this sounds crazy. We can't possibly know what kind of defenses they have or exactly how well guarded the Citadel Tower is. But, if we're going to prevent a war, there's going to be some risks involved. I can't ask you to risk your life for this. This is fully voluntary. If we are to do this, we do it as a team. If you want to leave, if it's just doomed to fail, go ahead and leave." He calmly aimed a pointed finger to the wooden front door of Ruana's cabin.

He looked up at the old clock on Ruana's wall, observing the time: "11:28 PM".

"Woah, it's late. Why don't we talk about this in the morning – sleep on what we have now and see if we can't come up with any other improvements to the plan?" Kado looked to each of the group expecting a measure of concurrence. All agreed.

"I'll sleep on the floor." Kado offered. That left room

for Yai, Dom and Troy to sleep on the couches and chairs, while Ruana slept in her own room. Kado was restlessly awake, his mind cycling through scenarios of how it could fail, how his plan could easily get them all killed. Worries filled his mind of the little partnership they have going could fall apart. More concerns flooded his thoughts; *Can I trust them? They just tried to kill me not 8 hours ago. Was it a mistake bringing them here to Ruana's private home? Possibly. She invited us in – she probably thought that I knew these people well. She may have unknowingly welcomed murderers into her house because of me!*

Shhhh. It was Xostir coming to his rescue.

Xostir, you don't understand.

Yes, I do, Kado. I've seen nearly every thought that's gone through your mind since we've first connected. I know exactly how you feel, I fully do understand. Listen, Ruana could've turned us away. We all need to have a little trust in each other if we're going to get through this and stop the Vanixx Corps.

Xostir, you're right. But I'm just so worried.

I know. You worry too much sometimes. You don't have enough confidence in yourself. You look like you do on the outside, but you don't trust yourself enough.

Yeah, well. I can't stop worrying that I've made a huge mistake.

Don't concern yourself any further about it. I don't need to sleep. I'll monitor their movements. If they go anywhere near Ruana's room I'll stop them. I know how you feel about her. Xostir continued the silent neural conversation.

Kado blushed.

It's nothing serious. She is very attractive, but she's out of my league.

There you go again – where is your confidence? She very likely has reciprocal feelings for you.

What? Kado's eyes widened with surprise.

Whenever I detect that she is near your company or in your presence her heart rate and blood pressure increases, her pupils dilate.

How can you tell if her pupils dilate? You can't actually see things.

Well I can see in ways you can't, and I can also see through your eyes with our neural link.

Oh. Well then.

Get some sleep, Kado. We really need to get these kids in shape if we're going to take on the V.C.

Alright, night.

The next morning, Ruana rose first and began

heating up a pot of coffee for everyone. She just loved looking out to the sunrise in the forest. It was her favorite time of the day. Peaceful, relaxing, birds chirping, wildlife roaming through the trees.

This was her favorite time of year. She began to put some frozen bacon onto a frying pan while she observed clumps of snow jump off of burdened boughs, coming to rest on the snow speckled forest floor.

The combination of sizzling bacon grease along with the welcome aroma filled the cabin. Kado was awoken and forced himself to be vertical slowly while his three newest allies were startled by the spitting, smacking sounds of cooking grease, jumping up alarmed.

"What's going on?" Troy shouted.

"It's fine, it's fine!" Ruana chuckled, "It's just bacon."

"Bacon?" Dom was confused, "There's something seriously wrong with your molecular resequencer."

"No silly, it's real food that's really cooked." Ruana returned an explanation, "This is how food used to be made hundreds of years ago. That molecular resquenced stuff isn't *real* food."

She placed three strips of bacon on a plate and handed it to him, "Here, try it." Dom, looked over to Kado with surprise and a poorly hidden element of glee, then picked up a strip and tasted it.

"Ohhhh man! That is incredible!" Dom exclaimed with unexpected enthusiasm, "How come we haven't learned how to do this?" Kado stepped up and patted him on the shoulder in a congratulatory manner, "Because molecular resequencing was 'easier' for us and 'easier' on the struggling environment."

Soon they all sat down with their own plates of eggs and bacon.

"So, you guys are wearing some pretty rough outfits. You were in hiding from the Vanixx Corps?" Kado gently prodded with his curiosity.

"Yeah," Troy answered sullenly, "It's been a rough time. Dom and I didn't really know each other back then, but we happened to be on the same patrol in this rough part of town when we encountered a mysterious chest, which was open and had a couple corpses beside it."

"It looked like they had killed each other fighting for whatever was inside the chest." Dom added, "So we took a look inside and saw these two Magna-Blades. They seemed to have been selling on the black market and something obviously went really wrong."

"Proper protocol was to report the incident, bring backup and a cleanup crew, but we picked up the Magna-Blade's first and..." Troy paused trying to articulate what he was going to say next.

"Our mental connection with the blades was remarkable. It felt so incredible to have this other intelligence 'speaking' to you. We just couldn't put them down." Dom continued the story.

"The next thing we know, there's a manhunt announcement for us because some video recording of us holding the blades and not immediately reporting them to our superiors." Troy added.

"We were in hiding for three months when we encountered Yai." Dom leaned back as he finished the last bite of the best breakfast he had ever enjoyed.

"Yeah, that was something else. She had been in hiding from the Vanixx Corps as well and she nearly killed us when she saw our uniforms. But when she realized that we were on the run from the V.C. as well she calmed down and after a discussion of our motives, we decided to work together to survive." Troy continued to explain the story of how they met Yai in detail.

"Wow, you guys. How did you make it so long?" Kado inquired between bites of his breakfast.

"We would rush into the city quickly, grab some supplies and then run back to the forest. Some rainy nights we would sneak into an abandoned part of a condo building and stay a few nights there." Dom remarked.

They continued to discuss their stories. Kado briefly explained his background; how he met Nicodem, learned about Magna-Blades, the life Nicodem saved him from.

Meanwhile Yai and Ruana were sitting on the couch across the room, discussing their Magna-Blades, their uniforms, their backgrounds. Ruana explained that her armored uniform was her grandfather's from the Gravity War, she had adapted it a little to fit her better.

"Where did your armor come from? It looks so elegant." Ruana invoked Yai as she observed the intricate details and curving lines in the designs on the armor.

"I was part of the Eurasian Military. I lived in the part of Hefei that was closest to where Japan used to be. My family was from Japan from centuries before the Gravity War, so the armor is a modern Japanese design honouring my ancient culture. They made this style of armor for all of our blade wielders during the Gravity War." Yai explained.

"Wow. What made you decide to join the Military?" Ruana queried.

"We don't have a choice in my city. Everyone needs to serve in the Military for two years when they reach 18 years old. After two years we are allowed to rescind our participation in the Military, or we are allowed to stay for as long as we want." Yai shrugged as she continued her explanation.

"So obviously, you decided to stay – what made you stick with the Military?"

"My entire family were caught in the middle of an assassination attempt by an undercover Vanixx Corps operative." Yai lowered her head, holding back tears, "The person – they, whoever they were, was after a well-known politician in Hefei named Varo Lee Yun. Twenty years ago, my family and I were just having a picnic in the park on a sunny day. The peacefulness of our city was profound compared to other cities at the time."

Ruana continued to listen on with great interest, her expression showing concern with her slightly furrowed brow. Yai continued after a brief pause of collecting her thoughts, "I was only eleven years old...and they...", she held her hand to her mouth trying to calm herself down.

"I'm sorry – I just – just haven't spoken about this to...anyone else before." A few streams of tears were visibly shiny on her cheeks now. She wiped them away and pressed on with her story, "We were eating in the middle of one of the safest parks in Hefei. It was a wide-open grassy field with bushes frequenting the area and beautiful cherry blossoms and a wonderfully landscaped creek in the distance. The park was made to commemorate the lost country of Japan when it sunk into the sea during the war. There were a few other families there, of course. Suddenly blasts from a gun came ripping into the grass all around us. There was dirt and grass flying into the air. My father pushed me, I rolled off into a nearby bush. When the firing stopped, I crawled to the edge of the bush. I saw a man walk up to my parents' bodies. He also inspected other corpses nearby. He was blonde American, wearing a fully black uniform. I remember a circular logo with a scorpion on his shoulder. I later came to find out that it was the Vanixx Corps logo. I also later found out that Varo Lee Yun was nearby us in the park with his family too."

"Oh Yai. That is terrible. I'm so sorry."

"Yeah. So, I vowed vengeance. I was already adept at using the blade which had been preserved and handed down through my family, but I devoted the next twenty years at mastering the Magna-Blade."

"How did you end up with Dom and Troy?"

"Oh, that's actually kind of a funny story."

"Oh yeah?"

"Yeah – I had come over to America from Eurasia in an effort to find whomever the operative was that killed my family. I had no idea who I was looking for – only that he had curly blonde hair and was young. After seeing a man who met that description, I stalked him until he was alone and made my move. Unfortunately, he was ready for me and I nearly lost my life in a duel with him. He was unexpectedly skilled at using his Magna-Blades and I barely escaped. I had to go into hiding because they issued a hunt warrant for me. They had mechs after me, soldiers tracking my whereabouts. A couple weeks later I encountered Dom and Troy in their Vanixx Corps outfits – all alone. I was bitter about losing to the blonde Officer and being hunted and wanted to take out my anger on these two Officers. They were terrible at using Magna-Blades compared to the blonde guy!" The two of them chuckled at the humor of it.

"After a brief – very brief – fight with them, they explained they that they were on the run from the Vanixx Corps as well. I nearly killed them, fortunately they got their story out before I did. We have been surviving together ever since for the next few months until we met you."

"Well, you three seem to be very genuine and I'm glad Kado brought you here. I've been very alone for quite some time and while it is peaceful for the most part, it was starting to get repetitive." Ruana grinned.

"How does everyone feel about going out to practice our skills with the blade?" Kado asked the group. All agreed so they got themselves ready and flew out to an open field nearby. All five of them landed, some rougher than others. Kado realized that they would need a lot more than just improved skills if they were going to face the V.C.

"Alright, so uh. Dom, why don't you show me what you can do." Kado stood ready with a defensive stance, Xostir in hand.

"Okay." Dom began to run towards Kado and swung his blade, leaving himself wide open to several vulnerable hits. Kado only took one opportunity, he simply aimed his blade towards Dom and threw him sideways several feet as if gravity shifted around him instantly.

While Dom was groaning, Kado looked to the rest of them, "Who's next?"

Yai volunteered, "Me." She stood a fair distance away from Kado, while Dom, Ruana and Troy stood farther back to what seemed like a safe zone.

"Come on." Kado urged Yai in a playful way.

"Oh you'll regret that." She mumbled to herself as she began a sprint towards him. She leapt through the air, allowing her blade to carry her as she completed a wide overhead swing down to the ground. She triggered a powerful gravity wave that blasted its way towards Kado.

Kado held Xostir up as a shield, effectively blocking the full force of the wave, skidding back six feet. As he was skidding backwards, Yai pressed on the attack, swinging her blade at him in several directions and multiple angles, trying to break past his defenses.

Xostir was much more advanced, hence faster so Kado had no issues keeping up with her strikes. She swung at him as if to slice him asunder, Kado leaned backwards at an impossible angle, knees bent, only Xostir was preventing him from falling. Upon straightening himself he lightly swung upwards, throwing Yai up into the air, flailing, causing her to land several yards away.

"What's the issue? Why is this easy for me?" he asked them all. They all shrugged as Yai recovered, making her way back to the group at the center of the field.

"You aren't strategizing with your blade. You aren't taking advantage of its incredible abilities. Yes, a blade is sharp, it's a sword. But the sword isn't its strength. The ability to control gravity and magnets is its true strength."

They continued to train and practice for the next few hours as Kado continued to utilize Xostir's database and share some of the wisdom he learned in his time training and practicing at the bunker.

"Good. That's a huge improvement." Kado encouraged Troy, and Troy properly blocked a graviton blast from Ruana.

"Yes. Just like that, excellent." He cheered on for Yai as she threw Dom backwards a hundred feet in a proton charged counter.

They were beginning to get better at using their blades and Xostir noted great improvements in their neural connections to each other.

Xostir had connected all of their minds to a point where they could open and close communication with each other.

As the sun reached its apex for the day, they continued to practice moves and try out some other abilities of their blades individually. Ruana was standing relatively closer to the forest edge than everyone else, she was attempting to uproot a tree with her blade and then return it back to the ground and replant it.

Suddenly a loud energy blast zipped by, echoing off the trees, just narrowly being blocked by Ruana.

***

"Greeg, your presence is required." The Mitigator spoke sternly into her wrist communicator. Greeg had a similar one on his new shiny white armoured uniform and held it up to his mouth as he announced succinctly, "On my way."

He had yet to be assigned a specialized room for a man of his position now as Vicero. It made sense that there wasn't a room for him, the decision was rather quick, and no one here knew what was about to happen, including the Mitigator. But a suit was provided to him already. It was almost identical to the Mitigator's, save for some design differences for her female body shape. Fully white with the most advanced armour plating that could adapt to any humanly possible position without allowing a vulnerability to be accessible. Next was a helmet that formed upon mental command to shape quickly around the head using nanotechnology stolen from the Vanixx Corps almost 10 years ago. To complete the ensemble was a white Cape with red as the lining.

Adrian immediately could sense tension from her as soon as it was announced that he was getting a never before used title among the Quell. He figured she felt threatened by his new role. He had wanted to mention that he had no intention of ever taking her place, but he'd let her squirm a little while – at least until she showed him an ounce of respect. He strode down the small tunnelled halls, every single Moderator he passed nodding with respect and admiration. The lights were strung along the ceiling like they used to do in mines hundreds of years ago, which made sense since part of the base connected to an old mine. It wasn't until you were in the Operations Center, a tall throne room, that you could see a more modern-day look and feel to the structure and design of the room. The Mitigator spent most of her time here, issuing orders and delegating assignments – keeping watch over the entire global operation. As Greeg strode in, he greeted her with pride in his voice, "To what do I owe this pleasure Mitigator?"

"I have your first task as Vicero."

"Oh? Do tell."

"You are to work closely with Moderator Kar. She will assist you in your endeavours to organize our global forces in each city." She ordered with a flat tone.

"Wha-really? Why? Wh-why her?" Adrian felt more flustered than he ever had been to his recollection.

"Is there a problem, Greeg?" The Mitigator inquired, deliberately not addressing him by his title.

"Well, no – it's just that there's a history-"

"It's settled then. You meet with her here at oh-nine-hundred hours, sharp, to begin your planning of the mobilization of our forces."

Adrian paused with a brief glance behind him. Lowering his voice and leaning in he implored, "Is there a particular reason you chose *her*?"

"Her aptitudes make her an ideal candidate for this

task at hand." The Mitigator replied with the same typical volume and commanding attitude that she always exuded.

"Alright then, oh-nine-hundred it is." Adrian responded, defeated in the aggressive discussion. Adrian left the throne room without another word as he seethed beneath his uniform. He didn't have to work with *her* again did he? Really? It had been over a decade since he last even spoke with her. He was in for a very uncomfortable conversation.

Ruana's blade detected the beam of energy flying towards them and while in her hands levitated to block the blast that was heading right for her face. Ruana's blade rose within an inch of Ruana's cheek, just in time to deflect the beam of green energy which split the beam off into several directions, some into the sky, and some right into the ground around her feet. She screamed, startled but quickly regained her attention and composure, standing at a defence-ready position, both hands on her blade's hilt.

The energy blast came from a rough looking bald man wearing a cloak at the forest line. He stepped into the light of the sun, Kado knew right away who that was. Their neural connection was still in place between the five of them so Kado's recollection of Orun gave the full story of his experience to the group in an instant of time. In less than a second, the entire group knew his name, his cybernetic adaptations, his aggression and why he might have tracked them down; all from the mental connection to Kado.

All five of the group had their attention poised at Orun. He began to run towards Ruana as Kado, Yai, Dom and Troy quickly glided with ease to her sides. Orun fired a few more quick blasts at them all before he leapt into the air. In his upgraded cybernetic feet, a blue glow emanated out of the bottom of the heels, arches and balls of the feet, causing Orun to jet off into the air with great speed. He began to fly a circle around them, firing with his right arm. His cybernetic arm, separated down the middle of the forearm and separated through the middle of the hand, causing two large gun barrels to be risen and expand out of the top and bottom of the arm. The barrels extended past his cybernetic hand, giving his weapon enough developed strength to fire at a great distance with incredible accuracy. Kado, Ruana, Dom, Troy and Yai soon all lifted off and took to the skies to fight this aggressor.

"Good thing we're already warmed up!" Kado

shouted in encouragement to them all.

Orun began to shout with rage as he looked behind to see a string of Magna-Blade wielders chasing after him and saw that they were catching up. While he did not expect to outrun them, it still infuriated him all the same. He aimed his arm towards them as he looked back, firing several blasts at his enemies. Kado flew to the front of the pack. Xostir was still faster than the other four blades so he could very easily catch up to the incredibly fast Orun's mag-lev-propelled cybernetic legs.

He kept looking back to see who was following him and soon saw that Kado was close behind while the other four were falling behind a bit, just as he had hoped. He looked forward again as he blasted ahead with a mischievous grin on his face. He was going to get his revenge and much sooner than he had expected.

Orun veered to the left heading closer towards the large city of Vancouver and farther from the wilderness. The city border was visible on the horizon now. He began to charge his arm cannon and with a twist and a rotation, he spun his body around midair to face Kado, aimed his charged, humming arm cannon right at Kado head on.

Kado, we've got a problem. That is an incredibly advanced antiparticle weapon and at its current charge, it could possibly cause a serious shock to my system or potentially even disable me. I'm not sure how to defend against this yet. Xostir relayed this information to Kado in a split second. All Kado could spit out was, "You gotta be kidding me."

Just then the crimson blast was fired and all Kado could do was either try to dodge or block the shot with Xostir. Without enough time to steer out of the way, Xostir helped him block the charged energy blast. The electrical bolt struck Xostir, causing jolts to zap around the blade's edges, zapping the gem of Xostir, causing it to crack.

Kado immediately felt a partial loss of connection to Xostir. The neural link was still there but the control of the blade was suddenly missing from his mental faculties.

In seconds, they began to fall towards the earth. Orun fired another green blast, less charged this time and it struck Kado in the right shoulder as he was plummeting downwards. The blast caused searing pain to pulse up and down through his whole arm, paralyzing it and causing it to twitch and convulse. All Kado could do as he fell was grasp his right shoulder with his left hand. A glitching Xostir was in his right grip, which couldn't be released, even if he wanted to since his right arm had seized.

Dom, Troy and Yai caught up to Orun, swinging their blades with fierce strikes and magnetronic blasts while Ruana dove to catch a hurtling Kado.

Kado was just a couple dozen feet from the ground as Ruana grabbed hold of his left hand. Her blade formed an anti-gravity field around the both of them as he struck the tops of a few trees in his uncontrolled descent.

"Gotcha!" She shouted as they slowly began to rise. Xostir was completely inactive on a functional level and could only communicate sentences to Kado. He finally realized just how heavy Xostir really was.

I'm sorry Kado. I don't know what happened. This has never happened before. You could've died! Xostir apologized. Kado replied silently with his own thoughts, *It's ok Xostir, we'll figure it out. We'll run diagnostics and figure out a way to prevent you from getting affected by this kind of blast ever again.*

"Thanks!" He shouted back up to Ruana as they continued to hold hands in their flight through the air. The anti-gravity field Ruana's blade was projecting allowed them to both position themselves side by side, chest down towards the ground and head forward, with her blade in-between them. They both held a portion of her hilt. Kado placed Xostir on his back for the next few minutes.

"Take this, you worthless piece of frex!" Yai shouted at Orun as she swung a negative neutron blast at him. He tried to dodge it but was thrown a few hundred feet, spinning uncontrollably from the powerful attack. He blasted off into the distance escaping from his failed, miscalculated bombardment.

"Xostir, how's your system?" Kado asked him.

I'm rebooting the physical systems, but something got fried...t-t-t-towards the-the-the final attack there. Xostir was beginning to glitch in his speech to Kado and it was giving him a pulsing headache.

Flight systems back online, Kado. Xostir added a few moments later.

"Alright, Xostir is feeling a little better now. I'll fly myself." He addressed Ruana. Within seconds they began to fly slightly father apart and Kado removed Xostir from his back, hopping back onto the blade, holding the hilt in his usual fashion.

"Thanks for your help back there, guys. Should we head back to the cabin?" He inquired of the group. All nodded with agreement, tired from the recent excitement. As they panned to the left, they headed back to the direction of the cabin.

"Sorry he got away, Kado." Yai apologized.

"Yeah, he's pretty quick." Dom added.

Suddenly Xostir's ability to fly froze up, causing them to drop to the ground once again. In a few seconds

Xostir re-enabled his flight controls and they ascended back to the altitude they were cruising at. This continued to happen a few more times as they all headed back to the cabin.

I-I-I-I will d-definitely be running diagnostics when we get home. Xostir reassured Kado.

Kado just thought to himself, *What kind of weapon could do this to the most advanced Magna-Blade? These things are basically indestructible.* For the first time ever, Kado was dreadfully concerned about the wellbeing of his friend.

The group returned back to the cabin for some reprieve from the recent attack. Xostir's continued glitching during the return caused Kado to be a little uneasy about flying with Xostir as his only flight lifeline.

"Alright buddy, let's get those diagnostics running." Kado spoke to Xostir as he laid him on the kitchen counter. Xostir remained levitating as Kado connected some magnetic cables to Xostir's orbs. Kado only knew what to do because Xostir was guiding him with the neural connection of how to hook him up to the diagnostic tools. Kado pulled out a small box from one of the pockets of his cloak.

Alright yes, plug those cables on the levitation orbs of my blade surface and make sure the white cable is attached to the p-port on the left and the green cable is attached to the port on the right of the diagnostic box. My diagnostic w-w-w-will take about three hours. His voice relay was glitching even worse now.

"How do you know how to do that?" Yai walked up beside Kado.

"Well Xostir knows how this all works so he just relays the instructions to me, and I do the work. It begins to make sense once its relayed through the link." Kado shrugged as he finished double checking the connections. He stepped back abruptly pressing his hand against his forehead, "Oh my head! It's pounding."

"Maybe you should take a nap." Yai suggested. Troy walked up behind them, curious of what was going on, "Is it a coincidence that Xostir was glitching out and now you have a migraine?"

"What, you think that my headache is connected to Xostir glitching out?" Kado looked over to the two of them, still pressing his hand against his forehead, "Yeah, perhaps there's a connection. Ok maybe I'll go lie down."

"Go rest in my room. Let us know if it gets worse." Ruana added as Kado stepped past her while she rested on the couch. Kado went into her room and lay down with the light out. He hoped that his headache would go away. This was the first time since his use of drugs that he actually wanted some sort of medication. The Immunoprofenalifen that was commonly used today was an excellent painkiller and he really could use some now.

The pounding struck to the beat of his heart and danced through the front of his skull and dove right down to the base of his neck, ripping through his mental pathways. He was beginning to believe that it was connected with the vengeful attack by Orun.

Kado cursed under his breath as he lay on his pillow, cringing from the intense throbbing pain that was beginning to take over his thoughts. All he could think about was wishing the stabbing would stop.

The group sat out in the living room discussing among themselves their present situation. Ruana sat sullen with concern written all over her face, "I hope he feels better soon."

"Yeah, let's hope this damage isn't permanent." Dom added.

"Permanent?" Ruana pleaded astonished.

"Well yeah, the blade was overpowered with some sort of antiparticle weapon. That's what my blade detected about the arm cannon." Dom continued.

"What does an antiparticle weapon do?" Ruana continued to bring her questions to the fore.

"Well, every particle can be associated with an

opposite particle that consists of the opposite characteristics. An electron is associated with an antielectron which is the opposite of an electron. An antielectron is also known as a positron since it has a positive electric charge instead of a negative electric charge." Troy began to explain.

"Okay, I'm not really following." Ruana responded slowly.

"Alright, well the antiparticle arm cannon that Orun had, is designed to douse something with the antiparticles of that material or a particular technological device which throws off the groove of that particular item and could possibly destroy such an item."

Ruana nodded as Dom continued.

"So, with a Magna-Blade which has positrons, electrons and neutrons flowing through it in very specific and set formations, having that disrupted so severely is a real shock on its system." Dom added to the explanation. Troy contributed even more, "And with the particle flow of the brain, having that interfered with even indirectly with just a neural connection to Xostir, it could cause permanent brain damage."

"Permanent brain damage, oh." Ruana shrunk in her seat despairing from the bad news. They were all sitting on the two couches having moved them closer together to discuss this. Yai shifted in her seat, "Is there anything we can do to help prevent this from affecting him worse?" Dom and Troy shook their heads, "This is uncharted territory. When we worked at the V.C. this kind of technology was not officially released and was only known as theoretical."

"Wait, well there's a hologram device here, right? Maybe there's information about it that we can look up." Yai stood up from the couch and walked towards the hologram device that Kado left on the mantle. As she got closer the visual representation of Nicodem appeared, "How may I help you?"

"Oh? Well, we, we uh, have some questions for you." Yai took a step back surprised by the intuitiveness of the technology of this device. It was more advanced than she had ever imagined.

"Go right ahead, Yai."

"Whoa, how do you know my name?"

"Oh well, Xostir relays all information he collects to me, so I know all of you and how you are Kado's helpful allies."

"Allies, huh?"

"Indeed. How may I help?"

"Well, we're wondering what kind of information you had on antiparticle weapons and the kind of harm it could do to a Magna-Blade or a human." Yai held her hands together in front of her in a polite Asian cultured fashion.

"Oh my, well I'm afraid that's quite serious. Antiparticle weapons were experimented on at the Vanixx Corps labs a few years ago, but they were said to have been discontinued from the hazardous results that they were encountering. They didn't actually stop the experiments contrary to popular belief and they finally did roll it out as an option for Military issue. You may encounter this kind of a weapon which has, by now, very likely been issued onto the black market." The Nicodem hologram thoroughly explained.

"Ok, well we have a situation." Yai went on to explain.

"Oh?"

"Yeah, Kado's blade, Xostir got struck by an antiparticle weapon and experienced some glitching issues."

"Ah yes, and I detect Xostir is going through diagnostics right now. It's very likely that he's going to be okay. Did Kado suffer from any symptoms?"

"He did start getting a pretty intense migraine."

"Oh I see, well if he isn't vomiting then he'll probably be ok, his symptoms should clear up in a couple of days." Nicodem smiled.

"Oh...oh, oh...Kay." Yai stammered. She looked back to the closed door of the Ruana's room with concern then looked over to the others as they had been listening to the whole conversation.

"We'll let him sleep a while and check up on him in a bit." Yai added, nodding to the group with a new shade of worry.

Kado opened the door to Ruana's room to rejoin the others in the living room of the cabin. He still had a headache, but the pain had eased off quite a bit. He had been embarrassed since he had thrown up into a garbage can in her room and brought it out to clean it.

He just hated throwing up and was wondering if he was coming down with one of those nasty flus. As he entered the kitchen, he saw a freshly brewed pot of tea steaming and ready for him. A note on a piece of paper beside it, "Drink Up".

He looked back over to the four of them conversing about the amazing abilities of their blades while pouring himself some tea. His head was hurting too much for him to care about anything. He desperately focused on emptying the garbage then on pouring his tea. Kado poured the tea out into a ceramic cup, breathing in the wonderful scent in the steam. He used the kitchen tap to rise out the soiled garbage can. Steam from the hot water rose into the air as he tried not to smell the fumes of warm vomit. His hands were full of tea and the bin and sat down beside Ruana on the couches.

He held the bin in his hand, "Not feeling so hot. Sorry."

"What do you mean?" Ruana raised an eyebrow.

"Oh, I threw up in your garbage can."

"Ah." She quickly looked over to the rest of them with nervousness and returned her gaze to him, "Kado, I think you need to talk to the Nicodem hologram on your little device about antiparticle weapons and side effects it can have."

"Oh?"

"Yeah, we think your headache has something to do with what happened from that guy with the arm cannon."

"Ah, I wasn't sure if that was connected or not. It's hard to think at all right now." He let out a nervous chuckle. He stood up, tea in hand, "Alright, I should look into this then." He got closer to the hologram display resting on the mantle, waiting until it automatically activated. In seconds a bust of Nicodem materialized, "Hello Kado, how are you feeling?"

"Well, I've got a bad headache and just vomited a few times, you tell me."

"Yes well, it sounds like you are suffering from a

rare case of antiparticle disruption; very serious if left untreated."

"What is the treatment?" Kado held a hand to his forehead, his headache worsening from the light of the hologram.

"The treatment is a particle rebalance session."

"How do I do that? Where?"

"Particle rebalance was an extensive experimental project Professor Wiltrite had going for almost two decades before he decided he wasn't making any progress. I recommend a visit to him to rebalance the particles in your brain. This visit should happen today, otherwise your symptoms could greatly worsen, you could die."

"How long before this condition becomes lethal?"

"Scanning your brain." He responded, followed by a brief pause.

"If left untreated you could die in 20 hours."

Kado's eyes widened at the shockingly short timeline. The group was standing beside Kado before he realized it, he looked over to them and started to speak slowly, "Do you mind if we..." Kado went unconscious and limp. Dom and Troy caught him before he fell and laid him down gently.

"He is unconscious." The Nicodem hologram continued, "Professor Wiltrite can be found either at

Union University or at his home in the Glanford Heights area."

"Give us the addresses." Dom commanded the hologram.

"I'll lead us there." Xostir's voice echoed through the minds of all four of them. His diagnostic completed now, he levitated there vertically with the cables unplugged and on the floor.

"Xostir, you alright?" Ruana pried.

"My system is not fully repaired yet but it will be soon. We need to get Kado to the professor before it's too late. It may be difficult to find him."

"Come on then, there's no time to lose!" Troy shouted. They laid an unconscious Kado onto Xostir and all flew out one by one heading towards the city as fast as possible.

"You two, head to the Professor's house and we'll take Kado to the university!" Ruana shouted over the wind, even though they could all detect her thoughts. They also sensed her deeper emotional connection to Kado; feelings she didn't realize that she had and emotions she couldn't contain. Xostir, Ruana and Dom headed to the center of the city. The Professor's house was quite a far distance away, but the university was even farther. It took them several minutes at unmatched speeds to reach the far end of the city a couple thousand miles away.

Troy and Yai arrived at the Professor's house first landing on the front lawn of his very large home. They looked around the gorgeous yard, filled with many bushes, trees and flowers as they knocked on the giant wooden door.

"He's well off, isn't he?" Troy observed.

"I should've gotten into teaching." Yai joked. They knocked again a little louder this time followed by hollow silence.

"Hey do you think that we can unlock the door with our blades?" Troy inquired.

"I don't see why not." Yai returned intrigued, "Let's try it." Troy used his mind to 'feel' the lock from the inside of the house and turned it. They both heard a click.

"Wow." Commented Yai.

"It worked." Troy was relieved. They walked in, gazing around the huge open concept living room that had high floor to ceiling windows, letting in plenty of natural light. Every light in the house was off and it was quiet. Every step they took echoed through the very minimalist open concept. The ceilings were 18 feet high and vaulted throughout.

"He's definitely not here. Let's go." Troy concluded.

"Wait, maybe we should take a quick peek." Yai contested mildly.

"Yai, I thought our days of theft were over." Troy raised a brow in disapproval.

"They are, yeah. But we should just – oh fine. You're right." She turned back from the hallway she was aiming to head down and led herself back to the living room. The house was eery with the lights off. They could make out the standard structure of the house, the light from the sky above refracting off the hand carved wood floor, the leather chair and couches, the fireplace and hearth. They couldn't make out much of the color scheme but the whole design was vintage yet somehow modern.

Troy's eye caught something shiny in the far corner and stepped over to take a closer look, "Yai, you gotta see this."

Everything was silent until a blaring alarm went off, flashing red lights appearing across the ceiling.

***

"Over there!" Ruana shouted as they neared the university. It was a huge building, sprawling across several city blocks. It was shaped like a giant circle and inside the thick outer ring consisted of courtyards and smaller structures. At the center of the interior of the campus was a large circular building with a domed top. It was a theatre but also doubled as a science center. Xostir fed information to Ruana and Dom about the most likely place the professor would be located and they homed in on that spot. As they neared the roof of the outer ring they swung to the right and then pulled a hard left in through the windows on the top floor, shattering the glass. They flew veering down the hall with their blades in hand trying not to decapitate anyone and trying not to knock anyone over. Xostir told them to head to room *406* and they finally found it. Ruana placed her blade on her back as she let her feet gracefully touchdown on the shiny polylaminate flooring. She walked over the threshold to the classroom and saw many students. Dom too let his feet touch down as he followed behind Xostir into the room. The class had alerted students all at their desks doing a science experiment and the professor with stark white hair, a tweed jacket and a bow tie began to shout as he walked up to them in the middle of the large circular desk arrangement, "Excuse me! You are interrupting a class! What is the meaning of this?"

"Sir, we're sorry but this is urgent." Ruana stepped forward gesturing to an unconscious Kado laying upon a horizontal levitating Xostir, "This young man is a dear friend of the late Nicodem Veradiun, and we believe he's suffering from antiparticle disruption. He's only got hours left. Can you help us?"

"Nicodem! You knew him? Wow look at those Magna-Blades." The professor was so astounded at the unexpected sight. He received a buzzing on his wrist watch. Looking at it he shouted, "Stop! My house alarm is going off! Someone is robbing me!"

Ruana and Dom looked to each other with concern and exchanged thoughts through their neural link, *You don't think Yai and Troy triggered it, do you?* She beckoned him.

Actually, I wouldn't be surprised. He responded.

"Oh well, false alarm. I don't see anyone or anything on my cameras. I'll have to get it looked at. Ah, you know, there's always something to fix." He deactivated the alarm from his watch and had a brief look of confusion as he looked at Ruana, Dom and an unconscious Kado.

"This man's life is on the line! We'll discuss the Magna-Blades after." Ruana was short on patience.

"Oh right yes, yes. Antiparticle you say?"

"Yes. Kado was using the blade here that he's lying on and it got hit with an antiparticle weapon, but his mind is now being severely affected by what we believe to be antiparticle disruption." Ruana continued to explain.

"Oh my, that's dreadful."

"Can you help him?" Ruana's patience was completely gone.

"Well how would I do that?"

"Didn't you do research on – what was that called?" Ruana trailed off forgetting the project name, looking back to Dom for help.

"Particle rebalance." Dom chimed in.

"Yes, particle rebalance. Didn't you do a ton of work and research on that?" Ruana swung her head back to face the professor.

"Well yes, yes I did", He started off hesitantly, "but sadly I could never get the machine to work."

"Where is the machine now?" Dom asked.

"It's in the basement here with about two inches of dust on it. I haven't touched it in almost twenty years." His face turned from hesitant to saddened.

"Take us to it." Ruana demanded as kindly as she could.

"It's not going to work." He shrugged.

"It has to!" She persisted; her voice raised with urgency.

"Alright, I'll show it to you, but it may not even turn on after all these years. Alright class dismissed – see you all tomorrow. Oh, and make sure you all read Heathcliff's

Dissolution Theory, chapters 10-20 for tomorrow."

***

The alarm, it stopped. Troy silently sent his thoughts to Yai.

Yes, I know that! She retorted with a snarl.

Well let's get outta here!

Yeah. Let's fly to the park down the street that we passed on the way here. Close the door and lock it.

Alright. He nodded. Just then Yai's blade interjected its thoughts, *There are security camera's, you can bend the light around us for a few seconds to 'cloak'.*

Cloak? Yai and Troy simultaneously inquired with surprise.

In other words, you'll become invisible for just a few seconds. Yai's blade clarified.

Let's do it! Troy ordered.

Instantly they became invisible to the cameras and in just seconds they bolted their way to a tree laden Park a few hundred feet away.

"Phew! That was close!" Troy wiped his brow. Yai looked around the park trying to make sure no one saw them materialize out of thin air.

"I wonder why the alarm stopped and why it took so

long to sound off in the first place." She looked to Troy with suspicion.

"I'm not sure. Maybe Ruana and Dom found him already and somehow got him to turn it off."

"Whatever it was, we need to tell them what we found immediately."

"Right." Troy added just before they both ascended and blasted off high into the air veering towards the university.

Dom, Xostir and Ruana followed the professor down to the basement of the university where Dom and Ruana laid Kado onto a dusty couch. The professor dug through some boxes of junk and after a few minutes he found something, "Aha! I wasn't sure if this was the right area but it sure turned out alright." He lifted a black cube which was about a foot and a half long in all dimensions with a deep circular opening in one of the surfaces, perfect for fitting something like a head. Holding it out to Ruana she held it uncomfortably, asking, "What do I do with this?"

"Well I'm not sure it's going to work, but you'd usually place it over his head." The professor responded hesitantly.

"You're too modest. No one else alive understands this science like you do. I've seen your books and read about some of the studies you've done." Ruana continued to observe each side of the cube. She was of course referring to the information that her blade was feeding to her with incredible speed as soon as they heard the name Professor Wiltrite. Her blade continued to relay the information to her through Nicodem's database.

She placed the cube over the unconscious Kado's head, it covered his entire face. Then on the outside edges, lights began to emit.

"Whoa there's lights on this thing? I couldn't tell." Ruana took a step back looking to the professor with a quick glance of intrigue. The lights where shaped like angled lines similar to the ancient computer structure design of Xostir; some lines were reaching all around every edge of the cube, some stopping at a circular circuit base. The colours flowed through every part of the spectrum at different points on various parts of the cube.

"So, what's it doing?" Dom imposed, pointing at the cube.

"The cube will detect where the particles in the brain are disrupted and hopefully nudge them into place. The particles - they aren't misplaced right now, otherwise he'd be completely braindead. Particle disruption is an attack on the cells of the brain, normally such an attack could kill a person. But perhaps there's a scenario when particle disruption doesn't mean death."

"Yes", Ruana conferred, "this antiparticle weapon that we encountered was an arm cannon attached to a cybernetic augment. I have to say that I think this blade absorbed most of the attack if not all of it. According to Nicodem, whatever effect Kado is experiencing seems to be related to his mental connection with the blade."

"Ah. That does explain it – wait. You said, 'according to Nicodem'. He's alive?" The professor suddenly grew excited.

"Uh no – I misspoke. I've done some – uh – reading around Nicodem's research and that's what he indicated in his research on particle disruption." Ruana tried to cover her tracks. The professor could not find out about the Nicodem hologram. That could really complicate things more so than they already were.

"Oh, how disappointing. I hoped he had somehow survived the attack on his house." The professor's shoulders dropped with sadness, his head lowered, "Well the good news is, this will be easier than expected. Since it wasn't a direct attack on Keda? Koda?"

"Kado." Both Dom and Ruana corrected him in unison.

"Yes, yes, Kado. Since it wasn't a direct attack on his brain and was a third-party effect through a neural connection, this particle rebalancer should be able to help him fully recover."

"Well that's a relief." Dom sat down on a nearby chair. Ruana's joy from the relief was overwhelming, so much to the point that she couldn't say anything for a few seconds. She was so concerned for his life and to think that he could fully recover was a greater source of joy for her than she expected.

"Yes, we should give him a couple hours. He'll likely wake up very thirsty." The professor gestured for them to head over to another part of the basement.

"Wait a moment." The professor stood up urgently.

"What – what is it?" Ruana darted her eyes back and forth between Kado and the professor.

"It's not working. It's lacking the appropriate amount of balanced particles to correct itself. This kid's brain was really messed up."

"Well-well-what do we do?" Ruana became more agitated.

"Someone needs to link to the particle rebalancer to ensure Kado recovers, the supporting neural activity from another mind is the only thing that can save him! If we don't link one of us to it, he could die in minutes. The device is starting to fail! But it's very, very dangerous to plug someone in. It could kill whoever connects to this device!"

The lights on the cube-shaped device began to strobe and flicker, causing Kado's body to convulse on the couch.

Dom stepped up to Kado, looking to the professor, "Plug me in, doc. Now!"

"But Dom! This could kill you!" Ruana shouted.

"You know your blade better than any of us! You can't risk your life for this! I'm doing it!" He hollered back. Ruana's shoulders dropped, accepting defeat, "Okay."

"Okay." The professor grabbed a couple nearby wires, plugging them into the black cube, then sitting Dom down on a chair beside the couch, he attached the cables to Dom's temples, "This won't hurt a-"

"Ow!" Dom shrieked in pain.

"bit.", the professor held a hand to his mouth with surprise. Dom stayed sitting there, keeping his eyes closed.

"Alright, now focus on helping Kado. Imagine a sphere. It should be pink, this represents Kado's mind." The professor guided Dom, "It will try to look green. But imagine it as entirely pink. If a portion of the sphere seems to look like it's becoming green, use your mind to force it to become pink."

"Yes, its mostly green."

"That – that is *not* good." The professor stammered.

"Yeah, yeah just leave me alone and let me focus. I think I've figured it out." Dom chastised the professor. Ruana's eyes were large out of fear for both Kado and Dom's life. She didn't want to lose them both right here, right now. *Where are Yai and Troy?* She asked herself, annoyed. She seethed with anger that this happened to Kado, that the horrible Oran did this to him. Her thoughts dwelt on vengeance.

"Now all we gotta do is wait. This area is where I used to spend quite a lot of time as a young scientist." The professor sat down on an old leather chair with scratches and rips all over it. Ruana and Dom sat in chairs opposite him in an open area of the basement just a few feet from where Kado was lying. The professor continued, "I wasn't yet a professor of science, but I was part of the faculty as a teacher. I did some experiments down here and read everything the famous Dr. Veradiun had written. I tried to recreate some of the science he had explained, but I failed many, many times. That man was a marvel."

"Had you ever met Nicodem before?" Ruana entreated.

"I did, once. We were at a science conference; he

was a speaker on the panel. This was before the war. It was the last conference before the war started. They haven't had one like it since."

"The war sounded awful. My grandfather was in it as a swordsman of the militia." Ruana stared at the old dusty carpet that completed the makeshift living room in the dark filthy basement.

"Ooh tough job. That would've been quite a lot of action for one man to see." The professor shook his head, "I was an artillery gunner at first. I was conscripted about halfway through the war. It was a dark time for the world. A dark, dark time."

"Well, Professor. We're trying to prevent another war." Ruana remarked; his eyebrows raised with seriousness. She looked over to Dom, perspiration beaded all over his forehead from his intense concentration. He was beginning to shake.

"Another war? Is that really possible?" the professor queried with astonishment. Ruana nodded, "It's more possible than anyone realizes." She looked over to an unconscious Kado and a struggling Dom, "And we can't do it without them."

***

Yai and Troy reached the perimeter of the university and were urgently trying to find Dom and Ruana. However, things had gotten complicated. There were Vanixx Corps forces surrounding the university.

Yai, here are Dom, Kado and Ruana's location. They are in the basement with another person. Her blade transmitted the thoughts to her mind. The blade helped her to see figures within the confines of the building.

"Alright, find us the way into the basement." Yai told her blade. In moments a path appeared in both her and Troy's vision of the curved and zigzagging line to the basement of the large university. They needed to discreetly get into that basement without drawing unwanted attention from the Vanixx Corps Officers. Both of them were crouching in the forest, trying to figure out a way into the university. The campus was swarming with Officers.

"Why are these guys here?" Troy looked to Yai for an answer.

"I'm not entirely sure but perhaps Ruana, Dom and Kado were seen with Magna-Blades. Somebody probably called it in. It's illegal to own these things now."

"Right. Can we make ourselves fly so fast that we're almost invisible?"

You could try but I'd run out of available energy

before you can get to the entrance of the building, even if you flew as fast as you could. Troy's blade relayed.

"What if we flew really fast through the forested part then while we're closer to the campus, just walk in, like students?" Yai suggested.

That would take more energy and we still can't avoid detection. Yai's blade explicated.

"Alright, what about this?" Yai put her hands on her hips continuing to gaze at the University in the distance through the brush, "What if we both fly as fast as we can and then blast through the doors and just fight off the V.C.?"

That isn't the best idea, there are innocent students everywhere that could get hurt. Yai's blade accounted with reticence.

"Blast through the doors?" Troy challenged incredulously.

There is a high concentration of V.C. Officers here, it makes a perfect entrance impossible. Troy's blade relayed.

"Okay. What do you think?" Yai coaxed Troy.

"It's a risk, but what choice do we have? We need to get to them before it's too late. They need to know the truth about the professor."

"Yeah, alright. On three, we run to the edge of the forest and once in the open we casually walk to the door.

Hold your arm around me and kiss me on the cheek just before we go through the door."

"What? Why?" Troy grilled.

"Public displays of affection make people uncomfortable; it will help us blend in with the other students."

"You think you wearing that armour will make you blend in? No matter what we do, we won't blend in."

"Ugh, you're right but we have to try. Maybe we'll get lucky." She shrugged.

"Well, what about cloaking?" Troy asked both Yai and his own blade.

We could enable a cloak but my system can only sustain a cloak for six seconds. Troy's blade relayed to both Troy and Yai.

"Well that could work. Look, the doors are not that far from the forest edge. We sprint from here to the edge of the forest, we clack–"

"Cloak." Yai corrected him with a slight giggle.

"Right, cloak, and while we continue sprinting through the doors, the blades can de-cloak."

"It will be tight." Yai shook her head hesitantly.

"What choice do we have? I think we've exhausted all other options."

"Yeah, I guess so."

"Alright. On three." Troy held out a gestured hand with three fingers.

In unison they counted down, "Three, two, one!" They sprinted through the campus forest, around trees, hopping over roots, ducking under fallen trunks until they reached the forest edge. Once at the edge their blades enabled the cloak and the two of them became invisible. It was fifty feet to the closest entrance and up a short flight of stairs.

As they neared the stairs, they saw a timer on their neural Heads-Up Display showing how much time was left on the cloak.

Five.

They crossed the open grassy lawn heading towards the closest flight of stairs.

Four.

Yai cut wide around a V.C. Officer in her path.

Three.

Troy started up the steps with Yai closely behind.

Two.

Troy threw the doors open.

One.

Yai dove through the doors as her cloak disengaged. Aside from a few estranged looks from some students, they narrowly avoided any V.C. attention.

"Oh, my head." Kado tried to hold his hand on his forehead but felt a surface covering his face. His head was pounding, but he wasn't nauseous anymore. Ruana, Dom and the professor ran over to see him.

"Kado, you're awake!" Ruana excitedly shouted. Dom opened his eyes relieved, yanking the cords off of his temples.

"Oh, oh, shhhh." He put a finger to his mouth with one hand, gesturing for silence, as he sat up on the couch. His head was still sensitive from the seemingly loud volume of her lovely voice. He took the cube off his head with his other hand.

"What's this thing?" He petitioned with exhaustion.

"That, my dear man, is an invention called a particle rebalancer. Your little run-in with the antiparticle arm cannon gave your brain a little jostle. So, we tried to fix it." The professor stood by Ruana with a friendly smile.

"Ah, and who are you?" Kado continued to ask with some confusion. He seemed to be missing some memories.

"Not who you think." Yai announced as she hurriedly stepped down the creaky wooden stairs.

"What? What's going on? Where even are we?" Kado inquired now standing looking for Xostir.

"Professor Wiltrite is not who he says he is." Troy added.

"What are you talking about?" The professor contested.

"We were at your house." Yai began her explanation.

"Oh, so *you* were at my house. You two are what triggered my alarm. Interesting. I didn't see anything on my security cameras." The professor noted.

"Yeah and we saw your picture on the wall." Troy added bravely as he stood beside Yai, "You were with Curt Weiss, the originator of the Quell. Your hand was on his shoulder. You two were clearly friends." Everyone looked to the professor, their expressions demanding an explanation. He calmly added, "I was an artillery gunner for the Military and was conscripted about halfway through the war." He looked to Dom and Ruana for their corroboration of what he mentioned.

He sat down on the nearby couch that Kado had been recovering on, "Well, Curt was one of my best friends growing up. He too was conscripted. When he lost his legs in the war after five years, he was excused from Military service. That picture is us in our first month of fighting the war. Back then, he was fighting for the Military like I was. After he left due to his injury, he was given a meagre pension and he wasn't quiet about it. They gave him half of what he needed to survive each month. He lived in the simplest, cheapest apartment. It became quite a well-known complaint in the media. I asked him why he was pressing the matter so publicly so he told me, 'Christopher, If I don't do this, then who will?'."

The five of them exchanged glances unsure if they should believe this whole story while the Professor continued, "He even had a few mysterious near-death experiences shortly after that. He claimed it was the Military trying to silence him. I didn't agree with him starting an organization like the Quell but I'm hardly surprised that it happened. Eventually, once the war was over, the V.C. got to him and took him out, but by then, the Quell was already global. I keep the photo as a reminder of why I keep going. Life can be unfair, but never give up." He looked to them all after his brief speech.

"Guys, he doesn't really seem like the 'Quell' type. He did just save Kado, you know." Dom shrugged.

"Guys, don't we kind of have some more pressing matters at hand?" Ruana interjected.

"Yeah," Yai added, "The Vanixx Corps have the building surrounded. There are flocks of them roaming around the halls and the immediate area of the buildings. It's only a short matter of time before they make it down here."

"Alright, we – we should go." Kado looked around for Xostir. He held his hand out and Xostir rose from behind the couch and placed his hilt into his hand. He felt the connection to Xostir again and it was refreshing. It felt like a door to a humongous universe of information had been reopened. A door with a personality. He had gotten used to having Xostir connected to his mind and always being there in the background for the past few months. It had felt like having a friend nearby always there instantly as soon as you called for them. He realized now just how badly he missed it for the several hours that they were disconnected.

"Well, how are you going to leave unnoticed?" The professor implored them.

"We have our ways." Yai replied abruptly, protective of their secrets of the Magna-Blades' abilities.

"You may not want to be seen with us, professor. The V.C. might connect you with us and we don't want you to get thrown into a mess." Ruana rested a hand on his shoulder with her natural kindness.

"Oh, you needn't worry about me. I'm pretty tough. I'll just hang back a few meters and we should be ok." He shuffled behind the five of them.

They started up the flight of old, creaky stairs to the old basic door to the hallway of the university. Kado rested his hand on the old-fashioned door handle and looked back to the rest of them, "Ready?" They all nodded, and he concluded, "Alright." As he opened the door, they all blasted off with a rapid jolt, one by one, almost simultaneously. As Ruana was about to zip off after the rest of them, she looked back to the professor, smiling as she saw his jaw drop. Astounded, he exaled, "Fascinating."

Adrian Greeg had a history with Moderator Kar, and he didn't want to talk with her about it. He summoned her to meet him at the briefing room of one of the largest hangars on the base. This briefing room had windows looking out onto the hangar filled with ships, smaller fighters, and hundreds of soldiers carrying out dozens of organizational duties. Adrian had already begun delegating tasks to hundreds of Moderators, but he was supposed to work with Kar to organize matters on a global scale. The longer she took to arrive, the more the butterflies in his stomach were agitated.

"Well, aren't you a sight for sore eyes." Moderator Ryla Kar mused as she stood leaning in the doorway with her arms crossed. As he turned around to her greeting, he noticed she was admiring his figure in the fancy white armored suit. Adrian immediately thought to himself, *oh boy, here we go.*

"Yes, well it's nice to see you too, Moderator Kar."

"Moderator Kar? Come on, why so formal?" She flirted as she stepped closer to him, "Has it been so long that you've forgotten our time together?"

"No, it's not that. It's just...bittersweet for me." Adrian tilted his head with an uncomfortable expression on his face.

"I know, you were married back then. But you didn't really put an end to my advancements, did you?"

"No, I didn't. But after a few months of our secret relationship I ended it with you. Then several months later, my family were killed, I never had worked up the nerve to tell Chloe about us. That really affected me. She died not knowing. Anyways, the point is, I don't want our history to interfere with the effectiveness of our mission. We need to keep things professional. As far as *we* are concerned" he gestured with a finger to each of them back and forth, "It's the distant past."

"Ah. Well then. Distant past it is, even if it was the best time of your life." She brought a hand up from resting on her hips, to point at him with emphasis. A part of her was offended that he pushed away their previous relationship with such ease.

"Yes, I will admit – er – well uh, anyways. On to business." He cleared his throat as he walked to the window overlooking the hangar. It was far more awkward than he had even anticipated to be in the same room with her after all these years. He raised his armored gauntlet on his arm which brought up a small holographic display, "We need to mobilize our forces in every single city, and we'll need your aptitude for your organizational skills."

"Is that my only skill set that you'll be needing?" She hinted. Having fully caught the innuendo, he tried to pacify the situation, "For the moment, yes." He spun the hologram around to show the cities that they needed to acquire strength in first, over in Africa and Australia.

"Here we'll need to pull heavy mechs and whatever weapons we can from the Military in these two countries. I have a couple dozen sources to give to you to negotiate the coordination effort. Meanwhile I'll coordinate with Eurasia and the rest of America."

"What kind of timeline are we working with?" She decided she'd put the flirting on the back burner for now and cooperate.

"Yesterday." He furrowed his brow with concentration, "But ASAP will work just fine."

"Alright good. And what organizations are we getting machines and tech from?"

"In Australia, you'll be able to get all the ships, vessels, handguns, support militia and if they have any, Magna-Blades as well, from their Australian Defense Force. For Africa, you'll find that the Egyptian Military is what they call their forces. There you'll be able to obtain a large plot of land for us to mobilize troops and ships in a secretive location safe from the eyes of the Military leaders. You'll also be able to get us possibly quite a few Magna-Blades and gravity weapons, in addition to the heavy mechs and ships."

"Sounds like overkill." Ryla raised her eyebrows with some surprise on the details.

"It usually would be if this was just a small skirmish. But this is a full-scale global war that we're waging. The Vanixx Corps have toyed with us for too long, as have the other Military forces out there. They've been trying to end the Quell since the Gravity War ended. Our intelligence Moderators have also reported that the Vanixx Corps may be developing relationships with other countries. We need to take on every city, every country and make it our own. This means tackling multiple different forms of government with a force so strong that they won't know what hit them. Once they see their own forces turn on them from the inside, they'll lose all motivation from the corruption and they will give up."

"Wow, so the rumors are true."

"What rumors?"

"We're actually at war with the world."

"Yeah. It's finally happening."

"Got it. I'll do whatever you need."

"Great, take this", he handed her a small drive containing all the contacts and specs of the equipment they would need from each city and each country, "and let me know when you make landfall overseas. I'll brief you on any new developments of the plan. You fly out as soon as you pack a bag."

"Right away, Sir." Ryla responded as she turned on her heel and headed out of the room. Just before she crossed the threshold leaving the room, "When this is over, let's chat over coffee." Before he could turn around and respond she ducked behind the corner. He shook his head, relieved that one of the most awkward conversations he could've ever imagined was over. He spoke into his collar communicator, "Hangar Control, this is the Vicero. Ready a ship for me."

They had blasted off out from the University just below the speed of sound avoiding detection from what they could tell. They followed Kado as he led them through the city, flying low, darting around the skyscrapers at dizzying speeds. Once they reached the outskirts, Dom flew closer to Kado, raising his voice over the wind, "Where are we headed?"

"Ruana tells me you risked your life to save me. That has shown that you're trustworthy. I'm taking us somewhere very special."

The sun had begun its descent on the distant skyline as the five of them stopped, hovering at the base of a large cliff face. Kado addressed them all, "Follow me and stay close, no matter what happens; this is going to get weird." He turned then flew immediately into the rock wall, vanishing through it like an open curtain. The four of them briefly looked to each other with a mixture of confusion and astonishment, then followed right after him.

After zipping through the twisting tunnels, they all landed in the bunker one after the other. The new visitors looked around at the advanced concrete oasis. It looked very old but had technology they had never seen – or even dreamed of – before. In addition to the lab tables, they saw holographic imagery in place along the domed walls and holo-screens showing some security footage in the surrounding area. Data from the first edition Magna-Blade was also displaying on one of the holo-screens.

Yai looked up to the second-floor walkway, her slight smirk betraying a hint of benevolence, "Seems like a formidable base of operations. You may be a worthy ally after all."

"What, you've never seen this place?" Ruana darted a look to Yai, slightly tilting her head.

Kado told them all, "This is the first time anyone, other than me, has been here. It's time to review our plan and in light of the recent attack we just suffered through, it clearly shows that we need an upgrade." He stepped over to the blue lockers, "First things first, we all need to get some rest and to freshen up. There's a shower over there by the restroom", he pointed to the doors by the kitchen. "Also, help yourselves to some fresh clothing," Kado offered to them as he opened the nearest locker, "It'll be nice to have a change of clothes, maybe even something with some sort of armor plating for our attack plan." He looked over to Dom and Troy, "Some of Nicodem's old clothes are still here in the lockers, help yourselves to pick out something you like." Dom and Troy looked through the surprising amount of clothing options.

"Now, we should probably all stay the night here. It's going to be safer than an abandoned condo in the city, and it will be better if we don't leave the bunker for the night. Since we were sighted at the University, Xostir says the patrols around the entire city border have increased tenfold. There are a couple private bunk rooms here, feel free to sleep on any one of them." Kado walked over to the kitchen and opened the doors, "There's a kitchen with some food and if you get hungry help yourself to something."

He headed for his room, "Have a good night, guys."

"Wait, Kado." Ruana followed after him, "Is this place safe? I-I mean, this close to the city? Won't they detect us?"

"This is the safest place on the planet. There are security countermeasures outside and within the base that protect against theft and will protect us from harm, just so long as we don't leave the bunker." He made sure his voice carried through the bunker for the next part just in case his new semi-trustworthy allies had any unsavory ideas, "We're so safe here, we couldn't even hurt each other in here if we tried." Kado headed into his room to inspect his gashes that he received from Yai and Dom in their earlier duel.

He sat down in his private room shirtless, noting that his recent injuries along his abdomen had nearly fully healed with barely a scar. His jacket was less royal blue with his blood staining a portion of it now. He took to stitching the bloodstained cuts on his coat, his giant open wounds in his leg and abdomen had been sealed and mostly healed by Xostir. His head was still gently pounding, as he seemed to have survived a lethal attack that nearly left him braindead. He owed Dom his life. He figured that he should be hungry since it had been so long since he ate, but from his earlier nausea, he still didn't have the stomach to eat anything. He would sleep as best as he could, despite how wound up he was. All he wanted to do was chase down Orun and slice another cybernetic limb off that bloody fool. He tried not to dwell on revenge, but it was all he could think about as he restlessly, slowly dozed off.

The next morning, he came out to the main bunker, sitting down at a metal hover chair by a circular table in the corner. Everyone else had awoken already, finding themselves a place to sit or practice their fighting moves in the wide-open area of the bunker. Ruana casually walked over to Kado, sitting down beside him. He opened with a friendly grin that he hoped was attractive to her, "How did you sleep?"

"Oh, I slept okay. It's not as comfortable as my bed at home."

"Yeah, your cabin is really nice."

"So, this is where you live. It's" She paused trying to find the right word, "cozy."

"Well is not as comfortable as your place, that's for sure. But it *is* safer." He replied kindly, focused on his jacket's repair that he started last night.

"Yeah, this place is pretty amazing. It's so hidden and impenetrable. But I'm still pretty nervous about our plan."

"Oh yeah?"

"Yeah well, I haven't fought that much and only know a little bit about how use the blade – the basics, you know; how to levitate, how to use some of the gravitational abilities. But I could use some guidance on how to be really effective with it." She shrugged. Kado's eyes met hers briefly. He thought about how Xostir helped him to become more skilled with the blade, "Maybe we can share some of the knowledge Xostir shared with me. That helped me to learn more about using a Magna-Blade properly. Before I met Nicodem, I barely knew how to use one."

"Well, that's a great idea!" She leaned back with an elated smile. Kado stood up as he finished his jacket, "Xostir, what resources can we share with our new friends here? We will need every advantage we can get." Xostir hovered down from the second level towards him, his manufactured voice echoing through the speakers of the bunker, "I was just inspecting some of the inventions Nicodem has catalogued and I believe the time has come to share those with you and our allies."

A hologram of Nicodem appeared at the central floor display, "Kado, I've recorded this holo-vid to help you install some important upgrades to your Magna-Blade. I have some helpful tools that I've kept hidden from everyone and kept secret especially from the Vanixx Corps." Everyone gathered around the hologram at the center of the room. Nicodem was facing the lockers along the far wall and gestured to them, "In these three lockers you will find three useful inventions that will assist you." Xostir opened the lockers.

"Inside you will find upgrades for Magna-Blades. First, the enhanced Xeno-Translators allow for triple the processing speed of what you are operating at. I've spent decades working on this and have a prototype in Xostir now. I've designed this quantum hardware to be a simple modular plug-in add-on for nearly all Magna-Blades."

Kado pulled out a box from the locker, carefully opening it. All of the team looked inside, seeing several tiny cylinders which would enhance their blades beyond their imagination.

"Next, you will see another modular plug-in I've worked on. A hybrid, positronic quantum processor. This will make your Magna-Blade ten times smarter. Again, this is designed to be an add on piece of hardware. Xostir had an earlier version of this and I was going to install one of these. I also have backup replacement pieces for years to come."

Ruana opened this locker, pulling out the small box. They all looked in to see incredibly small circular attachments.

"Lastly, the third invention to help you is a set of protocols that add to the abilities of any Magna-Blade. These protocols are only possible with the advanced processor and increased speed. Some of the abilities include short range teleportation, antiproton shield, and a neutron grenade." Nicodem's hologram continued to expound. They all exchanged glances between themselves, not really understanding the benefits of an antiproton shield or how a neutron grenade would work.

"There are other abilities as well, but you'll discover those over time. The teleport is fairly straightforward; you will be able to use gravity to literally fold space over yourself and move you to another nearby location. This took me several decades to perfect in secret. The antiproton shield will briefly protect you from virtually any kind of attack, be it electrical, electromagnetic, kinetic or tactile. It takes quite a lot of power to initiate it so make sure your timing is done properly; the shield can only last a few seconds without completely draining your blade for several moments. A neutron grenade generates from within your blade and stays stationary once it's charged, you then swing your blade lobbing the sphere of static neutrons a great distance towards an enemy. This weapon is designed to weaken or slow down whomever is hit by it. Depending on your commands to your blade you can tell it to generate a large number of neutrons which will irradiate an enemy or fry electronic devices or weapons. Commanding just a small number of neutrons will cause machinery to slow down or even be disabled. There are many options."

"When can we install these?" Yai needled. Xostir replied, "We can install these upgrades today."

Kado summoned a platform to raise from the floor near a lab table as he began to prepare installing the upgrades on each of their blades. All of the blades positioned themselves in a line; Kado helped each of the blade owners to learn how to properly open the hilt at the pommel. With a set of very small tools designed by Nicodem specifically for work on Magna-Blades, they inserted each of the upgrades, one by one.

Meanwhile, they were watching the news on one of the holo-screens that Ruana had projecting onto the wall. It wasn't long before something surprising was going on.

"Whoa! Check this out! The Grand Admiral of the

V.C. just executed a Quell agent, they caught it on camera." Dom described, unable to take his eyes off the viewer.

"What? Are you kidding me?" Kado was shocked. It seemed like things were escalating much faster than they had expected.

"We need to get a real plan in place. Time is running out." Kado addressed the team as he continued to finish the installation of the hardware on Troy's Blade.

After a few minutes, Kado had already upgraded, Ruana's blade, then Yai's and now Troy's. Next up was Dom's and lastly he would upgrade Xostir.

As he worked on Dom's blade he observed it's structure. Its alloy was even darker than Yai's blade, a darker mix of brown and grey resulting in a burnt umber color. It was mostly shaped like a big rectangle blended with an uneven hexagon sticking out on one edge making one unique geometric prism. On the flat wide edges of the blade were all sorts of geometric shapes, such as various rhombuses, triangles along with other odd sharp-angled designs, etched into the side of the blade all with a purpose.

"Hey guys" Yai addressed them all, "My blade has just decided to name itself Ptalojn."

"Tah-loan? How do you spell that?" Kado inquired.

"It's harder than it sounds. P-T-A-L-O-J-N."

"Interesting. I wonder why a blade feels the need to name itself." Troy briefly shook his head with a slight air of disdain, scoffing at the unique name.

"Well, think about it," Kado contributed, "You have a name. You are a sentient being. These blades are the closest thing to sentient that you can get without having a humanoid body. They strive for an identity like any sentient being; a huge part of an identity is having a name." Shortly all of the blades had been upgraded to their new hardware, needing an hour to reboot. Once they all had rebooted, the Magna-Blades had been communicating with each other while the wielders were resting, chatting or reviewing the plan of attack on the Vanixx Corps.

"Alright, now that our blades have rebooted, let's do a brief refresher on Magna-Blade maintenance." Kado stood out to the center of the bunker as everyone else remained resting on the nearby couches.

It was now late afternoon and the camera feeds to the security holo-displays on the walls showed the sun was still shining. Kado took a look at one of the holo-displays, "Anyone want to try these new improvements out?"

Everyone responded at once with smiling, enthused

expressions. He gestured to join him as he headed for the holographic secret entrance, "Let's go then."

All five of them flew out of the bunker one by one, either riding on the blade or flying with the blade in hand. They followed Kado at unbelievable speeds, all breaking the sound barrier almost immediately as they blasted off into the distance towards towering mountains. Yai, Ruana, Dom and Troy all had a new enhanced interface with their blade. To all of their minds, the blades' connection with their minds would display the speed that they were travelling at in their peripheral vision. They soon all reached Mach 2, Mach 3, Mach 4. The skies and the mountains became blurs to them, but they were in complete control, not frightened by the dizzying speeds. In just seconds they arrived at the distant wilderness, all landing in an open flat field in the middle of a heavily wooded forest.

"Alright guys, that was fun. Notice a difference already?" Kado addressed the crew, as he called to them with a synced connection with them all.

"Yeah, it feels like the blade is starting to have more of an actual telepathic conversation with me. It conversed before, but was more rigid, more robotic. Now, it's like a – a person!" Ruana commented.

Dom added, "Right, and we're able to fly at least

twice as fast as before. We weren't even close to our maximum speed coming here."

Troy followed, "Yes, you can tell we're strengthening our connection with our blades."

Ruana was holding her blade in both hands with a pleased look, "My blade is working on deciding a name for itself." Kado smiled to them all. He felt joy from being able to share his experiences with them. It was nice to no longer be alone. He trusted Ruana completely, but he still wasn't fully sure he could trust Yai or Troy without any small doubt. He reminded himself that he needed their help, and this was the only way he would get it. Ironically, he's made them the most dangerous potential foes on the planet, more so than the entire Vanixx Corps. He just hoped they didn't realize just how dangerous they could be yet.

"Okay guys, should we try these upgrades out?" Kado quizzed the team.

Yai chimed in first enthusiastically, "Let's do this." She swung her blade at nearby trees, effortlessly causing the trees to snap off their trunks, floating through the air. They remained stationary for a moment levitating in midair. She wound up then swung down to the ground, creating a gravitational hammer, throwing the trees into the ground, crushing and pulverizing them into tens of thousands of wooden shards. The impact of the trees on the ground shook the nearby area, causing the leaves and boughs of the surrounding trees to shudder. All of them felt the ground violently quake beneath their feet.

"Woah! That's awesome!" Ruana shouted excitedly. She next held her blade horizontally, bracing as she aimed it at some other nearby trees. She was commanding her blade to form a sphere of electro-statically charged particles which materialized. The gravity orb holding all of it in place. It looked like a ball of electricity had formed at the tip of her blade. Ruana let the charged particles escape in a beam that behaved like lightning towards the forest edge, causing a row of trees and forest several miles long to disintegrate. Seconds later they could all hear a few trees fall as they had been severed in half.

"Wow look at that!" Troy exclaimed.

"That was intense!" Dom added. They were almost like school kids again, experiencing the excitement of the incredibly enhanced abilities that their blades had now.

Kado decided that he would try to teleport. He stood there a moment focusing on reappearing fifty feet to the left. In moments he vanished then immediately reappeared further away.

"Whoa! That was weird!" he exclaimed.

I'm detecting a Sentinel incoming at a high velocity.

Xostir warned Kado. The other blades also warned all of their own wielders.

"What do we do?" Ruana implored Kado.

"We don't have time to hide in the forest." Yai replied.

"Make a gravity fold to form around you, it will be strong enough to bend the light around you and make you invisible." Kado shouted to the team.

"Just like we did back at the University." Yai looked over to Troy.

"Except our blades can cloak almost indefinitely now." He happily added.

"What about our heat signatures?" Dom beckoned.

"Oh. I'm not sure." Kado paused, trying to think. "Xostir?"

We haven't tried this before, but in theory, we could use gravity to slow the movements of the molecules and particles surrounding us, to the point where it will actually cool the air around us. It could possibly hide our heat signatures from the sentinel.

"Okay transmit that idea to the other blades." Kado ordered. In less than a second everyone understood what to do then initiated the action with their blades.

"Nobody move, everyone hold their breath."

Just then the sentinel came into view over the

treetops. Its scanner detected heat signatures briefly from further away, but they had instantly vanished. Unsure of how to investigate this since nothing in its protocols were programmed for such an event so it could see nothing on visual or auditory scanners, it carried on in its patrol, saying to itself, "I seem to require maintenance."

In a few seconds it was thousands of feet away and they all let out their breath.

"Phew! That was a close one." Troy sighed relieved.

"What's such a big deal with a single drone?" Ruana insisted, having destroyed a few quite easily in the past.

"Well, this in a very good area to practice and if one drone detects us today it can bring reinforcements - even if we destroy it right away." Dom explained.

"And then they will increase the patrols along this route for at least a year." Troy contributed to the explanation. Ruana nodded, "Makes sense."

"Now that we've tested out what our blades can do, let's get the details of the plan figured out." Kado addressed the team. They flew back to the bunker at a low altitude to ensure they wouldn't get detected by any other sentinels or patrols. Kado had some ideas for their raid on the Vanixx Corps, but it would take some complex coordination between all five of them. They were still very rusty and haven't even tried coordinating. They couldn't take on a single Vanixx Corps MAW, let alone the Citadel.

The following morning, Kado made breakfast for the entire group. He had gotten better at making breakfast the old-fashioned way.

"Holy cow, what smells so good in here." Dom asked enthused as he stepped into the kitchen.

"It's called toast and an omelet. *Not* made with a molecular resequencer, I'll have you know."

"Impressive!" He added, "I don't know the first thing about cooking."

"Neither did I, until I started living in the bunker." He added as the rest of the group came in. They all sat around on bar stools on the opposite end of the flat countertop across from the elements Kado was cooking on. He was able to face all four of them sitting down as he finished with frying the food.

"So guys, how are you feeling with your upgrades?" Kado inquired of all of them.

"I'm super excited about them myself, but still don't know so many of the things that the blade can do now." Ruana chimed in first.

"Yeah, I feel like I need more practice." Yai added. Dom and Troy nodded in agreement.

"Well maybe we should practice some of the moves that require some coordination today after breakfast." Kado suggested as he cut up the omelet into slices, laying the pieces on a stack of plates one at a time, "There's a few moves I need practice with too."

"Hey, has anyone else's blade named itself yet?" Dom inquired of the group as he leaned on the countertop.

"Mine hasn't." Ruana answered first.

"Not mine." Troy added.

"Just mine so far." Yai shrugged.

"Well mine has and it's a weird name. I don't really understand why it picked it." Dom responded to them all, "It told me its name is now Cnidus."

"That's an interesting name. How you do spell that?" Kado surveyed as he continued to lay the food on the plates, placing them in front of the group one by one.

"C-N-I-D-U-S. Ken-eye-diss." Dom responded slowly and clearly, spelling the unique name out for everyone.

"What does it mean?" Ruana implored.

"I don't know. I've looked it up and it was an Ancient Greek city but that's all I can find right now."

They all began to eat, bonding over stories from their past. Once they all finished breakfast, they flew off into the forest to practice their sword fighting.

The five of them were wielding their blades, trying out some of the new abilities to become more familiar with the personalities that their blades were developing.

"Guys! My blade just named itself!" Ruana shouted to the group. Now that her blade was developing an artificial personality, it was starting to surprise her.

"Well, what is it?" Dom inquired of her, since he was standing closest.

"It's See-yar, S-J-A-R. And it's relaying information to my mind in a woman's voice, sort of. I wonder why it chose that name." She commented excitedly looking at her blade with perplexity.

"Sometimes blades can isolate meanings of words and combinations of letters that we wouldn't usually think of. But the names always have some important meaning. Xostir still hasn't explained to me why he chose his name and gender." Kado explained as he stepped a bit closer to Ruana to explain the knowledge Xostir had just fed him an instant earlier.

Kado was then helping them orchestrate an interesting gravity mesh concept together, "Alright guys, so this is something I found in my research on gravitational abilities. With all of us working together, we can actually create a wall of impenetrable gravity, being able to lift almost anything."

"Sounds cool. Let's try it." Troy replied with a smile. They all stood in a circle, facing inward and held their blades out towards the center of their circle. Kado guided them, "Alright now everyone, imagine forming a disc shape." All five of them began to feel their minds merge through the five blades interconnecting. To Kado it felt like doors opened to the minds of the other four wielders simultaneously; he got a quick glimpse of what each one was thinking and desiring to enact with their blades. He could see that each one of them imagined a disc in a slightly different way, a different thickness or a different size. But in seconds they all started to form the same shape disc, same size and same position. From Kado's actual vision, Xostir overlaid the gravitational disc shape, positioning over his vision in the shape of a translucent white disc. The same thing occurred for everyone else's vision as well as their blades manipulated what their wielder could see.

"It's working!" Ruana shouted with her natural excitement.

Alright, let's move it around; make the disc larger. Kado sent a message through their neural connection to all four of the others. They positioned the disc to be parallel to the ground, raising it up about thirty feet, they made it quite large expanding past the distance they were standing apart from each other. They were developing control, becoming comfortable with sharing a small portion of each other's minds and thoughts, cooperating with their telepathic link.

Now let's try to push it into the ground. Kado issued another suggestion. They thought as one, shrinking the disc to be a bit smaller then they pushed it down into the grass by their feet. In seconds a circular patch formed at the center of them causing the ground to separate. A circular pattern sunk in between them all in moments. All five of them looked to each other with excitement and surprise.

I have an idea. Yai thought to the group and her idea appeared as a series of images to them all of the five of them standing in a line, firing an incredibly strong gravity blast through a line of trees. All issued agreement mentally then they soon stood in a line, aiming their blades towards each other, ripples began to distort the air in front of them. The gravity blast was powering up. When it reached its peak, they let the blast go. In an instant an invisible force of gravity, stronger than a dozen nuclear blasts, tore it's way through several miles of forest. The trees were struck so fiercely that they fully turned into powder like snow, drifting down through the air to the dirt floor.

"That was...insane!" Dom went from a gentle remark to an ecstatic shout. Everyone else's jaw dropped. With a renewed sense of purpose after the encouraging results they saw today, they felt more like a real team than ever before.

"Yes, that was great but let's try *not* to destroy a bunch of trees. These blades are powerful; too much damage could draw some unwanted attention to this area." Kado gestured to the shrapnel pile of wood that was once a chunk of forest.

"Yeah, yeah." Dom waved a hand dismissively.

At the bunker, Kado stood in front of the holo-projection of the Citadel tower and the surrounding Vanixx Corps buildings.

Ruana stepped up to him, "It's late. Can't sleep?"

"Whoa, 3am?" Kado looked at the time indicator on the holo-projection, "Yeah, I tried to sleep, but I can't help but feel that I'm missing something."

"Like what?"

"I don't know but it's really been bugging me."

"Well, maybe you need someone to talk it over with. Here, sit down, walk me through the whole plan." She stepped over to the couch with Kado following.

"Alright so, I've figured out that we need to fly in and hit the Citadel right away. But that building is so well guarded, we don't have any idea how insanely protected it is."

"Right. That is a challenge." Ruana nodded.

"Right, so the idea is we fly in, split up. You and I find an access port to the underground levels where they experiment in their Magnetics Division."

"Ahuh."

"Meanwhile Dom and Yai cause a distraction in the main Citadel lobby. At the same time, Troy will inflict as much damage as he can on the Citadel tower without actually toppling it."

"Right, a chaotic maneuver to cause panic."

"Yes. So, once we're down in the underground lab, I think we'll try to steal the data with Xostir, then wipe the data clean."

"Sounds like a solid plan so far." Ruana's hands were clasped playfully while listening as if she were in class.

"Alright, so my problem is then what? We just fly away? We don't have a proper exit strategy yet." Kado held his head in his hands, running his fingers through his hair with dismayed frustration.

"They will likely send a bunch of ships after us."

"Exactly. We'll be in the heart of the Vanixx Corps HQ and we'll have just rung the bell to trigger their highest emergency state ever. We'll be completely surrounded by hundreds of ships, MAWs or fighters in seconds. I don't see this being anything but a kamikaze mission."

"Kamikaze?"

"A suicide run."

"Oh." She hung her head in realization of the conundrum.

"We know that this will be dangerous. There's no escaping that. But a single attack on the Vanixx Corps Headquarters won't stop another Gravity War."

"Right! That's my point. This can't be a one-way ticket. We need a way out. We need...we need..."

"We need a miracle." She concluded with an overwhelmed chuckle.

"Yes. Yes that's it! You're a genius!" Kado jumped up, ecstatic. He leaned in, kissed her on the cheek with a peck of uncontrollable excitement then ran toward the holo-projector. She sat there a moment stunned. She didn't know what to think of what just happened. Ruana was flattered but also annoyed, yet at the same time enjoyed the kiss.

"Xostir, show me the hangar bays surrounding the Citadel tower." A new wave of energy surged through him as Ruana had just given him the epiphany he was hoping for. It was so crazy that it could actually work.

Three weeks later...

"Commander Trion, firstly, well done in the 'execution' we staged a few weeks back. You are a better actor than you thought. However, I've called you here to discuss our next steps in dealing with the Quell threat. They have been unsettlingly quiet since their attack last week on one of our hangars." François Vaux addressed the respectable Commander who had just sat down.

"Perhaps the loss of three operatives so wastefully got them to rethink their strategy." Rego added.

"Yes, well regardless, Operation: Pax Omnis is well under way, but it still has a few kinks to be ironed out." François sat in his hover chair leaning back informally with his feet on the desk. The office window displaying a gorgeous view of the endless city, it's hundreds of thousands of buildings glistening in the high sun.

"Oh? Such as?" Trion replied.

"Well, we're encountering logistical issues. Such as, how do we get three thousand MAWs distributed simultaneously to every city on the planet? How can we transport ten-thousand infantry to every city? What if our plans get discovered by another country, how do we tackle a leak?"

"Ah yes, those are all challenges that tend to complicate things."

"Yeah, and another thing-"

A massive explosion enveloped the room they were in. The deafening sound of the blast shattered the windows to Vaux's office. The desk they were sitting at began to flip through the air. Trion and Vaux were both thrown through the open window, a burning inferno engulfing everything around them. Their flailing selves were plunging through the air with the thousands of sparkling glass shards, spinning chunks of building along with shrapnel of office equipment.

Vaux's vision was only of a rapidly spinning horizon passing by; sky, ground, sky, ground. As he neared a briskly approaching rooftop, he felt a tug on his left ankle then looked to see Trion slowing their descent. In his hand was a Magna-Blade!

Rego Trion slowly lowered Vaux onto the rooftop, landing himself onto his feet. Vaux was astounded, "You carry a Magna-Blade with you everywhere you go?" He inquired over the wind resulting from their altitude on the roof of the tall skyscraper. They both looked up seeing the remnants of Vaux's office. Black searing marks framed the edge of the circular crater near the top of the building. Smoke and flames were billowing out of the opening. Chunks of building, glass and shrapnel were falling to the streets almost a thousand feet below them.

"Not always. But it is always close by." He turned back with a side grin to the Grand Admiral. Trion's blade was a 17th Edition blade, one of the more advanced blades that Nicodem had ever released during the war. The blade was unlike any other Edition. Trion held a cylindrical hilt in his hand, on either side of the cylinder's ends was a thin curved blade which formed a crescent. The shaft of the blade consisted of two long protruding extensions coming out to two sharp points that nearly touched. The blade was thin with the typical circuitry lines along with magnetic orbs embedded on both sides of the blade. It was translucent and could glow with pulsating energy whenever it wanted or whenever commanded.

His peripherals caught a shadow overhead speeding by almost avoiding detection.

That is the assailant, an agent of the Quell. Rego's blade, Zara informed him. The blade gave him the telemetry of his new mysterious opponent, flying right towards him coming down at a sharp angle. Trion timed it perfectly. The assassin came inches away, swinging his own Magna-Blade but narrowly missing as Trion effortlessly performed a front flip, dodging the attack. Rego swiped his blade at the attacker as he was upside down, commanding a gravitational push from his blade to throw the enemy over the edge of the roof. The push was incredibly powerful, causing the large man to almost cartwheel away uncontrollably as he neared the roof's edge. He finally gained control just in time to stand up to refrain from falling over the edge of the roof.

Trion landed on his feet, turning to get a proper look at this deadly foe. He was dark skinned, bald, impressively built with his overall size being enormous. It looked like he was wearing a uniform of some sort. It was bright red with a little white Q on the left side of the chest. Often Moderators never wore a uniform for an assassination or when out in public unless it was planned to give the Quell public recognition. The blade he wielded looked almost too small for him, despite him using an Edition that was one of the largest made. It was sharp on both edges and was shaped like a jagged question mark with acute angles and sharp points completing the unique shape.

That's a 5th Edition blade, but it's no match for me. Zara's female voice relayed to Rego confidently.

"Who are you?" Trion shouted.

"Your death warrant." He boasted loudly, his deep voice booming across the rooftop.

"Who sent you?" Trion continued to dig for answers that his opponent would openly verbalize. He wanted the man to verbally say who he was affiliated with since a news drone was nearing hastily from the distance trying to record a story about the explosion.

"You are about to be Moderated!" He shouted back fiercely. The two sliced at each other, blocking, dodging, parrying also using the gravitational abilities of their blades very minimally. It was obvious to Trion that this giant didn't really have the imagination to be effective with a blade. The large attacker leapt backwards flipping through the air to dodge an electrical attack from Trion's blade. He then began to aim his blade at Vaux who was equidistant to the two blade wielders. Instantly Trion leapt with inhuman speed, swinging his blade at him. The two slashed at each other as he pummeled into the large man's rigid body. The two fell off the edge of the roof before any harm could come to the Grand Admiral. They punched each other as they held each other's sword-wielding wrists, crashing towards the streets.

Trion understood Magna-Blades better than his rival, thus having the advantage. Trion lifted his feet up, planting them on the assailant's chest then pushed himself off of him with a graceful backflip, slicing upward issuing his enemy a large gash over his entire abdomen. As he made the cut, he also blasted a charged gravo-electrical wave, throwing the adversary down with lethal force to the streets below.

In seconds it was over. This was a Quell agent; a Moderator who failed; it was a rare sight to see. He landed with devastating force onto a parked hover car crushing part of it. He was now one with the car within the distorted, wrecked folds of the ruined metal frame of the vehicle.

After the sound of crumpling metal echoed off the buildings and through the streets, people in the nearby vicinity saw the aftermath, then ran off in all directions in a frenzy. Ones who looked up to see a man levitating with a Magna-Blade in hand screamed in fear. In seconds, Vaux's dark, glistening, elegant vessel flew overhead; a vessel that nearly everyone recognized as a Vanixx Corps ship. It took a moment to lower its boarding ramp as it hovered over the roof so the Grand Admiral could hitch a ride to safety in case there were any other assassins in place. As the *Traffinjo* lifted off, Rego flew along beside it as an escort, blade in hand.

The Quell had been dealt a hurtful, humiliating blow. One of their Moderators had been killed; fairly easily at that. Each moderator had a recording device on their uniform in the small Q logo offset to the left on the chest, sometimes an agent wouldn't even be aware of it.

The Vicero watched the live footage of the battle with frustration at this Vanixx Corps blade wielder. *Who was this guy; some sort of nobody that no one had even heard about? How could he have bested one of our own?* He thought to himself. He slammed his first on the desk, causing the holographic display to twitch briefly. The Vicero had left too much confidence in their agent and it made a negative impression on the Quell, having a counter-effect of the impression he was aiming for.

"Call in the clean-up crew." He spoke into his wrist communicator of his new glistening white armored suit, then stood up from the desk. He strode out of his office, his white and red cape flowing behind him. His suit was incredibly advanced with nanites materializing the helmet over his head. He had to accelerate the mobilization of their global forces. He held up his wrist communicator once more, "Kar, meet me in Chelyabinsk."

Kado sat in his room of the bunker and dwelled on how alone he felt during the time that he was disconnected from Xostir. It had been a few weeks ago when they were separated when he had felt so protected, so safe. Now that they were reconnected, their connection was stronger than ever. It was now early morning, however Kado was so exhausted from all the planning and training over the past few weeks, he wanted to go back to sleep. The rest of the group were hanging out in the main room of the bunker. He could hear laughter followed by chatting. He was glad that there was a bond forming between them. He never expected to have a group of associates working together for Nicodem's goal. Just then the laughter stopped; the bunker fell silent.

Curious, Kado headed out of his bunk into the main bunker and the group of four looked to him with various expressions of concern on their faces.

"What's wrong?" He raised a brow. He looked to see that they were watching the news again on the holo-screen.

"The Vanixx Corps and Quell just had a Magna-Blade duel in the middle of the city. A Quell Moderator was killed." Yai explained succinctly.

"Oh man," Kado stepped up to the couches, "That's escalating quickly."

"How are you feeling?" Ruana implored him.

"Oh, I seem to be getting a little better each day. Thanks for taking me to the professor."

"No problem. Are you sleeping well?"

"Not really."

"What do you mean?" Ruana's concern increased.

"Guys! Look the Vanixx Corps' Grand Admiral is addressing the city!" Troy shouted as his eyes were glued to the holo-screen. A figure of the authoritative leader sat at his desk, resolute as ever.

"Fellow Citizens of America. I just survived an assassination attempt on my life by the terrorist organization known as the Quell. They have been causing disarray and upset throughout the planet since the end of the Gravity War and they threaten our future – our very existence. It is the Vanixx Corps' mandate as protectors of peace to further our cause against them beyond just the confines of our country." They all watched on as the Grand Admiral's intensity increased, "We have begun negotiations with all other countries and will globally face this threat to peace, we will challenge these fierce terrorists and we will crush them so that they will never rise up to harm you ever again!"

Kado looked to the rest of the group as he felt forced to stand from sheer uneasiness, "Guys, we're out of time."

"Well let's go then!" Yai shouted with enthusiasm.

"Yeah!" Dom added.

"Right now?" Kado asked them.

"Sure, why not? We've spent every day now for more than three weeks practicing with our blades and we're getting really comfortable with them." Ruana added, looking to the rest of them. All of them had begun to stand.

"We've gone over the plan a few dozen times – we know what to do. Maybe we can steal enough of their research to stop them." Troy added.

"Alright," Kado summoned Xostir into his open hand, "let's go prevent a war!"

"The Quell are not to be trifled with. We are not to be viewed as a mere annoyance. We will suppress the very security the Vanixx Corps feel." The Vicero addressed a huge army of soldiers as his helpful assistant, Moderator Kar stood by his side. The soldiers were standing beside their flight-ready Cybernetic Assault Fighters – CAFs as they were more efficiently called. His voice echoed clearly through a microphone in his helmet paired with the speaker system of the entire hangar. This hangar was one of three in Chelyabinsk.

"At this very moment, somehow the Vanixx Corps are earning the support of every government in every city across the globe. Now is the time for us to organize our forces and prepare for a complete simultaneous global onslaught to their attempt at controlling the world."

The large crowd of soldiers began to cheer with great excitement. Their cheering echoed through the large underground hangar, which contained not only tens of thousands of CAFs but also dozens of Airborne Assault Carriers, absolutely huge vessels that could hold a thousand CAFs and ten thousand troopers. The underground hanger delved down eighty stories with simple catwalks connecting pathways to each level and each AAC. On each level, which were ten stories high, there were two AACs side by side. These massive flying freighters of death dealing destruction were running on the late Nicodem's maglev hover technology to propel them.

"We've all met before in a previous briefing to you all, but now that your machines are nearly ready, we wanted to announce just when the next stage of our operation will begin. We will be launching our forces collectively in exactly one month. If you know anyone willing to join our forces and fight to end the Vanixx Corps' reign of terror once and for all, please refer them to me." Adrian, the Vicero as everyone else would know him, stepped across the high catwalk as he continued the dramatic motivational speech, "You are the hand of the Quell that will finally bring true peace to our planet! Be proud in knowing that soon you will be responsible for the billions of lives saved thanks to your selflessness! You are the world's saviors!"

Another loud cheer erupted through the hangar as every soldier received his speech with pride and appreciation.

"You will be notified of the day and the hour to make your move. Until then, be ready. Dismissed."

Adrian Greeg and Ryla Kar stepped away from the handrail of the catwalk, heading to an interior office space to discuss the logistics of a worldwide launch of their forces.

"We'll need an organizing operative in each hangar in each city." Ryla quietly commented to Adrian.

"Yes, please arrange that. Only select Officers that have been with us for fifteen years or longer. We can't have someone inexperienced or someone who hasn't proven their loyalty to handle this."

"Right away, sir. Anything else?" She flirtatiously asked as they stood facing each other outside the entrance to the catwalk.

"No. That will be all." Greeg remained overtly serious, ignoring her advances. He wasn't over what happened years ago, he also wasn't about to start a relationship with her again. He also couldn't afford to be distracted, no matter how much he truly wanted such a distraction. As he strode away, keeping his posture in an authoritative fashion. He began to think that the Mitigator assigned Kar to him on purpose, perhaps knowing their history. Was she hoping Kar would distract him? He wouldn't put it past Mitigator Wren to try to set him up for failure. She was jealous, threatened by his demeanor and his potential to overtake her position of leadership. It was obvious to both of them that the Praetor had a liking towards Greeg for some mysterious reason; perhaps it was his self-sacrifice of 10 years under deep cover for the Quell's goals that made an impression on the Praetor. Others had done eight or five years undercover, but never ten. Whatever the reason, Wren was definitely not a friend to him, regardless he needed to be wary of her dangerous tactics. He would fly to Chatanga next to give an identical motivational speech to the troopers there, then on to every other city until they had everyone globally on the same page. It was just a matter of time before they would be fully ready to mobilize their forces to bring true peace.

***

Kado, Ruana, Yai, Troy and Dom soared as fast as they could towards the Vanixx Corps Headquarters in the heart of Vancouver. The clouds were like many fuchsia-tinted puffs of weightless décor strewn across the sky like confetti halted in midair. They were hardly obstacles for them as they blew right through effortlessly, leaving small disturbances in their wake. All five had reached supersonic speeds as they approached the tallest towers of the Vanixx Corps section of the city. They flew between the three tallest towers at blinding speeds, shattering the reinforced windows on several floors of these slender giants. Small shards of glass fell to the streets below. All five of them veered around, circling back towards the towers.

Ruana dove down rapidly towards an access port on the rear end of the building facing an alley, the plans showed this was the access they needed to get to the underground levels where the Magnetics Division lay untouched.

The concrete cracked below Kado's magnetically

shielded boots as he slammed to the ground right outside the main Citadel tower. He swung Xostir in the direction of the main entrance, causing the glass doors to be thrown inward, shattering with devastating force. The alarming sound of smashing tempered glass caused the receptionists inside to shriek.

Dom, Yai and Troy had circled around to fly in through that now openly accessible main entrance. Yai and Dom were halted in the tall lobby as Mechanical Assault Walkers greeted them with a violent barrage of energy blasts. The MAWs, were huge - standing nearly as tall as the three-story lobby that they were defending. Both of their arms existed to only serve as weapons, with a dozen small cannons placed in a circle at each wrist where the green death erupted from. At the center of these cannons was a larger cylinder which could fire a specialized high-powered beam of doom. Yai noted that these MAWs were outfitted with a set of jets on their back, probably in case they needed to engage in flight battle. These MAWs had as set of long stomping mechanical legs, inspired by the late ostrich, which could keep up with a standard hover car on ground.

Their rapid fire of energy blasts echoed unsettlingly through the tall foyer. Green sharp bolts sped through the air with nothing to hold them back as they pummeled their way into the ground and floor all around Dom and Yai's feet. They readied their blades to defend against the heavy onslaught. Chunks of granite floor and dirt flew into the air on each side. The two of them raised their blades in defense, blocking all of the shots from the massive murder machines.

Troy exchanged thoughts with Dom and Yai through the interconnectivity of all of their blades, which acted as the bridge for their minds. *I'm going to distract them on the upper levels to cause some more chaos for them.*

He continued to communicate neurally with them both as he was ascending rapidly, circling the outside of the building as he rose. If he saw a person in one of the hallways through the window, he would swing his blade with a mental command to throw that enemy or solider through the glass and outside the skyscraper.

Ruana, was trying to turn the seized handle for the access to the underground tunnels. The plans made it look like this was the easiest way to get to the lower basement. It was quite modern looking and appeared to be just a door. When she pulled on it or tried to turn it, nothing happened. She couldn't really do anything with this access door. Frustrated she removed her blade, Sjar from her back mount and sliced angrily at the door, breaking it to pieces, revealing underneath a partially rusted steel wheel latch from several hundred years earlier.

Kado was sent a mental image from Xostir of a MAW coming around the corner and aiming its arm blaster right at her back. He immediately flew himself as fast as he could towards her, landing between her and the MAW, shielding her just in time from a hundred electrical blasts. The impact of his Magna-Blade-shielded landing once again caused the concrete below his feet to crumble. He shouted to her over the loud blasting as he held Xostir like a shield against his shoulder, "How's it going?" The constant flow of lethal green energy was forming a curved dome over the two of them thanks to Xostir's highly focused gravitational counter.

Ruana was surprised at his sudden arrival. She was about to defend herself from the MAW but in retrospect wouldn't have been able to stop the oncoming barrage of dozens of energy beams at once.

She experienced a moment of euphoria at seeing Kado saving her life. She shook herself from her brief elated stupor, trying to keep her mind on the urgency of the mission. She turned back to the latch wheel, "Fine – just fine. Just...need...to..." Her voice strained as she was pulling the wheel shaped latch for the access door open;

it was much heavier than she had expected, or it was jammed from centuries of not being used. She took a step back and summoned help from Sjar, removing her from her back plate once more. With the creaking of rusted metal, the wheel turned and the circular access port swung open.

"Come on, lets go!" She yelled to him. As the ground shook, they both could tell there were two other mechs stomping their way toward them.

"Seriously, where are all these MAWs coming from?" He yelled, still shielding them from the onslaught of fatal fire.

"I have no idea but let's get out of here!"

"Yep!"

As they closed the door behind them, they fell down a short drop which housed a ladder. This was one of those areas that workers could climb up and out of the dark underground and back to the main streets. Ruana stopped her fall just before hitting the ground. Kado also stopped his fall inches away from her, coming face to face with her perfectly symmetrical features and her gorgeous dark blue eyes. He caught a glimmer of a pleasant expression in her eyes but shook himself from his entrancement. She too realized she was staring into his eyes. They both cleared their throats.

"We should – uh - get moving to safety." Kado stammered.

"Yes - right." She nodded as she turned over, crawling forward, leaving him space to land on his feet. They found themselves in a dark tunnel with weak lighting strung along the curved, rocky ceiling.

"Come on.", he insisted, his voice echoing through the dark tunnel, "It's this way." He walked past her then looked back to Ruana to make sure she was alright. They both had received some minor scratches and bruises; she nodded to him. They ran down the narrow tunnel, one in front of the other. Kado released the shield over the latch and in the distance, they could hear the mechs successfully blasting through the access port and firing down the shaft. They both briefly took a glance back as they ran to see green energy blasts crashing into the tunnel. Small rocks and chunks of dirt speckled down on their heads from the ceiling as they sprinted down the slow decline of the tunneled cavern. The distant firing continued as they began to curve through a veering tube. The stringed lights in the ceiling of the tunnel began to flicker.

"Keep going!" Kado hollered as the shaking increased intensely. Moments later the quaking became highly acute, causing the ceiling to fail, displacing large chunks, collapsing on top of them.

***

"Get me back-up!" Vaux shouted to his collar communicator. His office windows had been shattered. The winds were powerful at the hundred and ninety-ninth floor, gusting everything loose around. Some of the archaic processes being Grand Admiral still required actual paperwork, and those confidential papers flew out of the office and down towards the streets below. All of this greatly vexed him. Just then he noticed someone flying by with a blade and he immediately went to his bottom drawer in his desk, pulling out a small, yet powerful handgun. He stood up to the edge of the shattered window, feeling the stiff breeze push against him. He held out the gun as he saw the blade wielder flying around a nearby Vanixx Corps tower causing more damage at about the 50th floor. He looked down at the wielder as he was relatively stationary. He took aim. He fired. Purple blasts ripped out of the metallic gun, zooming their way toward the blade wielder wreaking havoc on his forces. He saw a few blasts get deflected by the blade handler. He persisted in firing, trying to hit the annoyingly agile target. Finally, he did it! One purple energy bolt vanished into the blade wielder's body.

***

Troy was swinging at the Citadel tower as he flew around the circular shape of it. The windows on most of the tower were completely shattered and he was structurally weakening the tower as much as he could. He put a few large dents and gashes in the tower as he spun his way around it. Next he flew over to an adjacent tower with the same procedure; smashing the side of the tower, weakening its structure, breaking windows where he could, and throwing enemies out. After a few moments of causing destruction on this second tower, he saw a purple energy bolt hit the building just beside his head, narrowly missing him. Startled he spun around seeing a string of purple energy bolts flying toward him with surprising accuracy. His blade boosted his adrenaline, assisting his mind to process everything faster. Time began to slow down just a little bit for him, and the bolts of purple energy were ever so slightly slower as they tried to lethally maim him. He swung his blade with unexpected ease and speed, deflecting one energy bolt, then another, and another. But the adrenaline could only be amplified for so long, and soon he could no longer deflect each blast. One energy bolt made it past his defenses and pierced its violet tip through his abdomen, making itself perfectly at home, compromising his internal organs.

Troy shouted in agony as he grasped at his midriff from the intense stabbing pain. More bolts of energy were enroute without relenting, so he made way for an escape while he could still think. Most of the thinking was done by his blade at this point, working hard to preserve his life and remove them from the situation. The blade pulled them through the building he was just beside, causing any obstacles in the way to be eradicated; glass, walls, support beams, any central concrete structure of the tower. They had just forced their way through the center of the tower with blinding speed and flew down towards the rooftop of another building nearby, yet far from danger.

Vaux looked as the young man had vanished into the building and out through the other side a fair distance away. *How could he survive that?* He thought to himself. Just then he noticed a shifting shadow on the building they landed on in the distance. The shadow was of the towering building the blade wielder had just blasted through. François' vision trailed back to the gaping hole of the adjacent tower that he was firing towards. The hole was large enough to greatly weaken its structural integrity. He noticed some odd movement on the building, and he began to process the fact that the top half of the building was beginning to change its position – it was angling. It was tipping! It was tipping towards...him!

The two adjacent towers were fairly close to each other. The main Citadel tower that held his office was the tallest of the Vanixx Corps sector, but this other building was only a little bit shorter – and now it was about to smash itself into the main Citadel!

François froze for just a moment with disbelief. *How could this be happening? I'm leader of the biggest Military force on the planet!*

He began to realize the greater half of the building was gaining speed as it toppled towards him. He cursed as he ran from the office, heading immediately to his personal craft's launch pad on the same floor.

"Get my ship ready to go now!" He shouted into his communicator as he sprinted down the hall. As he was near to the launch pad entrance door, the entire building shook with a jarring hit. The sound of metal creaking and concrete cracking was deafening at high decibels. The floor shifted slightly to the right underneath his feet causing him to stumble and take a moment to regain his footing. The other building struck with full force. Vaux could hear a continuous scraping occurring on the one side of the exterior as he ran out to the launch pad where the *Traffinjo* was. He turned to look at the neighboring skyscraper as he stood on the boarding ramp to his ship. In seconds, he could see the other towering mass emerge into view from behind the Citadel with shards of metal, glass and chunks of concrete flying in every direction. The tower had smashed into his building, skidded off the side of its round edge and now was careening towards the city streets below, much debris closely in tow.

***

Yai and Dom were busy fighting off the two MAWs. They both had managed to use the powerful graviton blasts of their blades to force one of them back with enough strength to throw the MAW through the lobby wall. Seconds later, they heard a loud crashing above them as the room shook violently. Yai was standing on top of the last mech that was left, stabbing her blade into the shoulder of the machine. Dom turned around, walking just outside the entrance of the lobby to see one building leaning against another.

"Yai! You gotta see this!" He shouted to her. She charged her blade, causing it rip the MAW apart from inside. It fell to a hundred pieces across the entire lobby, exposing the pilot inside who fell among the twisted wreckage, yet was trapped among it. She hopped off as it fell to the floor, then ran up beside him to see the nearby skyscraper leaning against the building they were just in.

"Whoa! What happened?" She asked, astounded.

"I think Troy was a little too vigilant with his distractions."

"Well, where is he?"

"No idea. I can't see him flying around anywhere."

Just then they could hear a continuous scraping of metal reverberating through the air. Small chunks of concrete and metal frame were falling from the sky. The tip of the building was partially impacted into the Citadel tower, the sheer weight of the structure was causing it to slide off the rounded edge of the Citadel; it was going to hit ground with a massive number of casualties.

Both Yai and Dom mentally consulted their blades with a way to stop the 60-story chunk of building from killing so many. Simultaneously they were presented with an image of them using the antigravity in their blades in a hyper focused manner to slow its fall then to gradually slow its descent to gently touch down on the ground.

This is the only way. Both blades sent the neural statement to them both. Almost in unison they flew with incredible speed, positioning themselves in the shadow of the huge, daunting edifice, crashing towards them, ready to plow through any obstacle. Yai was stationed near the tip of the careening tower while Dom positioned himself closer towards the shredded base. They held up their sections of the crashing metal column as they levitated at about fifty feet in the air, ready to 'catch' the enormous column of death.

The building made contact with their antigravity fields and began to slow its descent ineffectively. Dom and Yai rapidly approached the ground as they strived to slow the structures fall and they got closer and closer to the street.

Forty feet.

Thirty feet.

Twenty.

Ten.

Finally, the buildings descent reached a halt with both Dom and Yai struggling to control the positioning of not only themselves, but the now-horizontal structure hovering above them. It pitched and yawed slightly as they barely managed to ease it down to the ground. They positioned themselves to either side of the tower as they gently laid it to rest on the street.

Thousands of passersby and innocent civilians watched as Dom and Yai saved the lives that they were responsible for. Hundreds of hover cars were backed up in traffic as they sat and stared at the incredible event they just witnessed. Thousands cheered, including Vanixx Corps Officers, not knowing that the group were the cause of the incident. They looked around as three more MAWs appeared from the lobby of the Citadel, firing without concern of the many innocent all around. Green electrical bolts blasted outward at many angles, primarily in the direction of Dom and Yai. Yai hovered herself with a backflip, dodging fire, landing on top of the now stationary structure lying on its side beside Dom, blocking the fire raging towards them. They swung their blades to adjust their antigrav shielding to account for the various angles and areas that the bolts were about to strike.

"We need to find Troy and get some cover!" Yai shouted to Dom over the blaring, non-stop electrical blasts.

"Right!" He rejoined as they lifted off with immense speed upwards hundreds of feet into the air.

Dom summoned his blade to detect Troy and in seconds it homed in on his blade, "This way!" He yelled to Yai. They dashed towards the rooftop Troy was lying on. He had a large black burn mark on his chest and was conscious but looked in rough shape. Dom and Yai landed near him.

"What's going on?" Dom appealed.

"What happened?" Yai added immediately after.

"I'll be fine. My blade has been doing some sort of healing thing on me." He explained.

"No – why did you level a building? That wasn't part of the plan!" she retorted.

***

Kado awoke, covered by rubble and dirt. He used Xostir to lift the rocks and boulders off of him, kept them hovering and saw Ruana right in front of him unconscious, blade in hand and covered in dirt. He took a moment to detect her vital signs with Xostir's abilities and could immediately see she wasn't breathing. He grabbed her and flew her down the tunnel. As he flew towards caved in portions of the tunnel, he simply commanded the rocks and rubble to rise and move out of the way. They quickly darted ahead a couple hundred feet where the tunnel widened up a bit and hadn't caved in at all. He gently laid her down and knelt beside her, he could detect her breathing was stopped, as was her heart.

"What can we do, Xostir?" He asked his companion.

We can restart her heart with targeted electrical jolts.

"Let's do it." He ordered as he held out Xostir over her body. He let go and Xostir self-levitated over her. In seconds Xostir charged just the right amount of electrical current to zap her chest in the two appropriate spots simultaneously, one on her left side on her ribs and the other near her sternum. As he shocked her, her chest rose for a moment and then she went limp. The blue electricity lit up the dark tunnel each time. He repeated this process five more times.

Why would her heart stop? Kado thought to himself.

It's possible that she suffocated or that the sheer force of the rocks managed to hit her in just the right way to stop the heart. Her brain functions are currently still active, but we need to resuscitate her soon. Xostir commented. For a moment Kado forgot his thoughts could be heard. He also realized that Xostir would detect Kado's recently discovered feelings for her. He was so afraid to lose her, especially if it meant that he could never tell her how he felt. He wasn't sure how he felt for her exactly, but he did feel something.

Xostir defibrillated her again.

Once more.

We need breath to enter her lungs to help this process. Xostir suggested.

"Alright." He leaned over, nervous about giving mouth-to-mouth. It wasn't really how he imagined the first time his lips should touch hers, but he needed to save her. He closed her nostrils with one hand, and gently held her mouth open with the other and placed his lips over hers, sealing the gaps on all sides. He pushed his diaphragm to send a healthy dose of air into her lungs.

You may need to issue chest compressions. Xostir suggested. He sent a brief thought of how chest compressions are properly done, into Kado's mind and he mimicked the action exactly, counting to ten each time. He went in to continue the mouth-to-mouth but suddenly she took a breath in.

Her eyes opened to meet his. She took a moment to recover, taking in deep breaths while Kado sat back leaning against the rocky wall of the tunnel. He held his hands against his face, relieved but also emotionally distraught from almost having lost her.

***

"Yeah man, you could've killed a lot of people." Dom backed Yai up as they scolded Troy.

"I didn't mean to. I was near the tower and was shot so I just escaped as fast as I could!" Troy seemed genuine to Dom but Yai wasn't convinced, "Well when we're safe back at the bunker, we'll discuss this further. Let's see where Ruana and Kado are at." She turned to face the Citadel tower and sent out her thoughts through her blade to Kado and Ruana, *How are you guys doing down there?*

"What's that?" Ruana beckoned Kado, both of them were detecting Yai's neural messaging.

"That's Yai sending us a message through our blades' connection." He explained, sending a thought message back to Yai, Dom and Troy, *We got buried by rubble, but we're nearly to the underground lab.*

"Oh boy." Yai uttered, wiping her sweat beaded face. She turned back to the two men, "How's the injury, Troy?"

"It's doing a lot better but not a hundred percent yet."

"Dom, you all good?"

"Yeah, I'm ready to keep them distracted however long we need to."

"Alright." She nodded, satisfied. Just then they all heard the sound of ships engines humming getting louder as they approached from the distance. Seconds later, five large Heavy Assault Freighters veered out from behind a wall of tall skyscrapers in the distance, followed by about twenty smaller fighters, all barreling towards the three of them at frightening speeds.

"What the vealek is that?" Troy asked the rest.

"Those have to be at least five hundred feet long!" Dom commented in awe.

"Boys", Yai addressed them all, "get ready for a real fight this time."

"What have we here?" Ruana playfully remarked as she lifted a small metallic sphere from a desk in the underground lab. She had partially recovered from nearly dying earlier and they took a bit of a slower pace as they made it to the underground laboratory that Nicodem used to work in.

That is a gravity bomb in your hand. Sjar explained. Kado turned around as Xostir telepathically told him the same thing, "Oh you might want to put that down...gently."

"Right, yes. Okay then." She conferred uncomfortably, shocked by the devastating device that could fit in the palm of her hand.

"I think we've found the mother lode." Kado addressed her with a slightly raised voice from across the sizeable, obviously well-funded lab. Ruana was standing closest to the hole in the wall that they blasted through to enter the laboratory. She looked back to the series of underground tunnels hearing rumbling in the distance. She stepped over the three scientists that they incapacitated as soon as they broke into the lab. These laboratories weren't very heavily guarded, but perhaps they never expected someone to break-in through ancient abandoned tunnels that nobody knew about. She stepped up beside him to a viewing window that showed hundreds of shelves filled with various types of experimental weapons and at the end of the room was a hallway to a large sphere.

I've deactivated the alarm. Xostir notified them.

"How did you do that?" Kado was impressed yet again at the ingenuity of his companion blade.

Oh well, I used to live here. Nicodem gave me all the access codes necessary to access this base. I'm surprised the codes still work. Xostir explained carefully, starting to become suspicious of the ease of accessing the lab undetected.

There is some sort of gravity manipulation device located within that large orb shaped structure. Xostir relayed to both Kado and Ruana.

"This place is a proving ground for creating even more devastating weapons than ever before." Kado commented with sudden awareness of the self-destructive world they were living in.

None of this data is in my database. They've been very busy. Xostir added.

"We have to destroy this place." Kado resolved.

"Will a gravity bomb work?" She asked. Kado perked an eyebrow, impressed and intrigued, "Yes, yes it would."

They began to lay a couple gravity bombs in place throughout the experimental weapons room and rigged them to be set off with a timer. Xostir explained to them how to program them all to operate and to have a timed delay for exploding.

"Won't this number of explosives create a huge crater?" Ruana inquired of Kado. Not being fully sure, he telepathically asked Xostir for more specifics. Xostir related some statistical information to help clear their minds of any worry, *The structural integrity of this lab was built and fortified specifically to handle any potential accidental damage done by the gravity weapons, this was especially important when the gravity bomb was made. They didn't want to level the city in case a mistake happened, so Nicodem along with his associates at the time designed this room to be the strongest possible structure he could possibly imagine at the time. You should be able to lay five gravity bombs here to destroy most of this structure or at least the weapons. Above ground they will only feel a brief tremor.*

They continued to lay four gravity bombs in each corner of the experimental weapons room and Kado approached the door at the end of the room. This door led to a long hallway that opened up into a large room containing what appeared to be a concrete sphere. The sphere was a bit taller than the average human from top to bottom and was positioned at the center of a very large spherical room. Kado stepped onto the solitary path that was elevated, extending out cantilevered to the very center of the room. He looked down to the side, past the path he was walking on and saw the wall of the lower hemisphere disappear into complete darkness. An eerie feeling came over him as he was walking into the heart of the mysterious death machine. It felt like he was stepping right into a massive manmade cave and felt an element of prescience, even though the peculiar device wasn't active. Xostir didn't have any information on what this huge sphere was yet. His steps echoed loudly through the large, hollow, spherical room. It felt like the walls of the sphere were shrinking in around him. Perhaps it was just his imagination, he thought. He reminded himself that he just needed to place the bomb inside this sphere and get out of there. He adhered the gravity bomb to the small sphere positioned at then swiftly made his way out of the large sphere-shaped room.

Xostir had levitated up to Kado's side, he turned to look at his vertical hovering friend, "Where were you?"

I was collecting all of the data the Vanixx Corps had on all of Nicodem's experiments and all of the plans for the weapons they have constructed for the past several decades.

"Oh good, that might be useful."

I was planning to next attempt to wipe their data clean.

"Wha-what does that mean?" Kado raised a brow, a little confused at the concept he was hearing.

I am planning to permanently destroy all the data they have ever stored on the gravitational experiments and inventions in this lab. The Vanixx Corps will not be able to create more gravity weapons ever again.

"Great work! Awesome idea!" Kado bellowed excitedly.

"Well done, Xostir!" Ruana added, having heard the message projected to Sjar as well.

"Alright, let's wipe that data, set the timer on the explosives and get out of here." Kado concluded. He hoped that this would put enough of a dent in their experiments to perhaps end the possibility of another Gravity War.

Xostir approached a data screen and began to interface with it. Kado saw into Xostir's mind as he sped through the data files to see what was necessary to take and wipe. Xostir was flying through all the data incredibly quickly, brushing past many secret projects that even many of the V.C. Officers didn't know about. Suddenly Xostir encountered a wall. Xostir tried to disconnect but the system wouldn't let him.

I'm stuck.

"What do you mean stuck? Can't we just disconnect?"

There are failsafe's in place in case anyone tries to hack the database. It's preventing me from accessing any more data but it's also preventing me from disconnecting.

"Oh great."

I'm going to try a hard reset on the connection. I'd advise that we temporarily sever our neural link to each other just in case something goes wrong.

"Are you sure about this, Xostir?" Kado had edging

concern growing in his voice.

It's either this or we're stuck connected to this laboratory system and its starting to corrupt some of my higher functions – we don't have much time.

"Alright, let's disconnect our link and reboot. Let me know what to do when you boot back up." Kado stepped back as the feed from Xostir went silent. In seconds Xostir's glowing purple gem went dark and the blade violently clanked on the floor, the metal impact echoing throughout the lab.

Ruana and Kado just stood and stared at the dead, motionless blade for what seemed like an eternity. Kado, all the while, was feeling a deep sense of loneliness that he didn't know he would feel. He had no idea of the void that Xostir left when their minds weren't linked. He no longer had a constant companion in his mind, and it was unsettling, like the sudden removal of a security blanket. Frightening thoughts came to Kado's mind, *What if he doesn't boot back up again? What if there's no more Xostir? What will we do?*

Just then a welcome violet glow filled the darkened room, allowing Kado and Ruana to breathe a sigh of relief. Kado realized he had been holding his breath unintentionally.

Xostir rose from the ground and in seconds Kado's

mind was once again linked with Xostir.

It's good to be back.

"It's good to have you back." Kado returned the sentiment, "Do you feel any... different?

No. The failsafe's in place are incredibly advanced and effective, however Nicodem programmed in several different redundancies to protect from any data loss due to aggressive viruses.

"Viruses?" Ruana cocked her head to the side.

Yes, the system flooded my drives with a few dozen viruses intended to corrupt my entire system right down to the qubits. Fortunately, I have been outfitted with protective safeguards to defend against such an attack.

"Well that's some good news, my friend. Glad you're alright. Let's get outta here before anything else goes wrong."

Kado used Xostir to carry two of the unconscious scientists while Ruana used Sjar to carry the other one to fly out via the tunnel they entered through. They took a slightly different route back to the ground level by breaking through solid dirt, ground and rock to break through to the streets above. They wanted to reappear as far from the MAWs as possible. They left the unconscious scientists on the road as they took off to gain altitude. As they reached several hundred feet, they were greeted by many massive Military vessels baring down on them ready for a grossly outnumbered fight.

"Things escalated quickly out here!" Ruana exclaimed to Kado with surprise, fear and a touch of humor.

"Guys, we have a situation!" Yai shouted as she, Dom and Troy bolted past them towards the giant fleet.

"No kidding! What did you guys do?" Kado shouted.

"We'll explain later!" Dom hollered in return. All five of them began to enter a skirmish with the fleet, swinging, dodging, blocking, swiping. Kado dipped under a fighter and inserted the sharpest tip of his blade into the ship's fuselage, tearing through the belly of the ship like it was aluminum foil. He charged a graviton blast and as he neared the rear of the ship at its engine bay and fired it, blowing the fighter into a hundred pieces, its pilot resorting to their parachute as they fell to the streets. Ruana arced over another fighter and with a hyper focused electromagnetic charge, an incredible amount of force in a very thin line across the width of the small ship, she cut it clean in half. The ships two remaining pieces spun and flipped as they torpedoed into nearby buildings.

Kado saw the giant war freighters and the support fighters surrounding them. This was what he was worried about. He was not about to let this become a kamikaze run. They needed to get out of this alive.

"Xostir buddy, we're going to need that miracle we talked about."

On it.

Xostir, sent a command to interface with two of the closest assault freighters causing them to fire ballistic missiles, along with their energy blasts at one another.

"Just like we planned." Kado calmly resolved to himself.

***

"What in the blazes is happening, Captain!" The Commander of one of the V.C. assault vessels shouted.

"We can't control the ship anymore, sir!" A frightened young Officer weakly hollered back.

"Well get it under control, now!" His voice was gravely from screaming.

***

Two humongous assault frigates began to fire their full company of missiles and as much energy blasts at each other as possible, while positioning themselves for collision, thanks to Xostir.

***

"Sir, we're on a collision course with the other frigate!" Another Officer bawled terrified.

The Commander stood calmly on his bridge as he watched the chaos unfold from the main navigational windows. He stared on as the fellow frigate turning towards their vessel, threw jade energy blasts and smoke-trailed missiles towards them. The entire ship shook and creaked from the barrage of weapons fire. He watched on as the view filled up, no longer with sky, but with the careening metal hull of the other frigate. In seconds the bridge became aglow with a paroxysm of pandemonium.

***

"What happened?" Dom hollered to them all, seeing the two ships fly straight on into each other, merging into a flaming mass of falling wreckage.

"That was Xostir. He's able to temporarily control their ships!"

Troy and Dom quickly flew along both sides of the closest large freighter, their surging adrenaline helping them to be able to dodge the emerald green electrical bolts of lethal energy from the huge cannons on the top and bottom of the ships. Each of them dug their blades into the flat sides of the body of the giant vessel, tearing through the thick hull with incredible ease. Shards of metal flew off as their blades shredded the hull just like aluminum foil, the tearing metal screeching loudly.

Yai focused her attacks on the other smaller fighters who were zipping and rolling with evasive tactical expertise. She destroyed several smaller ships with just a simple swing and shielded herself from other fighters flying by, firing their jade green blasters. Yai spun and dove, slicing and dicing, blasting and smashing.

Kado threw himself at the next huge freighter, holding Xostir like a shield, energy bolts deflecting off of his heavy antigravity shield. As he plummeted near the bow of the ship, he swung a charged Xostir and drove the blade deep into the hull, causing the nose of the vessel to ripple and shudder. He mentally commanded Xostir to release the charged blast, sending a thick crack through the center of the humongous craft. The two sides drifted apart from each other, beginning to crash towards the streets.

"Can someone get that?" Kado shouted to the group through the neural connection they were sharing.

"I got it!" Dom told the group as he dove down

towards the streets, using his blade to catch the large falling chunks of broken ship. He zoomed past cars as he was just a few feet from the ground, catching nearly every chunk of ship, pulling the chunks behind him in tow. He worked with Cnidus to gently place the large pieces of shrapnel to the ground as Dom raced along the streets. Each hover car he blew by was flipped over from the velocity of his attempt to save the innocent.

Yai, Troy, Ruana and Kado lined up as they faced another freighter. This time they aimed their blades at the gargantuan vessel and charged a collected blast of graviton waves. In just seconds the ship angled upwards uncontrollably as if it was being picked up by an invisible giant and thrown backwards.

Yai and Troy veered off to the left while Ruana and Kado panned to the right. Dom continued to catch the falling pieces of the ships, while Kado, Ruana, Troy and Yai sliced through the remaining small fighters.

"What, now?" Troy yelled out loud. Yai looked over to him after destroying a couple more fighters, exasperated, "What are you talking about?"

"Oh sorry, my blade just named herself – it's Cymari!"

"Kai-mah-ree?", she added back questioningly, sounding out the syllables.

"Yeah! Cymari – oh look out!" He shouted as a charging fighter fired its energy cannons at them, both of them blocking the energy, deflecting it off the edges of their blades.

"It picked a lux of a time to name itself!" Yai hollered with frustration. They resumed swinging madly, throwing, crushing and dicing the dozens of support fighters storming them.

***

Vaux watched from the *Traffinjo* as his small fleet providing back-up was getting easily annihilated by those five little miscreants. He saw the destruction that they were causing and seethed with apoplexy as he watched on helplessly. He wasn't prepared to handle an attack like this. That's when he realized, he needed his back-up to consist of other Magna-Blade wielders. He had one more ace up his sleeve.

"Send in the twins." He ordered.

Shortly after the five of them finished destroying the fleet, they heard a rumbling through the air that shook the skyscrapers all around them. The group of five, remained levitating in place but turned to look behind to see where this noise was coming from.

Seven more humongous assault freighters accompanied by about fifty support fighters emerged from behind the wall of skyscrapers and with them, two very small flying figures.

"What in the blazes is that?" Troy shouted his question to the group over the noise of the distant engines.

"Uh...that's a big problem!" Kado hollered back.

"What are those?" Ruana asked, pointing and referring to the two small figures which were rapidly charging towards them.

Those are two Magna-Blade wielders. The Vanixx Corps database refers to these agents as 'The Twins'. Xostir relayed the detailed information telepathically to Kado and through the other four's blades in an instant, *They are known to be a ruthless pair of incredibly skilled, lethal blade wielders. The two are Heath and Luna, a brother and sister who underwent intense training to become the best possible sword fighters. They have been trained in the seven main primary techniques of swordplay by a specialized program setup in the Vanixx Corps. Use extreme caution with heavy defense strategy when in combat with them.*

"We're in over our heads, guys!" Dom shouted to the

team.

"Should we run?" Ruana looked to Kado.

"No time, we could never outrun them, but I have an idea." Kado answered her with confidence. He began to send his strategic plan telepathically through Xostir to the four of them. *Dom and Troy, go left. Yai and Ruana, go right. I'll take them head on, but I'll need you all to strike them from behind, then create a cyclone around us and throw us to the ground.* He continued to relay the instructions in great detail with visual representations to their mind.

***

"Sir, should we move the fleet to strike?" An Ensign implored their superior Officer. They were on the bridge of the lead assault ship.

"No. Let the twins do their job. Don't distract them or risk hitting them. We'll have the Grand Admiral to answer to if we did that." The Commander responded, perturbed at their seemingly insolent question. The fleet remained stationary to watch the mid-air fight ensue hundreds of feet above the ground.

***

The five of them worked as one as they sped towards the twins, blades drawn. As they got close, Dom and Troy veered to the left while Yai and Ruana jutted to the right. Kado swung a charged photonic wave which they seemed to have anticipated and blocked with an antiproton counter. It threw Kado backwards somersaulting through the air, narrowly able to dodge and block their swift strikes as they relentlessly began swinging at his flailing body.

Let's form that cyclone, they're giving him trouble! Ruana shot a thought out to the team. All gave affirmative responses in agreement and they began to fly in circles reaching supersonic speeds around Kado and the twins.

Kado straightened himself out and held out Xostir to block the next strike from Luna, while using his right gloved hand to halt Heath in his tracks, freezing him in midair.

Luna continued to swing and slice with incredible force, driven by her 16th Edition blade. Kado countered each attack, unable to continue his hold on Heath, he began to back himself up, blocking advances from both of the twins. Adrenaline raged through Kado's veins. Time moved slowly, allowing him to anticipate the directional assaults, and the various gravitational and electromagnetic charges that they employed on him. Their lethal three-way dance of death was so lightning quick it would appear as a hurried blur to any passerby.

Ruana, Troy, Dom and Yai were speeding up with their cyclical path surrounding Kado, Heath and Luna; beginning to form a powerful cyclone as intended.

Luna is using a 16th Edition blade, one of the more advanced blades made. Her brother Heath has an 18th Edition blade, which is even more advanced. Sjar explained to the group through their connection, pulling data from Nicodem's database. *Each are a dangerous challenge for Xostir since they nearly match him in his processing speed and capabilities. Two against one make Kado and Xostir seriously outnumbered.*

The cyclone is forming! Cnidus exclaimed excitedly to the group. A spinning tornado began to form above and below them, a tapered twister drove down into the ground below them, reaching all the way up to the clouds above.

The twins stopped for a moment, realizing that they were within the violent cyclone. They looked up and around, realizing that they had been distracted and drawn into a trap, Kado took the opportunity to strike. He unleashed a targeted EMP at them both. Blue electricity enveloped both of the twins' blades but took no effect. Luna's blade had elegant curves and crisp edges and was able to counteract against EMPs. Her swords curvy circuitry lines were unlike any other blade made

Heath's blade had a cylindrical cannon that ran parallel to the spine of the sword. There were circuitry lines lacing the blade. The cannon was nearly half as long as the blade itself, having the ability to be programmed in what kind of weapon to fire. It could shoot electromagnetic spheres of agony or be neurally commanded to fire an unstoppable gravity beam.

"Nice try." Heath scoffed. He rested his blade's cannon on his left hand, aiming it straight at Kado and fired! A ball of blue electrum with spikes of electricity shot out in all directions as it rushed towards Kado's head. He rapidly raised Xostir in front of his face as an effective shield, blocking the attack, causing the blue electricity to scatter and jitter in all directions.

Luna used all the gravitational force that she could to beam past Kado, her blade positioned horizontally to slice him asunder. Kado, his adrenaline pumping, had the help of Xostir to dodge, block and parry at blinding speeds. He swung the blade to block just in time to reject her attempted hemisection. Had he been just a half second too late, his life would be over. As Luna's blade bounced off of Xostir, she spun with her momentum, swung her blade around, and powered up a swing that aimed for his neck.

Kado moved with immeasurable speeds thanks to Xostir, blocking every strike and stroke she dealt him. In just a couple seconds, Heath was on his opposite side, dealing deadly blows at Kado's back. With nearly perfect precision, he dodged, parried, countered and struck with all of his speed and might.

These two really know their way around their blades! Kado thought to Xostir.

I have an idea. Xostir replied.

Kado continued to block and defend against the onslaught from the twins, while Xostir began to charge a boson helix blast. After a few more seconds of dueling, he repositioned himself so that Luna and Heath were side by side. Kado swung in a wide vertical circle to lock blades with both of them. He activated a gravity lock on Luna and Heath's blades. The three blades were connected near the tips, locked in place, unable to break free. Then he released the boson helix attack. A purple horizontal wave erupted from Xostir, his gem glowing a brilliant, almost blinding violet.

Luna and Heath were thrown backwards, losing their grip on their blades. Their airborne flailing began to slow until they eventually froze in midair, completely unable to move. This was the effect of the boson helix.

Now! Kado sent his thoughts to the team. The cyclone the four teammates created was at full power and they were able to control its behavior. All four of them seemingly disappeared, then their blurs could be seen blasting downwards towards the city streets. The synthetic tornado began to change shape, forming a cone which threw Luna and Heath down with staggering force.

As the cyclone faded, Kado looked down towards the crater that formed from the incredibly powerful twister, seeing the twins lying there at the bottom of the crater. Ruana, Yai, Dom and Troy rose up beside him on either side.

***

"What do you mean 'a disturbance'?" The Praetor pressed Mitigator Wren over the holographic video feed.

"There is unrest in Vancouver as a small band of terrorists are striking the Vanixx Corps' headquarters." She replied with succinct Military professionalism.

"Well good. Less for us to worry about. The less resources the V.C. have, the better. But out of curiosity, do we know them? The Xyl? The Rogue?"

"Neither, sir. It's a small group of five Magna-Blade wielders."

"Oh really? Interesting." He was intrigued, his helmet concealing any level of emotion that his voice embodied, "If they can successfully strike at the headquarters of the V.C. they could potentially cause us issues as well. Find out who they are and what their goals are. Send a couple of our closest cloaked scout ships. I want a better look at them."

"Yes, sir. Right away." She nodded then turned from the holo-viewer.

He disconnected his video feed with her, rotating around in his hover chair to look out his large office window to the empty wilderness. It always gave him a sense of peace to look upon the forest and mountains; no people, no technology, no war. He felt it was a foreshadowing of the time to come.

He paid his price for his nation, but it wasn't enough. The sacrifice they forced him to make made no difference in the war. He was just their lab rat, held against his will, never allowed to use his newfound abilities in the war effort. Always adhered to his prison of the testing facilities. There were the empty promises that he would be able to achieve great things with the results of this project. But before the tests were complete, they just abandoned it like it all never mattered. The experiments they ran on him left him shattered, broken mentally, shredded emotionally. It took him decades to recover to the point he was at now. That scientist leading it all kept apologizing as if he couldn't stop the tests and the experiment sessions. Nicodem. A great weight was lifted when he got word back that their operative in the field successfully ended that lead scientist's life, when Nicodem was shot down.

He was finally going to return the world back to a simpler, safer time; when there were no tachyon manipulations, gravity bombs, no more Magna-Blades or atomic bombs. They were nearly ready, but the waiting was agonizing.

***

"Whoa, that worked better than I expected!" Ruana exclaimed excitedly to the group, referring to the successful defeat of the twin Magna-Blade wielders.

"Where are their blades?" Yai asked. Everyone looked around the nearby buildings. They used their connection to their blades to scan and detect the blades signatures and they homed in on their location.

"One's over here on top of this skyscraper." Dom pointed to the left.

"The other one is in the streets a few hundred feet

that way." Troy looked ahead.

"Guys, we have another problem." Kado observed as he pointed at the huge fleet now surrounding them. They started to fire.

"Ok let's get those blades, and fast!" Yai shouted. A barrage of powerful emerald energy blasts flew at them. As it horizontally rained emerald green, Dom and Troy each darted off to obtain the blades, while Yai, Kado and Ruana charged the fleet. They dodged and blocked the electrical bolts speeding towards them.

Alright everyone, let's do this just like before! Kado relayed his thoughts to the team.

All three of them swung their blades with confidence and ferocity as they made contact with the first three huge assault freighters. Yai was at the left ship, Ruana took the one on the right and Kado went for the freighter in the center. Shards of ship, twisted alloy and shrapnel flew into the air.

Dom and Troy were side by side, zipping along to obtain the twins' blades when a large bolt of green energy made its way mercilessly through Dom's abdomen. Troy could hear Dom grunt as he went limp and began to plummet to the earth.

"Dom!" Troy dove to catch him before he would strike the nearby roofs below.

***

Yai finished slicing her blade through a support fighters' wing when she turned to see Kado and Ruana successfully taking down one of the large assault freighters. Just then, she felt searing pain in her back shortly followed by a lack of feeling in her legs. She looked down to see her armor smoking from within. She was hit and it wasn't good. She suddenly felt faint then passed out.

Ruana looked over to Yai just in time to see her drop her blade, Ptalojn, falling headfirst towards the city streets.

Yai's been hit! Ruana telepathically alerted the team as she bolted to catch her. Ptalojn repositioned themself to try and stop Yai's drop, allowing Yai to lay atop the wide edge of Ptalojn, but was not having much success. In just a few seconds, Ruana was there to catch her mere feet from the ground.

Dom's hit too! Troy announced as he flew back towards Ruana, Kado and an unconscious Yai. He had Dom resting over his shoulder.

"We need to get out of here!" Kado shouted, while simultaneously sending his thoughts to the team.

"Lets's book it to the bunker!" He added.

They all teleported a few hundred feet away from the battle lines, then took off in unison, blasting away from the ships, only causing minor damage to a few of the largest vessels of the fleet. The seven huge ships all panned around slowly as one, firing their energy cannons at them, missing every shot. As the blades focused on readjustments and avoiding attacks from behind, they didn't expect to deal with the twins collecting their blades and to join in the chase.

One of the green energy bolts which had strayed began to change its trajectory and to speed towards Ruana's head. Kado could detect that the twins were back on their tails. Ruana rapidly ducked as the emerald beam of death narrowly passed by her.

They sped past the hundreds of skyscrapers, zipping around buildings back and forth, staying below the skylines that formed the heart of the city with Vanixx Corps support fighters trailing closely behind firing spears of energy.

They were near to the perimeter of the city when Ruana spoke up, "Guys, what's that?" Her mind was relaying a brief snippet of her focused view to the team as they flew side by side. They all looked ahead and saw the outline of a ship, but it was unlike anything they had seen before. It was as if the ship was translucent but also holographic.

"Xostir, what are we seeing?" Kado begged of his companion. Xostir broadcast his explanation to them all, *You are seeing a representation of what we, your blades are detecting in the distance. There is a ship ahead, but it is cloaked. We are detecting the gravitational disturbances the ship is emitting and displaying it to your visual cortex.*

"Look there's one more!" Troy shouted to the group as another ship came into scanning range. Both were relatively small. They exchanged glances with each other briefly, while Troy turned to get a better look behind them. The Vanixx Corps support fighters were very close, firing at them profusely with the assault freighters not far behind.

"Are those V.C. ships?" Kado asked the group as they continued to race ahead.

Those are Quell vessels. Their ships' engines emit a different electromagnetic signature. Xostir explained to the crew.

"What in the blazes are *they* doing here?" Troy shouted to the team over the wind blowing against them.

"They are too small to be a threat. Let's just pass

them. They probably don't realize that we can see them."
Kado frowned. They all knew what he was thinking. The
Quell can't be allowed to find the bunker.

As they drew closer to the cloaked Quell ships, they
noticed that the two ships weren't beginning to fire or
change course, probably because they assumed that they
weren't detected.

The three of them that were still conscious were
sharing thoughts with their link, deciding what to do next.
In two and a half seconds they ruled out 23 options and
decided on firing a polarized charged photonic beam
behind them at the fighters giving chase. This calibration
of energy would disrupt the fighters' engines and would
disable the cloaks on the two smaller vessels, exposing
them to the view of the V.C.

They all continued to zip forward as they held their
blades in front of them, simultaneously charging up their
blades for the attack as one mind. A blinding white glow
began to form around all three blades, followed by
electrical bolts arcing between all of them. Loud cracks of
the lightning arcs could be heard from miles around. They
turned around to face the trailing fighters, flying
backwards to aim their blades at their followers. After a
couple seconds, a radiant beam of light, surrounded by
lightning exploded into view, relentlessly firing arcs

toward the closest V.C. fighters behind them. The white light enveloped the ship and spread to the two dozen fighters that were trailing closely behind on either side in their formation. Dozens of ships could be seen falling to the ground in pieces. As they passed the two scout ships, a few electrical arcs jumped out to them, causing their cloaking ability to immediately fail. In seconds both Quell ships that they were approaching were completely visible to the Vanixx Corps.

"Guys," Ruana addressed the team, "we need to get out of here!" They were soon to be surrounded by two of the biggest Military forces on the planet.

"Let's go supersonic!" Kado ordered the team. They blasted past the Quell ships at a supersonic velocity, leaving the two Quell scouts to face the Vanixx Corps armada at the edge of the city.

As the several Vanixx Corps ships fired upon the fleeing Quell scout vessels, myriads of red and green electrical bolts firing between the several ships were visible. Dozens of explosions from the ashen and ebony hulls of the gargantuan freighters filled the sky; dozens of smaller support fighters were flurrying in spirals around the assault freighters trying to defend their limping fleet.

The five of them stopped a few hundred miles away to look back at the explosive skirmish they initiated.

"This isn't going to fix anything. This encounter will only make things worse." Kado sullenly extenuated.

Back at the bunker, Xostir commanded the bunker to extract two tables up from out of the floor. Two rectangular slabs rose from the floor and began to hover at waist height. They immediately laid Yai and Dom down onto the two makeshift beds.

"Let's get their health statuses. Kado, do we have any equipment to read life signs here; a multimodal monitor of some kind or a heart rate monitor?" Ruana inquired. Shaking his head, he returned, "No, but we can get your blade to read their life signs for us."

"Right." She silently asked her blade to continuously read the life signs of both Yai and Dom. In her field of vision, she began to visually see the heart rate and blood pressure of their two injured friends. At her will, Sjar was displaying more data expanding on the serious injuries both Yai and Dom received.

"These wounds are really bad. Anyone have any medical experience?" Ruana beckoned Troy and Kado. Both responded with negative remarks.

"How are we going to save them? Their blood pressure is dropping!" Just then Sjar communicated to all three of them, *I can access a full library on emergency medical procedures. Let me transmit the most useful information to you in this scenario. Hopefully that will help.*

"Okay, good idea." Ruana lowered her head embracing the rapid collection of medical knowledge. After a few tense moments of silence, she raised her head, looked to Kado and Troy, "Their conditions are critical." Now having a better understanding of their situation, "I'm going to do all I can to stabilize them, but I can't make any promises. Do we have any medical equipment?"

The Nicodem hologram activated when it heard the question, "In the blue lockers, farthest left drawers."

Ruana, startled by the hologram, jumped a bit, "Forgot you were there! Alright good. Let's try that."

"I'll get it!" Troy called out, urgently running to the locker, pulling open the drawer and running the tools back to her. Another platform elevated up from the floor and levitated at the perfect height and was a perfect fit for the medical tools she was about to use.

"Alright, we need to make sure that their bleeding stops." She almost recited the newly acquired knowledge to herself to help her lead from one step to the next. For Yai, they removed the armor she was wearing, exposing a layer of black clothing worn specifically for under the armor.

Kado and Troy looked on in angst as they faced the possible loss of their two newly acquainted friends.

***

"Where did they go?" A furious Praetor shrieked at the Mitigator as they monitored the battle via video feed from a distant part of the planet.

"They were seen fleeing into the wilderness." She squared as factually succinct and emotionlessly as possible.

"Are you sure they triggered a weapon that caused our cloak to fail?" He continued to shout on with rage. She nodded, not risking further rage in her direction.

"Find them and bring them to me." He sat back down on the bridge commander's chair contemplating what his next steps were to be. It seemed like these five were up to something troublesome. Either way, his contempt for these five kids playing with swords was becoming the primary focus.

A few hours had passed, Kado and Troy were sitting on a nearby couch watching Ruana hard at work to save both Dom and Yai.

"I've stabilized them for now. But I've nearly lost them a few times over the past few hours. It's not looking good. I don't even know if they'll be able to really recover fully – if at all."

"Well done. You've clearly done great work." Kado gently patted an exhausted Ruana on the back, showing approval, "While we wait, why don't we look at what kind of data we got?" Ruana nodded, "Sjar, can you project their vitals into the bunker speakers if something needs my attention?"

Sure thing.

Kado stood by the holographic projector to see the data and scans they collected from the underground lab.

"Alright, Xostir, show us what you got."

A visual representation of files appeared zipping past the viewer, as if the camera was flying down a hallway of file cabinets at a ridiculous speed.

"We managed to collect three exabytes of data," Xostir projected through the speakers of the bunker, "We've extracted detailed holographic recording footage of nearly a century of experiments and projects, more detail on every Edition of Magna-Blade that was made public, and other Editions that never made it to production."

The three of them felt a little excitement at the idea of seeing Magna-Blade concepts that no one else had seen, but this news was overshadowed with worry for Dom and Yai.

"We also obtained details on other gravity weapons that the Vanixx Corps have been developing." Xostir continued, "As mentioned, I've wiped as many connected drives and their backups that I could. However, they have a huge network of drives throughout their system that I couldn't connect to, which means that they still have the capability to access most of their data again."

"We also downloaded a current map of the entire Vanixx Corps series of buildings with updated data."

A holographic display showed all of the buildings and underground tunnels.

"This is displaying the full tunnel structure and the buildings." Xostir continued. Then the visualization changed as Xostir broadcast the display from his incredibly advanced brain. New lines and sections appeared with a red overlay, "This indicates the areas that have been destroyed today from our bombardment of their headquarters."

Kado stepped up closer, getting a close look at the damage they did, critically analyzing what needed to happen next. His eyes trailed down to a familiar large sphere underground, he pointed down to the area that looked like a huge sphere.

"Xostir, what's that?" he beckoned.

Xostir spoke in the artificial yet realistic voice, "That is a portion that survived the blast. According to the records this is the Vanixx Corps' Quantum Mechanical Singularity Generator."

"A what?" petitioned Ruana.

"Speak English." Dom suggested, disgruntled.

Kado managed to elucidate the bleak reality having the knowledge Xostir has provided him on these theoretical concepts, "That device is designed to make" he paused, contemplating the consequences of the potential peril that lay before them, "black holes."

Suddenly, rapid beeping emanated from the bunker speakers. It was Yai's vitals – she was crashing!

The rapid beeping all of a sudden turned into a constant ringing. Her heart stopped! Ruana, Troy and Kado ran over to Yai lying on the floating medical bed, "She's coding! Paddles!" She grabbed two small semi-circular objects and held them over Yai, initiating a charge for defibrillation. She shouted, "Clear", to ensure no one was touching her. Pressing the two charging pads near Yai's heart and on her left side, Yai's entire torso raised from the electrical charge. An electrical thumping sound could be heard from the defibrillator.

"Again!" She shouted to herself. Wumph.

No response.

"Again!" Wumph.

No response.

"Again!"

Dramatis Personae

Organizations:

Worldwide Peace Committee: Group comprised of peace ambassadors that arranged the countries after the Gravity War

Vanixx Corps: Military rulership of America

The Quell: Secret global organization

Xyl: Worldwide underground organization

The Hawx: American gangster organization

Rogue: Eurasian underground gangster organization

Characters:

Nicodem Veradiun: Inventor of the Magna-Blade

Kado: Wields Xostir and learns much from Nicodem

Xostir (shoh-steer): First Magna-Blade created by Nicodem

François Vaux: Admiral of the Vanixx Corps

Adrian Greeg: Agent of the Vanixx Corps

Felix Lota: Grand Admiral of the Vanixx Corps

Vern Trelleck: Admiral of the Vanixx Corps

Rego Trion: Lieutenant of the Vanixx Corps

Wey Killarney: Officer of the Vanixx Corps

Vorace Dern: Commander of the Vanixx Corps

Orun Joppa: Cybernetically augmented blade wielder

Torrel Krux: Black market merchant

Ruana: Forest-dwelling blade wielder

Sjar (see-yar): Ruana's Blade

Yai: Escapee blade wielder hiding in forest from the Vanixx Corps

Ptalojn (tah-lohn): Yai's Blade

Dom: Escapee blade wielder, former officer hiding from the Vanixx Corps

Cnidus (ken-eye-diss): Dom's Blade

Troy: Escapee blade wielder, former officer hiding from the Vanixx Corps

Cymari (kai-mah-ree): Troy's Blade

Professor Wiltrite: Professor at University with knowledge of Magna-Blade technology

Praetor: Leader of the Quell

Mitigator: Second in command of the Quell

Vicero: Third in command of the Quell

Yuda Garrafor: Leader of the Hawx

Nima Veradiun: Wife of Nicodem

Alice Veradiun: Daughter of Nicodem

Chloe Greeg: Wife of Adrian

Xander Greeg: Son of Adrian

Lucious: Elderly homeless man

Heath: Male twin special blade wielder of the Vanixx Corps

Luna: Female twin special blade wielder of the Vanixx Corps

Maps

POST GRAVITY WAR

PRE GRAVITY WAR

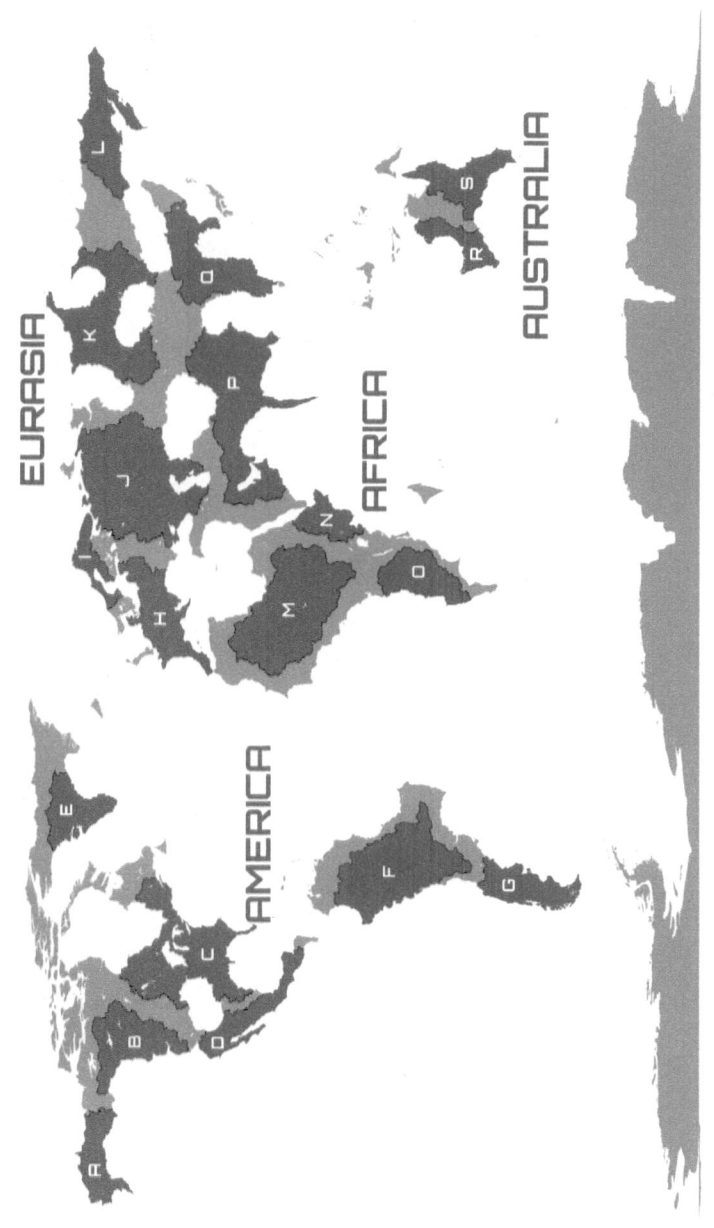

A: ANCHORAGE
B: VANCOUVER
C: WASHINGTON
D: ZAMORA
E: IKEQ
F: KAXARARI
G: ESCARPADA

H: GENOA
I: ÖSTNOR
J: CHELYABINSK [ЧЕЛЯБИНСК]
K: CHATANGA [ХАТАНГА]
L: OZERNOVSKIY [ОЗЕРНОВСКИЙ]
M: NEW TOGO
N: ADDIS ABABA

O: LESOTHO
P: DHAKA
Q: HEFEI [合肥市]
R: CERVANTES
S: WARRAMBOOL

www.ingramcontent.com/pod-product-compliance
Lightning Source LLC
Chambersburg PA
CBHW020501020726
47493CB00001B/133